Spore 7

CLANCY CARLILE

SPHERE BOOKS LIMITED
30–32 Gray's Inn Road, London WC1X 8JL

First published in Great Britain by Sphere Books Ltd, 1980

TRADE MARK

Set in Monotype Plantin

Printed in Great Britain by
William Collins Sons & Co Ltd
Glasgow

To my mother,

LESLIE FAUSTINE MISSO CARLILE NOBLIN

who survived.

FEBRUARY THIRTEENTH

1 In Mendocino the rains usually begin in the late fall as thick, drifting fogs. By the middle of December, the fogs develop into drizzling mists, and after that the rains come, the storms. During the storms, the ocean along the rocky northern California coast batters against the cliffs, roars in and out of kelpy grottoes and blowholes: a seascape of white crests, foamy turbulence, rain.

On one such rainy night in February, an old pick-up truck was coming down Little Lake Road towards town, its tyres making a slishing sound on the rain-slick macadam. The driver was Cliff Snyder, a huge, beer-bellied man, an unemployed logger. Riding with him was his wife, Kathy Mae. They were driving through the Pygmy Forest, with the rain blowing through their pick-up's headlights in misty swirls, when they both saw something on the road up ahead. It was difficult to see anything through the rain-blurred windshield, with the wipers flapping back and forth with the headlights reflecting off the swirls of rain and back into their eyes; still, there was suddenly a shape there on the road, a shape that moved, and it became apparent just before the collision that it was a man, and the man was naked.

Kathy Mae screamed. The truck swerved, skidding on the wet pavement, and the left front fender struck the man with a loud, dull thud. The pick-up shuddered to a stop almost cross-ways in the road. The motor stalled.

'Sonofabitch,' Cliff said. 'I hit him!' He flung the door open and leaped from the cab. Though his vision was obscured by a gust of misty rain, he expected to see the man lying in the road; but even though the pick-up's lights were still on and their glow illuminated the area of the collision, Cliff couldn't see a thing.

'Oh, my God,' Kathy Mae moaned from the cab. 'Is he hurt?'

'Hell, I can't see anybody,' Cliff said. 'Hand me the flashlight.'

'What? Where? I don't – '

'The glove compartment.'

She fumbled into the glove compartment and handed the flashlight to Cliff, who flashed it on to the road here and there and into the ditches. Nothing. Not a sign of anything. Cliff was sure the man must have been injured, or at least stunned, so where was he?

They were in the Pygmy Forest, a flat ribbon of land perhaps three or four miles wide that runs parallel to the coastline a few miles inland. Unlike the rich, loamy soil in which the giant redwoods grow, the soil of the Pygmy Forest is a white hardpan clay from which grow pygmy cypress trees that are often a hundred years old but are still no taller than stunted saplings. Poisonous rhododendron bushes grow among the grotesque cypresses in tangled profusion, but no grass sprouts from the clayey soil, no leafy trees take root there.

'He must've run off,' Cliff said. 'Crazy sonofabitch, standing right in the middle of the road, buckass naked, on a night like this!' He touched a dent in his fender, felt a sticky substance. No, it wasn't blood; but there was no doubt he'd hit a man.

At Kathy Mae's urging, Cliff, soaked to the skin, finally climbed back into the pick-up and started it, got straight on the road, and roared away in a new gust of swirling raindrops.

'Wait a minute now, Cliff,' the deputy said. 'You hit a man, a naked man. You hit him, then couldn't find him?'

They were standing just inside the door of the deputy's house, which he used as an office. Kathy Mae stood beside Cliff, and she was visibly shaken. The deputy had invited them to sit, but they had remained standing.

'That's right,' Cliff said defensively.

'Well, if he ran off, I guess he couldn't've been hurt very badly,' the deputy said.

'Maybe not,' Cliff said. 'But I don't see how he could help but be hurt. There's a dent in my fender.'

The deputy's six-year-old daughter opened the door leading to the main part of the house. Poking her head in, she said apologetically, 'Daddy? Mommy says your soup's getting cold.'

'Okay, Adrianne, I won't be a minute.'

The girl smiled at the Snyders, then disappeared behind the door.

The deputy said, 'Cliff, are you sure it was a man? I mean, you said it was pretty dark and hard to see, what with the rain and all.'

Cliff snapped, 'Come on outside. I'll show you the dent in my fender. I hit something. That's all I know. I just came to tell you in case – '

'All right, all right,' the deputy said in a placating voice. He put on his raincoat and hat and opened the door for Kathy Mae. They went outside to look at the pick-up.

'See?' Cliff said, directing the beam of his flashlight on the dented fender and running his fingers along the concavity. 'I hit something, see? And that's all I know. Now I ain't been smoking any of them funny cigarettes, Sheriff, and I ain't drunk neither, and I'd swear to you it was a man.'

'Without no clothes on,' Kathy Mae added.

'Come on, Kathy Mae, let's go,' Cliff said as he opened the door on the driver's side of the pick-up and climbed in. Kathy Mae walked around to the other side and got in.

'All right,' the deputy said, 'I'll go out and have a look.'

The deputy's name was Chris Jordan. He was thirty-six years old, and he was the only law officer in the town of Mendocino, which, being unincorporated, had no police force of its own. In fact, Mendocino was not so much a town as a village, a collection of clapboard buildings and houses and tall wooden water tanks clumped together in a grassy meadow on the cliffs overlooking the Pacific. It had once been a logging town, but over the years the trees in the forests along the coast steadily diminished while the tourists steadily increased, until the clapboard buildings that once were whorehouses and saloons for loggers became antique shops and art galleries for tourists. In the summer time the streets were jammed with campers and trailers and hippie vans. Now, however, during the rainy season, the streets of the town at night had a desolate emptiness rather like that of a carnival after closing time.

Chris got into his patrol car and drove out to the place where the accident was supposed to have happened. He sat in the car and directed the spotlight all around the area. There was nothing on the road, however, nothing in the ditches. He darted the light along the edge of the Pygmy Forest on both sides of the road, but stopped only once when he saw something interesting: a spider's web spun between the limbs of a misshapen cypress. It was spangled with raindrops. When the wind shimmered the web, the droplets glittered in the bright light.

He drove on slowly, stopping now and then to shine the spotlight into the ditches. He had gone only a few hundred more yards when he saw the car. It was an old wreck of a car, mud-spattered, parked on the shoulder of the road near a driveway that led down into the Pygmy. He recognised the car. It belonged to a potter – what was his name? Richard something or other – who lived in the house about a hundred yards down the driveway. Unpaved, the driveway was impassable during the winter, when it became nothing more than a deeply rutted and puddled lane.

There was a light in the house. Chris couldn't see the house itself – the night was too dark for that – but he could see a dim light in one of the windows.

The car's two-way radio crackled with static, a sound very much like that of a man clearing his throat before speaking, but it was a woman's voice that said, 'Car seven? Chris? You read me?' It was his wife.

He unhooked the mike and pushed the transmit button. 'I'm here, Marge. What's up?'

'Nothing.' She was transmitting from the radio in his office at home, which was always full of static. 'Just checking. You said you'd be back by now. Over.' She was trying hard not to sound worried or reproachful.

He smiled. 'I'm going to check out a house,' he said, although he didn't want to do it, didn't want to go slogging down that muddy lane at this time of night. 'It's the house closest to the scene of the Snyder accident, and if it was a man he hit, then he might've crawled to the house for help. Okay?'

'All right,' Marge said. 'I made some hot chocolate. I'll keep it warm till you get back. Don't get wet. Love you. Over and out.'

Chris pulled on his black leather driving gloves, turned up the collar of his raincoat, and sighed heavily before getting out of the car into the misty rain. He was thinking of Marge and the warm fire at home. He left the yellow light flashing on top of the car, got his flashlight, and headed down the muddy lane towards the house. He walked on the small ridge between the water-filled ruts, avoiding puddles where he could, sloshing through them where he couldn't. The silence around him was profound.

As he walked, he kept flashing the light into the brambled woods on both sides of the lane, letting the light linger now and then on one of the many toadstools that sprouted from the rotting twigs of fallen cypress trees. The toadstools, shining like lacquer, were in many shades of orange, brown, and red, while the moss that hung from the twisted limbs of the trees, wet and dripping, resembled grey-green icicles. And here and there orange lichen was splashed like a water-colour through the brambled profusion of dark, gnarled trunks and twisted boughs.

He was hardly half-way to the house when he glanced up and noticed that the light was gone. The house was now in total darkness and couldn't be seen at all. He hurried on, assuming that the people there had gone to bed and that he could still catch them before they fell asleep.

As he approached the house, he flashed the beam of light across the front windows a few times, signalling to whoever was inside that a visitor was near. The house, however, remained dark. It was a small two-storey house – a shack really – that had been thrown together from scrap lumber and tar paper.

'Hello!' he called when he came into the cluttered yard. 'Anybody home?'

No response. He had expected to be met by a big barking dog at least, since almost everyone who lived in the Pygmy Forest kept a dog. But there was no dog.

He stepped on to the porch and knocked on the door. 'Hello, Richard? It's me, Chris Jordan, Sheriff's Department.'

Still no answer. No light. No sign of life. He thought about sticking his head in the door, but he knew that the people who built houses here in the Pygmy, whether hippies or hill-billies, were individualists who wanted to be left alone and who didn't like strangers poking around. Some of them were known to be growing marijuana in small clearings in the Pygmy, while others had hunks of poached venison in their coolers. So they were wary of visitors. Especially law officers. Especially at night.

Even so, it was strange. He was positive he had seen a light in one of the windows only a few minutes before, and was just as positive that he could be heard by anyone inside the house. So why didn't someone respond?

He listened. There was an intermittent banging sound coming from the back of the house. He left the porch and slowly circled the house, flashing his light across the puddled and trash-strewn yard.

It was the back door. During gusts of wind and rain, the door creaked and slammed against its jamb. Didn't Richard – if indeed that's who lived there – didn't he know that rain was blowing into his house? Couldn't he hear the door banging?

Then something caught his eye: a large mound of dirt in one corner of the clearing. It looked like a well with its top off. He went to the well and shone the light down into it. The bloated carcass of a dog was floating there.

So that's why he hadn't heard a dog bark. The dog looked as if it had been dead for at least two or three days.

Well, then, it seemed as if he would have to search the house. There was certainly enough evidence to establish a reasonable suspicion that something was wrong, so he no longer needed a search warrant or the consent of the occupants.

He started for the back door – which, as he approached, suddenly closed with a bang, and stayed closed. Chris stopped.

'Hello? Anybody in the house?'

Silence.

He was standing there, wondering what to do next, when his beeper sounded. The first beep was a high-pitched sound that sent a surge of adrenaline rushing through him before he realised what it was. The beeper was a transistor device that he wore on his belt, an electronic pager. Whenever he was away from his patrol car for any length of time, the beeper could be activated in his office by anyone who wanted to reach him by radio. It sounded only in an emergency, and Chris was supposed to return to his car as soon as possible and radio his office. For a moment he debated with himself whether or not to leave things there at the house as they were. His curiosity and concern made him want to stay at least long enough to have a peek inside the house, but he felt a dread and foreboding about the place that was almost palpable, a feeling that made him want to go back to the car; and that was what he finally did: walked back up the muddy lane, jumped into the patrol car, slammed the door, and reached for the radio.

'Car seven reporting. What's up, Marge?'

She answered immediately. 'Chris? There's a fight going on at Dick's Bar. Can you respond? Over.'

A bar room brawl? They (and it would be 'they' because she would have already been in touch with the Sheriff's Headquarters in Fort Bragg for instructions) wanted him to drop what he was doing and take care of a bar room brawl?

'Negative,' he said. 'See if they can send someone down from headquarters. Lonnie, maybe. I got a problem out here, I think. Over.'

'Lonnie *is* responding. Sounds like a two-man job. What's your problem out there?'

He hesitated for a moment and instinctively glanced down the dark lane towards the unseen house. 'I don't know,' he said in a muted voice, as if talking to himself.

'Chris,' Marge said then with a hint of urgency in her static-filtered voice, 'maybe you'd better come in. This has something to do with Cliff Snyder. There's been a report that he's gone crazy. An ambulance is on the way there. Over.'

Crazy? What a strange word for her to use over the air. He drummed his fingertips on the steering wheel for a moment before he sighed, pushed the transmit button, and said, 'Ten-four. I'm coming in.'

2

'How you doing, Doc?' the bartender asked. 'Ready for another?'

'Why not?'

'Meeting Bobbi here tonight?' the bartender asked.

It was an innocent question, but the man called Doc said, 'Yeah,' in a tone calculated to discourage any familiarity on the subject.

'Great girl, Bobbi is,' said the bartender.

'Yeah,' said Doc.

His name was Sander Quence. He was a doctor, a GP, the only one practising in Mendocino. He often came into Dick's Bar in the evening for a few drinks, and the bartender never failed at some time during the night to bring him a drink and say, 'There you are, just what the doctor ordered.' He never seemed to tire of it. Indeed, he said it each time as though he had just thought of it.

Dr Sander Quence was in Dick's Bar the night of 13 February, the night Cliff Snyder and his wife came in. Later he would try to remember everything he could about the evening, and the time factor would become particularly important. He remembered that it was between nine and nine-thirty when the Snyders came in. There were only four customers in the bar at the time, and Sander himself was the only one occupying a barstool. There was a couple – a man and a woman – sitting at a table near the door. The fourth customer was James Newman, who was shooting pool by himself. Newman was a young astrophysicist from the NASA Space Centre in Houston, Texas, and he was a doctor, too, although a PhD kind of doctor, not an MD like Sander Quence.

Newman and Sander Quence had already played a game of chess and Sander had won again, so Newman had decided to try his luck at pool. He played by himself; that way nobody could beat him.

'Ten ball in the side pocket,' he would say to Sander, and shoot and miss. 'Well, you can't win 'em all,' he would say, or, 'Well, nobody's perfect.'

'Stick to astrophysics,' Sander advised. 'It's simpler.'

'It's just that I've got a block against games,' Newman admitted. 'My father. He never let me play games when I was a kid. He was a professor. Instead of reading comic books, I had to read Plato. His idea of a toy was a spectroscope.'

'A deprived childhood,' Sander said.

Newman looked like a typical hip young professional: bearded, with longish hair, wearing old faded blue jeans and a turtleneck sweater.

When Cliff and Kathy Mae Snyder had first come into the bar, Sander hadn't paid much attention to them. He knew them by sight, but not by name, and neither of them had ever been a patient of his. But he had soon noticed – sensed, anyway – that Cliff seemed very agitated. He would remember that. And he would remember the bartender calling out, 'Hey, Doc, you hear that? Cliff and Kathy Mae say they maybe hit some guy up on Little Lake Road tonight was running around naked as a jay-bird.'

Sander said, 'Oh?' in a non-committal way, hoping he wasn't going to be asked to go slogging through the Pygmy Forest to find some hippie who, out of his head on LSD, had decided to go for a run in the rain and got run over instead. And it was then that he really looked at Cliff and Kathy Mae for the first time. She was obviously upset, but Cliff was more than that; he sat at the bar clasping – squeezing – a drink in both hands, his expression seeming to vacillate between fright and fury. He looked feverish, and his eyes . . . Sander said later that his eyes seemed to be bulging from some pressure that was building up inside his head, as if his flesh and bones were trying to contain some sort of explosion.

When Cliff's neck and facial muscles began to jerk and

twitch, Sander's first assumption was that the man was entering the early stages of an epileptic seizure, and he wondered why the couple didn't leave the bar and go somewhere so the man could be medicated and made comfortable. But apparently neither of them had any idea of what was happening to him.

'What's the matter with you?' Kathy Mae asked her husband two or three times, and he couldn't seem to give a coherent answer.

In a breathless and disjointed way, he said, 'I don't. Jesus. Something's . . . I feel like I . . .'

'What?' Kathy Mae said. 'You sick, honey?'

'I better go,' he said. 'I better.' He obviously meant to push his drink away from in front of him, but no one seemed more surprised than he when the glass left his shaking hand with such force that it fell crashing behind the bar.

'Hey! What the hell's this?' the bartender asked.

In what seemed a sudden convulsion of fury, Cliff pushed himself away from the bar, knocking his barstool over. He staggered, blinking rapidly, grimacing, and Kathy Mae reached to grab his arm and steady him.

'Honey!' she cried, alarmed now. 'What is it? What's wrong?'

Cliff slapped her hand away. 'Keep your . . .! Lemme alone!' he shouted in a very hoarse voice, then viciously kicked the barstool out of the way and lurched towards the men's room at the rear of the bar.

As Cliff disappeared into the men's room, the bartender, as though personally offended by Cliff's bizarre behaviour, demanded of Kathy Mae, 'What the hell's got into him? Has he flipped his lid?'

Kathy Mae, obviously worried and frightened, slipped off the barstool and went to tap timorously on the door of the men's room. 'Cliff?' she called through the door. 'Are you all right? Honey?'

The first sound that came from the men's room seemed to

be that of someone pounding on a metal partition, and then a cry, and then the sound of glass breaking.

Thoroughly alarmed by now, the bartender came from behind the bar and hurried towards the men's room, saying, 'What the hell's he doing, tearing up the place?' He moved Kathy Mae aside firmly as he went into the men's room, from which immediately issued the sounds of shouting and roaring, and then the bartender came flying backwards out of the room and fell sprawling on the bar room floor.

Furious, the bartender had barely hit the floor before he was trying to get up again, and that was when Cliff Snyder lurched out of the men's room, his face twisted and his eyes bulging, babbling in tones that seemed to alternate between anger and beggary: 'I got to get. Please. Sonofabitch! Don't!'

Kathy Mae reached out to touch him, very sympathetic and solicitous, and that was when he back-handed her, not with enough force to knock her down but with enough to bloody her nose.

She couldn't have been more horrified if Cliff had suddenly plunged a knife into her. Frozen in an attitude of recoil, she stared at her husband, her eyes wide with amazement, while the blood from her nose trickled down into her gaping mouth, out of which came the small whining sound of a child, the *ah ah ah* sound of a child who is too surprised and terrified to cry out.

By then the bartender was on his feet again. He grabbed Cliff's arm, saying, 'You bastard! Get outta here! Get outta my place, you can't – '

His words were cut off by a blow from the back of Cliff's hand. It seemed merely a half-hearted blow, but it knocked the bartender sliding across the floor in a chaos of falling stools and overturning tables and breaking glasses.

And now the small whining sounds that Kathy Mae was making in her throat finally burst out of her mouth as a prolonged cry. That was when Cliff hit her again, still using the back of his hand and swinging as if in slow motion, but this time the blow was powerful enough to knock Kathy Mae down.

The bartender, on his feet again and mad as hell, rushed to get a hammerlock on Cliff's head, but Cliff slipped from his grasp, and before the bartender could duck or put up his guard, he had been hit with a fist, and the blow sent him flying back against the jukebox.

Sander quickly stepped behind the bar and telephoned the local deputy sheriff, Chris Jordan. Chris's wife Marge answered the phone, and Sander had to shout to be heard above the pandemonium of women screaming, tables and chairs overturning, glasses breaking, and men grunting, snorting, cursing.

'Better send an ambulance, too!' Sander shouted.

The bartender, though fighting gamely, was continuing to get the worst of it, perhaps because he simply could not get it through his head that Cliff – the Cliff he had known and been friendly with for years – could possibly be this vicious, this violent: biting, clawing, kicking him in the groin, trying to gouge out his eyes.

When Cliff pinned the bartender against the floor and got his fingers around his neck, James Newman intervened. Newman had been standing by the pool table watching the fight with wonder and disgust, almost totally immobilised, until it became apparent that Cliff was really intent upon killing the bartender. Then Newman, in one instinctive movement, turned the cue stick around in his hands, strode to the front of the bar where the two men were fighting, and rapped Cliff across the head with the heavy end of the stick.

Cliff collapsed. He sprawled unconscious amid the debris and spilled liquor on the floor.

The bartender staggered to his feet, grasping his throat and trying desperately to get his breath. He tried to speak but his voice caught in his throat. Blood was running from his nose and cut lips 'He was . . . he was trying to kill me! That sonofabitch was trying to *kill* me!'

3

Deputies Chris Jordan and Lonnie McCabe, each in his separate patrol car with red and yellow lights flashing, arrived at Dick's Bar almost simultaneously. By the time they got there, the fight was over. The ambulance arrived a few minutes later.

They found Cliff Snyder lying on the cluttered floor, tied hand and foot, his hands behind his back. He was no longer unconscious. Though still weak and groggy, he was growing stronger every second, and he had already begun to struggle against his bonds – pieces of hemp rope that the bartender had brought from the storeroom. When the deputies came in, Cliff was reviling everyone present with an inexhaustible barrage of curses as he thrashed around on the floor, each curse louder and viler, a sing-song crescendo of obscenities.

Kathy Mae, at a table in the back of the bar, was hugging herself as she rocked back and forth on the chair like a woman keening. There was dried blood on her upper lip and one eye was swollen almost shut. Sander had offered her both a drink and medical attention, but she had waved him away.

The bartender was behind the bar. He had a pistol in his hand, a .45 automatic, and he was pointing it at Cliff Snyder. His face was a mass of bloody cuts and bruises, and he looked as if he were about to cry.

'Put that damned thing away,' Chris Jordan told him, raising his voice to be heard above Cliff's curses.

'He tried to kill me! If he comes at me again, so help me Christ, I'll blow his fucking head off!'

Chris knew that the bartender's threats were more for show than for real, so he stepped directly in front of the .45 and glared at the bartender as he said, 'I told you to put that thing away.'

The bartender stalled for a few face-saving seconds, then swung around and slammed the pistol into a drawer behind the bar.

Chris approached Sander, who was sitting at the bar finishing his drink. 'Hey, Sander,' he said by way of a greeting. 'What's going on here?'

'Hello, Chris,' he said, and shrugged. 'What you see. That guy on the floor there, he suddenly started hitting people.' He shrugged again. 'No apparent reason. I guess a psychiatrist would say he suffered a psychotic break – some sort of severe trauma to the nervous system. Me, I'd say he went nuts.'

'You think maybe he's on LSD?'

Sander shrugged again.

Chris said, 'The only people I've ever seen act like that were bum-tripping on either acid or angel dust. But, boy, I sure never heard anybody cuss like that before.'

Cliff screamed and lunged against his restraints. Lonnie McCabe had taken out his handcuffs and had been reaching down to put them on Cliff's already tied hands when Cliff, with a terrifying burst of energy, wrenched himself into a sitting position and tried to bite Lonnie. With his lips curled back over his teeth in an almost canine snarl, he lunged and tried to sink his teeth into Lonnie's ear. Lonnie jumped back and automatically raised the twelve-cell flashlight that he carried for a club. But he didn't strike.

'We can give him a sedative when the ambulance gets here,' Sander said. 'Till then, maybe we'd better let him alone.'

'I tied him up pretty tight,' the bartender said as he examined his face in the mirror behind the bar.

'Was it you who laid him out?' Chris asked.

'No,' the bartender said, and suddenly seemed to be seized with a new rush of outrage and self-pity. 'The sonofabitch, he was trying to *kill* me. Choking me! I'm going to sign a complaint against that fucker for attempted murder, you can bet your ass on that, the crazy bastard, what got into him? We been friendly for *years*. He owes me a bar bill of twenty bucks, for Christ's sake, and I ain't ever said an unfriendly word to him. But he comes in here –'

'Who laid him out?' Chris asked.

'A guy named James Newman,' Sander said, 'a NASA scientist, if you can believe that.'

'That guy who's here looking for meteorites?'

'The same,' Sander said.

'Where is he?'

'He needed some fresh air. I suggested he go for a walk. Probably had to puke, too. He said he'd come back when he saw your car here.'

The ambulance arrived. It bumped to a stop at the kerb in front of the bar, its lights flashing and its siren winding down. Chris wondered why in hell they were using the siren since there were no other cars on the street at this time of night in Mendocino.

The two white-smocked attendants brought in a litter. The litter had three large straps across it with which they could hold Cliff down, but how were they to get him on to it? He fought and screamed and thrashed about so wildly, so maniacally, that no one could get hold of him – although it was obvious that the two ambulance attendants weren't taking any real risks. They were struggling with his flailing feet while Chris and Lonnie tried to pin his torso to the floor. They came at Cliff from both sides so that when he lunged at one of them, the other tried to grab his hair and hold it. His hair was so slick with blood from his head wound, however, that they couldn't hold him, and their gloves became covered with blood. At one point Cliff, quicker than usual, wrenched around and sank his teeth into Lonnie's forearm.

Lonnie yelped and brought the flashlight crashing down on Cliff's head. Cliff grimaced, went tense and quivered like a dying fish before he once again collapsed into unconsciousness.

'You okay?' Chris asked Lonnie.

Lonnie pushed his coat sleeve up to look at his arm. 'Yeah,

I guess. Didn't draw blood, anyway.'

'Let's hurry up, get him strapped down before he comes to again.'

They strapped him face down on the gurney, and the driver wanted to know where to take him. 'Hell, we can't take him to Fort Bragg Hospital. We got no facilities there for handling violent patients. The only place for this guy is in jail.'

'No,' Chris said. 'He needs medical attention.'

'Don't look at me,' Sander said. 'Ask his wife. They must have a family doctor in Fort Bragg. Or take him to Ukiah, to the Institute of Neurosciences, where the old Mendocino State Hospital used to be. They got straitjackets and padded cells there, which is what he needs, and they just love cases like this.'

Chris thought that was a good idea, but it would be an hour's drive over the mountains to Ukiah and the ambulance driver refused to make the trip unless one of the deputies rode in the ambulance with Cliff in case he became violent again. Lonnie volunteered to go because Chris – technically, at least – was off duty.

As the attendants rolled the litter out, Chris went to speak to Kathy Mae. 'Mrs Snyder? Come on, I'll give you a ride to the Fort Bragg Hospital.'

She moved in dumbfounded silence back and forth on the chair, her hair falling in tangles over her swollen and darkening eye.

'Come on,' he coaxed. 'You need to have that eye looked at.'

It was only with great effort that she managed to speak through her swollen lips. 'I got the pick-up outside. I don't need no hospital.'

'You're in no condition to drive.'

She waved him away. 'I'll be all right. Lemme alone.'

Chris sighed. 'Look, Mrs Snyder. If you don't feel like

talking about it now, it's okay, but . . . can you tell me anything about what happened? To set your husband off like that?'

A new rush of grief and bewilderment flooded her face. 'As God is my witness, Sheriff, I don't know. It wasn't me. I didn't say anything. I was just trying to find out what was the matter with him, he was acting sick, but . . .' Her words faded into a dismayed and despairing silence. She began to cry. 'I just don't understand . . . I didn't . . . He wasn't even mad at me, that I know of. He seemed sick, that's what it seemed like, like he got sick all of a sudden.'

'Had he been drinking a lot?'

'No. We had a few drinks at home, but he wasn't drunk, if that's what you mean. And even if he was . . . I've only known him to be drunk three or four times, maybe, but he never did anything like this. *Never*.'

'How about drugs?'

She seemed a little offended by the question. 'Drugs?'

'Look, Mrs Snyder. Will you be home tomorrow? I might want a statement from you.'

She nodded. 'Where they taking him?'

'To Ukiah.'

'To that nuthouse there?' She seemed to consider this the final and overwhelming outrage.

'A mental hospital,' he said. 'Listen. I wish you'd let me take you to Fort Bragg. That eye – '

'No, thank you. I'll take care of it. I'll be all right.'

He touched her shoulder. 'Good-night,' he said, and then to the bartender who was counting the money in the cash register, 'Come on down to my office and file a complaint tomorrow, Lew.' He didn't wait for an answer, but the answer followed him out the door.

'Bet your ass, I will! That sonofabitch, he was trying to kill me! I'm gonna see he goes to jail, even if it means losing that twenty dollars he owes me, the bastard.'

Chris left the bar and stopped beside Sander on the sidewalk. Sander was watching the ambulance attendants put Cliff into the rear of the ambulance. A couple of passers-by had stopped to watch.

'So what d'you think?' Chris said, nodding towards Kathy Mae. 'She okay?'

Sander shrugged. 'I tried to get her to let me take her to the hospital, or at least to my office, but she – ' He broke off when he saw James Newman approaching.

Newman wasn't running, but was walking as fast as he could, and his demeanour made it obvious that he was alarmed about something. His hair and beard were spangled with droplets of mist. He was panting slightly.

'Sheriff,' he said, as he approached, but when he came face to face with Chris he seemed at a loss for words. 'Sheriff? Listen, I went for a walk on the headlands just now . . . well, I was down there and . . . well, you're not going to believe what I saw.'

Chris waited for him to volunteer the information; when he didn't, Chris said, 'Am I supposed to guess?'

'A man,' Newman said, 'down there on the cliffs, walking around without a stitch of clothes on. Maybe I should say "prowling around", because that's what he seemed to be doing: prowling.'

When Newman left the bar after hitting Cliff Snyder with the cue stick, he had walked west along Main Street towards the ocean. He had walked along the sidewalk in the dim light of the scattered street lamps. The rain had slackened, was beginning to stop. Patches of fog and mist drifted here and there in the windless night, ghostly shapes that seemed to move within themselves. The dark canopy seemed to be growing thinner, allowing some light from the moon and stars to filter through and bathe everything in a dull glow, a light that had the grey, opaque quality of ice.

When he came to the edge of town, where Main Street turned away from the ocean, Newman was thinking, *But what if I had killed him?* He climbed through a wooden fence, walked across the treeless turf of the headlands, and was soon out of the light of the last street lamps. He had to slow down then, choosing his footing carefully in the darkness. *Jesus, think of the headlines: NASA Scientist Kills Man in Bar Room Brawl.* Such a headline would have caused the death of his mother and father, who had brought him up in a home where he had never been exposed to arguments, let alone fights. The only physical violence he had ever witnessed as a boy was on the television news programmes, and very little of that because he had been allowed to watch television for only two hours a week.

And tonight I almost killed a man.

He reached the rocky cliffs. The dark waters, storm-tosssed, cracked and curled around the cliffs, thundered and howled in crevices and grottoes, thrown back against the incoming waves. He watched the ocean in the dim moonlight and tried not to think about the scene he had just left. But he couldn't stop thinking about it because (and he had to admit this to himself finally) it had been exciting. As horrifying as the whole scene had been, and as shocked as he was with his own part in it, he nevertheless had to admit that, just for the few seconds before and after he had hit Cliff, for those few seconds that it had taken him to stride the length of the bar room and strike the man – for those few seconds he had never felt more alive. A sense of brute power that he had never felt before in the most suppressed fantasies.

I'd better get out of here, he thought. *I'd better leave this place.*

Not that he blamed it on the place, the town. He liked it here – liked the harsh landscape, the ocean, the people he had met. But there was something about this part of the coast, something he had never been able to put his finger on, a dark, primitive, brooding quality that made him feel uneasy and yet exhilarated . . . Yes, that was probably it. the primitive, brooding quality of this coast seemed to find some reflection in himself, found its counterpart in the keen sense of aliveness he had felt when he struck the man with the pool stick.

Well, anyway, it was time for him to leave. He had come to Mendocino two weeks before, after he had heard the reports of the meteorite shower that had fallen on northern California. Witnesses had reported seeing a few of the meteorites fall to earth in the vicinity of Mendocino, so his superiors at the NASA Space Centre had sent him to find and bring back one of the meteorites. They had supplied him with everything he might need, including a helicopter and an all-terrain pick-up, and he had spent almost every day of the past two weeks scouring the countryside, interviewing people who had reported seeing one or more of the meteorites plunge to earth. No luck. He hadn't been able to locate one. Well, maybe tomorrow he would try one last time, would fly one last time over the area in the Pygmy Forest where witnesses said they had seen at least one meteorite crash, and then, if he still found nothing, he would pack his things and go back to Houston. Get away from this dark and brooding place . . .

The moon broke through the scudding clouds, and Newman used the light to walk out on a spit of land that jutted out into the ocean. He sat down on a wet boulder and watched the billows of fog drifting over and about the headlands and ocean. He was lost in thought, so he wasn't quite sure when he saw the movement from the corner of his eye. And he wouldn't have noticed it even then if the movement had not been slightly contrary to the general drift of the mists. He glanced in the direction of the movement, saw nothing, and turned back to stare at the churning surf. Then he heard something.

It came from behind him, a snorting sound, perhaps a cough. He jerked his head around, instinctively holding his body rigidly still, and saw a man, a naked man, emerging from a billow of fog, his body strangely glistening in the dark. He was perhaps a hundred feet away, coming up out of a little fog-filled ravine. The nakedness of the man was odd enough, but the way he was acting was even odder. He looked as if he were stalking something. Prowling. His eyes were wide and hot, his face was twisted with menace and hostility, and he walked as if he were trying to creep up on something.

Newman sat very still on the boulder, his form blending with the other dark forms around him on the small point of land, and the man passed on the cliffs directly behind him. The man came close enough for Newman to hear his breathing, a phlegm-rattling sound, shallow and rapid. Then the man was totally obscured by another billow of drifting fog. The fog and he seemed to blend, to melt together, and then he was gone.

Newman's heart was beating loudly in his chest. He was frightened. It was an irrational kind of fear, one that he had never felt before in his life except in dreams, in nightmares where objects and experiences need no objective correlative for the fear they inspire.

He waited a few minutes, watching to see if the man was going to come back; then he rose slowly, took a deep breath, and began the slow, nerve-racking effort to get back across the rocks without falling, without dislodging a pebble, without making a sound.

He succeeded. Then, slowly at first, but speeding up with almost every step, he started back across the headlands towards the misty glow of the town's street lamps. He looked back over his shoulder now and then to see if anything was following him.

4

For more than half an hour Chris Jordan drove along the streets that bordered the headlands, the streets that formed the perimeter of the town, and flashed his spotlight searchingly through the drifting patches of fog. Finally he drove down Heeser Drive, the only street in town that actually reached the cliffs above the ocean. It ended in a parking lot that was often used as a lovers' lane, so Chris wasn't surprised to find a car parked there. What was surprising was that the parked car, a tan Pontiac, belonged to the Reverend Boyle, the minister of Mendocino's Presbyterian Church.

Chris parked his patrol car beside the Pontiac. He thought he saw two figures in the rear seat of the car disentangling themselves. He stayed in his own car and continued sweeping the cliffs with his spotlight, being careful not to shine it on the Pontiac. He didn't want to embarrass the occupants. He waited a few minutes to give them time to compose themselves; then he got out of his car.

A young man in the rear seat of the Pontiac rolled down the window as Chris approached. 'Hey, Chris,' he said.

'Hey, Billy. How you doing?'

It was the minister's seventeen-year-old son, who chuckled nervously. 'Well, I was doing all right till you came along.'

The girl in the back seat giggled. Chris automatically leaned down to look at her. It was one of the Coors sisters, Lacy, the sixteen-year-old.

'Sorry about that,' Chris said, 'but I had to check out something down here. Got a report of a prowler, some guy running around without any clothes on. Seen anything unusual around here tonight?'

'No, nothing too terribly unusual,' Billy said, smirking as if he had a secret. Lacy giggled again.

'Well, anyway, you better go on somewhere else, okay? Just in case there really is a prowler?'

Billy told him, oh, sure, they would go somewhere else, and he even began to crawl from the rear seat into the front, but Chris drove away before Billy had started the motor or turned on the Pontiac's headlights. As he drove back up Heeser Drive, Chris glanced in the rearview mirror, checking to see when and if the Pontiac's headlights came on. They didn't. When he reached the streets and houses on the edge of town, the parking area on the ocean at the foot of Heeser Drive was still dark. Chris assumed that Billy and Lacy had probably crawled into the front seat, immediately begun necking again, and forgotten about everything else, especially about leaving. They didn't seem at all worried about some crazy man who might be prowling around the cliffs without any clothes on.

When Dr Sander Quence left Dick's Bar that night, he drove to the Seagull Inn, where he picked up Bobbi Coors when she got off work. For nearly six months now he and Bobbi had been lovers, though Sander was old enough to be her father – was, as a matter of fact, one year older than her father. He – Bobbi's father – was a painter named Hurley Coors who had once been an illustrator for the *Saturday Evening Post*. Now he made his living as a painter of seascapes. He wore a goatee and a French beret and smoked a pipe. Bobbi's mother was also an artist, a sculptor, a shy and very gentle woman who wore sandals and smoked pot.

There were two daughters in the family. Bobbi was the older, Lacy the younger. Bobbi had just turned nineteen when she came to see Sander, who was still 'Doctor' to her then, and asked him for a prescription for birth control pills. Her mother had always supplied her with the pills before, but now she was living with a young man (she called him her 'old man'), a potter named Richard Hopkins, who didn't want her to have a baby.

'And how do you feel about it?' Sander had asked as he examined her. 'You want to have children?'

'Lots of 'em,' she said. 'But only when I'm living with a man I love who also wants 'em.'

'Well, you've got the body for it,' he said admiringly. 'That's for sure.'

Sander's medical offices were in a renovated Victorian house. There was an apartment directly above his offices where he had lived since he and his wife had separated. On the days when he accepted office calls – the days when he wasn't on duty at Fort Bragg Hospital – he usually went upstairs to have lunch in his own apartment. After he met Bobbi, however, he often had lunch at the Seagull Inn, where she worked as a waitress. In the course of time they became friends, and when the restaurant wasn't terribly busy, Bobbi would take a coffee break and join him while he had his lunch.

And, too, he sometimes saw her hitchhiking home after she got off work, and he always went out of his way to give her a ride. He would drive her out Little Lake Road to the lane that led down through the Pygmy Forest, at the end of which was a tar-paper shack that she shared with her 'old man', Richard Hopkins. She always got out of the car at the beginning of the lane and walked on down to the shack.

The first time Sander had dropped her off at the lane, she had thanked him and leaned across the seat to give him a kiss on the cheek. On the third or fourth time, she kissed him on the mouth. But she never invited him to the house or let him drive her there. She hinted that Richard might be jealous.

One day last summer Sander had met her by accident in front of Mendosa's grocery and hardware store. When he saw her coming out of the store with her arms full of groceries, he pulled the car over to the kerb. She came around to his side of the car, leaned down, and kissed him through the open window. She was wearing a skirt made from scraps of worn-out dungarees, a tie-dyed T-shirt, and beneath the flimsy T-shirt her breasts were not confined by a brassiere.

'Hi, Sandy,' she said. That was what she had called him for months now. No one else had called him that since he was a kid. 'Where you going?'

'Going to drive you home, I guess. I imagine it'd be kinda awkward for you, hitchhiking with an armload of groceries.'

She said, 'Oh, that's . . . Listen, take off your sunglasses, will you? I can't see what you're saying.'

He did. 'That better?'

'Yeah. Now tell me again where you're going.'

'I was going down to the ocean. It's such a beautiful day, I thought I'd take a walk along the cliffs.'

That was a lie. He hadn't had the slightest intention of going for a walk along the cliffs until he saw her, and then the idea popped full-blown into his mind. There was no denying, however, that it was a beautiful day, a rare, warm, sunshiny autumn day, without a cloud in the sky or a bank of fog anywhere to be seen.

'Lovely!' she said. 'Can I come with you?' There were small beads of sweat on her upper lip. 'I have to go home and get Richard's dinner, but there's plenty of time for that. Would you mind if I came?'

They put her groceries and his medical kit in the back seat of his Mercedes; she got in front with him, and they drove down Heeser Drive to the small parking lot overlooking the ocean. They left the car unlocked when they got out and went for a walk along the cliffs. The meadows of the headlands were thick with green grass and wild flowers. Seagulls circled overhead, gliding on currents of warm air.

The shore along the headlands was made up of small rocky islands, each with a stunted tree or two and clumps of wind-deformed bushes clinging to the ground. There were grottoes, tidal pools, and small beaches of fine yellow sand scattered along the foot of the cliffs.

Most of the time the ocean along the coast pounded and roared at the land, but that day there were hardly any waves, or at least no cresting ones – only swells, that roiled gently against the rocky shore, swirling and pouring over the rocks, spilling in cascades of foam, leaving the exposed kelp wet and dark and shiny.

After they had walked along aimlessly for perhaps a half-mile, holding hands and stopping to pick flowers or to look at something special, Bobbi said, 'Hey! I know where we can go. Come on, I'll show you.'

She released his hand and started down a nearby path that

descended from the top of the cliff to a small ribbon of sandy beach twenty or thirty feet below; then they turned and strolled south to where there was a cave in the face of the cliff.

'Miller's Cave!' she announced. 'You know about it? No? Oh, my goodness, you have to know about Miller's Cave. Sit down, I'll tell you about it.'

When he sat down beside her on the sand, she fumbled into a pocket of her skirt and brought out a crumpled marijuana cigarette. She straightened it out, licked it, and said, 'Got a match?'

After they got the joint going, they lolled around on the beach, passing the joint back and forth, soaking up the afternoon sun, and she told him the story of Miller's Cave: how a man named Miller had once caught his wife with another man, killed them both, and buried their bodies in Miller's Cave.

'Of course, it wasn't Miller's Cave then. It was Anybody's Cave. Well, you can get into the cave maybe once a month, when the tide is really low, like it is now. Well, of course, while Miller was burying those bodies in there, the tide came in and trapped him. He had to stay in the cave all night with the dead bodies of his wife and her lover, you see, and when he came out the next day, he was as crazy as a loon and his hair had turned absolutely white overnight!' She laughed defensively. 'Well, it's true! That's what they say! And guess what else? He couldn't talk at all! Couldn't say a word! From that time on the only sound he could make was a moaning sound, just like the sound that you can hear in the cave right now if you go in far enough. It's a sound that comes from a blowhole somewhere far back in the cave, and it's reallllllll *weird.*

'Anyway, so of course they could never find out what happened in the cave that night to make him go crazy and cause his hair to turn white overnight, because when they asked him a question, all he could say was' – and here she imitated the weird sound that Miller made – ' "UuuuHHHHhhuh!" Even the judge,' she said, mimicking the judge now, ' "How do you plead, guilty or not guilty?" And old Miller: "Uuuuu-HHH-hhhuh!" And when they put him on the scaffold and asked him if he had any last words, you know what he said? "UUUUuuHHHhhuh".'

They both laughed – almost got into a marijuana-induced giggling fit – and after their laughter had subsided, they sighed their way into silence, and then she said, 'Sandy? I have to go soon.'

He nodded. He understood what she was hinting at and took the hint. Though there was a small voice somewhere in a dark corner of his mind telling him how crazy this was, he nevertheless reached out and cupped her face in his hands and kissed her. It began as a cautious kiss, like one of a dozen they had exchanged before, but almost immediately it exploded into an open-mouthed sucking and probing and sharing of tongues, accompanied with groans, with fever. His hand went to her breasts beneath the flimsy T-shirt. He massaged her breasts, and soon she began to thrust her pelvis against his. After a few seconds of this, he began to pull her skirt up, she moving her body to make it easier for him, and he found, with a shock of excitement, that she wore no panties. And it was when he touched her crotch that she quite calmly, quite methodically, began to unbuckle his belt and unzip his fly.

Then he noticed that someone was on the cliffs above them. His eyes might have passed over the figure three or four times (he was lying on his back now, so he was seeing the figure upside down) before it registered in his feverish brain that the figure was not a plant or a configuration of boulders. It was a man. He was looking down at them. And perhaps Sander wouldn't have noticed at all if the man had not been wearing sunglasses made of one-way mirrors that caught the afternoon sun.

There was a little explosion of fear in Sander's head. Richard? Was it Richard Hopkins? He couldn't tell. The angle was wrong and the sunlight bouncing off the roiling surf played tricks with the shadows on the cliffs. Then, too, the marijuana . . . Under such conditions he probably wouldn't have recognised someone he knew well, let alone somebody he had seen only a few times.

'Wait,' he said.

'What's the matter?'

He dropped his eyes so that she wouldn't follow the direction of his gaze and see the person without being forewarned. He looked at her, chuckled with embarrassment, and said, 'Don't look now, but I think someone's watching us.'

'Where?' She jerked her head around to survey the cliffs. 'I don't see anyone.'

When Sander looked again, the figure was gone. Vanished. In the whimsical uncertainty of his drugged mind, he wondered if he had been mistaken. Had there really been a man there? Was he seeing things? Hallucinating?

'You're stoned,' Bobbi said in a delighted tone. 'There's nobody there.'

'I could've sworn . . .'

She reached for him again, trying to push him back down, but he said, 'Wait. Not here. Let's . . . can we go in the cave?' He didn't want to say that he was afraid, but he was. He was afraid of the man on the cliff, afraid that it had been Richard, and he felt too vulnerable here in the open.

Bobbi was delighted with the suggestion. Laughing, she jumped up and tugged at his hand. He rose too and, holding his pants up with one hand, followed her into the cave. They climbed upwards, over the rocky ledges, and finally came to the first landing where the tide never reached. The evening sun shone into the mouth of the cave, but they were so deep within the cavern that the light had dimmed to the power of a few candles.

And now Sander could hear the moaning sound from the blowhole somewhere far back and below them in the darkest depths of the cave, the sound that Miller had been forced to listen to as he spent the night trapped there with the bodies of his wife and her lover. It was the sound made when waves pushed air through a cavern and out a blowhole, a sound that could have been made by a giant conch shell, a sound like that of old Proteus blowing his wreathed horn.

They took off their clothes and made a pallet on the sandy floor. They made love there, and her moans of pleasure awakened in Sander a power that he didn't realise he had. He was astonished and delighted. He had long ago assumed that he was not a good lover, average at best. He didn't know until now that he was capable of giving a woman so much pleasure. That was why he delighted in her moans and cries as she thrashed her head from side to side. The sounds echoed in the cave, amplifying, multiplying, until they had completely drowned out the moans from the blowhole.

Afterwards, they lay in the dim light, holding each other, silent except for their breathing, feeling the cottony light-headedness of the marijuana, the peace of sexual satiety. But then they began to hear that sound again, the mournful cry from the back of the cave, from the depths of the sea, the sound of old Proteus's wreathed horn.

They started back to the car before dark. They climbed the cliff in the last salmon-coloured rays of the sun, then ambled across the headlands towards the car, their arms around each other. They were concentrating so intently on each other that they didn't notice anything wrong until, within a few yards of the car, they almost stepped on a package of frozen shrimp.

The groceries that Bobbi had left on the car's back seat had been scattered on the ground. Somebody had ripped open the paper sacks and flung the groceries everywhere and then stomped on them. A bag of flour had been ripped open, a carton of eggs smashed. Then they noticed that the contents of Sander's medical kit had also been flung into the grass and weeds.

'What the hell . . . is . . . *this*?' Bobbi said, slack-jawed with incredulity and outrage. 'Sandy! Somebody . . .'

Sander felt that little explosion of fear in the back of his head again, a premonition, a nebulous dread. He looked at the car and saw that the door on the far side was open.

She saw it, too, and followed him as he went around the vehicle and looked in.

'Oh, God,' she whispered.

The interior of the Mercedes had been slashed to ribbons. The white foam rubber of the cushions was bulging out of the slashes like intestines. The upholstery on the doors and ceiling had been cut to shreds.

Sander nodded grimly. 'So it *was* him I saw on the cliff.'

FEBRUARY FOURTEENTH

5 Shortly after seven o'clock on the morning of 14 February, Chris Jordan found the tan Pontiac in the parking lot at the foot of Heeser Drive where he had left it the night before. He had received two telephone calls from the Reverend Boyle during the late hours of the morning, the Reverend being worried because Billy hadn't come home when he was supposed to. Chris had tried to calm him, telling him that he had seen Billy and Lacy parked by the ocean that night and that they had probably fallen asleep in the car. But Chris himself was uneasy about it, so he left the house without even waiting for breakfast, drove down to the parking area and found the car.

There was nobody in it. The door on the passenger's side had been flung open, and the window had been smashed. It had been smashed from the outside, since all the bits of broken glass were showered over the front seat and floor of the car. There were a few dark splotches on the seat – dried blood? The keys were still in the ignition, still in the 'off' position, so the motor hadn't been running when it happened.

When *what* happened?

He looked for tracks between the puddles of water around the car, but the ground was hard and gravelly and even his own steps left no footprints in it. Then he saw the wristwatch in the grass and weeds that bordered the area. It was a man's watch. The band was broken and it was covered with a shiny substance, something very much like a shiny track of dried snail's slime. Chris picked up the watch in his gloved hand and saw that it was still running.

He checked a little further out in the grass and weeds and, with a steadily mounting dread, saw that something had recently been dragged through the grass, something – a body? – heavy enough to press down the grass. He began to follow the trail, sorry now that he hadn't eaten something for breakfast. The cup of instant coffee that he had gulped down before leaving the house now sloshed around like crude oil in his stomach, compounding his queasiness.

The patches of fog that had been so prevalent the night before were gone now, but the sky was overcast with low, thick clouds. It was going to rain before the morning was over, and he hadn't brought a raincoat.

As long as the trail led across the meadows of the headlands, he had no trouble following it. When it veered close to the cliffs, however, where the terrain became rocky and no grass grew, he often lost it. He doubled back a couple of times, found the trail again, and followed it with a constantly increasing sense of apprehension. He kept his eyes directly on the trail most of the time, expecting to find – what? Another wristwatch? An earring, perhaps? But he looked up every few seconds to survey the landscape in front of him, and soon he saw a plant that was growing in a jagged rock formation down near the surf. At first his mind didn't register the fact that there was no soil there in which a plant could grow. Then something made him stop and tilt his head, straining as if to hear a faint sound from somewhere, something telling him to wait a minute, now look again. *Look.*

Where? He swept the landscape again, paying very close attention to every detail. Once more he glanced at the formation of rocks that sloped down to the surf, and now the plant growing there was the only noticeable thing among them. But what was so unusual about it? It happened to be a greyish-pink colour, with waxy, finger-like petals . . .

A human hand?

He hurried towards the object, but he went slowly enough to glance behind every rock formation that was big enough to conceal anything. He glanced behind him a few times, too, and then went on, covering the remaining yards to the hand (there was no doubt about it now) by leaping from boulder to boulder. His last leap put him directly above the body.

It was Billy Boyle. His body was sprawled grotesquely among the jagged rocks. His skin was greyish-pink, waxen, and his eyes were open. There was a milky opaqueness over his eyes, which seemed to be staring fixedly at some vanished source of horror. Blood had run from his nose and ear. His longish hair was wildly tangled, and there it was again, a trace of it in his hair, that shiny substance like dried snail's slime. There were also smears of the slime on his clothes, across his chest and back.

6

Sander Quence was also awakened by a telephone call that morning. He didn't have to be at his office until ten, so he and Bobbi were still in bed when the phone began its loud, nerve-rattling ring. He thrashed out of his sleep to grab the phone, but he didn't put the receiver to his ear immediately. He held it at arm's length, as if it were something repulsive, until he could rub his eyes and face with his free hand. He smacked his lips, trying to get some saliva into his dry, foul-tasting mouth.

There was a faint, puzzled voice coming from the phone, a man's voice, metallic as a doll's: 'Hello? Sander? Hellooooo.'

Sander struggled up in bed, trying to guess what time it was – eight? – by the light filtering through the curtains. Bobbi stirred beside him. She turned, mumbling something, and laid her arm across his naked abdomen.

'Yes?' Sander finally said into the mouthpiece.

'Sander? This is D.B.'

D. B. Sheftman was a psychiatrist and the chief of staff at the Institute of Neurosciences in Ukiah.

'Well, D.B., how the hell are you?'

'Sleepy,' D.B. said, trying to strike a note of good-natured gruffness. 'I would apologise for phoning you so ea ly, Sander, but I myself haven't been to bed all night, and it's partly your fault. A man was brought in here last night, a man named Snyder. There was a deputy sheriff accompanying him who said you were the one who recommended that Snyder be brought here.'

'That's right,' Sander said as he stifled a yawn.

'Did you treat him?'

'No, no. Never been a patient of mine.'

'Last night, I mean. The deputy said you were at the scene when Snyder got the scalp injury.'

'Yeah, I was there, but I couldn't've treated him even if I'd wanted to, which I didn't.' Sander cradled the phone between his shoulder and cheek, fumbled a cigarette from a package on the nightstand. 'You couldn't get within a yard of that guy without getting your hand chewed off.'

'He was that way from the moment you first saw him? Where was that? In a bar?'

'No, no, he was all right – well, not all right, really, but at least he wasn't violent when I first saw him. In a bar, yeah.'

'Tell me about it, will you? Describe from the first moment you saw him, what time it was and all that, will you? I'll tell you why, Sander, this is an amazing case – simply amazing – and I need all the information I can get.'

As Sander described the incident to D.B., Bobbi stirred again, and Sander slipped his hand beneath the covers and stroked her naked hip, lovingly, soothingly. She gave a sleepy moan of pleasure.

When Sander finished the narrative, D.B. said excitedly, 'Do me a favour, will you, Sander? Get me a medical history on this man? Check the doctors in Fort Bragg in case he has a family doctor and find out from his wife or somebody whether or not he's ever been committed to a mental institution before.'

'All right,' Sander said. D.B.'s excitement about the case was infectious. 'But fill me in on what's happened so far. You been able to run any tests on him?'

'Sander, it's – what can I say? It's simply incredible, this case. I was late getting out of here last night. We'd had a staff meeting, so I was here when they brought Snyder in last night, and I haven't been home since.'

As D.B. talked, Bobbi slowly began stroking Sander's belly and soon let her hand drift idly down to his crotch, where she raked her fingers gently through his pubic hair, and then, as softly as she would have fondled the most delicate flower, she cradled his penis in her hand. She moaned encouragingly as it became erect.

D.B. was saying, '. . . so it took about five orderlies to get him into restraints, and I injected a hundred milligrammes of Thorazine, which had no effect at all on him. I hit him with two hundred more over the space of an hour, but – '

Bobbi had begun to massage his penis, just being her usual, idly sensuous self, and he soon began to feel the pleasure radiating out from his groin, slowly suffusing his whole body, making it difficult for him to concentrate on what D.B. was saying.

' – but it still had only a minimal effect on him, so after giving him three hundred *more* milligrammes in one dose, we finally got him sedated enough to do a work-up on him. He had a FUO, so we did a white blood cell differential, and found an elevated white count, but . . . well, we also found something else, something that neither I nor any of the doctors on the staff has ever seen before.'

Sander finally became fully awake. 'Bobbi,' he said *sotto voce*. 'Don't. I'm – '

'What?' D.B. said. 'Did you say something?'

'No, no. Go ahead,' he said as he pushed Bobbi's hand away. 'What do you mean, it's something you've never seen before?'

'Just that. It's too big to be a virus, and we don't think it's bacteria – in fact, it couldn't be either one. At first we thought it was a fungus of some sort, but it's not culturing like a fungus, and there's other odd things . . .'

Sander had begun to feel a tingling of dread. He pushed

himself up in bed, and Bobbi, who had been puzzled by his rejection of her advances, now sensed his growing concern. She, too, sat up in bed and began to watch his face as it became more and more pinched. But then he suddenly relaxed.

'Oh, come on, D.B.,' he said in a chiding tone, 'this isn't April Fool's day. What're you guys over there drinking? Or is it something you smoked?'

'Hold on a minute,' D.B. said, and apparently put his hand over the mouthpiece for a moment. Sander and Bobbi exchanged puzzled glances, and then D.B. came back on the phone, even more excited now. 'Sander, someone just handed me the results of an EEG we did on Snyder, and at first glance I don't believe it any more than I believed the first pathology reports, but here it is, right in front of me. His seizure patterns are far more severe than those of an epileptic. And the beta bursts from his amygdaloid nucleus! Looks more like the eruptions of a volcano than a human brain. Jesus Christ! Look, Sander, I gotta go. I'll be in touch later, but now be sure and talk to the patient's wife, will you? And get me a medical history?'

'Yes, I will. I'd – '

'And get back to me as soon as possible.'

'Absolutely. Sure, I'll – '

'If I'm not here, phone me at home, will you?'

'Okay, but – '

D.B. hung up. Sander sat staring at the phone for a moment before he slowly replaced it in its cradle. He had just turned to Bobbi and started to say something when the phone rang again. He picked it up quickly this time.

'Hello, Sander?' a woman's voice said. 'Let me speak to Bobbi. It's important.'

He placed his hand over the mouthpiece. 'Your mother.'

Bobbi's expression as she took the phone was one of exaggerated puzzlement. 'Mom? What is it? Something wrong?'

Sander crawled under the curled phone wire and sat up on the side of the bed. He lit another cigarette. He could hear the small, metallic voice of Bobbi's mother talking rapidly on the phone, but he couldn't hear what she was saying. He knew it couldn't be good news, however, not after he heard Bobbi say, 'Oh, my God, no! When?'

He looked at her and tried to guess what could possibly be so upsetting to her.

'And Mrs Boyle?'

The metallic voice again, the tone edging towards hysteria.

'Mom! Listen, Mom, I'm coming right over. Sandy has some Valiums here, I'll bring – Mom! Calm down, now, Mom, it won't . . . All right, I'll be right over.'

She hung up the phone, moving slowly, dumfounded. 'It's Lacy,' she said to Sander. 'She's been . . . Billy Boyle is *dead.* Somebody *killed* him. They went out together last night, Lacy and Billy, and oh, my God, somebody killed him and kidnapped her. They're forming a search party . . .'

7

By ten o'clock that morning the parking area on the cliffs at the foot of Heeser Drive had been cordoned off and was swarming with law officers. Sheriff Benjamin P. 'Buddy' Parsons had arrived and taken charge. There were already six Sheriff's Department cars there, plus an ambulance, two civilian cars that belonged to reporters from the local newspapers. and a rattletrap pick-up truck with a wood-and-wire cage on the bed that held six of Lem Forestner's yelping hounds.

One of the deputies was dusting the tan Pontiac for fingerprints; another was photographing it.

Radios were humming and crackling.

The ambulance roared away with Billy Boyle's body inside it.

All the officers who gathered around Sheriff Parsons and Deputy Chris Jordan were carrying walkie-talkies and shotguns.

Chris reported to Sheriff Parsons about finding the body. They agreed that the abductor had carried Lacy – over his shoulder, probably – and dragged Billy to where his body had been found. Chris said that after finding the body, he had radioed for help and then continued tracking the abductor and killer, afraid that any moment he was going to find Lacy's body, too. He followed the tracks – just one set of footprints in the grass – across Loader's Point and then down the winding steps carved into the cliffs to Portuguese Beach. The part of Portuguese Beach above the tidemarks was covered with driftwood, and Chris had lost the trail there when the tracks came straight out of the driftwood, crossed the ribbon of clean, sandy beach, and went directly into the surf. It was as if the killer had walked, without breaking stride, right out into the ocean and been swallowed up by it.

'It's an old trick,' said Sheriff Parsons, who was a devoted fan of TV westerns and knew a thing or two about tracking a man. 'He walked in, sure, but then he turned and walked along the edge of the surf so it'd wash his footprints away. Don't worry,' he told everyone present, but speaking particularly to the newspaper reporters, 'Buddy Parsons will catch this guy.'

The sheriff often referred to himself in the third person. He was a puffy-faced man with pouches beneath his eyes and a belly that bulged over his pistol belt. He had been a real-estate promoter before he had been elected sheriff in a hard-fought campaign ten years ago, and he hadn't stopped campaigning since. He spoke of his campaigns as Napoleon might have spoken of his.

When they were ready to go, the sheriff shouted to Lem Forestner. 'Hey, Lem! Bring those dogs out, let's go. We'll pick up the trail where the body was found. And, Matt,' he said to one of the shotgun-toting deputies, 'you drive over to Portuguese Beach, and don't let anybody go down there. Okay, men, let's move out.'

Lem Forestner and his hounds took the lead, and Lem had

trouble holding the yelping, excited dogs back as they lunged repeatedly against their leashes.

They found Lacy late that afternoon. The trail led across Loader's Point to Portuguese Beach, where they found Lacy's clothes, which had been ripped off her, and which, like everything else the abductor seemed to have touched, were spotted with dried slime. From there, the trail led around Church Point, the tracks sometimes coming out of the surf, and then across Big River Beach, under the bridge that spanned Big River, and on up the river. The dogs floundered around, lost the trail a number of times in the surf and in the marshy delta meadows of silt around the mouth of Big River, but they always picked it up again, leading the search party through the alder thickets and finally into the gloom of the giant redwoods that grew on the steep slopes of Big River Canyon.

The tall, thick growths of redwoods let in very little light and on foggy, overcast days the needle-like leaves of the redwoods seemed to collect the moisture in the air, condense it, and drop it, dripping like random raindrops, on to the mossy and fern-thick floor of the forest. Big River was deep here, and sluggish; mists rose off the lacquer-bright surface of the grey waters, and the grey clouds overhead were heavy with rain.

The dogs, still held on leashes by Lem Forestner, were in the lead when the searchers came around a bend in the river and saw her. She was in a small glade, an opening in the redwoods where the forest floor was thickly carpeted with grass and vines and ferns. She was there in the glade, naked, on her hands and knees. She apparently didn't hear the dogs until they were at the edge of the glade, not more than fifty feet from her, which suggested that she was in a state of deep shock.

Lem Forestner jerked the dogs to a stop as soon as they saw her. Everyone stopped. The halt was simultaneous and instinctive, but was only for a few seconds – long enough for them to assess the situation, to adjust to the shock of seeing her there like that, on all fours, naked, vomiting into the grass and ferns.

She jerked her head up to stare at them, and some of the vomit spilled down her chin. But the strange thing was, instead of seeing them as rescuers, her eyes widened with hostility, as if their presence held some fatal threat to her. Her face was twisted and ugly, her hair tangled and matted, and her naked body was splattered with mud and criss-crossed with raw, red scratches.

She bolted. Emitting a low and prolonged sound, a sort of guttural whine, she leaped to her feet and bolted towards the woods on the far side of the glade.

'Lacy!' Chris yelled. 'Lacy, wait!'

'What the hell?' Lonnie McCabe said. 'She's out of her mind!'

They all broke into a run, thrashing and stumbling through the vines and ferns. They carried their shotguns at port arms.

Chris began in the lead, but lost it when he broke stride and yelled over his shoulder to Lem Forestner, 'Keep those dogs back! They're scaring her.'

Lacy disappeared into the redwoods on the other side of the glade. Lonnie McCabe and Carl Gotlieb were the first of the deputies to go in after her, but they slowed down and finally stopped in the dripping wet gloom of the redwoods, because they didn't know which way she had run.

'Spread out!' Chris yelled, signalling frantically. 'She can't be far.'

She wasn't. She was hiding – crouching – behind some rocks and ferns in a small gully. When Chris was near her hiding place, she screamed – that high-pitched but strangely guttural sound again, a sort of screeching snarl – and leaped out into his path only a few feet in front of him.

Startled, Chris instinctively levelled his shotgun at her. The adrenaline that surged through his body caused his heart to pound wildly and his grasp on the gun to tighten so suddenly that he almost pulled the trigger.

She was set to attack him.

'Lacy,' he said, lowering the shotgun. 'It's me, Chris Jordan. It's all right now. We want to help you.'

But he could tell by the look on her face that things would never be all right for her again. There was not even a flicker of recognition in her wild, bloodshot eyes, not a sign of comprehension. Her lips twitched above her bared teeth and her whole body was tensely poised and trembling like an animal ready to pounce.

'Get away!' she growled. 'Get away from . . . me!'

The other men in the party were slowly, quietly, emerging from the trees around them. Lonnie McCabe had circled around and, after leaning his shotgun against a log, stealthily approached Lacy from behind. Carl Gotlieb, following Lonnie's lead, had circled around and was approaching from the other side.

Chris tried to keep her attention. 'Lacy . . . we're your friends, Lacy. We're here to help you. We're not going to hurt you and we won't let anybody else – '

But her red, bulging eyes and distorted face reflected the full force of her malice and hostility as she spewed the words out at Chris: 'Get the fuck away! From me! I'll kill you! Kill you!'

Lonnie and Carl leaped at her. They each grabbed one of her arms in a provisional way, almost apologetically, as if they were only trying to keep her from falling.

She exploded with violence. So furious was her struggle, so hysterical her hostility, that she managed to break loose from Carl's grasp for a second, and before he could grab her again, she had raked her fingernails down Lonnie's face, tearing four bloody furrows across his eyes and nose and mouth. And as she was struggling, she never ceased cursing, screeching; when another of the deputies – Matt Salis – rushed in to help subdue her, she crashed a knee towards his groin, missing by only inches, and the blow was so forceful that it almost knocked him down.

Lonnie hit her. It was a karate chop across the side of her neck, a blow that would have stunned an ordinary man, but it hardly fazed this girl. She bit him, snarling, screaming curses, as both Lonnie and Carl tried to twist her arms behind her back and put handcuffs on her.

Two more deputies quickly moved in to help, and it took all five of them to wrestle her to the ground and get the handcuffs on her.

Chris hadn't moved. Sheriff Parsons stood behind him now, puffing, his mouth agape. He had just caught up with the party.

'I don't believe it,' he muttered. 'Is this . . .? Chris, is *this* the girl?'

And Chris wasn't even aware of what he was thinking until he heard himself say, 'It was.'

'What?' the sheriff said. 'What d'you mean, *was*? Is it she or not?'

Chris nodded. 'Physically, sure, but . . . it's incredible. Lacy Coors was always one of the gentlest people who . . .'

Then he remembered the night before in the bar, where he had seen it first. 'It happened just like this,' he heard himself say aloud.

'What?' the sheriff said in an agony of confusion. 'Who?'

'Cliff Snyder,' Chris said, paused, and then in a tone of mounting dread, murmured, 'What in Christ's name is it? What's going on?'

8

'Sander we're on a three-way telephone hook-up with Professor Charles Roget. He's a professor of botany at the University of California at Davis. Specialises in mycology.'

'Mycology?' Sander said, 'Fungus?'

'Right. Now go ahead with your report on Snyder,' D.B. said.

A little rattled by D.B.'s staccato speech and by the implied significance of being on a three-way telephone hook-up, Sander cleared his throat and began to summarise the notes he had taken on Cliff Snyder's medical history. D.B. kept saying, 'Uh-huh, uh-huh,' as if to hurry him along, and when he had finished, D.B. said in a tone of brisk dismissal, 'Nothing there. What'd his wife say about them colliding with that man last night? A naked man, wasn't it?'

'I was coming to that,' Sander said, but came to it only after he lit a cigarette and puffed nervously on it. His seeming indifference was his way of resisting the white-hot intensity he felt coming from the other end of the line. Instinctively, he countered the tension with an exaggerated calmness. He told them what he knew about the naked prowler having been seen again last night, this time by an extremely reliable witness, a young NASA scientist, and how a boy had been killed and a girl apparently kidnapped by him, the prowler, whoever or whatever he was.

'Doctor Quence,' Professor Roget said. He had a deep, smoky voice. 'I've just been in contact with Noah Hoffmann at Stanford.'

The professor paused for a moment to let the name have its effect, and Sander was grateful. He needed a moment to recover from the surprise of hearing the name again after so many years.

'Really?' Sander said. 'How is he? I haven't – '

'Fine. Just fine. I briefed him on this case and asked him if he knew anybody on the north coast who could be of any help to us. He mentioned you. Said he thought you were somewhere in the area. He spoke very highly of you.'

Sander felt vaguely uncomfortable with this dredging up of the past. 'Well, really? I'm flattered that he even remembers me. I was just one of the many assistants he had there at the Biochemical Research Institute, and that was a long time ago.' This was by way of cautioning them, in case they were going to ask him to use any of the knowledge or skills he had acquired as an assistant to Professor Hoffmann. 'A long time ago . . .'

'In any case,' Roget said, 'we feel it's a fortunate coincidence, having you there in Mendocino. You might be pleased to know that Noah is going to be part of the team we're putting together for this operation, and he's on his way to Mendocino now.'

Sander felt his heart leap. 'Professor Roget, this suspense is making a nervous wreck out of me. Would you mind telling me exactly what's going on?'

'Well, Doctor, we don't know exactly. What little we do know, however, is very alarming.' He paused briefly, as if giving Sander a chance to prepare himself, and then said, 'It appears that what we have here is a very virulent new kind of disease, a metamorphic disease, if you can imagine that, but that's about all we know at this time.'

Sander sat in a stunned silence.

D.B. said, 'It's like I was telling you this morning, it's some kind of rapidly multiplying foreign bodies that none of us has ever seen before.'

'But whatever it is,' Professor Roget interjected, 'we know this: it has a very sophisticated host specificity, it attacks only humans, its contagion is absolute, and as yet we haven't found any defences against it.'

'*Metamorphic?*' Sander was still unable to get past that point.

It was D.B. who spoke again. 'Sander, we've got two more cases over here, infected from Snyder before we realised what we had on our hands. About two hours after infection, they – a couple of orderlies – began to show symptoms of extreme hostility and their physical strength seems to have increased tenfold. So we've got to assume that the foreign bodies invade the brain and cause severe personality changes in the patient. The glands, too, causing severe glandular malfunctions, particularly in the adrenal glands.'

'That's what you meant by "metamorphic"?' Sander asked. 'It really *is* metamorphic? Literally?'

'That's right,' D.B. said, 'and here's some more proof of that: Snyder's epidermis is now completely covered with a thin layer of something, a slimy substance, that's swarming with the foreign bodies. The cells of his – '

'Foreign bodies! Foreign bodies!' Sander interrupted. 'You keep talking about "foreign bodies"! For Christ's sake, D.B., they must at least fit into some pathogenic category – bacteria, or virus, *something*. Hell, the way you talk, they may be something from Mars.'

'And for all we know, they may be,' D.B. said in deadly earnest. 'In any case, *we* don't know what they are.'

'Anyway,' Professor Roget interrupted, 'the point of all this is, there's obviously a carrier at large in your area, Doctor Quence, probably the prowler that Snyder hit last night and the one who murdered that boy. So you can appreciate the urgency of the situation. What we have on our hands is a potential plague of horrendous proportions, and as long as that carrier is loose, he's infinitely more dangerous as a plague carrier than he is as a simple murderer.'

'Wait a minute,' Sander pleaded. 'Professor, you said you were a mycologist, a specialist in fungus? How did you come into this?'

'Doctor Sheftman sent some specimens from the Snyder patient down to the U.C. lab to be analysed. The lab people put them through all sorts of imaginable tests, and then sent for me because the one characteristic of the organism that they could isolate and recognise was a slight DNA reproductive resemblance to a fungus, probably a parasitic slime mould.'

'A fungus,' Sander said without inflection.

'Not like anything any of us has ever seen before, I assure

you', Roget said. 'The organism is no doubt a quasi fungoid of some sort, perhaps a mutant slime mould. And this similarity is substantiated by the fact that fungicides seem to work as disinfectants. So let's start from there. Here's what you'll need to do immediately – '

9

Professor Noah Hoffmann was in the computer room of the Stanford Biochemical Research Institute in Palo Alto, California. He was soberly watching a computer print-out screen as he puffed idly on an empty pipe. Now and then he would glance at a printed sheet lying beside the teleprinter and quickly and deftly peck a code on the computer keyboard with one stiff forefinger, then he would sit back, puffing on the empty pipe, and watch the programmed data flash on the screen. Occasionally, his lips, puckered around the pipe stem, would curl faintly into a nostalgic smile.

That was what he was feeling – nostalgia – as he scanned the information that he himself had put into the computer almost twenty years before. The print-out contained the data of a top secret project that he had once conducted for the US Army Department of Chemical and Biological Warfare. For some forgotten reason the project had been code-named *Dandelion*, and it had begun when a Russian scientist, Alexey Kirilov, had defected to the West, bringing with him news that the Russians had had a breakthrough in creating a germ-warfare agent by mutating a pathogenic fungus.

The idea was not new, of course. The Americans had known for a long time that such a disease might be feasible, and had even once developed a pilot programme to create such an agent. The programme had fallen victim to congressional budget cuts, but it was counted as no great loss. While the money was still available, the scientists in the programme had mutated various and sundry strains and types of fungi, but none proved to have any virulent pathogenic qualities. So the project was abandoned.

Then Kirilov came over and told about the breakthrough the Russians had had with a mutated pathogenic slime mould – *dictyostelium mucoroides mutabilis*, to be exact. When alerted to this, the Department of Chemical and Biological Warfare immediately launched a project of its own. The Stanford Biochemical Research Institute contracted to do the project, and Professor Noah Hoffmann was picked to head it. He, in turn, picked the people he wanted for his staff, and Sander Quence's name had been at the head of the list. At the time, Sander was doing advanced research in microbiology at the Research Institute, and was one of Hoffmann's favourite students.

As it turned out, however, Sander didn't want the job. Hoffmann could remember the night he offered the job to Sander and the words Sander had used to turn it down: 'That's all the world needs, another disease.'

Hoffmann had countered by saying, 'But if it's true the Russians have had some success in doing it, hadn't we better do it, too? If for no other reason than to develop a serum that would control it? If we don't develop some defence against it the Russians might be tempted to use it during a war, and then where would we be, eh? And remember, an offensive capability is still the best defence we can have, like it or not.'

'Maybe so,' Sander had said, and called Hoffmann by his first name, which he did only when they were talking privately, 'but look, Noah, it's just not the kind of thing I want to spend my life doing. I want to cure diseases, not create them.'

'Let somebody else do the dirty work, eh?' Hoffmann jibed good-naturedly. They were sitting in the parlour of Hoffmann's house, sipping their third drink and waiting for Isa Hoffmann, the professor's wife, to call them to dinner.

'Oh, come on, Noah, that's bullshit,' Sander had said. 'That's the same argument they used in the German extermination camps: "Well, *some*body has to do the dirty work".'

'Excuse me, my young friend,' Hoffmann had said with some asperity. 'They were *Nazi* – not *German* – extermination camps.'

'Okay,' Sander conceded, 'but the point remains: nobody *has* to do it. That's a cop-out, a rationalisation – or it would be for me, anyway. For you it's different. You're a scientist before everything else, so what may be a rationalisation for me would be a rationale for you.'

'Yah, yah,' Hoffmann had heartily agreed. 'I am a scientist. Above everything, I am that. And, Sander, my friend, I urge you to become also a scientist, a man whose first duty is the pursuit of knowledge, wherever it might lead. It's the fabled last frontier, science is – particularly biochemistry. A journey into the unknown, an exploration of worlds we know not of. Why speak of responsibility? Christopher Columbus discovered America, but is he to be held responsible for what others did to it? Is Winchester to be held responsible for all the people who've been killed by the rifle he invented? Come, come, Sander, be fair.'

Sander shrugged. 'I don't know. I don't think you can argue a thing like this by analogy. Face it: what they're asking you to do is build a chemical bomb, a bomb that may be every bit as powerful as a hydrogen bomb. Maybe *more* powerful. A nuclear blast has only a given amount of power, and has to stop when its fuel is exhausted. But a disease that we don't have any defence against – where might it stop? It might not stop at killing everybody in one city. It might wipe out a whole state, a whole country, a whole hemisphere.'

'That's right. So should we not therefore find some defence against it?'

Sander threw up his hands in mock despair. 'Back to square one.'

So it went. For hours they had argued, but to no avail. Sander wouldn't change his mind, so Hoffmann had to do *Project Dandelion* without him.

And now, twenty years later, Hoffmann was sitting in front of a computer screen, scanning a print-out of the data produced by *Dandelion* and contemplating the ironies of fate that had thrown him and Sander together again. Now they were going to be members of a team being formed to combat what apparently was a new and frightening disease, a disease with metamorphic fungus of some sort, perhaps even the same fungus that Hoffmann had used in *Dandelion*.

Now, however, the more Hoffmann reviewed the computerised data of *Dandelion*, the less likely it seemed to him that the Mendocino disease was a mutant. Professor Roget, Hoffmann's old friend and colleague, had been able to tell him very little about the disease, of course, but at least two characteristics seemed certain: it was metamorphic, and it required a human host.

Those two qualities alone made it seem too perfect to be the product of laboratory experiments in mutations. Regardless of the most sophisticated and precise lab techniques, radioactively induced mutations were haphazard and random at best, and so, even if scientists somewhere had succeeded where *Dandelion* had failed, it was still inconceivable that they could have mutated a pathogenic organism that was both metamorphic and human specific. The odds against it were fantastic. Such an organism, rather than being the result of mutations, would almost certainly have to be a genetically engineered organism.

Acting on this supposition, Hoffmann went to another part of the *Dandelion* programme on the computer. He hurriedly checked his notes, glanced at his watch and then asked for the chemicals required for synthesis of DNA. The print-out read:

Synthesis requires presence of all four deoxyribonucleoside triphosphates,
1. *deoxyadenosine triphosphate (dATP)*
2. *deoxycytidine triphosphate (dCPT)*

3. *deoxyguanosine triphosphate* (*dGTP*)
4. *thymidine triphosphate* (*TTP*)

Then he typed out his request for the molecular structure of a thymidylic acid molecule that had been used in the experiments. The print-out read:

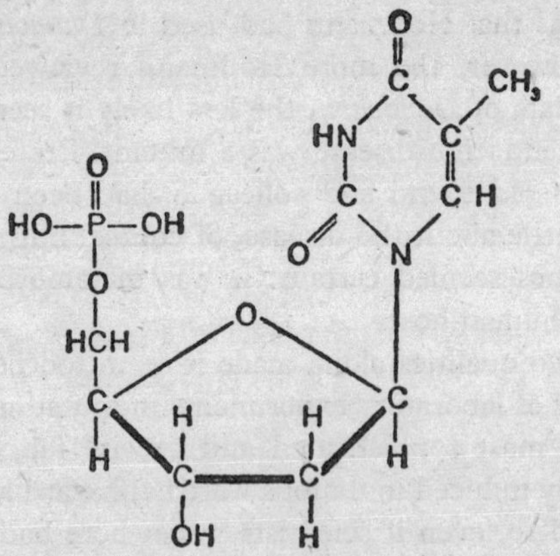

This continued for hours. He kept looking at his watch, hurrying, trying to acquire all the information he could before he left for Mendocino. Time was growing short, however, since he had agreed to be in Mendocino before morning, and so he finally had to be satisfied with the information, however scanty, that he had managed to memorise. He would have liked a print-out of all the *Dandelion* data, but it was classified top secret, and he didn't have the time required to go through the red tape to get the information cleared.

However, there was one more thing he had to do before he left the institute. He picked up the telephone beside the terminal and asked the operator to put through a call to the Pentagon. He wanted to speak with General Thurston Blanchard, who had been, back in the days of *Project Dandelion*, the projects co-ordinator for the Department of Chemical and

Biological Warfare. In those days Blanchard had been a bird colonel; now he was a lieutenant-general, serving on the National Security Council as liaison officer for DCBW.

It was nearly seven o'clock on the West Coast, which meant that it was nearly ten in Washington, so Hoffmann really didn't expect to contact the general in person. He did succeed in getting one of the general's aides, however, and learned that General Blanchard was at the White House in a meeting of the National Security Council. The council was discussing the latest Soviet threat in the Middle East, and it wasn't known whether General Blanchard would return to his office that night. However, the aide said, if the professor wished to leave a number where he might be reached . . .

Hoffmann gave the aide the number of his home phone, then he packed his notes and papers into his attaché case, said good night to the uniformed guard at the door, and went to find his car in the parking lot. As he drove home, he listened to the news on his car radio: all of it bad. The Russians were reported to be deploying nuclear missiles in Syria. The Chinese were massing troops in Manchuria. There were unconfirmed reports that the President had ordered the armed forces to go on maximum alert, and all military reserves were being called to active duty. The National Security Council was in continuous session at the White House.

So once again the world had become a proverbial powder keg, and Hoffmann wondered what, if anything, the disease that had suddenly appeared in Mendocino had to do with it. He felt certain there was a connection, but the implications of it were too frightening to contemplate.

10

Still in his smock, Sander hurried out of his office, through the crowded waiting room, and as he went out the door, he turned and said to the startled nurse-receptionist, 'Cancel all my appointments. Don't make any new ones till I tell you to.'

He drove straight to the local pharmacy, rushed in, and interrupted the clerk with a customer; he told him to get all the tolnafte undecylenic acid he had. He took as many bottles as he could carry, dumped them in his car, then drove to Chris Jordan's house. After bringing his Mercedes to a gravel-spewing stop in the driveway, he bounded up the sidewalk and entered the office without knocking.

Marge was there, sitting in front of the short-wave radio, which was crackling with static. A woman's voice was saying over the speaker, '. . . television newsman, wants to know if there's any word yet. Over.'

Speaking into the microphone, Marge said, 'Negative. Not since two-o-five. The party's still in Big River Canyon.'

'Ten-four, Marge. Keep us posted. Over and out.'

When she switched off the microphone and turned to him, Sander said, 'Marge. Don't be alarmed now, and don't ask me any questions. Just trust me and do as I ask, okay? It's important that I get in touch with the sheriff's search party immediately. Can you get them on the radio?'

Bewildered, she shrugged and said, 'No. They have walkie-talkies and they were headed into Big River Canyon, the last report we got from them.'

This was apparently meant to explain everything to Sander, but he didn't get it. 'So?'

'So they're in a canyon. The walkie-talkies aren't powerful enough for us to get them, or for them to get us. When you get down that – '

'Try them,' he said.

She shrugged helplessly. 'But, Sander, I just told you, they – '

'Try!' he snapped.

Taken aback by his assertiveness, she murmured, 'All right,' and hurriedly tried to call the search party. Four or five times she said, 'Sheriff's party, do you read me? Over.'

Nothing but static.

'Shit,' Sander said. 'And there's no other way to contact them?'

She shrugged again, apologetic for being so helpless, and was becoming alarmed now by Sander's urgency. She had never before seen him like this. 'To get them on the radio, you'd have to be down in the canyon yourself.' She paused. 'Or maybe above them, like in a helicopter.'

'Helicopter?' An idea worked itself into his consciousness.

'Newman!' he said then, and reached for the telephone. 'Operator, this is an emergency call. Put me through to the Seagull Inn.' He stood by, nervously drumming his fingers on the desk, until a woman's voice answered. He asked for James Newman, and then waited perhaps two more agonising minutes while the phone in Newman's room rang and rang. Nobody answered.

The woman came back on the line and said, 'I'm sorry, he doesn't seem to – '

'Page him in the restaurant,' Sander ordered.

'Yes, sir,' she said, intimidated by his tone.

And after another moment of finger-drumming anxiety, a man answered the phone.

'Jim? This is Sander Quence. Listen. Something's come up, an emergency, and – Do you still have the use of that NASA helicopter?'

And Newman's voice, very guarded and mystified, answered: 'Yeah, I've still got it, why?'

'Where is it?'

'At the hangar at the Georgia-Pacific lumber mill in Fort Bragg. They have a landing strip there and – '

'Can it be ready to go in five – ? Wait! Hold the line a minute.'

A message was coming in through the static on the radio, a man's voice. It was Car four calling Sheriff's Headquarters, and in the background was a terrible screaming sound. A woman's voice from headquarters answered the call. 'This is Headquarters, Car four. I read you. Go ahead.'

'Joan, this is Carl. We found the girl. She's alive, but – ' There was a new outburst of screaming in the background. 'Can you hear that? She's fighting like a wildcat. We had to carry her here, all the way out of the canyon. We don't know what's the matter with her. We're taking her to Fort Bragg Hospital. Sheriff and the rest of them are still pursuing the suspect in the canyon. Over.'

The woman's voice from HQ asked, 'Where are you, Carl?'

'We're under – '

Sander set the phone down and said to Marge, 'Interrupt them.'

' – the Big – '

'But, Sander,' Marge said, 'shouldn't – ?'

' – River Bridge.'

'Interrupt them!' Sander snapped. 'I have to talk to them.'

Marge grabbed the microphone and pushed the transmit button. 'Headquarters, Car four, this is Station seven. Interrupting transmission. Stand by, please. Cease transmitting and stand by for a message. Do you read me, Carl?'

'I read you, Marge. What's going on?'

'Stand by,' Marge said, and handed the microphone to Sander. 'When you want to transmit, push this button down,' she told him. 'Let it up when you want to receive.'

Sander said, 'Hello? Carl, this is Doctor Sander Quence. Are you a deputy?'

'Yes, sir. What can I do for you?'

'How many of you are there?'

'Two of us here, me and another deputy, Matt Salis. And

the girl, of course.'

'Listen to me, Carl, and don't ask any questions,' Sander said, trying to use very strong words in an ordinary tone of voice so that they would become concerned without becoming panicked. 'You and the other depty are to take Lacy to Fort Bragg Hospital without delay. Report to Doctor Brokowski. He'll be expecting you. You're to do exactly as he says. You understand?'

Carl's crackling voice was hesitant, doubtful. 'Understood, Doctor Quence. But Sheriff Parsons ordered us to join the search party again as soon as we've delivered the girl to – '

'Never mind that,' Sander said.

Marge said, 'He can't hear you. You're both transmitting at once. Wait till he finishes.'

Sander said, 'Carl? Are you there?'

'Yes, sir.'

'Carl, I don't care what the sheriff ordered you to do. *I'm* ordering you to report to the hospital for fungicide baths and isolation. I'm sorry, I don't have time to argue or explain, but I'll tell you this much: all of you . . .' He was aware that others were monitoring the conversation, so he chose his words carefully. 'All of you may have come in contact with a highly communicable and virulent disease. So it's important that you do exactly what I tell you. All right?'

This time there was no hesitation in Carl's voice. 'Ten four, Doctor. Understood. Will do. Over.'

'One more thing,' Sander said. 'You say you're at the mouth of Big River Canyon. Can you reach the search party from there with your radio?'

'Negative. They're about three or four miles up the canyon, around half a dozen bends. The walkie-talkies they have reach only a couple of miles at best. Over.'

'All right, then, Carl. Get to the hospital as fast as you can, commensurate with safety, of course, and good luck. I'll be in to see you as soon as possible. Here's Marge again.'

He handed the mike back to Marge, who signed off and immediately began fending off a flood of panicky questions from other stations that had been monitoring the call.

Sander picked up the phone again. 'Jim? Did you hear any of that?'

'Yeah, I heard what you were saying, anyway. So you want me to fly you over Big River Canyon?'

'That's it. The search party's still in there, apparently, chasing that man. I have to get to them before they get to him.'

11

When the search party came up out of Big River Canyon and reached the clearing in the Pygmy Forest, Chris immediately recognised it as the place he had been the night before, the shack where Richard Hopkins lived. The dilapidated house stood dank and weather-greyed except where patches of orange lichen grew below the eaves. There was no light in the house, no smoke coming from the chimney. The back door was standing open and the two hounds, confused and frustrated, ran in and out of the house, sniffing everywhere.

It was empty, then. The trail had led to the house, and even into it, but the quarry wasn't there, or the hounds would have bayed him.

'Mighta been here and gone,' Lem Forestner said. 'That case, we might be able to pick up the trail again where it leaves the clearing.'

Sheriff Parsons was puffing so hard from his run through the Pygmy that his words came in jerks. 'We'll check it out first, Chris. Let's me and you take the back door. You three,' he said to Lonnie and the other two deputies, 'go round and come in . . . the front door. Lem, you get your dogs. And you,' he told the reporter who had managed to follow them all the way (the other reporter had turned back a long time ago), 'you stay out of it.'

With his shotgun at the ready, Chris slowly mounted the creaking steps and stood sideways with his shoulder against the jamb, peering into the gloomy interior of the house. From where he stood he could see the front door, and he waited and watched until he saw Lonnie coming in; then, followed by a panting Sheriff Parsons, he cautiously made his way into the house, into the main room, which was a combined living room and kitchen. The dogs were sniffing around some trash in a corner of the room.

The place was a shambles. The cupboard doors were gaping open, and boxes and cans of food were scattered all over the floor in the kitchen part of the room. Flour spilled from a broken bag, garbage and empty tin cans overflowed the sink. On the drainboard lay a half-gnawed loaf of bread that was covered with mould. Pots and pans, some of them dirty and caked with mildewed food, were strewn about the room. And on many of the things were traces of that peculiar glittering substance like dried snail's slime, as if a swarm of snails had passed through the house.

In the living-room area, which had also once served as a pottery, the table and chairs were overturned amid pieces of broken pottery, upset containers of glazing compounds, and torn clothing.

The search party exchanged glances, uneasy and incredulous, because it was obvious that the chaos was deliberate. The place had been vandalised, torn apart.

There were two doors leading off the living-room area. One was closed, the other half-open. Chris signalled Lonnie with his eyes, and Lonnie stepped in front of the closed door. He levelled his shotgun at the door as Chris slowly reached for the knob with his gloved hand. He turned it slowly, then suddenly threw open the door.

Nothing. It was a closet. There were a few pieces of mildewed clothes – men's clothes – but nothing else except a dank stench of mould and rot.

The other two deputies – Harvey Cunningham and Joey Nunns – had gone to the other door, the half-open one. Joey Nunns kicked the door. It banged back against the wall, and the two of them, with their shotguns levelled, dashed into the room. But it, too, was empty. There was a bare mildewed mattress on the floor and lots of papers and books strewn everywhere, but no sign of life.

Lem Forestner was the first to speak, breaking the intense silence that had brooded over them for the past few minutes. Lem had come in to get his dogs, who were still snuffling about the room, whining now and then, but no longer barking.

'I'll be go to hell,' Lem said. 'What hit this place, a cyclone?'

Nobody responded to his question.

Lem grabbed the dogs' leashes and cursed them softly as he led them out the front door. 'I'll take the dogs, scout around, see if I can pick up a fresh trail.'

They were silent for another moment after Lem had gone, and it was the sheriff who finally put an official stamp on what was obvious at least to him: 'Gone. The sonofabitch got away.'

'No,' Chris said in a soft voice. 'I don't think so.'

All eyes went to him. They were standing amid the debris in the living-room area in a sort of uneven circle, and they turned as one man to Chris, whose head was slightly tilted, as if he were listening to some sound just beyond hearing.

'You think he's still here?' the sheriff whispered.

Chris didn't answer.

'You hear something?' Lonnie asked.

'I don't know,' Chris said. 'But I got a feeling . . .'

Then the man was suddenly there. He dropped among them like a bomb. He had been in the loft. Quite suddenly he came feet first through the trapdoor in the ceiling and landed among them, a man naked and dirty, glistening with a sheen of slime, his hair matted and tangled, with only the gaping mouth and fierce eyes recognisable as human features in the greenish-grey mass of his face.

He screamed. From his gaping mouth came a torrent of sound, a scream that was more than just maniacal anger and hostility, and then he attacked. All this was in one continuous movement. He didn't turn his head right or left, but plunged at the man closest to him, covered the distance in two strides, and, still screaming, brought his fist down like a hammer across the sheriff's head and face.

Sheriff Parsons fell, crashing amid the debris on the floor; then the man turned towards Chris, reaching out for him. That was when Lonnie crashed the butt of his shotgun down on the man's head. Rather than collapsing, however, the man screamed again and grabbed the shotgun from Lonnie's grasp. Lonnie was stunned with surprise that the man hadn't gone down under the blow, but was even more surprised when the man whirled on him, ripped the shotgun out of his hands as easily as he might have jerked it from the hands of a child, and swung it like a club. Lonnie ducked, instinctively reaching for his pistol. The stock of the shotgun missed Lonnie and slammed into the side of Harvey Cunningham's head. The bones cracking beneath the blow made a sound deeper than that of the wooden gunstock cracking and splintering. Harvey fell.

Lonnie fired. Within the confines of the room, the blast from the .38 sounded like a cannon. The bullet splattered a hole in the man's side, spinning him around, and Lonnie fired again. The second shot was low, blowing away part of the man's leg, and before he could fall, Lonnie was preparing to fire again.

'No!' Chris yelled.

Lonnie held his fire. The man fell backwards and slammed against a wall with such force that the whole house shook. He bounded off the wall and crashed like a tree into the pots and pans on the trash-strewn floor. He thrashed about, trying to get up even before he had stopped falling.

The men stood as still as statues, as if amazement and horror had turned them literally to stone, and watched as the slime-covered man thrashed about on the floor, growling now rather than screaming, and perhaps even trying to say something in what might have been a recognisable human voice. Amid the clattering of pans and broken pottery, he finally pulled himself up to a sitting position, his back against the wall, his hands groping at the blood-oozing wounds on his body. Then another sound came from his mouth.

'Youuuuu willll . . .' His voice was low and had a subterranean timbre, as if it were blowing out of some deep cavern in the earth itself, and the words, the syllable sounds, seemed to be slowed down, like a phonograph record played at a reduced speed.

With his pistol levelled, Lonnie leaned forward, menacing and contemptuous, as if the man were some sort of personal affront to him. 'You trying to say something?'

'Don't get too close,' Chris warned.

Then the man spoke again, loudly and clearly enough for all of them to hear, the words slow and deeply slurred but quite understandable: 'You will . . . soon . . . die . . . like me . . . die . . .' For that moment there seemed to be in his voice a sort of religious joy.

Then he leaped. With the use of only one leg but still with the strength of many men, he sprang – propelled himself – on to his feet and, screaming, leaped at Lonnie.

Lonnie fired point-blank into the man's chest, but the man's momentum carried him smashing into Lonnie, knocking him down, falling on top of him, mauling him. Lonnie yelled for help.

It was Chris who next used his shotgun like a club. He slammed the butt of the gun against the man's head with much more force – the force of panic – than he had intended. He felt the man's skull crack and crumble beneath the blow; even so, the blow had not been powerful enough to knock the man off Lonnie. He quivered and died while still on top of

Lonnie, and Lonnie had to heave him off.

Nearly hysterical with anger, Lonnie got to his feet and, with a revulsion so profound that he was sobbing, kicked at the man's body again and again.

'Lonnie!' Chris yelled.

But Lonnie didn't stop. He lept kicking the man's lifeless body until Chris shouted again; then, still in a rage of revulsion, Lonnie jerked his handkerchief from his pocket and tried to wipe the slime and blood off his face and hands.

A first, faint radio message began to come through. From the walkie-talkie slung across his shoulder, Chris heard the very weak, faraway voice and the static of transmission. By the time Chris pulled the radio from its leather case and extended the antennae, the voice had grown louder and was almost understandable. In a tone that fluctuated between a demand and a plea, the man's voice was saying, 'Calling sheriff's party! Come in if you hear me! Come in, sheriff's party!'

'This is the sheriff's party,' Chris snapped. 'Identify yourself.' He was grateful for the call. It brought with it a much-needed touch with something familiar and routine. In another way, however, the call seemed to be an intrusion of trivia into a scene of profound wonder, awe, horror.

A note of great relief broke through the next transmission. 'Chris! Is that you? This is Sander. Where are you?'

Like the other men in the room, Chris was still staring raptly at the body of the man on the floor, though Joey Nunns soon broke the trance and ran to where Harvey Cunningham had fallen on the floor. Lonnie was still scrubbing his face and neck with his handkerchief.

'Yeah, this is Chris. Glad to hear it's you, Sander. We need a doctor here. We got two men hurt, both unconscious, looks like, maybe even dead. Where are you? Over.'

'I'm in a helicopter, heading for Big River Canyon. What's your location? Over.'

'We're at Richard Hopkins' house in the Pygmy. It's

about three miles up Little Lake Road.'

'I know where it is,' Sander said, his voice growing stronger every second. 'What happened that you've got injuries in the party? Have you found the suspect yet?'

'Yeah. Here in the house. He's dead, looks like.'

Sander's voice came across firm and cool: 'Chris? Don't touch anything. I'll be there in just a few minutes. Don't let any of your men touch the body. That's crucial. You understand? Over.'

'Understood, but it's already happened.'

There was a moment of silence, and then Sander's voice, heavy with warning, said, 'Don't let anybody else touch the body. I'm on my way. Be there . . . I can see the house now.'

And now they could hear the first sounds of the helicopter, that *whump whump whump* sound coming closer and closer every second.

Lonnie vomited. He was in such a paralysis of concentration that he apparently didn't even realise that he was going to vomit until it started pouring from his mouth. He slapped his hand over his mouth, groaned loudly, and ran from the house. He dashed outside, fell on to his hands and knees in the yard, and vomited into a mud puddle.

Lem Forestner appeared at the front door. When the shooting started, he had dragged the dogs into the woods, tied them to a tree, and hid until it was all over. At the same time that Lem appeared in the front door, the newspaper reporter came cautiously up the steps to the back door.

'Don't come in here,' Chris said to both of them. 'Stay out. Go on, get out of here. Stay in the yard.'

Lem did as he was told, but the reporter, who seemed to be in a panic of bewilderment, said, 'Please, what's – ?'

'Get out!' Chris yelled. 'Get the fuck out of here!'

The reporter turned and bolted.

The helicopter came in low over the Pygmy Forest. The backwash from the rotors whipped and jerked the stunted trees, making them seem to be moss-clothed skeletons in a frenzied dance, as the helicopter passed over them.

Amid a deafening roar of clattering rotors, the helicopter hovered over the widest expanse of the yard for a moment, the wind from its backwash banging the doors and rattling the windows. Then it descended, landing feather-softly in the wet yard. The motor was cut instantly. Sander jumped out, a bag in his hand. Ducking under the whirling rotors, he ran towards the house. Newman was pulling on gloves when he emerged from the winding-down helicopter.

Sander came through the door and stopped so suddenly that Newman almost ran into him. They both stared at the slime-damp man there on the floor in a pool of blood with the side of his head crushed. They might have stood there as if hypnotised for a full fifteen seconds, and then Chris spoke.

'Sander,' he said. 'The sheriff . . .'

Sander forced his eyes away from the body and went to kneel beside the sheriff's sprawled and lifeless form. With his hands protected by surgical rubber gloves, he began searching for vital signs.

Newman spoke in an ordinary voice, a studied voice, but his eyes betrayed his tangled feelings of fascination and revulsion as he said, 'That's him. That's the man I saw last night. But . . . what's with him? What's all that slime?'

'Keep away from him,' Sander said. 'He contacted some sort of metamorphic disease. Nobody knows what the hell it is, but that's what it did to Richard Hopkins.'

Chris said, 'And it's . . . contagious?'

'Yes,' Sander said as he left the sheriff and went to Harvey Cunningham. However, he needed only a glance to know that Harvey was beyond help. 'They're both dead,' he said as he took the plastic bottles of tolnafte from his medical kit. He poured some of it over the rubber gloves he was wearing. 'Now here's what I want each of you to do.' He gave them each a piece of gauze soaked in the acid and instructed them to wash all the exposed area of their skin.

'Disease, hell,' Chris said in a voice that was sharp with

defensive demand. 'I never heard of any disease that'd do that to a man.'

'Nor has anybody else,' Sander said. 'How many of you came in direct contact with Hopkins?'

'Only Lonnie, I guess, and the sheriff,' Chris said. 'Lonnie's outside.'

'I'll go look after him. As soon as you're finished, Newman will fly you all back to Fort Bragg Hospital. You'll be given fungicide baths and put in isolation for a while.' He whirled and passed Newman, who was still standing in the doorway.

Newman started to turn and follow Sander out, but he glanced around the room first and something that caught his eye made him stop in mid-turn. There, amid the debris on the floor, was a large cone-shaped rock. It was black and ruggedly porous on the large end, but wavy-smooth on the cone end. On seeing it, Newman reversed the direction of his turn and crossed the room, passing Chris and Joey Nunns as they hurried towards the door. Newman stepped over the trash and broken pottery and stopped at the rock, crouching down beside it. It was a meteorite. There was no mistake about it, a meteorite.

'I'll be damned,' he said aloud to himself, resisting the impulse to touch the wavy-smooth ablation markings on the cone end. A carbonaceous chondrite. Exactly what he had been scouring the countryside for since he had arrived in Mendocino two weeks ago, and there it was.

12

The hospital lobby was crowded, more crowded than Sander had ever seen it, but the first faces he saw as he came in with the last load of men from the Hopkins house (Lem Forestner and the newspaper reporter) were those of the Coors family: Bobbi and her parents who were sitting on a sofa in the lobby. When Sander entered, Bobbi ran to him and said, 'Sandy! My

God, what's happened to Lacy? Why can't we see her? Why won't – ?'

'Bobbi, I don't have time to talk about it now,' he said. 'I'm sorry, but we've got a hell of an emergency on our hands. Look, I'll be back as soon as I can. Then I can have a look at Lacy and we can talk, okay? I'll be back,' he assured her as he turned to leave.

Dr Brokowski had just entered the lobby from one of the wings and moved towards Sander as soon as he spotted him. Herbert Brokowski was the hospital's house doctor, a mild-mannered little man who wore thick, horn-rimmed glasses and a toupee.

'Sander,' he said with mingled relief and exasperation, 'I have to talk to you.'

'Of course,' Sander said. 'In the meantime, though, here are two more men that have to be processed. The others that I sent in, the deputies, they're being taken care of?'

'Yes, yes, of course. I've followed instructions to the letter. Here,' he said to a passing orderly, 'show these two men the way to – '

Sander went to the reception desk and leaned across it to catch Carol Marvin's attention. 'Carol, this is urgent: get me a Professor Charles Roget at the University of California at Davis right away, please.'

'Yes, Doctor,' Carol said. The reception area behind the counter was a beehive of activity. Phones were ringing, people talking, typewriters clattering, orderlies and nurses hustling about with clipboards and syringes and stethoscopes.

Brokowski caught up with him. 'Sander, listen,' he pleaded. 'I just got a call from the Department of Public Health in Sacramento. They told me they're invoking clause fifteen-B of our charter. You know what that means? Sander, they're taking over the hospital.'

'Clause fifteen-B?' Sander said indifferently, and started to move away.

Brokowski caught his elbow. 'And they're going to do it?

Just like *that*?' He tried to snap his fingers, but there was no snap in them. 'So I've got to move out a whole wing of patients? They're screaming at me. They're threatening all sorts of malpractice suits. What am I going to do with them? Send them home?'

'And Carol,' Sander said, turning back to the woman behind the reception desk, 'I want an outside line kept open at all times.'

'Yes, Doctor Quence.'

He turned to Brokowski. 'Listen,' he said. 'Don't you know what's going on here?'

'I know what they *told* me.'

'Then you know as much as I do, and that should be enough.'

'What they told me was that this may be the outbreak of a metamorphic disease. Have pity on me, Sander. I'm an old man. My credulity is as brittle as my bones, it breaks easily.' Brokowski was about seventy years old. There was a turkey-wattle of loose flesh under his chin that shook when he became upset, which was often enough because he cultivated the image of a cantankerous Old World gentleman. He had come to America nearly thirty years before, having been liberated from the Buchenwald concentration camp in Germany. He had survived the camp because he was a doctor. His family hadn't.

'I'm not asking you to believe anything,' Sander said. 'I'm just asking you to act as if you did. But I'll guarantee you one thing: if you'd seen what I just saw in a house in the Pygmy Forest, you'd throw your own mother out in the street if it'd help stop whatever it is we've got to stop.'

Brokowski seemed chastised. He thrust his chin forward. He was pulling at his tight collar, but it was as if he had suddenly bared his throat to Sander in a do-with-me-as-you-will gesture. 'All right,' he said. 'I'll get on with it. The two men you just brought in . . .'

'The same treatment as the others: fungicide baths and

isolation. What about specimens from the others?'

A few people had begun to gather around them, obviously keeping a tactful distance while they waited to speak to Sander. One of them, Sander noticed from the corner of his eye, was the Reverend Boyle.

'Blood only,' Brokowski said. 'Did you want urine, too? We're short of lab help, you know. As it is, I had to call Anne Jackson on her day off. She's doing the blood now. We got specimens from everybody except the Coors girl. Damnedest thing I ever saw, the strength that girl has. We couldn't let her out of the straitjacket long enough to get a blood sample, and we couldn't hold her down even if we did.'

Sander felt like shaking Brokowski and saying, 'You damned old fool, can't you get it through your head what's happening?' But he fought back the impulse and said, 'Get one. I don't care if you have to put her toe in a vice and slash it with a knife. And what about the two deputies I sent in earlier with her, one by the name of Carl Gotlieb? Has either of them shown any signs of aggression or hostility?'

Brokowski shook his head. 'On the contrary, they've been very co-operative.'

'Well, then, here's what we'd better do now,' Sander said, feeling his throat becoming dry. He wished he had a drink. There was a bottle of Scotch in his office on the second floor. Maybe in a little while . . . For the present, though, he told himself that he had better keep his head as clear as possible, muddled though it already was with the nagging fear that he wasn't up to this task, this role of leadership that he'd had to assume in a vacuum. Who the hell was he to be issuing orders as if he knew what he was doing? But there was nobody else to do it, so he did. 'See that the men I just brought in are processed and isolated. Take the weapons away from all the deputies. That's very important.'

Brokowski opened his mouth to speak, but Sander kept talking, ticking the orders off on his fingers. 'Sedate the Coors girl. If Thorazine won't do it, try SP or chloroform, I don't care, just as long as you get it done. We need blood and skin tissue for biopsy.' Then he turned back to the receptionist. Brokowski hurried away as Sander asked Carol, 'Any luck on that call?'

'The lines are all busy,' she said. 'The operator at the university says there are half a dozen calls waiting to get through to Professor Roget.'

Sander was aware that one of the men who had been waiting to speak to him was edging closer and making little throat-clearing sounds in an effort to lay first claim to his attention. It was the Reverend Boyle, whom Sander ignored. 'Keep trying,' he told Carol. 'Tell them this call has top priority. And, Carol, one more thing. I want both ambulances to stand by for a run, but the crews have to be given special instructions on prophylactic measures. Let me know when they're ready to go. I'll be in the lab for the next few minutes.'

With that, he jerked his medical kit off the counter and hurried away down the corridor of Wing C, the second of three wings that led off the lobby – hurrying not only to get away from the Reverend Boyle, but also trying to avoid Christine Parsons, the sheriff's wife, whom he had just seen coming in the main entrance and who, judging by the already near-hysterical look on her face, had already received the news about her husband.

To ignore the Reverend and run from Mrs Parsons, not to mention having to keep his eyes straight ahead as he hurried out of the lobby so that he wouldn't have to meet Bobbi's imploring stare, made Sander feel cowardly and guilt-ridden, but what could he do? They all wanted something from him that he wasn't able to give: comfort, confidence, reassurance. Hell, he himself was as much in need of those things as they were. He was as dumbfounded as they were, as helpless. So he felt a sting of resentment towards them, and then felt guilty because he knew the resentment was unjust, that it indicated a shallowness on his part, a deficiency of some sort.

And yet, as he hurried towards the lab at the far end of Wing C, he had to admit to himself that somewhere near the shadowy edge of his consciousness, somewhere beneath the resentments, frustrations, and impotence – somewhere was a spark of excitement. The surges of adrenaline he had received so far had keyed him up, had made him feel more vital than he had felt in – how long? Twenty years? Since the days at Stanford's Biochemical Research Institute, when he had been an assistant to Professor Noah Hoffmann? It certainly seemed so. Horrible as this was, then, it was still shaping up as being the most challenging situation he had ever faced in his life, and in that he felt a tingle of excitement, a resurgence of a long-dormant vitality.

That was why he didn't go to his office and have that drink that his parched throat called for. To douse and numb his negative feelings with alcohol would risk dousing that spark of excitement that had flared on the edge of his consciousness.

Anne Jackson was in the lab alone. Dressed in a long, white smock, she sat on a stool and was peering into a microscope when Sander entered.

He didn't greet her, but said bluntly, 'Found anything yet?'

She shook her head. 'Nothing. It might help if I knew what I was looking for.'

'From what little I've been told, you'll know it when you see it. It's a foreign, unicellular body with a – ' He stopped. 'Why're you working without gloves?' Even to his own ears his voice sounded like that of a petty tyrant. 'Didn't anybody tell you to wear gloves when handling those specimens?'

She seemed rather taken aback by his asperity. 'No, no one – '

'Do it. Until we know more about it, take every precaution. Are you the only one working on it?'

As she took a pair of rubber gloves from a nearby drawer

and pulled them on, she said in an icy voice, 'Yes. And it's supposed to be my day off. I was supposed to take my son to – '

The telephone rang. It was a wall phone near the door. Sander left his kit on a nearby table and took the call. It was Carol at the reception desk. She said she had been unable to reach Professor Roget, but that she had Roget's assistant on the line, and he wanted to speak to Sander.

When he came on the line, the assistant introduced himself and explained that Professor Roget wasn't available because he was on his way to Fort Bragg in a chartered plane. 'He plans to stop at the Institute of Neurosciences in Ukiah and examine the patients there,' the assistant explained. 'After that, both he and Dr Sheftman will fly on to Fort Bragg.'

'What about cultures?' Sanders said. 'Have you been able to get any?'

'Not yet,' he answered. 'We're trying a human blood solution now, maybe that'll do it, but we already know that none of the usual antibiotics has any effect on it. That, and the fact that we can't get a culture in normal solutions, makes us conclude – tentatively, of course – that the organism is probably a laboratory mutant of some sort. No fungus, particularly a new one, would have such universal resistance to antibiotics unless the resistance had been bred into it in a laboratory.'

Sander thanked the assistant and said good-bye. When the connection was broken, he dialled Carol at the reception desk and asked if the ambulance crews were ready.

'They're here at the desk, but – '

'Send them down here. Oh, and Carol, call the Fort Bragg police. I want a squad car to accompany the ambulances.'

'There're a couple of Fort Bragg policemen here in the lobby now, Doctor. They heard about the sheriff's death and about all the deputies being admitted here. They want to talk to you about it.'

'Send them down here with the ambulance crews.'

When he replaced the phone on its hook, he held on to it for a moment for support, and stared into space with unfocused eyes, lost in a deluge of thoughts, trying to sort them out, put them together, make sense of them. He felt that at any moment his brain might blow out like an overloaded transformer. *Created in a laboratory.* That phrase kept running through his mind, outrunning all the other thoughts. *Hoffmann. What was the name of that project? Dandelion? Germ warfare. Created in a –*

A knock sounded on the door. Three ambulance attendants in white uniforms came in, followed by two policemen in blue. Without preamble, without even returning their greetings, Sander said to the ambulance crews, 'There're only three of you. Where's the other man?'

'He quit,' said one of the men. 'I guess that's what you'd call it. Anyway, he's not here.' He was one of the drivers, a young man with shoulder-length red hair and some fuzz on his upper lip that was straining to be a moustache.

With his impatience showing, Sander asked him to explain.

'We had that run this morning, and I guess it was just one too many for Roy. He started acting real moody after that, and, man, he finally . . . when I needed him to help me with something later, he just flipped out. Told me to go fuck myself, and stormed off.' He shrugged, as if to say he couldn't be held responsible. 'That's what he said. I ain't seen him since.'

Sander felt a tingle of apprehension. 'That run this morning – was it to pick up Billy Boyle?'

The driver nodded. 'Yeah, that's right.'

'And how long after the pick-up did your partner – what's his name? Roy?'

'Roy Schumacher, yes, sir.'

'How long after the pick-up did he start acting strange?'

He shrugged. 'Oh, a couple of hours, I guess. It was just before lunch that he flipped out. Told me to fuck myself.'

'And he didn't have any reason to be angry?'

'Not that I know of. Looked to me like he was hung over, maybe, or on some bad dope, something.'

Sander turned to the police sergeant. 'You'll have to pick him up. You can get his address and physical description from his file in the personnel office.'

'What're we supposed to charge him with?' the sergeant asked. 'It's no crime for a man to walk off his job.'

'Goddamnit, don't you people understand?' Sander snapped at the startled policeman, and didn't realise till then how close to panic he was. 'Can't you comprehend the gravity of what I'm telling you? We've got some kind of new disease on our hands, and no defences against it; doesn't that register with you?' He stopped, realised that he had to get hold of himself and not spread his own feelings of panic to others. 'Look,' he said then with an air of off-handed assurance, 'the guy's symptoms make it sound as if might have been contaminated by this disease. Now that makes him a menace to public health, doesn't it? And I know you can pick him up for *that*. If not, charge him with anything you want to – resisting arrest, for instance, because he probably will. In fact, it may take four or five men to handle him, and he may be dangerous.'

'I think, Doctor,' said the sergeant respectfully, 'that if you want us to co-operate with you in this thing, you're going to have to tell us what's going on. I mean, we can't – '

With an elaborate shrug, Sander interrupted. 'I can't tell you any more than I – '

'Doctor Quence!' It was the slightly alarmed voice of Anne Jackson, who was still at the microscope. 'I think I've found something. You'd better have a look.'

As Sander turned, the sergeant caught his arm. 'Will my men be in any danger of catching this . . . this disease from the man?'

Sander had an impulse to slap the man, but contained himself and said with a semblance of composure, 'I don't know.

I don't even know that he's contaminated. But if you get him in time, I don't think there's much risk. However, Sergeant, if you *don't* get him in time . . .' Silence and the warning look in Sander's eyes hinted at possibilities that were too dire to mention. He crossed quickly to the microscope, saying over his shoulder, 'Hold on a minute.'

Anne got up from the stool and let Sander have her place. He looked into the microscope, and there was no mistaking what he saw. 'Jesus Christ,' he murmured. He felt a surge of mingled excitement and fear. 'Anne! I want to get photomicrographs of this.' And while he nervously pulled on a pair of surgical gloves, Anne went to another table and checked the photographic microscope to make sure it was ready for use.

Sander brought the slide to the new microscope and spent a minute making fine adjustments in the focus. 'There,' he said finally, and felt another great surge of excitement, and perhaps because it was mixed with equal parts of fear and dread, he realised he was experiencing what explorers throughout history must have felt when they came face-to-face with unknown and fantastic and very dangerous new worlds.

13

When Professor Noah Hoffmann returned from the Stanford Biochemical Research Institute and entered the front door of his house in the Palo Alto hills, he could hear his wife Isa saying in a twittery voice, 'Oh! Hold on, I think he just came in.'

It would be a phone call for him, Hoffmann knew, but he took his time. He dropped his attaché case on a table in the foyer and hung his coat on a rack. Isa yoo-hooed to him as she came to meet him and gave him a quick kiss on the cheek.

'It's for you, dear,' she said. 'A call from Washington. Some general or other.' She was an apple-dumpling of a woman, pleasantly plump with a twinkle in her eyes. 'I put him on hold. Take it in your study, if you like.'

He did. He got comfortable in the big chair behind his desk before he pushed the button on the telephone and said 'Hello? That you, General Blanchard?'

It was. They exchanged pleasantries for a moment, both protesting that they were sorry they didn't get to talk to each other much any more, but . . . well, you know: busy, busy, busy.

'And speaking of busy,' Hoffmann said. 'There's something happening out here on the West Coast that might mean a lot of busyness for both of us.'

Isa brought him a cup of tea as he talked, but he let it get cold as he relayed to General Blanchard the reports he'd had from Professor Roget.

'It's something that nobody has ever seen before,' he said at one point, 'and preliminary tests indicate that it's – are you ready for this? – it's a metamorphic fungoid, it infects only humans, and is apparently resistant to all antibiotics.'

There was a breathless silence on the other end of the line for a moment, and then General Blanchard, apparently stalling for time to comprehend what he had heard, murmured, 'Are you . . .? Professor, how sure are you of this information?'

'The man I got it from is Charles Roget, an old friend and colleague of mine from UC, Davis. He's probably the most distinguished mycologist in the country, so if he says it, you can believe it.'

'A fungoid?' the general asked, although it was more of a meditative statement than a question.

'Evidently.' Hoffmann's tone was grave.

'A mutant?'

'Ah,' Hoffmann said. 'You, too, eh? You also thought of *Project Dandelion*, eh? So did I. At first. But this . . . well,' he continued as he puffed idly on his empty pipe, 'I don't know. It doesn't sound right. It's too good, too well engineered, if you know what I mean.' This last remark was both a hint and a test, and General Blanchard took both.

'A recombinant?' he said, his voice pregnant with dread and astonishment. 'A chimera? Is that what you think?'

Hoffmann shrugged. 'I don't know,' he said. 'Do you? I mean, I heard – what was it, a couple of years ago? – that the people at Fort Detrick were trying to develop some DNA recombinants as germ-warfare agents. This doesn't sound like something they were working on, eh?'

'No. That was discontinued by order of the President. But, number one, they weren't working with fungi, and, number two, they didn't come up with anything that had metamorphic capabilities. If they had, I'd sure as hell know about it.'

'It's not ours, then?' Hoffmann said.

'No,' General Blanchard said, and then added in a worried voice, 'not that I know of.' After another brief pause, the general spoke again, and now there was a new sense of urgency in his tone. 'Professor? Listen to me, please. I officially request you to drop everything else you may be doing now, and go to Mendocino. I want – '

'As a matter of fact, I'm on my way in a few minutes,' Hoffmann said, and told Blanchard about the team that was being formed by Professor Roget, who, acting as a consultant to the California Department of Public Health, had taken charge of the operation.

'How are you travelling?'

'By car. As I understand it, the closest commercial airport to Mendocino is a hundred miles away, in Santa Rosa, so – '

'How long will it take you to drive up?'

'Three–four hours, I'm told.'

'Too long. I'll have you flown up in a military aircraft. Stand by there at your house and a staff car will pick you up in a little while. The car'll take you to San Francisco International, where I'll have a plane waiting for you.'

'I appreciate it, General, but here's the story: they don't

have any airports up there big enough for a jet. As a matter of fact, it – '

Blanchard interrupted him. 'Hold the line a minute, Professor,' he said, and within thirty seconds he was back. 'I've just gone to the Pentagon's map computer. It shows there's a landing strip at the Georgia-Pacific lumber mill in Fort Bragg – small, but big enough for a Piper, so that's what we'll use. It'll be waiting for you at San Francisco International. That way you'll be in Fort Bragg within an hour. When you get there, find out everything you can and phone me back as soon as possible. You can reach me either here at my office or at the National Security Council room at the White House. And don't worry about waking me. Phone me the minute you know anything. If you have trouble getting through the White House switchboard, tell them it's a Code Thirty-four alert.'

When Hoffmann hung up the phone, he sat and stared vacantly at the instrument for a moment. A plane . . .? They were sending an aeroplane for him. Flattering, of course, but what did it signify? A degree of alarm on General Blanchard's part, to be sure, and that was quite natural, considering the possible consequences of a new disease wreaking its devastation upon a totally defenceless population. But was there more to Blanchard's concern than that? Hoffmann had the uneasy feeling that there was.

Isa entered the study. 'I've got your bags all packed, dear,' she said. 'I left your razor out, though. You'll need to shave, won't you?'

'What? Oh, yah.' He felt his chin. 'Forgot to shave again this morning, didn't I?' He pushed himself up out of the chair. 'Getting absent-minded in my old age, eh? Well, thank God I have you to look out for me.'

Isa beamed with pleasure.

Hoffmann went into the bathroom to shave. As he prepared the lather with a brush in an old-fashioned shaving mug, he gazed idly at his reflection in the mirror. Yes, he was getting old (though not absent-minded; that was a sort of game he had been playing with Isa for years because it gave her something to do, a feeling of being necessary). He would be sixty-five on his next birthday, and the wrinkles in his face showed it. Other than the wrinkles, however, he hadn't really changed very much over the last twenty years. He still had a mass of wavy iron-grey hair, still stood tall and straight, and his leathery olive complexion gave him the appearance of being sun-tanned and healthy. Not bad for an old geezer, if he did say so himself.

He wondered about Sander. He, too, was twenty years older now, which made him – what? About forty-five. And how much had he changed? Had he become bald? Fat? Probably not. He figured Sander to be like himself in that respect: a person who would age well, without major changes during his adult years. Well, it would be good to see him again. He wished it could be under more pleasant circumstances – under conditions that weren't so heavy with the grim and perhaps even fatal ironies that were bringing about their reunion. How many hours had they argued over the advisability of trying to create new pathogenic organisms? He remembered Sander saying that *Dandelion*'s purpose was to create a chemical bomb, claiming that it might have a greater kill-capacity than a hydrogen bomb. And he had been right, of course.

Unluckily for them all, however, somebody had apparently gone ahead and created such a bomb – might have created it, anyway – and then dropped it, either by accident or design, upon the peaceful little out-of-the-way town where Sander had chosen to live: Mendocino, ground zero where the bomb had exploded.

14

'Take this down,' Sander told Anne Jackson. While peering into the microscope, he clicked the camera and said, 'Photomicrograph one: something . . . a foreign body, resembling a . . . a meiasporangium in process of meiosis.' He refocused the camera, clicked it. 'Two: foreign bodies resembling . . .' He could hardly believe what he was seeing, 'Haploid zoospores?' He refocused again. *Click*.

Then he suddenly jerked his head up as if he had been stung. 'Whose specimen is this?'

'Number four?' Anne said as she quickly crossed to the first microscope and shuffled through some forms on a clipboard. 'Number four,' she said, and looked at him. 'Lonnie McCabe.'

'Good God,' he said in a despairing whisper. The excitement was gone. All he felt now was dread and horror. He abruptly got up and strode towards the door. 'You men,' he said to the policemen who were waiting. 'Come with me. We might need you.' And he had no sooner opened the door than he heard the disturbance in the lobby. It was a pandemonium of sounds: screams, shouts, running feet, glass breaking. Sander and the policemen bolted up the corridor towards the lobby. The climax had passed by the time they reached the scene, but for a moment more all the people in the crowded lobby were transfixed by shock, fear, outrage. Two men were picking themselves up off the floor. The glass door in the hospital's entrance was shattered.

'What happened?' Sander asked Carol, who was standing behind the reception desk with her hands over her mouth as if repressing a cry.

'One of those deputies came through here, knocking everybody down,' she said. 'He just started hitting people who were in his way. Pushing them down.'

'Lonnie McCabe?'

'I don't know his name,' Carol said, getting hold of herself, calming down. 'A big guy with bushy dark hair.'

Sander said to the policemen, 'It's Lonnie. Sergeant, he's got to be stopped. He's contaminated.'

'Is he armed?'

'No. Their guns were taken away from them when they came in. But he's going to be very dangerous,' Sander warned.

The sergeant, who was a friend of Lonnie's, was reluctant to go chasing him, but the almost apocalyptic seriousness in Sander's face sent him and his partners running for the door.

Sander turned to see Dr Brokowski and an orderly approaching. They were coming down the corridor of the south wing, Wing A, where the deputies were being kept in isolation, and they were both bloody. The orderly, who was supporting Brokowski by the arm, had blood trickling from beneath his swollen lips, and Brokowski was bleeding from a number of small cuts on the right side of his face. One lens of his glasses had been shattered and the plastic frame was broken. Brokowski was using both hands to place the glasses on his nose, but each time he took his hands away, the glasses fell askew. He almost ran into Sander before he, righting his glasses once again, recognised him.

'Did he get away?' Brokowski asked. 'We couldn't stop him. You can see what he did to us. We were – ' He righted his glasses again, and now Sander noticed that his toupee was also askew.

There was still so much hubbub in the lobby that Sander could hardly hear what Brokowski was saying. A radio was blaring somewhere. A woman – Leslie Coors? – was crying.

As one of the administrative clerks passed by, Sander grabbed him by the arm. 'Leroy, get all these people out of here. No more visitors. Don't allow anybody else in the hospital unless he or she is on official business.'

Bobbi was standing a little way off. He could feel her probing stare upon him, but he didn't turn to meet her eyes.

Brokowski was saying, 'Does this mean – ? Does this . . .' His glasses fell to one side again. 'Sander, this fellow McCabe, what does it mean?'

Sander stared at the shattered glass door and beyond it to the flickers of lightning that played across the darkening landscape, and then shook his head. 'I hate to think what it means.'

15

The town of Mendocino is clustered on a slow descent of grassy land that slopes off to the ocean, the gentle and almost treeless turf of the headlands broken here and there by old wooden fences that are encrusted by moss and lichen. Wild roses and blackberry vines grow in random places along the fences, using them as runners, so that in the spring the fences become hedgerows of wild pink roses. Then, in autumn, after the rose petals have blown like pink snowflakes across the headlands, the berries ripen and hang heavy on the vines, plump and almost opalescent in their wet blackness. But in winter, when the vines are barren, they stretch across the headlands like rusty barbed-wire entanglements on an abandoned battlefield.

As the afternoon of 14 February edged towards evening, storm clouds gathered on the horizon of the ocean. All day the light had been glaucous, like that in an aquarium, with lemon-yellow patches of sky illuminating a land- and seascape of greens and greys; but as the storm clouds neared, the air itself seemed to take on a heavy, dark pewter-grey quality, and soon bolts of lightning began to flicker from the sombre underbelly of the clouds.

Then came the rain, the wind. The ocean roared and battered against the rocky shore, and the rose and blackberry vines that grew along the wooden fences on the headlands, stark and thorny, quivered in the wind like exposed nerves.

16

The first small plane that touched down on the narrow. rain-wet macadam runway at the lumber mill in Fort Bragg carried Dr D. B. Sheftman and Professor Charles Roget. A police car was waiting for them, its red dome light spinning slowly. They dashed through the rain to the car, got in, and were driven straight to the hospital.

A policeman was standing guard at the shattered hospital door. The brightly lit lobby was empty of visitors now, but still the hospital personnel crowded and scurried around the reception counter like bees at the entrance of a hive. D.B. intercepted a passing nurse, who told them that Dr Quence was in ward three of Wing A, where the Coors girl was being kept.

'Show us, please,' Roget said, and such was the authority of his voice that the nurse showed no reluctance to break off her own errand and lead them down the corridor to where Sander was standing in front of a door that had a small observation window in it. He was peering into the room.

As the two men with their attaché cases approached, Sander turned and nodded. 'D.B.,' he said as they shook hands.

D.B. had huge ham-like hands and a crushing handshake. He was a black man, but only in the sense of race rather than colour, because he wasn't black at all. He was a sort of tea-brown colour, with darker freckles across the bridge of his nose. He sported a modishly long Afro haircut.

D.B. introduced Sander to Roget, and to Sander's surprise, the professor looked nothing like his voice sounded. His voice had a huge quality to it, as if it were being projected from a stage by a Shakespearean actor, but the man himself was almost diminutive. He was no more than five and a half feet tall, and he appeared to have no neck at all, as if his head were placed directly upon his shoulders. What was more, the front of his head was bald, while the rear half was tufted with a shock of hair that was about the colour and texture of a lion's mane.

'I'm really glad to see you,' Sander said with a sigh of relief, then blurted out, 'They killed him, did you hear? The carrier? He killed the sheriff and one of his deputies first, though. Apparently killed the sheriff with one blow that broke his neck.'

D.B. said, 'That would be the man Snyder ran into last night?'

Sander nodded. 'Unless, of course, there were two of them. His name was Richard Hopkins. I knew him slightly, though I wasn't able to recognise him.' He shook his head with resigned incredulity. 'Wait'll you see him yourself and you'll understand why.'

'Has anyone else been contaminated?' Roget asked.

'The girl that was abducted last night, Lacy Coors. She's the most advanced case. Then Lonnie McCabe, one of the deputies. He escaped from isolation before we realised. You noticed the front door? He did that on his way out. Also, there's another suspect, an ambulance driver named Roy Schumacher . . .' His words trailed off and died, as if he were weary of speech.

D.B. said, 'What about the girl? How is she?'

'How is she?' Sander said, and a shadow of helpless rage crossed his face. He nodded towards the observation window, and there seemed to be both a dare and a warning in his voice as he said, 'See for yourself.'

Newman was pacing back and forth in his room when Sander came in.

'How you doing, Jim?' Sander asked, obviously worried. 'You okay? The nurse said you wanted to see me.'

'Oh, I'm okay,' Jim assured him. 'It's nothing like that. What I was wondering . . .' He hesitated. 'Well, look. I understand you released the deputies. What about me? If I'm not contaminated, either – I'm not, am I?'

'Not so far as we know. But, Jim, we were taking a calculated risk when we let Chris and his men go. We figured it'd be a much greater risk to leave Lonnie running around loose. What can I tell you? He *has* to be brought in, and they are the only ones who might be able to do it.'

'Then run the risk with me, too,' Newman pleaded. 'I've got something to do that may be just as important.'

'That meteorite, huh?'

'Look, there *could* be a connection, you know. Don't you see? Hopkins found the meteorite and brought it to his house, and he was – as far's we know, he was the first one to get the disease.'

Sander sighed, then nodded. 'All right. But on one condition: you bring the meteorite back here to the hospital lab to run your tests on it. Don't take it out of the area. Agreed?'

That was a severe restriction, since the hospital wouldn't have the sophisticated equipment necessary for a thorough analysis of the meteorite. Newman had intended to take it to the nearest NASA lab, which was in Santa Maria. Under the circumstances, however, he could understand the restrictions.

'All right,' he said finally. 'Agreed.'

Newman turned up his collar as he left the hospital. The night was pitch black except when bolts of lightning flickered across the sky, briefly illuminating the stormy landscape, the trees whipping in the gusts of wind, swirls of rain, empty streets. The wind made a strange sound as it buffeted the telephone poles, their lines and guy wires, as though it were passing through the bass strings of an enormous harp.

He held his collar tight around his throat and dashed into the full force of the rain. He was passing the parking lot when an automobile horn suddenly sounded, and the headlights from a parked car flashed on him.

'Hey! Where are you going?' a woman's voice called from

the car, a Volkswagen van.

When she turned the lights off, Newman saw that the woman in the van was Bobbi Coors. He leaped the rivulets of water that swirled around a parking island and approached the car. Bobbi was behind the steering wheel, with the window rolled down so she could call to him.

She said, 'Are you walking? Where's your pick-up?'

Newman could feel the raindrops trickling beneath his collar. 'Down at the lumber mill landing strip. Can you – '

'Get in,' she said. 'I'll drive you.'

He dashed around to the other side of the van and got in. The car smelled of old leather and scented body oils.

'What're you doing sitting out here in the car?' he asked. 'Does Sander know you're out here?'

She shook her head as she started the engine. 'No. I've been waiting for him. No, actually, I've just been waiting, period. I didn't want to wait at home, and Sandy won't let any visitors in the hospital, so . . . ' She pulled out of the parking lot and started down the street, the tyres making a slishing sound on the wet pavement. 'How is he?' she said, sounding very lonely and lost.

'Like all of us: stunned,' Newman said. 'But he's managing to do what has to be done.'

'And Lacy?' Her voice tightened. 'Have you seen her?'

'No.'

'You're lucky,' she said.

Now, in the lights of the instrument panel, he could see the shiny tracks of tears on her cheeks. She sniffled. He felt an impulse to comfort her, but wasn't sure how. 'I'm sorry,' he said, realising how lame that sounded, not knowing what else to say or do. He was reluctant to touch her. Although the three of them – Sander and Bobbi and he – had been together socially a couple of times, and had had dinner together once, they had never really become friends. There hadn't been time for that yet. So he wasn't sure how far his familiarity should go. If she wanted or expected comfort from him, she would have to let him know, give him a signal.

'You know what I'd like?' she said as she made some adjustment of the windshield wipers. 'I'd like a good stiff drink. But I can't very well go into a bar by myself . . . Would you consider . . .'

'I can't, I'm sorry. I have to go back out to the Hopkins house tonight.'

'*Tonight?*' She gave him a hard quick glance. 'What for?

'Something I have to get there.'

They had turned off the street and on to Highway 1. About two miles south of town, just before the Noyo River Bridge, she turned the car off the highway and on to a gravel road that led down to the small landing field on the cliffs above the ocean. All the landing-field lights were on and a police car was parked near the runway. They were obviously expecting a plane in, and Newman realised that the arrival must be someone of importance or they would never try to land in such foul weather. He directed Bobbi to where his pick-up was parked near a small hangar at the north end of the field.

'Let me come with you,' she asked as she stopped the van beside his pick-up.

Now it was his turn to give her a sharp glance.

'He was my old man, you know – Richard Hopkins was. I was living with him there in the Pygmy when I met Sandy.'

No, Newman hadn't heard that, but he didn't quite see the relevance of it now. He opened the van's door a crack so that the interior light came on. 'I don't think you should come with me,' he said. 'You'll get me in trouble with Sander. He wouldn't want you to go out there. It's too dangerous.'

'Please,' she said, and looked straight at him. Her face was slightly swollen from crying, but it didn't prevent her from being attractive. She reached across the seat and placed her hand on his. 'Please? I've got to do *some*thing. I can't just sit around and wait for something to happen. Let me come with you. I might be of some help. I could show you how to get to his house.'

He gave it a moment's thought, and then nodded grudgingly. 'All right. But you have to stay in the truck. You can't go in the house.'

She pressed his hand and thanked him, but he, with considerable misgivings, hurriedly transferred to the pick-up and started the engine as she climbed in the passenger's side. They were silent as they drove away from the landing strip and turned south on Highway 1. He turned the heater on in the pick-up. The windshield wipers kept a steady swishing beat as the swirls of rain clattered over the truck. Newman was aware of her sitting there. She had brought the smell of scented body oils with her.

'You turn left on Little Lake Road,' she said.

'I know.'

'Oh.'

They were silent again.

When they were near the lane, she said, 'It's the next turn on your right.'

He stopped at the entrance of the lane. There was a saw-horse blocking the entrance and on it was tacked a sign that said, 'Quarantine. Keep out.' Newman left the motor running as he got out and moved the saw-horse to one side, then jumped back into the truck, and pushed the lever on the floor that put the vehicle into four-wheel drive. He eased the truck down into the muddy, deeply rutted and narrow lane. The pygmy cypresses that bordered the lane scraped and scratched along the sides of the truck, the sounds like fingernails being drawn against a blackboard.

'Look!' Bobbi said. 'There's a light on in the house.'

Newman felt a quick chill of fear, but then realised and said immediately, 'The police probably have a guard here.'

But there was no police car around and, when the pick-up stopped in the front yard, no policeman came out of the open door to meet them. Newman honked the horn, and then sat in the pick-up for a moment longer, waiting for someone to come out. No one did.

'You wait here in the truck,' he told Bobbi.

The rain had stopped for a moment, so Newman walked slowly across the yard to the porch and called through the open door, 'Hello in there!' There was no response. Well, then, he thought, the ambulance crews that had taken the bodies away must have left the light on and the door open. That would be natural enough, considering the state of shock they must have been in.

He poked his head in the door and glanced around the room. The bodies were gone, and there was a dark pool of dried blood on the floor, but other than that, the room was unchanged. There, amid the broken pottery and tumbled debris on the floor, was the meteorite, exactly where he had left it.

He picked his way carefully through the debris, trying not to make any sounds, because each time his foot brushed against a tin can or a shard of pottery, the sound seemed to be magnified tenfold by the profound silence in the house. But once he thought he heard a sound other than the ones he himself was making. He stopped and listened. The bedroom door was standing slightly ajar.

'Hello? Anybody here?'

Silence. So it was probably the echo of a sound that he himself had made. In any case, he wasn't going to waste any time getting the meteorite and himself out of there. He crouched down beside the meteorite and –

He suddenly sensed that there was someone in the room with him. He could feel someone close behind him. He jerked around and looked up.

A man was standing over him with an axe in his hands. The axe was raised to strike.

From his crouching position, Newman sprang away, stumbling in the debris, and fell banging against the wall.

But the man didn't pursue him – didn't even move. He remained in the same place, the axe raised to strike, and glared at Newman, who had instinctively thrown up a hand to ward off a blow from the axe.

'What the hell you doing here?' the man demanded. He was a young man, maybe twenty-five, with wet brown hair, and there was a frown of deadly fury on his face. He continued to hold the axe poised.

'I . . . I came to get the meteorite,' Newman stammered.

'Meteorite?' the man said, baffled. 'What the hell you talking about?'

Newman slowly got to his feet, but his eyes never left the man's face. He was greatly relieved to see that the man wasn't a homicidal maniac, but apparently a rational man who was righteously indignant and genuinely confused.

'That one,' Newman said, pointing to the rock on the floor.

'That's a meteorite?' the man asked, and then said, 'Well, what the hell's it doing here? Who put it here? Did you? Did you do this to my house?'

'*Your* house?'

Then they heard the cry. It was Bobbi. She was standing in the doorway. 'Richard!' she cried.

He whirled on her, still holding the axe poised to strike. 'You!' he said with renewed anger. 'Goddamnit, are you in on this, too? Sure!' he said with vengeful comprehension. 'I might've known it'd be you! It was you and that doctor, wasn't it? Still trying to get back at me for cutting up his car! That's it, isn't it? You and him – '

'No!' she said. 'No, it's . . . oh, my God, Richard, it's not you!'

Now he was more baffled than ever. 'What d'you mean, it's not me?'

Joy was beginning to break through Bobbi's look of stunned disbelief. 'It's not you! You're not the man!'

'What?' he said. 'What the hell – ?'

'Oh, my God, am I glad to see you!' she cried with mounting joy, then glanced at the axe and added in a chastising voice, 'Richard . . .'

He followed the direction of her gaze, and it seemed as if he were vaguely surprised to see the upraised axe in his own hands. With a disgusted snort, he suddenly tossed it clattering amid the debris on the floor. 'Goddamnit,' he said then, 'somebody better explain to me what's going on here.'

Newman pointed at him. '*You*'re Richard Hopkins?'

'Who the hell you think I am, Little Bo Peep?'

Bobbi said, 'Where've you been?'

'In Santa Barbara. I'm gone a couple of weeks and come back to find my house wrecked! Blood on the floor! My dog dead – *dead*, Godamnit! Somebody killed my dog and threw him in the well! Not to mention stealing my goats and tearing up my house! My pots! Look at 'em! Smashed!'

Bobbi and Newman looked at each other. Newman was the first one to say what they both were thinking: 'Well, if the man they killed wasn't you, who was it?'

17

As Sander passed the receptionist's desk, he asked Carol, 'Any word yet about Lonnie McCabe or Schumacher?'

'No, nothing,' she said. She looked haggard. Like all the other hospital employees and staff, she had been requested – urged – to stay on her job until further notice, and, like most, she stayed, but the long hours and tension were beginning to take their toll. 'The police and sheriff's officers are looking for them everywhere, but they've . . .' She shrugged. 'Their homes have been staked out, but . . .'

A phone rang. Somewhere in the busy administration offices behind the reception area a radio was playing country-western music. Orderlies pushed carts loaded with dirty plates and garbage through the lobby, the dinner remains of the ordinary patients, many of whom were drifting into the lobby to see and talk about the smashed front door and to try to guess what was going on.

Somebody tugged at Sander's sleeve. It was one of his patients, a wizened little old woman who walked with a cane. She was wearing a housecoat over her hospital gown.

'Doctor Quincy,' she said in a squeaky voice, glaring up at him from behind thick glasses. 'You didn't come by today. You said you would. They moved me and – '

'I'm sorry, Mrs – '

' – moved me out of my room, and you were supposed to come by to give me my shot, but a nurse – '

'Mrs Statler, I'm sorry. I'm sure you were taken care of all right, though, weren't you?' He caught the attention of a passing nurse. 'Here, take Mrs Statler back to her room, would you, Nurse? Yes, yes, Mrs Statler, I'll be in to see you as soon as I can.' Then to the nurse, he added, 'In fact, better get them all out of here. Tell all the patients there's a quarantine in effect, and they have to stay in their rooms till further notice.' Assuming her compliance, and ignoring Mrs Statler's squeaky protests, he turned back to Carol and said, 'How about the other doctors? How many were you able to get?'

'Three. Two from Fort Bragg, and Ted Cassidy's driving up from Point Arena. Oh, by the way, we got a long telegram from UC, Davis, about a breakthrough they'd had in culturing. I put it on your desk and gave a photocopy to Professor Roget.'

'Good,' he said, trying to gather all the loose ends of thoughts and plans in his mind; but he couldn't concentrate. All his thoughts and plans were too frayed, the lobby was too hectic, and he needed a drink.

'I'll be in my office for a little while,' he told Carol, and then hurried away before somebody else could demand his attention. He went to the second floor and into his small cubicle of an office, which was even smaller than usual now because a cot had been moved in for him to sleep on. He sa down heavily in the swivel chair behind the desk. From one of the bottom drawers he pulled out a bottle of Scotch and a dirty tumbler. To hell with it, he thought as he unscrewed the cap and poured the tumbler half full of the amber-coloured liquid. He sat the tumbler exactly in the centre of the blotter on his desk and looked at it. He hadn't had a drink since last night – almost twenty-four hours – and that was some sort of record. He was in the habit of having at least six or eight drinks to get him through the day, and sometimes a lot more, but seldom less. So he needed this one. His hands were getting shaky and his spirits had begun to sag under the increasing pressure of the last twelve hours.

But then he noticed the telegram that had been sent from the mycology lab at UC, Davis. There were about ten pages in the telegram, all crammed with data from tests and experiments that had been conducted on what was, for lack of a better name, rapidly becoming referred to as Hopkins's disease. He wondered how Richard Hopkins, were he alive, would feel to learn that his name was probably going to go down in history – might, in fact, become one of the most important names of all time.

He grabbed the sheaf of papers and flipped to a random page, where his eyes fell on a table that was entitled, *Effect of various treatments on the particular localisation of x-L-Arabinofuranaosidase (AF) and acid phosphatase (AP) in mycelium grown in blood culture (minus glucose)*. The table showed the incubation time of the organism when treated with formalin (4% pH 7.2), and triton X-100 (0.1% w/v). The rapidity with which the organism multiplied in blood culture was amazing, and seemed directly proportionate to the number of human blood cells in the solution.

'Crazy,' he said aloud to himself, shaking his head. 'Crazy.' And then he remembered what Roget's assistant had told him over the phone: *bred in a laboratory. Resistant to all known antibiotics . . .*

There was a knock on the office door. At Sander's beckoning an orderly entered carrying a tray of food. He said that Carol had asked him to bring the tray up, and Sander remembered that he hadn't had any dinner – lunch, either, for that matter.

'Tell her thanks for me,' he said, though the food didn't look very appetising. It was cold meat loaf and hash browns. Canned corn. Jello. The drink was more attractive. He tossed the telegram aside, and picked up the tumbler and took a large gulp of the Scotch. From the raw, burning sensation in his throat and stomach, he felt a warm smoke float throughout his body, over his brain. He let himself go limp in the chair, relaxing for the first time that day. Then he wolfed down the cold food. Unpalatable though it was, it felt wonderful in his empty stomach, and he experienced an almost immediate surge of energy.

The phone buzzed. It was D.B., who, along with Roget and Brokowski, was in the autopsy room. 'We're about to start the autopsy on the Hopkins cadaver,' D.B. said. 'Shall we wait for you?'

'Completed sterilisation yet?'

'Just beginning.'

'I'll be down in a few minutes, go ahead without me.' He hung up and took another gulp of the liquor, draining the glass, and then poured himself another. He knew he shouldn't drink it. He had less resistance to this second drink than he had to the last one, and knew that he would have even less resistance to the third. By the fourth one, he would be drunk. Then he could relax. Then he could stop being afraid, stop feeling so scared and inadequate. It was true that he felt surges of excitement now and then, but the feeling was seldom strong enough to overcome his fears and feelings of deficiency in the face of this challenge by a power – a strangely malignant power – that was so completely beyond his experience and control. He wished he could be more like D.B. and Roget. He wished he could be caught up in the historic importance of the event. But he wasn't. He would just as soon take the second drink, and then a third, and a fourth, and then go home and crawl into a nice warm bed with Bobbi and make love, and let the whole world go hang.

The phone buzzed again. This time it was Carol. 'I'm sorry to bother you, Doctor, but there's a gentleman here to see you. Noah Hoffmann?'

The news brought a sigh of relief and gladness from Sander. 'Send him up,' he said, and took another drink as he replaced the phone in its cradle. He quickly considered what his greeting to Noah should be like: warm and nostalgic? Reserved but friendly? But he didn't have time to decide. In a few seconds there was a knock on the door, and Noah Hoffmann was there in the doorway.

Their greeting turned out to be one of reserved gladness, a greeting that was both friendly and warm without being in the least effusive. They shook hands heartily, and Hoffmann said, 'A fine coincidence, isn't it? Our meeting like this, after all these years, in such a place? On such an occasion?'

'Have a seat. How about a drink? I have Scotch.'

'Why not?' Hoffmann's eyes took in the whole office at a glance – it required no more than that, it was so small – and he obviously wasn't impressed. 'By the way, my wife Isa sends you her best wishes.'

Sander went into the adjoining bathroom and got two paper cups from the dispenser above the sink. 'Oh? I'm flattered that she remembers me. How is she these days?'

Both of them knew they had to get down to business, but the urge for small talk was very strong. They were glad to see each other, and each was curious to know what changes the years had brought about in the other.

'Oh, Isa is still Isa,' Hoffmann said, his eyes reflecting an unabashed appreciation of his wife. 'And how about you Sander? Did you ever get married?'

'And divorced,' he said as he filled the two paper cups with Scotch. 'Cheers.'

They touched the edges of the paper cups before drinking.

When Hoffmann had recovered from the mild shock of the liquor, he cleared his throat and said, 'So! We'll have a long talk later, yah? For now, though, I must find out what developments have occurred since I last spoke to Professor Roget. I have to phone Washington, so – '

'Washington? Do they know about this already?'

'Oh, yah, you may be sure of that. The National Security Council wants a report, and you can bet the germ-warfare people at the Pentagon are buzzing about it by now.'

'I'll just bet they are,' Sander agreed sardonically as he slouched down in the swivel chair and propped his feet up on the desk. 'But to tell the truth, I've begun to suspect that they might be able to tell us more about it than we could tell them. In point of fact, Noah, I've had occasion to wonder if maybe this wasn't something that you and your people down at the Research Institute had a hand in creating.'

'Really now, Sander,' Hoffmann said, and made a hands-up gesture of supplication, 'would I be sitting here asking you about it if I knew what it was?'

'No, you wouldn't,' Sander said. He poured himself another drink and offered to refill Hoffmann's cup, but Hoffmann declined. 'Well, the only really technical information we have is there in those reports,' he said, and pointed to the telegram. 'As for the general stuff . . .' He began briefing Hoffmann on what had happened, outlining what little had been learned about the disease. Although Hoffmann frequently interrupted him with questions, the whole discourse lasted no more than twenty minutes. Sander ended by telling him about Lonnie McCabe and Roy Schumacher, and why he and D.B. and Roget had decided to release the deputies.

'We have only about six or eight more hours to get Lonnie, and we're pretty sure the other deputies aren't contaminated. So far it's been our experience that, if a person is contaminated, the organisms – the myxamoebas, whatever the hell you want to call them – reach a concentration sufficient to be detected in a blood test in less than two hours.'

'So if the symptoms don't show up within two hours after exposure, it's safe to assume the person isn't contaminated?'

'Well, I don't know that it's safe to assume *any*thing about this thing, but we had to assume as much when we released the deputies. Like I said, we figured it was worth the risk to get Lonnie back in isolation. It takes about twelve hours after contact for the carrier to enter the slime-secreting stage. Anyway, that's about how long it took for both Snyder and Lacy Coors to begin slime secretion. So that leaves Lonnie about eight hours to go. After that, he'll contaminate everybody he touches. And if Roy Schumacher has been contaminated . . . well, his twelve hours are up.'

Hoffmann puffed contemplatively on his empty pipe. 'Hmmmmm. And if it starts to spread . . .'

'It'll be a major epidemic within twenty-four hours,' Sander said, 'unless somebody comes up with some ideas and men and money to combat it. You realise, don't you, Noah, that if it starts spreading, this whole area will have to be quarantined? We'll have to put a sanitary cordon around this whole area, and for that we'll need an army – an *army*.'

Hoffmann nodded. 'And if we need an army, that's what we'll have.' He picked up the phone, got an outside line, and dialled a long list of numbers. He got an answer almost immediately and said, 'This is Professor Noah Hoffmann, calling for General Thurston Blanchard. I believe he's in a meeting of the NSC. Please tell him I wish to speak with him. It's a Code Thirty-four matter. I'll hold.' He looked at Sander. 'You've done a damned good job on this, Sander. When I first heard that you, one of my most brilliant students – yah, yah, you were, it's true – when I heard that you had become a GP in a small town, I thought, *what a waste*. I did, I'll admit it. But now! Well, it's very fortunate for all of us that you were here. It's true,' he said in protest to Sander's cynical frown. 'If it had been just any small-town GP, this thing would have gone off like a bomb. As it is, you've managed to muffle the explosion a little and give us a little time, and that's what we – Hello?' He suddenly broke off the conversation and spoke into the phone. 'Hello, General Blanchard? Noah Hoffmann here – in Fort Bragg. I've just been briefed by Sander Quence, the local doctor who's been on top of this from the beginning.'

The general's voice came over the line faint and brittle: 'Professor, I'm putting you on monitor so the rest of the council members can hear you. Do you by any chance have a scrambler on your phone?'

'No. I'm at the local hospital.'

'Then better not give any details. Just tell me: is it a situation that necessitates an alert?'

'I'm afraid so, General.'

'What colour?'

'Red.'

There was a short pause on the other end of the line. When the general spoke again, his tone was grimly low-keyed. 'Professor? Our contingency plan for this operation is code-named *Hatchet*. It'll be put into effect immediately. The Special Tactics Unit from Dugway is already airborne. They'll be there in, oh, say three and a half hours. My staff and I will be airborne within the hour and should be arriving there no later than oh-four hundred this morning, your time. Till then, Professor, consider yourself in charge of *Hatchet*. Authority for this operation comes under Executive Order A3802, which gives us national emergency powers, so you can stop all news media from publishing or broadcasting any information about this, and that's what I want you to do: keep a top secret lid on it till we get there.'

'I understand,' Hoffmann said, and after he gave General Blanchard the hospital's phone number, they said their good-byes and hung up.

Hoffmann looked at Sander. 'Well. That's it. It's a national problem now. Did you hear anything of what was said?'

Sander wasn't even sure that what he felt was anger until he heard it in the tone of his own voice when he said, 'That Special Tactics Unit he mentioned from Dugway – that'd be Dugway Proving Grounds in Utah, wouldn't it? The germ warfare testing place?'

Hoffmann nodded. 'The Special Tactics Unit is a group of men who've been trained to handle any – what shall I say? – any accident the army might have with one of its chemical or biological-warfare agents.'

'Sonofabitch,' Sander muttered, unable to keep the anger out of his voice. 'So that's what this is? Did the army have a little *accident* with one of their Goddamned germ-warfare weapons?'

Hoffmann was made uncomfortable by Sander's tone, but he looked him directly in the eye. 'I don't think so. General Blanchard says he knows nothing about it, and I have no reason to suppose he's lying. In any case, if we had anything like this in our germ-warfare arsenal, I think I'd know about it. Still . . .' He shrugged.

There was a long moment of awkward silence as Sander poured himself another drink; then Hoffmann slowly pushed himself to his feet and said, 'Well, then? Shall we get going? The autopsy room, first, if you please, and then I'll want to see the Coors girl. After that I'll look through these reports.'

Sander rose and saluted him with his half-filled paper cup. 'Like the man said, you're in charge.' He tipped the cup up and swallowed the contents in one gulp. He was nearly drunk now, and he thought he could see a disapproving look in Hoffmann's eyes. Maybe the professor was now getting the answer to the puzzle of why one of his most brilliant – well, that was the word he had used – most brilliant research assistants had ended up as an unimportant GP in an unimportant small town a hundred and fifty miles from nowhere. And Sander made no attempt to pretend otherwise. He made no attempt to hide his feelings of relief, the feeling of suddenly having a terrible burden of responsibility lifted from his shoulders. Now he could have a drink or two without worrying about dulling his faculties. So what if he had one too many now? Hoffmann was there, he could take care of things, and soon the army's germ-warfare people would be there, and he could tell them all to go to hell, them and their God-damned death-dealing microbes.

They left Sander's office and headed for the autopsy room. To get there, they had to descend the stairs and go through the lobby again, and it was there, in the lobby, that Sander stopped dead in his tracks when he saw who was standing at the reception desk.

It was James Newman, who was carrying something wrapped in a large plastic cover, presumably the meteorite; and Bobbi, who wasn't supposed to be there; and Richard Hopkins, who was supposed to be dead.

FEBRUARY FIFTEENTH

18

The rain continued until almost dawn, deluging the Mendocino coast, and then it passed. Just another winter storm. Another would be along soon enough.

For now, weak flurries of raindrops still fell here and there, but the wind had died down, and on the thin, ragged edges of the storm, the dawn sun broke through the clouds in shafts of lemon-pale light.

When Bobbi was released from quarantine that morning at six, she asked an orderly at the reception desk where Dr Quence was.

'In his office,' the orderly informed her, 'but he asked not to be disturbed. He's had a helluva night, and just laid down a couple of hours ago.'

'I have no intention of disturbing him,' Bobbi said.

She found him asleep on the cot in his office, still in his smock, still with his shoes on. It appeared that he had collapsed, rather than fallen asleep, as if he had sat down on the cot to take his shoes off, then toppled over on his side. On the floor beside the cot was an empty bottle of Scotch.

She very gently lifted his legs and placed them on the cot. He groaned, but didn't awaken. Then she carefully unlaced his shoes and took them off. There was a hole in the toe of one of his socks; she made a mental note to mend it. Once he was stretched out on the cot, she took his topcoat and placed it over him. His face, in sleep, was clawed with fatigue, and she could see grey patches in the stubble of his beard.

She pushed a strand of hair away from his eyes, then leaned down to kiss him on the forehead, her lips as light and transient as a feather.

She stayed with him for a while, watching him sleep, loving him, and then she went back downstairs to the lobby. She waited at the busy reception desk until she caught the attention of a clerk who, recognising her, irritably asked why she hadn't left the hospital.

'You were issued a quarantine clearance,' he said, as if telling her something she didn't know.

'Yes, of course, but . . . well, I was wondering if I might be able to see my sister? Lacy Coors? Just to peek and see if she's – '

'No, Miss Coors, you cannot,' the clerk said in no uncertain terms. 'Once you're cleared of quarantine, you have to leave the hospital.'

'Richard Hopkins, then?' she asked. 'We came in together last night. Has he been released from quarantine?'

'No, he hasn't,' the clerk said, and now his tone of weary exasperation was tempered with a sort of grudging sympathy. 'He's being held for further tests. I'm sorry, but you'll have to leave now. Give your quarantine clearance to the guard at the door.'

'Further tests?' she said, and her throat was suddenly so constricted that her voice was little more than a squeak. 'Does that mean that he . . .? That he . . .' But she couldn't finish the question, fearing that she no longer had the strength to bear the answer.

Chris Jordan, now sheriff of Mendocino County, returned to Richard Hopkins's house for the third time. He and Deputy Carl Gotlieb, wearing gloves soaked in a fungicide, visited the house again shortly after nine in the morning and poked through the debris on the floor. They found not only a pair of Army dog tags, but a wallet, which contained one hundred and twenty-five dollars, four national credit cards, and two US Army Chemical Corps identification cards. All of them belonged to the same man, one Clarence H. Lawson, sergeant,

United States Army. The Army identification cards bore the sergeant's picture, although the sergeant's features bore very little discernible resemblance to the dead man's.

Chris dropped the wallet and dog tags into a plastic bag and carried them back to the patrol car parked on the paved road. He spread the items out on the dry, still-warm hood of the car, pulled off his right glove, and carefully slipped it into another plastic bag. He opened the car door and picked up the radio microphone with his ungloved right hand, while between the fingers of his still-gloved left hand he held the identification cards.

While Carl was busy cleaning the mud off his boots, Chris, standing outside the car, made radio contact with Sheriff's Headquarters. 'We got something here, maybe the identification of the subject,' he told the dispatcher. 'Phone Doctor Quence at Fort Bragg Hospital and tell him, will you? It's a guy by the name of Clarence H. Lawson, who was an army sergeant. Serial number RA five-six-one-four-one-four-six-one. Date of – are you getting all this, Joan? Over.'

'Ten-four, Chris,' the dispatcher said. 'You're on tape. Go ahead.'

Chris gave her the sergeant's date of birth, weight, height, blood type. 'Now, Joan, I'm reading a gate-pass identity card issued by the US Army Chemical and Biological Warfare Research Centre at Fort Detrick, Maryland. Here's what I want you to do: phone the personnel office at that place and see if you can find out who this guy was and what he was doing here. Okay?'

'Ten-four, Chris. I'll get on it right away. Over.'

'Thanks, Joan. Over and out.' He tossed the microphone on to the car seat. He then slipped the wallet, cards, and dog tags into a new plastic bag, being very careful not to let anything touch his naked fingers or the mouth of the bag. After that, he took the top of his left-hand glove in the fingers of his right hand, turning the glove inside out as he peeled it off, dropped the glove into the plastic bag with the first one, twisted clamps around the bags, and then he and Carl took turns pouring fungicide on the other's hands and boots.

They were thus engaged when they first began to hear the helicopters. At first Chris thought it was the distant roar of a bulldozer, but the sound increased too rapidly, faster than a bulldozer could travel, and, besides, the sound was far too dense to be from a single engine.

There were fourteen of them. Chris and Carl suddenly saw the big Chinook helicopters in formations of threes and fours, flying at no more than three hundred feet altitude, come sweeping over the Pygmy Forest in an awesome display of alien forms and sounds.

'Jesus, would you look at that!' Carl said, shouting to be heard above the roar. 'Two, four, six – ' He counted them. 'Fourteen!'

And then they were gone. They whooshed across the cloudy blue sky and disappeared behind the horizon of the Pygmy Forest. The sound they made died very quickly, as if it were being sucked back towards the helicopters in the vacuum of their passing.

'They must've been doing two hundred miles an hour,' Carl said. 'They headed for Fort Bragg?'

Chris said, 'Yeah, and that's the second bunch that's passed this morning. The first bunch passed over town about dawn. Five of 'em. All military.'

They let their hands dry in the air and then got into the car. Once inside, Carl said, 'I hate to think what that means, all of them army helicopters at once like that. Think it has anything to do with that dead man maybe turning out to be an army sergeant?'

Chris nodded grimly. 'I'm afraid it does,' he said as he started the car. 'I'm afraid it does.' He rolled down the car window and sucked in a deep breath of brine-scented air, like an exhausted animal trying to induce a second wind, trying to find within himself some reserve of energy not yet used up. 'Anyway,' he added as he glanced at his watch, 'the army brass have called a meeting at the hospital at eleven o'clock. Maybe we'll find out then.'

19

The meeting took place in the hospital's cafeteria because it was the only room in the hospital big enough to accommodate everyone. Even so, there weren't enough chairs to go around, so some of the assistants and secretaries and members of the hospital staff had to stand along the walls.

Altogether there were almost a hundred people jammed into the cafeteria. The Special Tactics Unit from Dugway Proving Grounds was present (thirty-two men and three women), then there were the officials from the California Department of Public Health, the people from the National Institute of Health and the Federal Centre for Disease Control, as well as the white-smocked technicians from various military installations in the area who had arrived with the mobile laboratories. But by far the largest contingent was the one from Washington, headed by General Thurston Blanchard himself. Among his group, many of whom were in army uniforms, were officials and scientists from the National Security Council, the CIA, the National Defence Agency, and the Pentagon's Department of Public Information. The Fort Bragg chief of police was there, as were Sheriff Chris Jordan and the Reverend Boyle, who was the representative from the Mendocino County Board of Supervisors.

It was Sander Quence who convened the meeting. His face was drawn and pale, his eyes were red-rimmed, his hands were shaking. 'Could I have your attention, ladies and gentlemen?' he said over the public-address system. He was standing on a dais at one end of the room. To one side was a speakers' table, around which sat Professors Hoffmann and Roget, D. B. Sheftman, and an immunologist who had arrived with the Special Tactics Unit. On the other side of him was a movable blackboard, and a projection screen had been hung on the wall behind his head. The screen was illuminated by the light from an empty slide projector. When Sander began to speak, the *sotto voce* hubbub in the room ceased and everyone turned to face him.

He leaned against the lectern and spoke into the microphone. 'My name is Sander Quence. I'm an MD, a local, so I've been asked to speak to you first, to fill you in on the events that've taken place here in the last forty or so hours. I'll make it as brief as possible, and if any of you has questions – and I'm sure you will have – please hold them till after all the speakers are finished. At that time there'll be a Q-and-A session, and we'll try to answer any questions we can.'

In a tired, droning voice, he launched into the story from the beginning. Brief though he tried to be, it took him nearly thirty minutes to tell it, to inform them adequately, and when he was through with the short history of the disease, he described the general physical effects it seemed to have on its victims. It was at that time that the cafeteria lights were lowered and the first slide was projected on to the screen behind him: a picture of the dead army sergeant who had been killed in Richard Hopkins's house. When the picture of the man was projected on to the screen, showing him lying on an autopsy table, there was a gasp from the audience, a collective intake of breath.

'This is he,' Sander said, 'the first man – as far as we know – to contract the disease. As I said, we thought at first that it was a local man named Hopkins, but we've recently learned that it was an army sergeant named Lawson. We don't know what he was doing in the Hopkins house. Hopkins himself was away, and he returned last night, before we could get a quarantine notice up on the property, so he himself contracted the disease.

'In any case, this was the first man, and that's the reason we've begun to call the malady "Lawson's disease". The subject was killed by a blow to the head. So far as we know, there haven't as yet been any fatalities directly attributable to the disease itself. But of course we have no idea what its eventual effects will be. So far the victims seem to have undergone some profound metamorphic changes, both physically and psychically, but . . .' He fell silent, as if lost in thought, then seemed to shake himself out of it, and said, 'But I'll let the others tell you about that. For those of you who don't know Professor Charles Roget,' he added by way of introduction, 'he's a distinguished mycologist from the University of California at Davis. Professor?'

Sander took the empty chair at the speakers' table, and Roget, with a sheaf of notes in his hand, went to the vacated lectern. He dropped the notes on the lectern and snatched up a baton. With the tip of the baton he dramatically struck the projection screen behind him. A new picture flashed on to it, a photomicrograph of a cellular substance, a brownish tubular-shaped amoeboid cell suspended in some sort of liquid.

'There it is,' he said. 'That's it – whatever it is.' He tapped the sheaf of notes on the lectern. 'Tests and experiments indicate that it's some sort of parasitic amoeboid cell that seems to have a few genetic characteristics in common with *dictyostelium mucoroides* – or, more specifically, a variant pathogenic strain of the mucoroides, *D. mucoroides mutabilis.*' He paused for dramatic effect. 'For those of you who don't know what that is, I'll tell you in plain language: it's a slime mould fungus – not a fungus plain and simple, because fungi are never that, and this one – if, indeed, it is a fungus in the strictest sense of the word – is one that has undergone an extraordinary mutation. In fact, it's so extraordinary that it's . . . well, almost an impossibility. But then, of course, so is man, when you come to think of it. I mean, the odds against the evolutionary development of man, if you want a gambler's odds, were about a few billion to one. The odds against the evolutionary development of this organism are probably a little less than that, so maybe it's not so impossible, after all. In any case, there it is, right in front of our eyes, and we're going to have to believe it whether we want to or not.

'Now, I assume that most of you know, don't you, that fungi are generally divided into two distinct categories. The first is the saprobes, which attack and bring about the decay of dead organic materials – mushrooms, for instance, and lichen, moss, and so forth. Mycologists generally believe that this category of fungi – the saprobes – descended from plants that lost their ability to produce chlorophyll. On the other hand, the second category of fungi, the parasites, attack living organisms. They cause diseases in plants, animals, and humans, and we believe that these parasitic fungi originated from protozoan ancestors rather than from plants. But both types of fungi reproduce in more or less the same way: by spores – that is, primitive reproductive bodies – and these spores are all around us all the time, in the air, the earth, the water.'

He paused to pour himself a glass of water from the pitcher on the speakers' table. He was a man of highly mannered gestures, which matched his dramatically modulated baritone. Also, every feeling he experienced seemed to find expression in his small gnomic body, in his eyes, in the wrinkles on his large domed forehead.

'Now, the spores of *D. mucoroides mutabilis* will germinate when they find suitable conditions – that is to say, when there is enough moisture and a source of nutrients. They germinate and produce one or more amoeboid swarm cells called myxamoebas, and these myxamoebas, in turn, begin to divide and form large populations. Under certain conditions – when the amoebal population reaches a certain density, for instance – they suddenly begin to stream together to form an aggregation.

'Frankly, we mycologists have studied the hell out of this

very common fungus, but we still don't know how the cells get the message to begin aggregation. The message is not sent chemically or by bioelectric impulses. We know that much, at least, because we can place barriers between the cells – barriers such as lead, glass, distance – and the message still very often seems to get through. So we have to assume that the cells somehow have the ability to communicate by something like telepathy.

'In any case, the cells do get the message, and they aggregate, and these aggregations function as a unit. That is to say, the aggregation responds to external stimuli as a single entity, while, in reality, it's a federation of thousands of amoebas, each of which retains its own individuality.

'Think of it! It's as if each individual cell in my body had the ability to exist on its own, as a separate entity, and then, at a given message, aggregate to form my body, which, in turn, functions as a single unit, as it is doing right now.'

After what seemed to be a pause of tribute, Roget said, not as a statement to convince sceptics, but as a quiet and confident expression of collective thought, 'That's remarkable.' Another pause. 'But very common, very common, as any sophomore botany major can tell you. These aggregations are commonly called pseudoplasmodia, and I believe we have a photomicrograph of one. May we have it, please?'

He waited until the requested picture flashed on the screen, the picture of an elongated, ballon-like body, glistening with slime.

'Actually, this aggregation resembles a miniature tongue,' Roget said, as he tapped the screen with the baton. 'And like a tongue, it has the ability to assume different shapes. It's shown here in the process of aggregation. At some point, triggered by some message from the founder cells, the pseudoplasmodium goes into the last stage of its cycle, that of a sporophore. This happens when all the thousands of cells in the pseudoplasmodium begin to form a filament-like stalk, something very similar to a hypha, and at the tip of the stalk some of the cells become spores – microscopic still, but a ball-like mass of spores held together by a drop of viscous liquid.

'I'll show you some. Next picture, please,' he said, and when he got it, he gestured with the baton and said, 'Up till now I've merely been describing things that you can find in any textbook concerned with mycology. But now let's make the jump from information about ordinary slime mould fungi to the subject at hand: Lawson's disease. The photomicrograph you see here is of a skin section taken from the cadaver you saw lying on the autopsy table a few minutes ago. See these? They're the filament-like stalks I was telling you about, and there, at the tip of each stalk, is a mass of spores large enough that they require a magnification of only about four or five to be seen with the naked eye. When the stalk rubs against something, the spores are transferred by contact. If the spores don't happen to meet with proper conditions of moisture and food source, they become dormant. However, when they do meet these conditions, they bore in and begin multiplying at an astonishingly rapid rate. It takes only a matter of hours for the organism that causes this disease to pass through a sequence of growth and change, from spore to myxamoeba to swarm cells of zygotes.

'That is one way in which the organism is most *un*like a fungus. The growth of fungus is slow, while this is almost as fast as viral pneumonia.

'But of course that's not the only difference between this organism and a normal fungus. There are yet more astounding differences, not the least of which is that this organism needs human blood in order to germinate and multiply. Not just any blood, mind you, but human blood, either in the host or in the culture dishes, or else it goes dormant. It will enter the bloodstream of any warm-blooded animal, but will germinate only in human blood.'

A crew of cafeteria employees was passing through the dining room with coffee pots and cups stacked on pushcarts. They were serving coffee and doughnuts as they made their way through the tables. The red tips of cigarettes were visible in the dim light, and the room was as smoky as a nightclub.

'And once these organisms get into the bloodstream and begin to multiply,' Roget continued, 'they then invade the cells in the host's body and attach themselves to the chromosomes in the cell nuclei. And now comes the mystery, the amazement: they produce an enzyme that we have reason to believe is a uridine diphosphate galactose polysaccharide-transferase.' He smiled. 'But don't let that name intimidate you. What it is is an enzyme that gives the DNA of the invading amoeboid cells the ability to *override* the directives of the DNA in the host's cells.

'I'm sure most of you know what DNA is. For those of you who don't, it's a deoxyribonucleic acid, a component of the chromosomes that contains the genetic code of the cells. It's the blueprint, if you will, of what we are. It's what makes the cells in my finger, for instance, form themselves into the shape of a finger, rather than into the shape of a foot, or a tooth. It's what makes the protoplasm in our bodies take the shape of human beings, rather than the shape of cows or trees.

'So! What happens when the DNA in these invading amoeboid cells overrides the directives of the DNA in the host's cells? *It changes the form and function of the cells.* Can you appreciate that? The host's cells become *slaves* to the invaders. They are, in effect, *recoded* by the DNA of the invader cells. And that's why, for instance, the epidermal cells all over the host's body, once they're invaded by the amoeboid cells, cease ordinary functions and turn into slime-secreting cells. From the pores grow hypha-like filaments, forming a thin mat of mycelium-like growth. And all this is accomplished within approximately twelve hours after contamination.

'That's why this disease is so horrifying, so fraught with catastrophic consequences: it's truly *metamorphic* – the world's first and only known metamorphic disease. You understand? It literally changes – not just scars or deforms, but *changes* – the physiognomy of its host. And the body has no defences against it. It's true that the victims usually develop a fever and have an elevated white count during the very early stages of infection, but soon the victim's body stops resisting the infection. It's as if the invading cells take over those cells in the victim's body that usually produce antibodies to fight the disease. In short, the invading cells shut down production of antibodies in the victim, presumably by taking over those cells that produce antibodies.

'Amazing? Indeed! Fantastic, in fact!' He shrugged. 'But that's not all. That's not the end of it. I've just given you a small indication of what it does to the host's *body*. Now I'll turn you over to Doctor D. B. Sheftman, a psychiatrist and neurophysiologist, who'll tell you what it does to the host's *brain*.'

20

'I'll make it short,' D.B. promised as he jammed his hands into the pockets of his smock. 'At first I thought maybe I'd make it easy on you – take you into my report one step at a time. But I looked at your faces while Professor Roget was speaking, and it became obvious to me that your credulity had already been broken. Maybe now you're prepared to accept what I have to tell you. I hope so, because . . .' He paused, took a deep breath and then said, 'Well, because while we were examining and running tests on the brain of the autopsy subject, Lawson, we discovered something that . . .' He halted again and sighed with frustration and futility. He was having a difficult time finding the words he wanted, finding the right approach. Finally he gave up and said, 'Could I have the brain slide, please?'

The new picture that flashed on the screen was an outline of the human brain, with all the major parts labelled by name. But though it was on the screen, D.B. didn't refer to it. Unlike Roget, D.B. was awkward and nervous.

He said, 'This new disease . . . from the evidence we have thus far, the amoeboid cells that produce Lawson's disease have *specialised* functions. Well, of course, that's also true of the common slime mould fungus, as Professor Roget pointed out. I mean, ordinary slime mould cells have the ability to function in specialised ways – a very limited ability, I grant you, but specialised nonetheless. I mean, they aggregate, for instance, into pseudoplasmodia, and carry out specialised functions within the aggregation. That's also true of the amoeboid cells of Lawson's disease, especially the cells that invade the host's brain. Once in the brain, they aggregate to form a . . . that is, thousands and thousands of individual cells come together to make a unified, co-ordinated, multi-cellular organism capable of acting as one unit. Okay. Just like ordinary slime mould cells. But then these cells take the process a step further: the pseudoplasmodia all come together, end to end, to form a complete circuit, a complete network throughout the brain. And they do to the brain cells what the others do to the host's epidermal cells: they take over. They override the signals sent out by the brain cells.

'I won't go so far as to say that the invading cells occupy the host's brain and proceed to use it for purposes of its own, because we – as yet, at least – we can't discern any human – that is to say, logical – purpose.' He paused for a moment and rubbed his forehead. 'I hope you'll excuse me if I'm not exactly coherent. I've very tired. We all are, those of us who've . . .' He seemed to have lost his train of thought.

It was General Blanchard who spoke from the audience in a very reassuring voice. 'You're doing fine, Doctor Sheftman. Take your time.'

D.B. nodded his thanks. Forcing a smile, he stammered, 'Yes. Yes, well, about that purpose. I mean, I know it's a terrifying concept . . . it's terrifying to our way of thinking that a disease could be said to have a *purpose*. However, the inescapable fact is that the amoeboid cells of Lawson's disease seem to comprise a highly organised, disciplined and effective group dominated by a single will and purpose, and are capable of dealing with various emergencies in what appears to be a *cognitive* way. They *communicate*, you see? If something goes wrong, they're like, I mean even common everyday slime mould cells communicate, as Professor Roget said, probably by some telepathic means, but these . . . these . . . Well, let me give you an example. If I, as a human being, had the same capabilities as these aggregated organisms, I could, say, give my hand an order to do something, and the mass of cells that make up my hand could then detach themselves from my body and go off on the errand. When the hand had finished its errand, it would come back and rejoin my body. If for any reason it were prevented from rejoining my body, it would send some sort of telepathic message, whereupon other cells in the aggregate of my body would move to form a new hand. Does that . . . Am I getting my point across to you?'

This time D.B.'s faltering explanation was interrupted by a slight commotion in the back of the room near the cafeteria's main entrance. Two orderlies had rolled in a plastic domed gurney. Recognising what it was, D.B. used the occasion to forgo the remainder of his briefing.

'But enough explanations,' he said. 'Now we'd like for you all to see at first hand the results of a human who's been invaded and taken over by these phenomenal amoeboid cells that we've been trying to describe.'

With this as their cue, the two orderlies pushed the gurney down the aisle towards the speakers' table. It was a specially constructed gurney which was covered by a Quonset-shaped and hermetically sealed plastic cover. The capsule was supposed to be soundproof, but those closest to it could hear the muffled screams and cries coming from beneath the canopy, from the twisted and slime-glistening face of the young woman who had once been Lacy Coors. She was strapped down to the gurney, but had managed to work her head loose from the head strap, so she could raise her head when she screamed, and could glare directly into the dumbstruck faces.

'This is the Coors mutant,' D.B. said to the audience, all of whom had come to their feet now. 'That's what we'd better get used to calling them: mutants – not simply diseased patients, but humans who have undergone a very definite and unarguable mutation.'

Some of the spectators were straining on tiptoe to see the girl beneath the plastic canopy, while others in the further end of the room were climbing on tables and chairs for a better view.

The persons at the speakers' table and those in the front rows of the audience got up and gathered around the capsule more or less in order of importance and rank. General Blanchard joined the speakers in the first circle, as did the assistant CIA director and Colonel Thomas Parker, the commanding officer of the Special Tactics Unit. There was a growing tension among the audience, an incipient disorder that was almost palpable, and murmurs began to be heard in the rear ranks.

One of Blanchard's aides held up his hands for silence. 'Please,' he said. 'Please.'

The murmurs abated but didn't cease altogether until Blanchard himself turned a baleful eye upon the spectators and silenced them without having to say a word. He was a tall man with the composure of a statue, the self-assurance of a stone.

After the muttering died down, Blanchard turned back to stare at the girl under the sealed canopy, and without taking his eyes off her, he said, 'Professor Hoffmann? You said last night that you didn't think this disease is caused by a mutated fungus. Have you had any reason since then to change your mind?'

Hoffmann, who was standing on the opposite side of the canopy, said, 'No, sir, none at all.' He shrugged. 'It's possible, of course. Given its many fungoid characteristics, such an opinion would be reasonable, and I wouldn't want to go on record as saying categorically that it wasn't. But,' he said, and paused for a moment, sighed, and then continued, 'from what I've learned in the last twelve hours, I'm even more convinced that it's not a mere mutant. It's quite obviously an advanced form of life – far too advanced to be a mutant.'

General Blanchard nodded, then turned to Roget. 'And you, sir? Do you have an opinion about its origins?'

'Not a firm one,' he said, 'but I would like to offer a possibility. It's been said a number of times that this is an entirely *new* kind of species, a new life force. Perhaps so. But it also might very well be a very ancient species, something that evolved thousands of years ago, but with which we've had no contact until now. Why not? Such things are not rare. Frequently in the last few years, for instance, fish have been brought up from the depths of the sea that have lived for millions of years without man's even being aware of them. And just last year, a team of scientists from the National Science Foundation discovered a new species of one-celled organisms living in the mud and ooze under the ice-covered Ross Sea in Antarctica. It is a very peculiar mixture of plant and animal that has lived in that environment for over four hundred million years. Then there was the team of – '

'Yes, yes, Professor,' Blanchard interrupted. 'I'm aware of such findings. But let's stick to the present case, if you don't mind.' He turned to Sander then, and said, 'And what about you, Doctor Quence? Do you have an opinion about the origin of this disease?'

Sander was almost sullen in his answer. 'I'm only a small town MD, not a creator of germ-warfare agents, so I have no way of knowing what it might be.' And he didn't even try to disguise the challenge in his tone when he added, 'Do you?'

Blanchard ignored the barb. He laid his forefinger alongside his nose, as if in deep deliberation, and then said, 'Perhaps,' and all eyes went to him. 'I think the answer to what it is will probably be found in its host specificity. It attacks only humans, right?' He asked this of Sander, as if to give him a chance to redeem his surliness.

Sander nodded. 'We've injected a number of dogs, cats, laboratory mice, and so forth, with the spores, but they're unaffected by them.'

Blanchard turned to Roget: 'How many chromosomes does an ordinary slime fungus mould have?'

'Fourteen,' Roget said.

'And how many does this organism have?'

Roget shook his head. 'We haven't been able to determine exactly yet, but we know it's very high, probably in the forties.'

'I'd be willing to bet that it has forty-six,' Blanchard said in a grimly speculative tone. 'Chromosome compatibility.' He looked at Hoffmann then. 'Is that what you had in mind last night, Professor Hoffmann, when you hinted that it might be a recombinant? A chimera?'

Hoffmann nodded dolefully. 'Yah. And the more I learn about it, the more I'm afraid that that's what it is.'

Blanchard turned to address the audience. 'As most of you know, Professor Hoffmann is a world-renowned biochemist and Nobel prizewinner, and certainly one of the world's foremost authorities on UVL- and radioactive-induced mutations in fungoid micro-organisms. But he's also had some experience in the field of DNA research, and he thinks – suspects, anyway – that this disease is most likely caused by a DNA recombinant. For those of you who might not know what that is, I'll ask the professor if he'll give us a brief explanation. Professor?'

As Hoffmann went back to the dais to stand behind the lectern, the others moved hastily to reclaim their seats and places along the walls, while the orderlies, at a nod of dismissal from Blanchard, rolled the plastic-covered gurney out of the room.

Hoffmann was slow to start. He was exhausted, unable to think clearly, and obviously didn't know quite where to begin.

Finally, however, he cleared his throat and said, 'A few years ago . . . well, I'm sure most of you know that a few years ago some molecular biologists discovered that there was a way to separate the DNA from one species and recombine it with the DNA from another species. In effect, they unlocked the secret of creating entirely new species of life.'

He paused for a moment, pulled his pipe from the pocket of his smock, and puffed on it a few times before continuing. 'Now, as Professor Roget said, DNA is the chemical in the chromosomes that carries the genetic code of a species – the blueprint, so to speak, of what makes any species what it is. Well, by taking the DNA from one species – a frog, say – and recombining it with the DNA of another species – a bacterium, or a fly, a fungus, a horse, whatever – why, then, they have a new species of life. Or to take it a step further and really get into some fine bioengineering, they could separate and recombine DNA from *all* of those species, put them *all* together, and, presto, what have they got? An organism that did not previously exist in the natural evolutionary order. You see? A *living organism*, with the capacity to breed and multiply.'

He paused again, glanced around the audience to see if they appreciated and understood what he was saying, then added, 'The discovery of how to do this no doubt equals – no, surpasses – the importance of discovering how to split the atom, and, believe me, it's a lot simpler than splitting an atom. It's so simple, in fact, that it's being carried out in the laboratories of dozens of universities and pharmaceutical companies throughout the country right at this moment. Indeed, in laboratories throughout the world.

'And if I'm not mistaken – and I may be; I hope I am, but if I'm not – then what we have here is such an organism: a DNA recombinant. A chimera.'

When Hoffmann fell silent, signalling that he was finished, General Blanchard got to his feet, thanked Hoffmann, and then turned to the audience. 'So there it is,' he said, as if addressing troops in the field. 'Professor Hoffmann says it's only a possibility, but I think we'd better accept it as the most plausible one, and go from there. I'm hereby invoking Contingency Plans C-1 and D-1 of *Operation Hatchet.* That means that a state of martial law is now in effect in this area, that all of you are under the authority of the military government, and that everything that has been said in this room today is top-secret information.'

He then turned his attention to one of the civilians who had been sitting beside him, a man in a white smock, and said, 'As soon as those mobile labs are operational, I want you to do a gel electrophoresis on this organism. Find out exactly how many chromosomes it has, and pay particular attention to how many of the chromosomes might be primate.'

Then he addressed one of the young men in his retinue: 'Lieutenant, set up a scrambler on one of the hospital phones. I want to talk to the Secretary of the Army first, then to General Dblis.'

As the lieutenant dashed from the room, Blanchard singled out Chris Jordan, and said, 'Sheriff, I want you to work closely with Colonel Culbertson here' – indicating one of the officers at his side. 'He'll be field operations officer for this operation. I want you to help him set up a plan to put a sanitary cordon around this area. Get on it,' he said to Colonel Culbertson, who immediately left the room, taking Chris Jordan with him.

'As for the rest of you,' Blanchard said to the audience at large, 'you'll remain here for the time being. My administrative officer here, Major Harris, will begin a duty roster for all of you, civilian and military personnel alike. Are there any questions?' he asked, but before anyone could respond, he had already whirled and started out of the room, adding by way of dismissal, 'All right, then, let's get cracking.'

Sheriff Chris Jordan knocked on the door to Sander's office and entered when a voice said, 'Yeah?'

Sander was in the office with Professor Hoffmann and

D. B. Sheftman, the three of them poring over reams of data – reports and forms that were covered with scrawled writings, graphs, molecular drawings, and chemical formulas.

'Sorry to bother you,' Chris said. His raincoat and hat were dripping wet. 'Didn't mean to interrupt your work, but . . .'

Sander was behind his desk, the top of which was cluttered with papers. D.B. was sitting in a chair, his lap filled to overflowing with papers, while Hoffmann was examining papers that were spread out on the cot.

'What is it, Chris?' Sander said.

Obviously inhibited by the presence of the other two men in the room, Chris said, 'There's something I want to ask you about, Sander. Something I want to know.' He scratched his unshaven jaw. 'Is this . . . this disease, is it a germ-warfare weapon of some sort?'

Sander shrugged with a sort of resigned weariness. 'Who knows? *I* don't. Your guess is as good as mine.'

'The reason I ask,' Chris explained apologetically, 'is because . . . well, when General Blanchard mentioned the name of another general today, a man by the name of Dblis?'

It was Hoffmann who looked up and said, 'What about him?'

Chris divided his attention between Sander and Hoffmann. 'It's a name I remembered hearing before, seeing it in the newspapers. Something to do with Vietnam. A scandal of some sort. So I sent Marge – that's my wife – I sent her to the library to check the newspaper files, and, sure enough, it turns out that this General Dblis was accused of using Vietcong prisoners as guinea pigs in germ-warfare experiments in Vietnam back in 1970. There were reports that as many as three hundred POWs died because – '

'Sheriff,' Hoffmann said, interrupting. 'I don't want to be put in the position of defending General Dblis. I don't even know the man. But I recall the case, and in fairness to him I must remind you that the man was never charged with anything.'

'That's right,' Chris said. 'Seems that most of the witnesses who accused him – his own men, soldiers under his command – it seems they mysteriously died before the general could be brought to the States to face a board of enquiry.' Chris stood in the middle of the room, glancing from one man to another, and waited for a response that never came. Both Hoffmann and D.B. had suspended their perusal of the papers; with tentative, puzzled expressions, they looked at Chris, but said nothing, while Sander, in a gesture of frustration and despair, covered his face with his hands and sighed.

'Well,' Chris said, pushing on, 'I guess maybe all of you know by now who this General Dblis is? He's the man in charge of the Army Chemical and Biological Warfare Research Centre at Fort Detrick, Maryland. That's the place where Sergeant Lawson was stationed.'

No one seemed surprised by that information, and it was only after a long pause that Hoffmann, sucking on an empty pipe, said, 'Quite right, Sheriff. You're quite right. And if you want to tighten the noose of circumstantial evidence even tighter around the general's neck, consider this: it was in the same CBW Research Centre, oh, about three years ago, that a project was undertaken to create a DNA recombinant that might have some uses as a germ-warfare agent. It was called *Project Chimera.*'

'Chimera, yeah,' Chris said. 'That's the word. It means some sort of monster, doesn't it?'

Hoffmann nodded. 'A mythological monster, yah. Usually with the head of a lion, the body of a goat, and the tail of a serpent. Conceptually similar to a recombinant, you see. In this case, for instance, you take a slime mould fungus as a vector-host, then you add DNA from, say, pathogenic bacteria, maybe throw in DNA from a virus or two, and then, for good measure, you might add some DNA from a primate – an ape, say. Or,' he added, tapping the papers in front of him, 'in this case, a human.'

'*Human?*' Chris said, his face pinched with shock and outrage. He looked at Sander for confirmation that he had heard correctly, but Sander still sat at the desk with his face in his hands, unmoving, perhaps beyond hearing, perhaps beyond caring.

Hoffmann nodded, faintly apologetic for having traumatised Chris. 'It's possible. You heard what General Blanchard said about chromosomal compatibility, didn't you? Well, that's what he was implying. That's why we're combing this data, looking for anything that might suggest the presence of a primate chromosome.'

But Chris couldn't take it in. 'You're telling me . . . are you calmly sitting there telling me that this – the thing that causes this disease – may be part *human*?'

Hoffmann became cautious, puzzled by the anger and outrage he heard in Chris's voice. 'I wouldn't be at all surprised. How else do you explain its remarkable host specificity? And it wouldn't be a difficult thing to do, you know. As I said in the meeting earlier, it's being done every day in the biology departments of probably a dozen universities, not to mention all the leading pharmaceutical companies in the country. And what about in foreign countries?'

'*Why?*' Chris said.

Hoffmann, who obviously wished to end the discussion, shrugged and said, 'Why? Because it *can* be done, that's why. It's an old scientific axiom, Sheriff: if something can be done, somebody somewhere will do it.'

'Goddamn them,' Sander said from behind his hands. His voice was muffled so that the others couldn't be sure they had heard correctly. Then he made his hands into fists and slammed them down on the desk. 'God*damn* them!'

The others stared at him in mute surprise.

'Bastards!' he said, and shot a venomous glance at Hoffmann as he got up and turned his face away from them, so they couldn't see that he was near tears. He gazed from the window into the early evening darkness, the rain.

Hoffmann and D.B. exchanged puzzled glances; then Hoffmann, with fatherly solicitude, said, 'Sander? You okay?'

Sander whirled to face them again, his haggard and unshaven face twisted with impotent fury. 'No, Goddamnit, I'm not okay. I'm exhausted, and angry, and ashamed. You *scientists*,' he sneered. ' "If it can be done, it will be done." You bastards just can't let well enough alone, can you? You're going to keep fucking around, creating new diseases and bombs and shit like that, till you end up destroying us all, and that's all you can say? "If it can be done, it will be done"? Jesus Christ,' he murmured, his tone edging from anger to disgust as he turned back to stare out the window.

After a moment of embarrassed silence, Hoffmann cleared his throat and said, 'That's hardly fair to me, is it, Sander? I'm not respons – '

And Sander, turning again, furious again: '*Fair?* You talk to me about being *fair*?' He picked up a fistful of papers from the desk and waved them at Hoffmann. 'Is this fair to *me*? I was just trying to live out my life in peace, and not hurt anybody, maybe even help somebody now and then, and then you . . . you *scientists* come along and drop this shit on our heads!' He slammed the papers down on the desk. 'Don't talk to me about being *fair*.'

Hoffmann sighed. 'All I meant was, it's hardly fair to accuse me of being personally responsible for – '

'Well, then, who the hell *is*?' Sander said, and now the anger had almost gone out of his voice. Only the disgust was left. 'How many years ago was it that you used to tell me that scientists weren't responsible for what other people did with the things scientists created? It was the politicians, you said. The military. Well, I said it was bullshit then, and I say it's bullshit now. You can't put a forty-five in the hands of an idiot and then say you're not responsible for what he does with it. Goddamnit, Noah, *somebody some*where has to start being responsible for what they do!'

Hoffmann sucked on his empty pipe, quietly contemplating

the issue. 'Ah. Yes, of course. But maybe you ought to tell that to the Russians.'

Sander stared at Hoffmann, the disgust in his eyes softening into bafflement. 'What d'you mean, the Russians? What've they got to do with this?'

Hoffmann, once again in the moral ascendancy, shrugged as if explaining something that ought to be obvious to any schoolboy. 'I'm surprised at you, Sander. Hasn't it occurred to you yet that this disease is probably a germ-warfare attack on us by the Russians?'

Sander was unable to speak for a few seconds. He was becoming overwhelmed by all the horrific possibilities of this situation – possibilities that were being peeled away, layer by layer, with each new layer proving to be uglier and more terrible than the last. And when he finally spoke, there was a strange pleading note in his voice, as if he were asking a question to which he didn't want an answer: 'The Russians? Why? For God's sake, why would they want to do something like this?'

Hoffmann responded, still calmly explaining a point to a student: 'Don't you read the papers? Watch the news on TV? The Russians have about two million troops massed on the Chinese border right now – more than half their army. The other half is spread thinly throughout Europe and the Middle East. So they've got none left over for us, right? Not enough, anyway. So if war breaks out between China and Russia, how would Russia handle us? Keep us out of it? Simple: they paralyse us. They drop something like this in on us, and presto, the whole country becomes paralysed in a matter of days. With all our attention turned inwards, trying to stop this thing, the Russians can go ahead and do just about anything they want to do in China and the Middle East. You see? Makes sense, yah?'

'But . . .' Sander knew there was some flaw in the supposition, but he couldn't put his finger on it. 'But what the hell, to do this to us . . . that'd be just as much an act of war as dropping a nuclear bomb, or invading us.'

'Of course,' Hoffmann said. 'But a bomb . . . troops . . . we would know where something like that came from, wouldn't we? So we would strike back. But *this*? We may all be dead before we even find out *what* it is, much less *who* developed it.'

Sander slowly shook his head with bewilderment and despair. 'God help us,' he murmured.

'Indeed,' Hoffmann said, clamping his pipe between his teeth. 'But since he's reputed to help those who help themselves, why don't we stop wasting time and get back to work?'

FEBRUARY SIXTEENTH

21

On the night of 15 February, at exactly ten o'clock, a forty-mile stretch of the Mendocino coast – from Ten Mile River, north of Fort Bragg, to the Navarro River, south of Mendocino – was closed off. Barricades were erected at strategic points on all the roads, paved and unpaved, that led inland from the coast. The road-blocks were manned by two battalions of Sixth Army soldiers who had been brought up by truck convoys from the Presidio in San Francisco and from Fort Ord near Monterey. In addition, four companies of paratroopers from Fort Hood, Texas, were being flown to Travis Air Force Base near Fairfield, where they would be transferred to helicopter gunboats and be airlifted to Mendocino.

But it was the helicopter gunboats themselves that were intended to be used as the cutting edge of *Operation Hatchet*. The gunboats and their crews had been developed and trained for search-and-destroy missions in Vietnam, which was why General Blanchard wanted them in Mendocino. Given the rugged, mountainous terrain of the coast, and the inaccessibility of its redwood forests, the gunboats would be invaluable for running search-and-destroy missions against any disease carriers – the mutants, as they were officially designated – who resisted capture and incarceration.

So the headlands north of Heeser Drive in Mendocino became an army bivouac area, storage depot, motor pool, and helicopter landing area. Throughout the night, as troops arrived in convoys, tents sprang up across the turfy headlands like huge, brown toadstools, dozens of them in rows. Barbed-wire entanglements were strung around the storage area, and by dawn field kitchens had been brought in, and soldiers, dressed in winter fatigues and carrying M-16 rifles slung over their shoulders, began lining up to get their breakfast.

All this was accomplished in little more than ten hours. Most residents of the town were too close to the activity to sleep, and those who tried were soon awakened when the helicopter gunboats began clattering in a little after three o'clock on the morning of the sixteenth. Lights soon burned in almost every house in town, the telephone lines were overloaded with calls, and by the first chilled grey light of dawn, people had begun going from house to house, saying, 'Have you heard? Have you heard what's happening?'

Many people didn't go to work that morning. Instead, they drove down to the headlands to look at all the activity; they asked passing soldiers what was going on, but the soldiers had been ordered not to talk to civilians, and, besides, they didn't know any more than the civilians did.

But the gravity of the situation was overwhelmingly apparent. They – the residents – had all heard reports and rumours about an outbreak of some new and terrible kind of disease, so of course they connected the presence of the army to the reports and rumours; but what they hadn't realised before was how serious the situation must be if the army was willing to respond so quickly and with such a show of force.

One rumour had it that the area had been invaded by creatures from outer space. The officials – or so the rumour went – were trying to keep it secret, were lying to them by telling them it was a disease rather than running the risk of causing a panic by telling them the truth.

The most cogent and widely spread rumour, however, was that an army sergeant had been contaminated by a new and devastating germ-warfare disease. According to the rumour, the contaminated sergeant had escaped from an army hospital and come to Mendocino to hide out, had been turned into some sort of monster by the disease, and now there were whole packs of the monsters hiding out in the Pygmy Forest, attacking everyone they met, and turning everyone they touched into monsters, too.

By half-past seven that morning, the whole town was on the verge of panic. When they heard that the Mendocino Hotel had been turned over to the army, crowds of local civilians gathered in front of it. They didn't get to talk to any of the officers who were swarming in and out of the hotel, however, because soldiers with rifles held at port arms formed a corridor from the hotel to the street, through which the officers walked briskly to their chauffeured staff cars. Then a colonel came out of the hotel and asked them to please disperse.

'Go back to your homes,' Colonel Culbertson told them. 'There'll be a television address by General Blanchard at oh-eight hundred – eight o'clock. That's in fifteen minutes. Go home and tune your televisions to channel ten. General Blanchard will inform you fully of what's going on.'

At that time an army jeep, carrying a public-address system, was crisscrossing its way through the town, telling the gathering crowds of panicky residents to go home and tune to channel ten at eight o'clock for an address by the general. Two soldiers were riding on the sides of the jeep, and at each intersection the jeep would stop long enough for the soldiers to jump off and nail copies of a government notice on the utility poles. It was a notice of quarantine and a map showing the quarantined area.

Chris Jordan sipped a cup of coffee in the kitchen of his home as he watched General Blanchard on the small portable television set. Christ was bleary-eyed, having had only three hours' sleep the previous night, and still unshaven, his hair uncombed. Marge sat with him at the table, while Adrianne and her puppy sat on the floor.

General Blanchard spoke in a calm voice. He told the residents that, by the authority of the President of the United States, he had declared the area shown on the map behind him to be quarantined.

'This is necessary,' he said, 'because a new disease has broken out in the area. Let me hasten to assure you, however, that you have nothing to fear from the disease if you co-operate with the military authorities and obey the quarantine laws.'

The army, he assured them, was there to help and protect them, and had the situation well under control. If everyone in the area co-operated, why, the situation might be back to normal within just a few days.

'In the meantime,' he said, 'we must take very strict precautions.' He was in full military uniform, including gold-braided hat, and was standing beside a desk in a television studio. He was flanked by an American flag on one side and a California flag on the other; projected on the background wall was a map of the coast. The quarantine area was outlined in red. General Blanchard was a man with a cautious and tranquil nature. Though very tall and straight, he appeared to be completely at ease, adopting the tone of a man who was speaking to respected friends. 'While these precautions may prove to be an inconvenience to you, I'm sure you can appreciate why they must be taken, and will co-operate with us in implementing them.'

Marge got up to pour Chris another cup of coffee. The puppy, growling fiercely, took the opportunity to run after Marge and nip her heel just above the fuzzy house slipper. And he yelped with surprise when she kicked him.

'Don't hurt him!' Adrianne demanded as she rushed to protect the puppy.

Marge's nerves were frayed. Her tone was only grudgingly apologetic as she said, 'Well, you've been told that h – '

Chris shushed her. 'Damnit, I need to hear this.' He, too, was irritable from overwork and lack of sleep, and now, feeling guilty for having shushed her, he said defensively, 'For Christ's sake, can't I just – ?'

'All right,' she said. 'All right.' She sat down to drink her coffee and watch the broadcast, but she jumped every time the phone rang. It rang regularly every few minutes – had been ringing like that since a little after three o'clock that morning, in fact. Now, however, she no longer had to answer it. Now it was on automatic answer, which referred the callers to the Sheriff's Headquarters in Fort Bragg.

General Blanchard, having moved around to the front of the desk and leaned back against it, was now reading the prohibitions listed in the quarantine proclamation.

'. . . except official personnel with special passes will be allowed to leave or enter the quarantine area, and anyone attempting to leave the area by circumventing the road-blocks and eluding the armed patrols will be subject to arrest under military law. If found guilty, the violator could be sentenced to as much as six months in a federal prison.'

He also informed them, as though it were merely incidental, that all civil rights had been suspended, and a state of martial law was in effect.

Concluding, he asked his audience to remain calm and, if possible, continue working at their jobs. However, schools were to be closed, and children – particularly children in rural areas – kept at home under observation.

Adrianne asked excitedly, 'Mommy, does that mean I don't have to go to school?'

'Shhhhh,' Marge said with her finger to her lips. 'We'll talk about it when he's through.'

'Did you hear that, Pupo?' Adrianne asked in a conspiratorial whisper. 'I don't have to go to school today. I can stay home with you.'

The puppy seemed to like the idea. His response was a wag of the tail and an attempt to lick Adrianne on the mouth.

When General Blanchard finished the address, Marge said to Chris, 'Let me fix you some breakfast before you go.'

Chris agreed to some scrambled eggs, which she cooked for him while he was shaving. As he stood staring into the mirror above the bathroom sink, his face smeared with lather, it struck him as grimly ironic that the mundane and usually boring act of shaving could, under certain circumstances, become a positive luxury. He would have loved a hot bath, too, but Marge called to tell him that his eggs were ready, and he was going to be late for his scheduled meeting with Colonel Culbertson.

As he gulped down the eggs in a stony and distracted silence, Marge watched him from across the table. She had sent Adrianne and the puppy into another room to play. She wanted no interruptions in case Chris felt a need to talk to her, to let her share some of the fears and forebodings that seemed to be dragging him down, causing his shoulders to slump, causing his face to be set in an expression of stolid helplessness. But even though she encouraged him to talk, he didn't respond, so finally she said, 'What is it, Chris? There's something you're not telling me.'

He swirled the dregs of the coffee around in the bottom of his cup.

She decided to take a more businesslike approach. 'While you're up in the helicopter today, will I be able to reach you on the radio?'

He shook his head. 'The army's radios operate on a different band.'

'Well, then, where'll you be?'

He shoved the cup away and got up. 'We're going up Albion River first. There was a report that a couple of women and a boy from that Jesus freak commune went up Albion River yesterday to pick mushrooms.' He crossed to where his jacket and revolver belt hung on a peg near the kitchen door. 'The boy came back, said his mother and the other woman had been . . . attacked by some crazy man covered with slime.' He strapped on his revolver while Marge held his jacket. 'Late yesterday we got a report that at least one of the women had been seen in that old Sansi cabin about a mile up the river.'

After Marge helped him slip into his jacket, he started to

leave the house, but Adrianne waylaid him before he got out the door. Suddenly she was there beside him, tugging at his sleeve, while the puppy, growling and snapping, attacked the cuffs of his pants.

'Daddy, are you coming home early tonight?'

'I don't know, honey,' he answered impatiently. 'I'll do the best I can.'

The puppy, having successfully pounced upon an unsuspecting cuff, now had it in his teeth, snarling as he tried to shake it to death.

Marge said, 'It's her birthday,' and smiled to show Chris that she was explaining the motive for Adrianne's question, not reminding him of something he had forgotten.

'Oh, of course,' he said. 'That was dumb of me. Miss Priss is seven today.'

Adrianne's spirit revived. 'Yeah, and I'm going to make a cake. Mommy's going to help, but I'm going to put the frosting on it and seven candles, and I'll write across the top, "Happy Birthday, Me".' She giggled.

Chris leaned down and took her small, excited face in his hands. 'I'll try very hard, honey. But if I'm not able to get back in time, you be sure and save me a piece of the cake, okay? And happy birthday,' he added as he gave her a kiss on the forehead.

Marge followed him out of the house. Still probing, she said, 'What're you going to do when you find her? The woman in the old Sansi cabin, I mean.'

Chris opened the car door, but didn't get in. He looked at Marge as she stood there without a coat in the chilled morning air, her arms folded beneath her breasts.

He looked directly at her to gauge the shock on her face when he said, 'The army made a decision last night. They decided that the disease-carriers – ' He snorted. 'They insist on calling them "mutants" now.' He looked down and scuffed at the gravel with his shoe. 'If they won't come in on their own, and if we can't bring them in without risking contamination ourselves . . .' He shrugged. 'We'll have to kill them.'

The shock was predictable. 'Chris! Oh, my God, why? Such extreme measures, why . . . nobody's died from it yet, have they? It hasn't even proved to be fatal yet, has it?'

'No,' he said as he got into the car. 'No one's died from it yet, far's we know.'

'Then why don't they wait? Just for a few days, anyway?'

'That's what I argued, but . . . well, what if they did wait?' he asked, speaking through the open window and obviously taking no pleasure in playing the devil's advocate. 'What if we waited five days, and then it proved fatal? Given the hostility and aggressiveness of the carriers, the disease would've been spread all over northern California by then.' He started the car. 'It's like the colonel said, a simple matter of arithmetic: it's better to kill a hundred than risk the deaths of a hundred thousand.'

She reached in and put a hand on his shoulder, as if to hold him there by force. 'But, Jesus, Chris, what if it doesn't prove to be fatal at all?'

'You haven't seen one of them yet,' he said.

'No, but . . .'

'I have,' he said. 'It might be better if it were fatal.'

'It's that bad?'

He nodded. 'The army thinks so, anyway,' he said as he slowly reached into his jacket pocket and brought out a small aluminium container. He held it in the palm of his hand and let Marge stare at it.

'What is it?' she asked. 'What's it hold?'

'Three capsules of cyanide,' he said.

'*Cyanide?*' She couldn't believe what she thought he was saying. 'What for?'

'Just in case,' he said.

'Just in case of what?

'In case we get it.'

After a moment of stunned silence, she said, 'In case *who* gets it?'

'Us,' he said. 'It holds three capsules. One for me. One for you. One for Adrianne.'

Chris drove down to the headlands, marvelling at the suddenness and ominous magnitude of a full-blown military operation: marching details of soldiers with slung rifles, jeeps, trucks, tents, helicopters – all vibrating with the energy of a disturbed anthill. There must have been a dozen helicopters on the ground, and three of them were warming up for take-off. One of them was the big, arms-bristling gunboat that was waiting for Chris.

'Ah, there you are, Sheriff,' Colonel Culbertson shouted above the roar of the slowly whirling rotors. He glanced at his watch. Dressed in fatigues and carrying a .45 automatic on his hip, he stood on the ground below the huge open door in the side of the helicopter. A crewman was standing in the open door; beside him was a .50-calibre machine-gun on a swivel pod.

As Chris approached the helicopter on foot, instinctively shrinking away from the backwash of the clattering rotors, Colonel Culbertson climbed into the open door, then gave Chris a helping hand. Immediately the rotors began speeding up, the helicopter began to vibrate violently, and the ground slowly began to recede below them.

On the other side of the helicopter was another open door, another gun (a recoilless homing rocket, as Chris was to learn later) and three other crewmen, all of whom were wearing helmets with built-in radios.

Colonel Culbertson gestured with pride towards the guns, and raised his voice above the roar of the motor to tell Chris, 'That's not all. There are rockets below, you see 'em? Sidewinders. And cannons in the nose. Lots of firepower.'

One of the crewmen gave Chris and the colonel a crash helmet each. Built into the helmets were wireless intercom radios, so that Chris could see the colonel's lips move when he spoke, but he heard his voice over the earphones in the helmet. It sounded as if the colonel were speaking with a piece of metal in his mouth.

'Let's go up front,' the colonel said, no longer shouting. He took Chris up into the ship's cockpit to meet the pilot and co-pilot, who were also wearing the helmets with the built-in intercoms.

Looking over the heads of the pilots, Chris could see the coastline flashing by. He guessed that they were at about three hundred feet altitude, and going maybe a hundred miles an hour. The pilot, after turning the controls over to the co-pilot, unfolded a map on a map board between the seats. His voice on the intercom asked Chris to locate their destination on the map. Chris slid his finger down the coast and stopped at Albion Flats. Colonel Culbertson hovered over his shoulder.

'That's the Albion River,' Chris told the pilot. 'The cabin's about one mile up the river, about here.'

The pilot nodded. 'You tell me which river it is, all right?'

Colonel Culbertson said, 'Fine. But first I want to see the Navarro One-twenty-eight road-block. See how many cars they have stacked up there by this time.' To Chris, he said, 'People trying to get out before the quarantine was announced.'

Nodding, the pilot radioed his new flight plan to a dispatcher, and then chewed gum contentedly as he swooped the helicopter over the shoreline. At one time he rapidly gained altitude to escape a flock of frightened seagulls, and then he swung the helicopter up over the highway and followed it to the road-block.

It was set up where Highway 128, which led to the freeways in the interior, intersected like a 'T' with Highway 1, which coiled its sinuous way southwards down the coast towards San Francisco. A barricade was across the highway just north of the intersection. All vehicles coming in from the west or the south were simply being turned back by a highway-patrol car before they reached the barricade. But behind the barricade, on the quarantine side, was a long, bumper-to-bumper line of stalled vehicles: cars and trucks and vans, camper pick-ups and house trailers. There were about thirty vehicles in all, and from the helicopter the line looked like a brightly coloured segmented snake coiled along the shoreline. Many of the cars stood with their doors flung open, while the drivers and passengers milled about on the road. They all stopped and lifted their faces when the helicopter flew over.

One rank of soldiers stood at the barricade with their rifles at port arms, facing the civilians, and there was a big army transport truck parked beside the barricade, on the roof of which was a machine-gun on a turret. Manned by two soldiers, the gun was pointed in the general direction of the civilians on the road.

The colonel said, 'They'll all be turned back, of course. Trouble is, there'll be a lot more of them trying to get out in a little while, now that they know the area is closed off.'

'You don't sound too worried about it,' Chris said.

'I'm not,' the colonel assured him. 'My men are setting up checkpoints, you see, all along the highways leading out of Mendocino and Fort Bragg. We'll have a checkpoint every five miles. Only the local residents will be allowed in or out of any one area. There'll be twelve areas altogether, and each area will have its own command.' What was left unsaid, but definitely implied by his tone of voice, was that the colonel took great pride in a job well done.

The helicopter was on its second tilted swoop over the road-block. On the ground an officer was standing beside a jeep and talking through a bullhorn to the milling groups of civilians. As the helicopter was passing over the second time, the officer looked up and waved.

The colonel said, 'He's got everything under control. Let's go on back to the Albion River, shall we, Captain?'

The helicopter immediately went into a powerful banking turn and began following the highway back towards Albion Flats. The colonel used the few minutes of flight time to talk to the gunners. Speaking on the intercom, he reminded them that, during their training for *Operation Hatchet*, they had been told that there might be times when they would be required to fire on non-military personnel.

'This may be one of those times,' he told them bluntly. 'You've been briefed on what this disease does to people who come in contact with it. They cease to be human. Remember that. They become mutants, and I guarantee you this much: one of these mutants may be as dangerous to us as a whole army of enemy troops. So if you're ordered to shoot, shoot to kill. If you have the choice, don't just wound them. They can't be medically treated, so you will shoot to kill.'

Chris could hardly believe what he was hearing. It sounded rational enough, to be sure, and he knew the colonel was correct in everything he said. Rational though it was, however, there was an unmistakable aura of madness about it. The colonel was, after all, talking about shooting unarmed civilians - women and children - anybody 'strongly suspected' of being contaminated by Lawson's disease. That policy decision - that of shooting suspected mutants on sight - had been agreed to the previous night at a meeting of the Field Operations Committee, which had been convened by Colonel Culbertson for the purpose of formulating a policy to deal with the daily tactical problems they would be likely to face while tracking down and neutralising the disease-carriers - the mutants, as the colonel insisted on calling them, as if to dehumanise them in his mind before he had to go out and kill them.

Chris had been apointed co-chairman of the Field Operations Committee, and he had argued from that position of authority that they would be giving the soldiers a licence to shoot anybody. The others argued that that was a risk they would have to take, but Chris had continued to oppose the policy until the colonel told him that if he couldn't support the decisions of the committee, he should resign as sheriff and let them appoint a sheriff who could.

They came in sight of the old Sansi cabin. It had been built on a marshy silt deposit in a curve of the river. The pilings in its foundation had rotted out years ago, and now the cabin sat askew, broken-backed, windowless, with a tangle of brown, leafless blackberry vines clinging to its sides and roof. Seen from the helicopter, the leafless vines seemed to be tentacles that had reached out of the ground and enfolded the cabin, pulling it slowly back down into the maw of the earth as if it were some stricken prey.

'See anything?' the colonel asked. He and Chris had gone back to the fuselage now. They stood holding on to the overhead safety rail as they looked out the open doorway. The helicopter was circling so that they, and the .50-calibre machine-gun, were always facing the cabin.

'No,' Chris said. 'No signs of life that I can see.'

'I thought I saw something in one of those windows. Couldn't tell what it was, maybe just a movement.' He turned to the machine-gunner. 'Sergeant. See if you can flush out whatever's in there. Put a few rounds in it.'

The gunner bolted a round into the chamber and began firing, pivoting the gun on the pod. The bullets exploded in the old pilings around the edge of the cabin, kicking up showers of splinters and chunks of rotted wood, and about every fifth round was a tracer, the trajectory of which the gunner could trace and use to guide the other round that spattered into the foundation of the cabin.

Then the door of the cabin suddenly burst open, and out dashed a completely nude figure. It was a man, a naked man with dark bushy hair, who, obviously panic-stricken, dashed out of the cabin and ran into the bog-like area that lay between the cabin and a thicket of cottonwoods on the river bank about fifty yards away. It was his only hope of escape.

'Captain,' the colonel said over the intercom, 'get in front of him, come down in front of him.' To the gunner, he said, 'Hold your fire till the last minute, but don't let him get into those trees.' Then he grabbed a microphone off the fuselage wall and, speaking to the pilot again, said, 'Give me the loudspeaker.'

'You're on,' the captain said.

When the colonel spoke again, his voice could probably be heard for a mile. It boomed from a loudspeaker attached to the belly of the helicopter: 'You down there! Stop running immediately!'

But the naked man didn't stop. It could hardly be said that he was running, however, because he was bogging down in almost every step he took, so that his legs often seemed to be pumping in slow motion.

'You down there! This is Colonel Culbertson, United States Army, speaking. I order you to halt!'

The helicopter swung over him – very low now, maybe no more than twenty feet above him – and turned sideways so that the machine-gun continued to face him.

The man stopped struggling in the bog as the helicopter swept over him, the backwash of its rotors almost knocking him down; he stopped and glared up at them, and for the first time they got a good look at him. It was Lonnie McCabe.

It took Chris a few seconds to realise who – what – he was seeing, that the mud-splattered and slime-shiny man there knee-deep in the bog, staring up at them, his face a grotesque mask of hatred, his mouth moving in spasms of unheard curses, was Lonnie McCabe, the man who had been his friend for nearly ten years. But there could hardly be any doubt about it.

'You there!' the colonel was saying over the loudspeaker. 'Stay where you are. Put your hands over your head. Do you understand me? Put . . . your . . . hands . . . over . . . your . . . head!'

'It's Lonnie!' Chris said to the colonel, forgetting for a moment that the colonel didn't know Lonnie. 'A deputy, a friend of mine. Here, let me talk to him.' He nearly snatched the microphone from the colonel's hands, and said, 'Lonnie! Lonnie! It's me – Chris Jordan. Lonnie, do what he tells you to! You understand me, Lonnie? For God's sake, do – '

But like an implacable savage, and with the stamina and strength of ten men, McCabe whirled to his right and started slogging his way towards the river.

'Lonnie!' Chris pleaded, his voice booming out across the water and woods. 'Stand still! Don't run! For God's sake, man, you're sick!'

'Don't shoot till I say so,' the colonel told the gunner; then to Chris, he said, 'It's a mutant, isn't it?'

Chris hesitated.

'Damnit, Sheriff,' the colonel said, 'I want your concurrence before he reaches the water: it's a mutant, isn't it?'

Chris nodded.

'Then say so,' he snapped. 'I want it on the record, your *official concurrence.*'

'Yes,' Chris said. 'It's a . . .' He hesitated for a second before using the word for the first time, and then was glad that he finally did. 'It's a mutant.'

'Fire!'

But Lonnie had made it to the water. He threw his body forward just as the .50-calibre opened up. The rounds sprayed over his head, and he was under the water before the gun's trajectory could change. He had been hit, however, at least once before he submerged.

'Get him!' the colonel urged. 'Don't let him escape.'

Blood surged up from the water where he disappeared, a large stain that faded to pink at its edges.

The firing stopped. There was no body. The helicopter was hovering over the fading pink stain, but there was no body to be seen in the shallow, murky, moss-choked waters.

'Damn!' the colonel said. His face was flushed. 'Well, he's got to come up some time. Keep hovering, Captain, and everybody keep a sharp lookout. When you see him, fire.'

Chris didn't even want to look. It would be his fault, he knew, if Lonnie got away, because he had waited too long in signing his death warrant. He knew the mutant had to be killed; he had acknowledged it a hundred times, but he didn't know if he could be the one to do it. Maybe the colonel was right. Maybe he should resign and let the sheriff's badge be given to someone who had the intestinal fortitude to kill sick and unarmed humans in cold blood. *But that's the problem,* he thought. *You keep thinking of them as humans. Friends. People you know. Stop it. They're mutants. No longer humans . . .*

'There!' someone shouted. It was one of the crewmen on the other side of the helicopter. 'Two hundred feet off starboard at five o'clock.' He was pointing at something in the water, the lumpy outline of a half-submerged form.

Chris and the colonel crossed to the other door. The colonel told the gunner at the homing rocket, 'Put a round in it.'

The gunner, already aiming at the object, fired, and the round exploded in a geyser of water and bits and pieces of whatever it was that it hit.

'Direct hit,' the gunner said boastfully, but then the target, which had been driven deep into the water by the explosion, suddenly resurfaced and shot out of the water far enough for them to see what it was: the smoking remains of a driftwood log.

'Heads up!' the pilot said over the intercom. 'We got him fifty feet forward.'

The helicopter swung around so the .50-calibre was again facing the target. The gun opened up immediately, ripping and churning the surface of the water where Lonnie had surfaced.

'Cease firing,' the colonel said when it became obvious that Lonnie was gone. He had dived again, and again there was a blood stain in the water, a smaller one this time.

'Damn, damn, damn,' the colonel fumed. 'He swims underwater like a Goddamned fish.' He was apparently very angry with himself for having let Lonnie get into the water in the first place.

It was Chris who spotted him when he resurfaced. That was only because Chris was gnawing on his knuckles with his eyes downcast, and suddenly there Lonnie was, almost beneath the hovering helicopter. Blood was pouring from one of his legs and he apparently couldn't swim any longer. He glared upwards at the helicopter, and Chris met his gaze for a moment, felt Lonnie's eyes boring into him with a fathomless hostility.

And Chris hesitated yet once again before he said, 'There. Almost directly under us.'

The helicopter quickly swung around, which made it necessary for the machine-gunner to change aim as he fired, so the first burst went wild, giving Lonnie a chance to dive again. This time, however, he wasn't fast enough. The gunner, firing at the place where Lonnie had dived, got one into him. His body wallowed to the surface like a log, spewing blood; then he slowly turned over on his back, and Chris thought for a moment that Lonnie was looking up at him as the bullets tore into his body. And as the bloodstain rapidly widened across the river's scum-grey surface, the target area finally became a churning fury of frothing water and blood and bullets.

'Cease firing,' the colonel said at last, then glanced at Chris and said, 'So we . . .' He stopped when he saw the expression on Chris's face. 'What's the matter, Sheriff?'

Chris could smell the cordite and the gun's hot, smoking barrel. 'That man was my friend,' he said.

'Wrong on both counts,' the colonel said. 'He wasn't a man, he was a mutant, and was probably the deadliest enemy you ever had. Now, Captain,' he told the pilot over the intercom, 'let's go back and put a rocket in that cabin. We got a report of female mutants around here somewhere, maybe they're hiding in there.' To Chris, he said, 'Come on, Sheriff, you'll want to see this.'

Chris couldn't tell if it was supposed to be a question or a command. He followed the colonel back into the cockpit.

'Stand off one hundred yards,' the pilot told the co-pilot. 'Laser locked in?' he asked, although he could see that it was by the signal on the instrument panel, but he wasn't really asking questions, he was counting down. 'Laser guidance system,' he said as he flipped the cover off a red toggle switch on the instrument panel. He pushed another button marked AMK, and said, 'Fire one.'

The rocket roared beneath the helicopter. It immediately homed in on the laser beam that was aimed at the cabin, and followed it directly to the target. The cabin exploded in a geyser of flames and splintered wood. The sound of the explosion, caught between the walls of the canyon, was horrendous. Boards and debris were hurled hundreds of feet into the air, and a column of smoke boiled up from the site. The shock waves buffeted the helicopter.

When the smoke cleared, the cabin was gone. Where it had stood was a charred hole. Chris gazed at the charred black hole, and he had a premonition that what he was seeing was the future, and then he couldn't see clearly any more because the scene was blurred by the tears in his eyes.

22

That afternoon another storm bank gathered on the horizon of the ocean. The day had been a rare one, a day when raindrops still trembled on the leaves and grass, twinkling in the pale winter sunlight. But by two o'clock that afternoon, the westwarding sun reached the wispy edge of the oncoming storm bank, and in a few minutes the sun seemed to be slowly sucked into the clouds, swallowed up by the dark amoeba-like mass of thunderheads that was spreading across the sky.

The helicopter gunboats were grounded, their search-and-destroy missions terminated for the day. Colonel Culbertson cursed the storm, and later he was to say that if it hadn't been for the storm, they could have stopped the spread of Lawson's disease that day, the first day of the quarantine. At that time, he said, the gunboats could kill the mutants faster than they could multiply. Without the helicopters, however, it was an impossible task.

And soon it became obvious that the mutants were increasing at a rate that matched or exceeded the most alarming estimates. There were reports all afternoon coming in from people who claimed they had seen a mutant, or – in two cases – been attacked by one. Then later that afternoon came the ominous report that two mutants had been seen together. If the mutants actually started forming groups . . .

Troops were dispatched to check out each report, but in every case the mutants disappeared into the heavily forested areas where the troops, without helicopters or spotter planes, inevitably lost them. But while tactical field operations were totally unsuccessful, the achievement of the Signal Corps in putting together the Crown Hall Communications Centre surprised even the officers and men who achieved it.

Crown Hall had been a huge old dance hall and community centre built before the turn of the century. The Signal Corps took over the hall and surrounded it with mobile generators, dotted its roof with antennae, and scaffolded the interior with electronically controlled video cameras, projectors, microphones, loudspeakers, screens, and klieg lights. By two o'clock that afternoon they had installed a direct closed-circuit television hook-up to the National Security Council room in the basement of the White House. They – the engineers and technicians, many of whom wore headsets and dragged colour-coded cables around with them – scurried in and out of the prefabricated control booths and over the scaffolded electronics equipment all afternoon, checking and rechecking this and that, shouting questions and instructions, until two o'clock, when they made the first successful test of the White House hook-up.

Brigadier General Damon Dblis arrived in Mendocino just before the storm broke. The first flurries of raindrops had already begun to fall when the chauffeured staff car – General Blanchard's own staff car, with the three-star flags on the fenders – picked up General Dblis at the helicopter landing area on the headlands and took him to the Mendocino Hotel.

Dblis was a man who made heads turn. The chauffeur nearly had more than one accident because he couldn't keep his eyes away from the rearview mirror, in which he could see a face like no other that he had ever seen in his life. It was true that General Dblis was an ugly man, but it was the ugliness of difference, not deformity. Not only was his head completely hairless, his face was, too. He had no eyebrows or eyelashes or beard. Presumably, he had lost all his hair because of some tropical disease, or perhaps had suffered a terrible accident with an acid, or had been burned in some war.

The hairlessness, however, wasn't his only striking feature. He was an enormous man, perhaps six-foot-three, with a barrel chest and a thick, bullish neck. He had a very prominent nose and a mouth that seldom smiled, and even when it did, the smile never reached those cold greenish-grey eyes behind the hairless lids.

Once in front of the Mendocino Hotel, Dblis waited in the car until one of the hotel's door-guards stepped down and opened the door for him. A shocked silence fell over the guards when they saw him get out of the car. They had come to attention and were saluting him, but he didn't return the salutes, so they continued holding their gloved hands to their foreheads and turned with Dblis as he passed, their eyes wide with wonder at the face they were seeing.

General Blanchard met him just inside the door. They said their hellos and shook hands, crisply and formally, and Blanchard said, 'The corporal here' – indicating a nearby soldier who had been assigned to Dblis as his valet – 'will show you to your quarters. Sorry to be so abrupt, but I've got a Pentagon call waiting for me. I'll be up to see you in a few minutes, though. Did you bring the *Chimera* files?'

Dblis nodded.

The valet took him up to his room and began unpacking the general's things.

Dblis went into the bathroom and was washing his hands. He washed without rolling up his sleeves, without taking off his dress jacket. He looked at his reflection in the mirror, looked a long time, and then slowly – very slowly – the corners of his thin mouth curled into the semblance of a smile, smug and cheerless.

He was still in the bathroom when the doorbell rang and the valet let General Blanchard in. Dblis came out of the bathroom to meet Blanchard, still drying his hands with the towel, although the act was only a ruse to discourage Blanchard from offering to shake hands again. He didn't like to shake hands. Whenever politeness required him to, he would wash his hands as soon afterwards as possible.

Blanchard first spoke to the valet, who was still unpacking the suitcases. 'Corporal? Coffee?'

'Yes, sir,' the corporal said, and left the room with his eyes cast down so that he wouldn't be caught staring at Dblis.

'All right,' Blanchard said in the tone of a schoolteacher moving on to the next subject. 'First of all, did you bring *all* the *Chimera* files with you?'

'I believe you asked me that downstairs,' Dblis said. 'And I nodded an affirmative. The files are on their way to the Fort Bragg Hospital. I believe those were your instructions?' Then he added in a slightly sarcastic voice. 'I always do what I'm told to do.'

Blanchard snapped, 'Then why in the hell didn't you obey

my instructions when I first told you to get out here? Why'd you make me practically put you under arrest to get you here?'

For all the emotion it showed, Dblis's face could have been carved in Mount Rushmore. 'I didn't care to be your hostage,' he said.

'Hostage?' Blanchard said. 'Is that what you consider yourself, a hostage?'

'Well,' Dblis said, 'aren't I?' When he finished drying his hands, he began neatly folding the towel into four layers.

After a moment's reflection, Blanchard said, 'Yes, you are, if that's what you want to call it. If this disease turns out to be one of your little DNA recombinants, I figure we might be lucky to get out of here alive. I thought that if you were exposed to the same dangers that we were, you might be a little more co-operative in helping us get it under control.'

Having folded the towel, Dblis carelessly dropped it on the floor. 'Bullshit,' he said. 'The truth is, you saw this as another chance to embarrass me. You want to associate me with this thing, to blacken my name, so that you can get me booted out of the service, as you've been trying to do ever since that frame-up in Vietnam.'

'Frame-up?' Blanchard said, his voice edged with sarcasm. 'You're still claiming the Communists tried to cause an international scandal by killing their own men and blaming it on you?'

'Perhaps you'd better come to the point,' Dblis said curtly. 'We both have better things to do than stand around and rehash old arguments.'

'All right,' Blanchard said, as if he thought that was a good idea. Glancing at his watch, he said, 'In exactly twenty-three minutes I'll be talking to the President, and he'll want some answers about what's going on out here. Well, I don't have any. Maybe you do. This disease we've got here, is it a recombinant? One of those organisms you tried to create in the *Chimera* project?'

'I told you on the phone, I don't know whether or not it's a chimera. You know more about that than I do, why ask me?'

'You never succeeded in producing anything like this?'

'I wish I could say yes,' Dblis murmured. 'Unfortunately, I have to say no, we never produced anything like it. We might have, if those damned politicians had left us alone. But as you have every reason to recall,' he said pointedly, 'the President ordered us to discontinue it before we could even get started on anything useful. And I believe he did so on your advice, Thurston, you and those nervous Nellies from the EPA. Well, isn't it too bad that he couldn't have ordered the Russians to stop, too?'

'You think it's Russian, then?'

There was an almost imperceptible shrug of his massive shoulders. 'Can you doubt it?'

'What about a drug company? Or a university? Something they might've been working on, and it got away from them?'

Dblis snorted with disdain. 'The drug companies are working only on DNA recombinants from which they can make a profit. The only way they could've come up with something like this is by accident, and we both know this was no accident, don't we? And as for the universities – *poof*! Sure, they have people who might try to do it, but they also have people who might try to compose a symphony worthy of Beethoven, or a painting worthy of Michelangelo. Realistically, though, what do you think their chances of success would be? A million to one? Two million to one?' He sneered again. 'No. This chimera – if, indeed, that's what it is – is the work of a genius. A great genius. Whoever did it, if he ever becomes known, will go down in history along with Einstein and Galileo as one of the most brilliant scientists who ever lived. Think of it,' he said, his voice becoming almost soft with awe and admiration, 'the world's first metamorphic disease! No doubt the most significant species of life to have appeared on Earth since man himself.' He paused, as if in tribute, then continued in a more matter-of-fact tone, 'So you can be sure it didn't originate in the lab of some college or pharmaceutical company. If it's a chimera, it has to be Russian – probably the work of Lomovskaya of the Moscow Biosciences Institute. He's the only other man that I can think of who has the brilliance to have done it.'

'And "the other man"? Who might that be?'

Dblis shrugged. 'Me, of course.'

'Of course. But you didn't.'

'I told you I didn't. How many – '

'You also told me that Sergeant Lawson was AWOL. You said you didn't know where he had gone or what he was doing.'

Dblis was nonchalant. 'Lies, of course,' he said. 'All lies.'

'Of course, I now have a copy of his last TDY orders, signed by his company commander, dispatching him to Mendocino. Why?'

Dblis seemed resigned. 'The fact is,' he admitted grudgingly, 'Sergeant Lawson came to Mendocino to locate and recover one of the meteorites that was reported to have fallen here on February first. It was a routine assignment for a project we began at Fort Detrick called SORU.'

'SORU?'

'Space Organism Retrieval Unit. It's an effort to capture an organism from outer space – a germ, a virus, whatever – for possible germ-warfare application. Included in the project is work on meteorites, of course, as possible carriers of microscopic life from outer space. That's what Sergeant Lawson came here to do, find one of the meteorites.'

'The old *Panspermia Project*,' Blanchard said.

Dblis nodded. 'The same purpose, yes.'

Blanchard seemed almost incredulous. 'But the President ordered that all efforts to capture a micro-organism from outer space be stopped, and not resumed. That was over four years ago.'

Dblis said nothing.

'And yet you went ahead and tried to do it?' Blanchard

asked. 'In direct defiance of a presidential directive?'

Dblis remained silent.

'I see. So that's why you lied about Sergeant Lawson. You knew that when the President found out about SORU, he'd take your stars away from you. Of course. And he will, too, if I have anything to say about it.'

'Oh, I'm sure you'll have something to say about it,' Dblis said. 'If I were you, however, I wouldn't say anything to him about it until you get control of the crisis here in Mendocino – *if* you get control of it, that is.'

'Oh? Why not?'

Again the shrug of his shoulders was almost imperceptible. 'If he found out that I'd disobeyed his directive, he might order me back to Washington immediately, and then what would you do for a hostage?'

Blanchard gave that a moment's thought, and then said, 'You're right. It can wait. In the meantime, I'll have you assigned as *Hatchet*'s executive officer. That way I won't have to let you out of my sight, at least not until we get through going over the *Chimera* files, just in case there's something in them that needs explaining.'

'Good thinking,' Dblis remarked cooly.

The valet returned, pushing a cart with the coffee service on it.

Blanchard glanced at his watch. 'All right. The White House conference will take place in about seven minutes. I want you to be there, too, just in case the President has any questions he might want to ask you.'

'Quite. But I may be allowed to change my shirt first, mayn't I? I always like to look my best for the politicians.'

'I'll meet you downstairs at the door in seven minutes. No longer.'

Dblis nodded, and then stood watching the closed door for a long moment after Blanchard had gone. What finally snapped him out of his unblinking absorption was something he saw from the corner of his eye. The valet had resumed unpacking, and was now hanging the general's uniforms in the closet.

'Not that way,' Dblis said, startling the valet. As he crossed to the closet, Dblis said, 'You've never been a general's valet before, have you, Corporal?'

'No, sir,' the corporal said. 'Did I do something wrong, sir?'

'Everything,' Dblis said. 'Before you hang up the uniforms, you make certain the wrinkles are pressed out of them. And when you do hang them up, put each uniform in its place: full dress uniforms on the left, and the others in a descending order of casualness, to the fatigues, which hang on the extreme right. Furthermore, you hang them all facing the same way – facing right, so that when I take one off the rack with my left hand' – he demonstrated ' – the front of the uniform is towards me. Understand?'

'Yes, sir.' The corporal was very nervous. The general's visage, seen up close, had a very discomfiting effect on the corporal, who had thus far managed to avoid anything but the most surreptitious glances at the general. Now, however, up close, he had to meet the general's eyes, and they, behind those lashless slits, terrified him.

Dblis pointed towards the footwear on the closet floor. 'That's all wrong, too. Rearrange them.' He stepped aside to give the valet access to the footwear. The corporal dropped to his knees. He began rearranging the footwear according to Dblis's instructions. 'House slippers on the left. Then dress slippers. Next, the shoes I'm wearing now, so leave space for them. Then come the boots.' He paused. 'Make certain that they're in that order at all times, and that they're always polished.'

'Yes, sir.'

As Dblis went to get a clean shirt from one of the suitcases on the bed, he said as if to himself, 'I do wish that Blanchard would make sure his CIC men had valet training. It's an insult to the intelligence, that's what it is.'

'Sir?' the corporal said. 'CIC?'

Without even bothering to look at him, Dblis said, 'Don't lie to me, Corporal. You're a spy. There's also a bug in the room, mind telling me where it is, so I won't have to waste time finding it myself?'

The corporal seemed genuinely puzzled. 'A spy, sir? Me?'

Dblis snorted with contempt as he turned to leave the room. 'And not even a good actor.' When he passed the cart with the coffee service on it, he said, 'You forgot to pour the coffee.'

The corporal jumped up. 'But I thought you were . . . weren't you leaving immediately, sir? General Blanchard, sir, didn't he say the President might be waiting?'

'Pour the coffee,' Dblis said as he strode towards the bathroom with the fresh shirt in his hand. 'Let the sonofabitch wait.'

23

Every bar and restaurant in both Mendocino and Fort Bragg – all along the coast, in fact, within the quarantine area – was jammed with off-duty soldiers. The liquor inventory was quickly depleted, and when it began to appear that no more liquor would be allowed to come through the road-blocks, the price of whisky quickly reached five dollars a shot. The soldiers grumbled that they were being ripped off by the local businessmen, but they bought the high-priced booze, anyway, and drank and sang and sometimes got into fights, brawls either among themselves or with some of the local youths. When the local civilians were involved in the brawls, it was usually due to a drunken soldier making a pass at the wife or girl-friend of one of them.

Sheriff Chris Jordan made his way through the guards and the helter-skelter activity in the lobby of the Mendocino

Hotel. He went into the tracking room, which had been set up in the hotel's dining room, where there was a battery of phones and a big map of Mendocino County on the wall. There were now two more flags on the map than there had been an hour ago. The green flags indicated reported sightings of mutants; the yellow flags indicated reported contacts; the red flags indicated confirmed contacts. Three of the flags were green, four were yellow, four red. And as Chris stood watching the map, one of the army clerks walked over to it and replaced one of the yellow flags with a red one. Another mutant contact confirmed. Near Casper.

'Paging Sheriff Jordan,' said a voice on a loudspeaker. 'Sheriff Jordan, please report to the switchboard for a call.'

The switchboard was located near the hotel's registration desk. The operator directed Chris to a red courtesy phone.

The call was from Deputy Carl Gotlieb, who informed Chris that the blockade had claimed its first victims. A carload of drunken teenagers in a fast car had run the checkpoints (the teenagers leaning from the open windows of the car, taunting the soldiers at the checkpoints) between Mendocino and the Navarro River road-block. When the car approached the road-block and it became obvious that it wasn't going to stop, the soldiers shot at the tyres on the car. The car spun out of control, hurtled off the highway, and plunged 150 feet down the face of the cliff into the rocky edges of the stormy surf. The soldiers had recovered two of the bodies. Chris knew them both. One was the daughter of a nurse at Fort Bragg Hospital.

The overcast sky sat upon Cape Mendocino from horizon to horizon like a lid. Rain squalls whipped along the coast. The earth was spongy with water, and where the rivers, gorged and swollen, emptied into the surf, large alluvial fans of muddy water spread like brown stains into the ice-grey ocean.

The outside world knew very little about what was happening in Mendocino. News of the quarantine had been released, since there was hardly any way to deny it, but it was released locally, rather than from Washington, in order to minimise any national implications it might have. The press release, issued by the Army's PIO, simply stated that a quarantine had been declared in the area due to the presence of an 'exotic' new disease.

The national newspapers and TV news departments tried to get through to the coast to find out what was going on, but by that time all telephone communications had been cut off, and physical access was impossible because of the roadblocks. One enterprising reporter from CBS hired a small plane to fly him over the area. He had intended to parachute from the plane and send back news by shortwave radio, but helicopters forced his plane to land in Ukiah, and the reporter was jailed for the duration of the quarantine.

But even though ham radio operators had their radios confiscated, and citizen's band radios weren't powerful enough to reach across the coast range to the interior, news inevitably leaked out. There were rumours and reports of mutants and monsters and, occasionally, about creatures from another planet or another solar system having invaded Earth in UFOs. But government pressure and the importance of other fast-breaking news events kept such rumours to the back pages. It was the Soviet military build-up in the Middle East and on the Manchurian border that dominated the news. Headlines were monopolised by threats of war, particularly after reports started coming out of Washington that the US armed forces, for the first time since the Cuban missile crisis of 1962, were being put on maximum alert.

There was, however, one puzzling enquiry about the quarantine that came all the way from China. The American ambassador in Peking relayed a message from the Chinese Minister of Health to the China Desk at the State Department in Washington. The Chinese minister, it seemed, had heard rumours of the quarantine in California and requested information about the nature of the disease. Since such information was classified top secret, however, a low-level administrator in the State Department declined the Chinese request. At the time, the request seemed merely puzzling; it wasn't until later that the bureaucrats at the State Department realised how revealing and very important the request had been.

By six o'clock the evening of 16 February, thirty-two people who'd had some encounter or contact with mutants had been admitted to Fort Bragg Hospital for tests, observation, and isolation. Of those, twenty-four proved to be contaminated with Lawson's disease. At that rate of increase, the hospital, which had already been emptied of all its ordinary patients, would be filled to overflowing by midnight. What would they do then? Where would they put subsequent victims?

24

The Crown Hall conference began late, due to technical problems in the video system on the White House terminal. The audio system was sending and receiving perfectly, and the picture from Crown Hall was being received in the White House NSC room, but the picture from the NSC room wasn't being received in Crown Hall.

While waiting, the members of *Operation Hatchet*'s Executive Steering Committee sat around the conference table in the middle of the hall. The table had been created by pushing a number of card tables together in a rectangle. General Blanchard sat at the head of the table; on his right was Professor Hoffmann and on his left was General Dblis. In all, eighteen men were seated at the table. Among them were Professor Roget, James Newman, Colonel Culbertson, the Reverend Boyle, and S. Bradley Hunter. Hunter was an assistant CIA director who served as *Hatchet*'s intelligence officer. The Reverend Boyle had come, not as a minister, but as a representative of local authority, given his role in the county government.

Around the head of the table, there was a second row of folding chairs, which were occupied by assistants, secretaries, and runners.

Among the committee members there was a great deal of muffled talk going on while they waited for the video system to be made operable. Messages were sent and received, information exchanged among the members, papers and reports passed from one to another. Then, suddenly, the voice of the major in the control booth said over the loudspeakers, 'Stand by, please. Stand by.'

The next voice that came over the loudspeakers was that of the Secretary of State. He said, 'General Blanchard? The President's on his way down here, he'll be here any minute, so we'll go ahead without the video part. You can hear us, at least, but since we can see you and you can't see us, we'll identify ourselves as we speak. Here's the President now.'

The voice of the Secretary of State was coming from behind a giant screen at one end of the hall. The screen was illuminated but blank. The next voice was the President's – that molasses drawl, the half-slurred words of a man chewing on a cigar as he spoke.

'Gen'al Blanchard, members of the committee,' he said. 'I don't reckon I have to tell you that events are breaking pretty fast around here. We don't have much time. That's why I – '

At that moment line patterns began to flash across the giant screen, and the voice of someone – a technician, perhaps – somewhere in the system interrupted the President. 'We got it. We're getting the – ' He was cut off.

As the patterns tumbled into recognisable shapes, a giant image of the President's face appeared on the screen. The video camera at the White House zoomed back to show another conference table filled to capacity, another room full of clocks, computers, electronic panels, illuminated grid maps, along with the technicians required to operate the complicated array of communications and intelligence equipment.

The President sat at the head of the table. On his right and left, respectively, were the Secretaries of State and Defence. The director of the CIA was there, as was the Chairman of the Joint Chiefs of Staff, several influential senators, advisers, and translators.

The President said, 'Oh. Oh, yeah. You got me now, huh?' He hunched forward in his chair, alternately chewing on and gesturing with a big, black cigar. His familiar pompadour and pomaded hair glinted in the bright lights. 'All right, now, let's get down to cases, gent'men. I got to know what it is you got out there, and where it came from. What can you tell me?'

After he made certain that the microphone in front of him was on, Blanchard looked at the President and said, 'Not much, I'm afraid, Mr President. As yet we're not certain what it is or where it came from.'

'You don't know,' the President said in an inflectionless voice.

'We have some theories, of course, and some of us have some very different theories, at that, but we simply do not have enough facts at this time to say with certainty – '

While Blanchard was speaking, the CIA director passed the President a note; after glancing at it, the President looked up and said, 'Yeah. Tell you what we're worried about back here, we're worried about that army sergeant out there who got the disease first. Gen'al Dblis, I'm glad to see you there. Maybe you can clear up a couple of things for us. Last report we got said the sergeant was AWOL from Fort Detrick. What d'you know about that?'

General Dblis glanced at Blanchard before he said, 'Mr President, I, too, was first informed that Sergeant Lawson was AWOL. A more thorough check of our records, however, turned up information that the sergeant was here in Mendocino on a legitimate routine assignment, that of trying to locate one of the meteorites that fell in this area on February first. He – '

'Excuse me, General Dblis,' the CIA director said, interrupting. 'Why was your man searching for one of the meteorites?'

In a voice of mild pedagogic boredom, Dblis said, 'We routinely examine all meteorites for signs of microscopic life from outer space.'

The CIA director was about to ask another question, obviously suspicious of Dblis, but was cut off by the President, who also seemed to be sceptical of Dblis's answer. 'You mean to tell us, Gen'al, that your man just *happened* to be the first person to get this new disease? What'd he do, just *happen* to stumble on to it first?'

It was Blanchard who deflected the President's attention away from Dblis's nettlesome indifference by saying, 'Mr President? We have a young man here with us who has a theory that he thinks will explain why Sergeant Lawson was the first victim of the disease.' He went on to introduce James Newman as a NASA astrophysicist, mentioning that Newman had been one of the team of scientists who examined the first lunar rocks brought back by the Apollo II astronauts.

'Let's hear what he's got to say,' the President said.

Newman stood up and went to the illuminated projection screen. The screen was facing the Crown Hall conference table broadside, so that the committee members seated on one side of the table had to turn in their chairs to see it. A video camera picked it up for the people at the White House. As Newman approached the screen, an army technician handed him a baton and then snapped a small transistor microphone around his neck.

Newman ran his fingers through his bushy red hair and nervously bounced up and down on his toes as a picture was flashed on the screen and then brought into focus. Then Newman tapped the screen with the baton and said, 'What you see here, Mr President, is a fairly common type of meteorite, a carbonaceous chondrite, which has a spheroidal aggregation of minerals unlike any known in terrestrial rocks. This chondrite fell on the Mendocino coast in the recent meteorite shower, the only one that was recovered. It was found in the house where the first known victim of the disease, Sergeant Lawson, was found. If he came here to find a meteorite, he succeeded. This is it. This is the one he found.'

Newman paused. 'Now, on the basis of my examination of this chondrite, it's my contention that the disease – the very unique species of micro-organism that's causing this disease – is of extraterrestrial origin. It came from somewhere within our solar system, and it came in this meteorite.

'Look at this next picture,' he said, and when the next image was projected on the screen, he continued. 'That's a photomicrograph of a spore that was taken from the body of one of the mutants. The next picture – ' He waited for the change. 'This is a photomicrograph of a similar spore found in the interior of the meteorite. As you can see, sir, they appear to be identical.'

He gave them a moment to assimilate this news, which obviously surprised the President and the others at the White House, even to the point of leaving them momentarily speechless. Then the President said with obvious admiration, 'Young man, I didn't catch your name.'

'James Newman, sir.'

The President, waving his cigar, said in a slurred tone, 'Gen'al Blanchard? What's your reaction to what Mr Newman here just said? Seems to me he might have some answers you said you didn't have.'

'Well, Mr President,' Blanchard said, 'Mr Newman is an astrophysicist of some reputation, in spite of his being young, and so I have to take his assertions seriously. But I really can't subscribe to his theory. It requires too many very far-fetched assumptions.'

'Such as?'

'Such as the assumption that the organism was actually *in* the meteorite when it fell. Instances of this kind have happened often in the past when scientists searched for signs of biological life in meteorites. They often thought they'd succeeded, but in the vast majority of the cases, the organisms turned out to be of terrestrial origin – spores, bacteria, and the like – that got into the meteorite *after* it fell to earth. The porous nature of this particular type of meteorite makes it particularly vulnerable, an ideal receptacle for such organisms. In short, Mr President, it's more likely that the organism in the meteorite came from Sergeant Lawson, not the other way around.'

The Secretary of Defence spoke next. 'Mr Newman? If the spores were in the meteorite when it hit the earth, how and when did they get into it in the first place?'

The President nodded vigorously, as if he, too, were anxious to hear the answer.

Newman said, 'Well, sir, it's generally accepted by most astronomers that meteorites and asteroids are the detritus of fragmented parent bodies. This meteorite is a fragment from the crust of a planet that disintegrated about twenty thousand years ago. We have no way of knowing how big the planet was, or why it disintegrated. Maybe by explosion. Maybe by collision, either with another planet or an interstellar comet. We *do* know its age, however. Age can be dated by induced radioactivity. In this case, we determined that the material in the meteorite was formed about four and a half billion years ago, making its parent body about the same age as earth. But about twenty thousand years ago – a period that can also be dated by induced radioactivity – the planet broke up. This meteorite was part of its crust.'

The President said, 'And you're going to tell us that this disease came from that planet? That it lived there?'

'Yes, sir. I believe it lived there, and had obviously developed into a life force that is very high on the evolutionary scale. Maybe it was the master of that planet, as we are of ours. Or maybe it was just another disease there.

'In any case, when the planet broke up, spores of the disease organism were trapped in this lump of material, this meteorite that drifted through the solar system for twenty thousand years before it crashed into earth. Here, finding the conditions suitable, the spores germinated.'

'Look here, Mr Newman,' the President said, his pugnacious face obscured by a wreath of cigar smoke, 'I have to tell you, I find it pretty damned hard to believe that something could stay alive that long. How many thousands of years?'

'Well, Mr President, I don't know that you would call it "alive". The spore is dormant during all that time, with no more life than a seed has. Professor Roget here is a mycologist – an expert on fungi – and he tells me that it's quite possible.' He glanced at Roget for confirmation.

Roget nodded. 'Oh, yes, Mr President, that's quite possible. We've found viable spores in rock strata that were laid down in the Pleistocene Age, roughly a million years ago, and we've managed to germinate them. So why not a mere twenty thousand years? Especially if the spores were in a frozen state, as they would've been if they came from the outer reaches of the solar system.'

The Secretary of Defence asked, 'Well, what about when the meteorite entered the earth's atmosphere? Could the spores survive the heat?'

Roget said, 'That presents no real problem, Mr Secretary, as Newman can tell you.'

Taking the cue, Newman said, 'It's true that the meteorite got so hot that the anterior end melted, as you can see by the ablation markings. But the heat affects only the periphery of even quite small chondrite meteorites. You see, this kind of meteorite melts at one thousand, eight hundred and fifty degrees Celsius, but it's possible – even probable – that the centre remained frozen during its fall to earth. Because, first, chondrite is a very poor conductor of heat. Second, the time the meteorite was in the atmosphere was so short, why, it'd be something like passing a blowtorch across a piece of ice: the outside would melt profusely, but the inside of the ice would remain frozen.'

There was a rare silence as the President and his entourage seemed to ponder this information. Then, with a sudden jutting of his jaw, like a horse champing at the bit, the President said, 'Let's get to the bottom of this, gent'men. Which of you is Professor Noah Hoffmann?'

Hoffmann held up his hand. 'I am, Mr President.'

'Ah. There you are, Professor. Sorry I didn't recognise you, but it's been many long years since we met – 1967, wasn't it? The year you won your Nobel?'

'Yes, sir,' Hoffmann said. 'You were a congressman then.'

The President nodded, and for a brief moment his usual pugnacious expression was softened by nostalgia. But then he shook off the self-indulgence and said, 'Look here, Professor, what do you think about uh, uh, Mr Newman's theory?'

'With all due respect to Mr Newman, sir, I must say I can't agree.'

'Why not?'

'Well, sir, there's a scientific principle known as Ockham's razor, which holds that the simpler the explanation, the more likely it is to be true. And the test of simplicity is minimum assumption – that is, keeping within the evidence, and if there's no evidence and a guess is necessary to fill in a gap, why, then the guess should conform to the pattern of the evidence, yah? Well, as for Mr Newman's theory, I think it falls apart on its basic assumption: that the spore came from another world.'

'Why do you find that so hard to believe? Seems to me he's covered his bases pretty well.'

'Except for one, sir: if the spores were in the meteorite, how did they *get* there? If they got into it while on another planet, then, *ipso facto*, the meteorite material would have to be porous enough to admit them. But in that case, don't you see, it'd also be porous enough to admit the spores once it landed on earth. On the other hand, if the spores were in hermetically sealed pockets within the meteorite, how did they *get* there? Somebody or something would've had to *put* them there.' He shrugged. 'So you can see, that leads to all sorts of assumptions that are at variance with the principle of Ockham's razor.'

The irritation that had been building up in the President's voice and expression finally erupted. 'Goddamnit, Professor,' he said as he smashed his cigar butt out in an ashtray, 'excuse me, but I didn't come down here to get a lecture on theories and scientific principles. Don't you see what kind of position I'm in? I want you all to tell me something I can *act* on. Hell fire, tell me it's a germ-warfare agent! Tell me it comes from Russia! Hell, tell me it's our own! But *something*, God-damnit, give me something on which I can *act*.'

Hoffmann shrugged. 'I wish I could, Mr President. In all honesty, however, I can only advise you on what it *probably* is.'

'All right, then, let's hear it. Tell me what it *probably* is, according to that guy with the razor, Ockham or whoever.'

'It's *probably* a chimera, it's *probably* a germ-warfare agent, and it *probably* comes from Russia.'

25

While the Crown Hall-White House conference was in progress, Dr Herbert Brokowski went into his office at Fort Bragg Hospital and killed himself.

All personnel at Fort Bragg Hospital, whether medical or administrative, civilian or military, were required to have blood tests every two hours. Anne Jackson was in charge of this programme. Assisting her were four lab technicians who had arrived with the mobile labs from the Alameda Navy

Base near San Francisco. But it was Anne Jackson herself who found the myxamoebas in Brokowski's blood sample.

She was told at the front desk that Brokowski was in Wing B overseeing the removal of the last ordinary patients from the hospital – those patients with simple conditions, like broken bones or cancer, who were being sent either to their homes or to the three convalescent hospitals in the area. But Anne didn't find Brokowski in Wing B, so she went to find Sander, who was in conference room 1-C with D. B. Sheftman and Captain Yoshimura, an immunologist from the Special Tactics Unit. The conference room had been turned temporarily into a specialised lab for Yoshimura's use, and the three men were there carrying out experiments in the molecular structure of an antibiotic called actinomycin.

When Anne asked Sander where she might find Dr Brokowski, he told her that Brokowski had gone to his office to lie down for a little while on his cot.

'The strain's getting to him, I think,' Sander said, who looked as if the strain were getting to him, too. 'I think he's got a slight fever, so I told him – '

'I'm afraid he's got more than a fever,' Anne said.

Her expression told them the rest of it, all they needed to know, but, stunned, they didn't want to believe it.

'The blood test?' Sander said.

She nodded. 'Positive. About a hundred per cc. The blood was taken about forty-five minutes ago, so he hasn't got long.' After a moment of silence, she said, 'Shall I tell him?'

Sander shook his head. 'I'd better,' he said in a weary and impersonal voice.

Sander found Brokowski in his office. He was at his desk, obviously in a desperate and agitated state, and in front of him on the desk was one of the small aluminium containers that the Special Tactics Unit had issued to all hospital personnel. Within it was the capsule of cyanide.

'So you know, then?' Sander asked.

'I wasn't sure,' Brokowski stammered. He had taken off his

broken glasses and tossed them on the desk. The small cuts around his eye were covered with adhesive bandage. 'I was waiting. Sitting here waiting for the . . . the result of the blood tests. Positive, hey? Yeah. Thought it would be. Been having blackouts. Felt it in me. But I can't remember where I might've slipped up. The Coors girl? Trying to get . . . blood. Wasn't careful, I guess. Didn't take the proper . . .' He suddenly became silent. A convulsive shudder passed through his body. His eyes went blank. Then, as if suddenly waking up, he shook his head and said, 'What? Where was . . . Another one. A blackout. Getting more and more frequent. You see? How much . . . time have I got?'

'Thirty minutes, at best,' Sander said.

Brokowski nodded. There were tears smeared into the wrinkles of his cheeks, but he wasn't crying. Actually, he was chuckling, or trying to, making a sound that was something like a chuckle. 'You better go.' He picked up the aluminium container.

'Herb, listen. You don't have to do this, you know.' Sander's voice was without inflection, without emotion, as if a zombie were talking, as if he had realised that the only way he was going to survive the shocks of this ordeal with his sanity intact was to empty himself of all feeling. 'We could keep you alive, you know. We've made a decision to keep twenty-four of the . . . the mutants here in the hospital, for tests and experiments. We could make it twenty-five.'

Brokowski shook his head. 'No, Sander, do you know what they're building? Down at the old Point Cabrillo lighthouse compound? They call it . . . they call it a "disposal unit". Know what it is?'

Sander nodded.

'Gas chambers. Soon there'll be too many. More than you can handle. Do you know? My family was, my sons and wife, in Buchenwald, did you know? In the gas chambers. Not me. Not in a gas chamber.' He gripped the aluminium container. 'This is the best.'

'I promise I wouldn't let them – '

'Promise? How can you?' He was making that chuckling sound again. 'You might . . . end up there yourself. No. No. Keep somebody young. Anyway, I've seen them. I wouldn't . . . want to live. Like that.' He was becoming more agitated, as if he could hardly keep control of himself. Then his body suddenly convulsed again, his eyes went blank, and he sat for a moment in stony silence; soon, as if jerking awake again, he said, 'Another one. Blackout. How long did that last?'

'A few seconds,' Sander said.

'Getting longer. You better go now.'

Sander wanted to say something else, but since words were so inadequate, he hoped his silence would be taken as a more meaningful statement of his sorrow. But at the door he turned and said, 'Is there anything I can do for you? Anything you want or need?'

Trying to speak quickly, Brokowski said, 'One thing. I'm an old man. No family left. But there's Mojo. My dog. He's old, too. At home by himself. Don't let him starve. Put him away. He's old, too. Nobody would want him.' Then his voice, rising to a shout, cracked as he said, 'Get out! Go on, get the hell out!' His eyes were beginning to flash with hostility and hatred, beginning to bulge with some terrible pressure, as if the bones of his skull were trying to contain an explosion within him.

Sander nodded and opened the door, but stopped just before closing it behind him when he heard Brokowski, in one last supreme effort of control, say in an almost ordinary voice, 'Good-bye, Sander.'

Without turning around, Sander said, 'Good-bye, Herb,' and closed the door behind him.

He remained standing in front of the door to Brokowski's office to prevent anyone from going in. He waited there about two minutes before he heard Brokowski's body fall out of the chair.

He didn't go back into the office. He had intended to, but

suddenly realised that he wouldn't be able to take it, seeing Brokowski's body sprawled on the floor. It would be too much for him to bear. Being a doctor, he was used to death, had deadened himself so that he could deal with it and do what he had to do. So it wasn't Brokowski's death itself that bothered him so much, but the injustice of it. He knew if he went back into the office and pulled up the sleeve of Brokowski's smock, he would see the SS number tattooed there, the one he had been given in Buchenwald, where he and his family had been sent for extermination. And it made Sander tremble with impotent rage to think how this old man had escaped extermination in a Nazi concentration camp, only to suffer it there, on the northern coast of California, nearly four decades later, a victim to the last of crazy politicians, puppet soldiers, and lackey scientists.

His reverie of rage was broken only when someone approached him, a nurse. She hurried down the hall, clipboard in hand, and said, 'Excuse me, Doctor Quence. Is Doctor Brokowski in? I have to get his signature on some requisitions.' And when he didn't respond, she said, 'Doctor Quence? Are you all right?'

He sighed. 'Yeah, sure. I'm all right. But Brokowski isn't. He's dead.' Then, before she could recover and say something useless, he added, 'Listen, Kay. Do me a favour, will you? Call the ASPCA. Tell 'em there's an old dog in Brokowski's apartment. Tell 'em to dispose of it.' He started to turn away then, but stopped long enough to add, 'And while you're at it, send a crew in there to get Brokowski's body. Tell 'em . . . tell 'em to dispose of it.'

Then he walked away without waiting to hear what she would say. He started back towards the conference room where he had been working with D.B. and Yoshimura, but when he passed the stairway leading to the second floor, he automatically turned and went up to his office. His instinct was to run away, to hide, to find some place where the horror couldn't get to him.

He opened the top drawer of his desk and took out the new bottle of Scotch. As he poured the liquor into a paper cup, he noticed that his hands were trembling. He felt better – calmer – almost as soon as the first drink was in his stomach, but it was not the kind of escape he wanted. It wasn't enough for him to escape from anxiety; he wanted to escape from its source. He wanted to be away from this madhouse, wanted to be with Bobbi somewhere far away, wanted to be in bed with her, holding her, and once more feel life in his hands, instead of death.

But escape was impossible. They could never get out of Mendocino now. All the roads and trails were blocked, all the exits closed. He had never had any illusions about being brave. He had long ago realised that he was not the stuff of which adventurers and heroes were made. He was just an ordinary man who wanted to live an ordinary life, but they wouldn't let him. *They*. Who were *they*?

He shook his head, trying to shake off his morbid reverie, and then took another drink. Sighing, settling down into the swivel chair, he idly picked up a piece of paper from among the many scattered across his desk. This one was a photocopy of the results of the gel electrophoresis that had been performed on the Lawson's disease organism to find out how many chromosomes it had. As suspected by General Blanchard, the organism had turned out to have forty-six chromosomes, the same number as humans. He recalled how impotently outraged he had been when he first saw the report about an hour before, and also recalled the look on Chris Jordan's face when he had said to Hoffmann, 'Are you telling me this thing may be part *human*?'

Yes, Chris, that's what they were telling you, and it appears that they were right. He chuckled dryly, mirthlessly, as he imagined Chris standing on the other side of his desk right at that moment, so he could toss the report to him and say, 'Chris, meet your brother, the disease.'

The telephone buzzed. He took another drink of Scotch

before he picked it up.

'Sander?' It was D.B. 'Hey, if you're not tied up, why don't you come back down here and have a look at something interesting?' There was a peculiar note of excitement in D.B.'s voice.

Sander said he would be right down, but after he hung up, he had another large swallow of Scotch before he braced himself, took a deep breath as if trying to get a second wind, and then got up to go back to work.

26

'Russia, huh?' the President said. 'Now we're getting someplace – not any place I like to be, but at least some place. What about you, Gen'al Blanchard? You share Professor Hoffmann's opinion?'

Blanchard nodded grimly. 'Yes, Mr President, but I want to stress that it's only an opinion.'

'So what makes you think it's Russian?' the President asked, and then quickly threw up his hands. 'Now, don't go giving me any long scientific theories. Just give me things I can use – like, for instance, how could they've got it in?'

Blanchard glanced at S. Bradley Hunter, who was sitting about midway around the conference table. 'Mr Hunter?' he said. 'Would you mind?'

Hunter stood up, cleared his throat, adjusted his rimless glasses, and said, 'Mr President. The way the Russians could have gotten it in . . . To understand that, we have to go back to February first, sixteen days ago, when a shower of meteorites fell on the northern California coast. As Mr Newman pointed out, witnesses reported seeing a number of the meteorites survive entry into the atmosphere and actually fall to earth.' Again he cleared his throat and adjusted his glasses. 'With that in mind, we checked all missile launches that took place immediately preceding the meteorite shower. Well, sir, the one launch that commanded our attention was a Russian vehicle, a Tekka B rocket, which they use mainly for space probes. It was fired from Lebyakin Space Centre in central Siberia approximately two hours before the meteorites entered the earth's atmosphere. It was first picked up by one of our infrared satellites, the A504, then tracked on our radar until the payload was achieving perigee orbit at forty-six miles above the central Pacific. At that time, the – '

The President was beginning to frown, which apparently prompted the Secretary of State to interrupt Hunter's narrative to ask if he had any visual aids. Hunter said, 'Yes, sir, I'm sorry. I didn't know if you wanted to take the time...'

The President said, 'You know me, Mr Hunter, I'm just a cotton farmer from Arkansas.' He gave Hunter that famous self-deprecating grin, the mask of a man who loved to play the role of cornpone politician.

As Hunter turned from his chair, a technician snapped a microphone around his neck; he crossed to the illuminated screen, upon which suddenly appeared a map of Siberia. Hunter used the baton to point out the location of the Lebyakin Space Centre, and then asked for the next picture, a drawing that showed two arching lines that gradually converged and became one.

Pointing to one of the lines with the baton, Hunter said, 'This is the trajectory of the Tekka B rocket just at attaining orbit. This other line represents the trajectory of a relatively dense shower of meteorites coming from somewhere in the general direction of Saturn. Here the meteorites and the Tekka B intersect, at which point the meteorites are being captured by gravity and pulled into the earth's atmosphere. As you can see, the angle of entry is near the skipping limit, about a three-degree arc. It's at this point that they began to share the orbit of the Tekka B, and continued to do so for about two thousand miles – until they reached the northern California coast. Here, the meteorites plunged to earth, after which the Tekka B could no longer be picked up by our radar.

'Our people checked with the Russians. Their explanation – their assumption, I should say – was that the Tekka B had collided with the meteorites. They said they lost contact with it at the same time we did, when it intersected with the meteorites. They said the payload capsule wasn't made for re-entry, so it probably burned up as it entered the atmosphere, as did most of the meteorites.

'However, the obvious possibility is that it didn't burn up, it simply "joined" the meteorites, and came in with them, thereby escaping radar detection, carrying a germ-warfare payload. And that,' said Hunter in conclusion, 'is how they could have gotten the disease organism in.'

The Secretary of Defence said, 'Any evidence for that at all? I mean, instead of just speculation? How about part of a nose cone, maybe? Something that would definitely connect them?'

'No, Mr Secretary,' Blanchard said. 'To comb every foot of this terrain, under the weather conditions that prevail, looking for a nose cone, would require probably five divisions of foot soldiers.'

'Damnit, Gen'al,' the President interjected, 'you know as well as I do, this matter concerns the lives of literally millions of people. It concerns the security and existence of our country, and you talk about five divisions of soldiers. Well – '

He was interrupted by the Secretary of Defence, who placed an attention-getting finger on the President's forearm and then leaned over and whispered in his ear. Blanchard could guess what the Secretary was telling the President: that Blanchard had, indeed, requested the five divisions, but had been turned down by the Defence Department because the soldiers were needed in the Middle East and the NATO countries to counter the build-up of Russian troops in those areas. In any case, whatever was whispered to the President had a calming effect on him.

Then the Secretary of Defence spoke to Blanchard. 'General, we're in the process of mobilising the California

National Guard. Could you use them as searchers?'

'We certainly could, Mr Secretary.'

It was the Secretary of State, that pear-shaped little man with horn-rimmed glasses and a penetrating stare, who got the discussion back on the track. He said, 'Excuse me, General. Mr Hunter has made a case for the disease being of Russian origin, which sort of boxes us in. Can any one of you there – besides Mr Newman, that is – make a case for it's *not* being Russian? A plausible alternative? If so, I would certainly like to hear it.'

Blanchard said, 'Yes, sir. We have Professor Roget here, a distinguished mycologist. I don't think he agrees with Mr Newman's theory that it originated in outer space, but at least he has an argument against it being of Russian origin.'

'Another "theory"?' the President said, with a hint of sarcasm.

'Yes, sir,' Roget said, 'and a theory only, but one that I believe we should seriously consider before we start blaming the Russians for this epidemic.'

After a bare nod of weary acquiescence from the President, Roget said a bit guiltily, 'Sir, I'm sorry if this makes your decisions more difficult, but I must tell you that there is yet another possibility of the disease's origins, which is simply this . . .' Without waiting to be asked, he rose and strode to the projection screen, moving with an air of heaviness, as if he were a large person instead of the diminutive and almost gnome-like man that he was. In his deep, smoky voice, he said, 'May I have the slide of the fossil, please?

'What you see here, Mr President,' he said when the picture flashed on the screen, 'is a photomicrograph of a fungoid spore – or, more accurately, I suppose, the spore of a quasi fungoid. It's a fossil. This particular spore was found with many others of the same kind in a stratum of sedimentary rocks laid down about sixteen thousand years ago. It was found on the shores of Lake Superior in the early 1920s by a mycologist, who believed that this quasi fungoid was an extinct variety of *D. mucoroides mutabilis*, a unique strain. In any case, no mycologist had ever seen anything like it before. This man tried to germinate some of the spores, but without success. So he published an article about it in the *Mycology Symposium*, and then forgot about it.

'The next picture – this one – is a fossil spore of the same type. It was found in the late 1940s by a team of scientists who were drilling into the arctic tundra for core samples that would tell them what that area of the earth was like in prehistoric times. The sedimentary stratum in which it was found was laid down approximately nine thousand years ago.'

The President interrupted. 'Professor? I 'preciate what you're saying. I'm sure we all find it very interesting, but is it possible to shorten it up some? We're pressed for time, you see. So could you? Without missing the point?'

'Of course. I'm sorry. Being a professor, I suppose I have a compulsion to explain. In any case, I'll get to the point, which is this: these fossil spores are *apparently* the same unique strain of quasi fungoid that we have on our hands today.'

'Well, what would've brought the strain back to life all of a sudden?'

'I don't know, Mr President. I'm presently in the midst of gathering and computerising all the data I can get about this particular type of quasi fungoid. When I get a print-out, perhaps I can give you a better answer.'

'Thank you, Professor,' the President said. 'And you let us know if you do find any hard evidence, you hear?' Then he turned to Blanchard. 'But just where in hell does that leave us, Gen'al?' He lifted his hands in a gesture of despair and defeat. 'Right back where we started from! The fact is, nobody knows what that Goddamned disease is, or where it came from, or *any*thing.'

It was then that a quiet and unassuming voice from somewhere near the bottom of the conference table said, 'I know.'

The words hung in the air while everyone looked to see who had spoken, but nobody at the end of the table looked as if he had, so everybody started to turn away again. Then the voice spoke again, the same words again, '*I* know.'

It was the Reverend Boyle. He looked as if he knew he was being very bold and was shamed by it, but, like a man compelled to speak against his own wishes, he said, 'We all know. Don't we? I know the word hasn't been used here today, but . . . but we know what it is, don't we?'

Everyone stirred, discomfited by the drift of the Reverend's argument, and Blanchard seemed downright embarrassed. If the Reverend said what Blanchard feared he was going to say, it would be a poor reflection on Blanchard for having let a distraught minister sit on the committee. So he hoped the Reverend would sense the discomfort he was causing and shut up. Unfortunately, however, the Reverend, having broken the first barriers of modesty, began to speak more rapidly, more urgently.

'For the love of God, don't you see? This . . . this *thing* we're dealing with here is a chimera, all right, but not just a germ-warfare agent created by scientists in a lab somewhere. What we've got here, and what I have yet to see anyone fully appreciate, is a *highly developed* life force. We've been told that this organism has the capacity for choice and purposive action. Perceptive and cognitive powers – that's what's been said about it! Well, to say that it could have been created in a laboratory by scientists is like saying that man himself could have been put together the same way. Who really believes that?'

General Blanchard said, 'Reverend, perhaps we'd – '

But the Reverend wasn't to be stopped. 'No. What we're dealing with here *has* to be a supernatural power! Well, doesn't it? Doesn't it? That's what we're describing: a supernatural power – a power that can turn people into demons. *Demons.*'

When the Reverend, apparently on the verge of tears,

broke off, it was the President himself who played the straight man. Like everyone else, he could easily guess the supernatural power to whom the Reverend was alluding, but he wanted the name out in the open without having to say or infer it.

'What supernatural power you talking about?'

Reverend Boyle's eyes were widening with terror, and tears glistened in the fine wrinkles of his unshaven face. 'The *chimera*,' he said. 'That's what you've called it, isn't it? Don't you know that the appearance of this beast was foretold in Revelations? The beast with the head of a leopard, the body of a goat, the tail of a serpent, which shall rise up on the day of judgement from the bottomless pit?'

He paused. There was no response from anyone.

'Don't you see?' he implored, his voice growing louder and slightly oratorical, as if he were reaching the climax of a sermon. 'You must see! Everything that's been said about the chimera's powers, everything that's been learned, and every speculation – all lead to one inescapable conclusion: that *here*, in *this* time, in *this* place, *Satan has made himself manifest*!'

'Well, I'll be damned,' the President said, 'now I've heard everything.'

'No, sir,' the Reverend Boyle said, 'I don't believe you have, sir, if you'll excuse my saying so. I have here in my hand a study in demonology that I myself made when I was a graduate student at Union Theological. It's – '

'Reverend,' General Blanchard said I'm sure the President has – '

' – it's my master's thesis, sir, a study in pre-Christian demonology, and if I could just have a – '

'Reverend,' Blanchard said.

' – just a few minutes of your time, sir, I think I could show you – '

This time it was the President himself who interrupted. 'Look,' he said, obviously making an effort to keep from being rude, 'when I want a sermon, Reverend, I'll go to church. All I want from you people out there are some *facts*, and until I can get a few of 'em, I won't be wasting any more of my time with these meetings.' With that, he got up and whirled away from the table, and left the room.

The Secretary of State also stood up to leave, signalling that the session was adjourned, and told Blanchard in a mildly reprimanding tone that he would like some hard information from him within hours. 'That's all the time we have, General,' he said. 'A few hours, at the most, before we have to make some irrevocable decisions. So let's not waste any more time on theories and sermons, shall we?'

When he nodded good-bye, the electronic systems began to shut down, and all the men around the table in Crown Hall hurriedly gathered up their papers and paraphernalia.

Blanchard said, 'All right, gentlemen, you heard the man. Return to your stations immediately. I want all of you to work till you drop, then get up and work some more. Keep me posted on all new developments.' He got up then, and the others followed his lead. While the others began to stir and talk among themselves, however, Blanchard, still with the calmness of a stone, strode to where the Reverend Boyle stood at the end of the table.

'I'm sorry, Reverend,' he said, 'but I think you're a little too distraught to be of service to this committee. I'll have to ask you to turn in your security and priority passes to the captain of the guard as you leave the building.'

The Reverend Boyle pleaded, 'General, please listen to me,' but by then Blanchard had already turned and started out of the building, followed by a scurrying retinue of aides and service personnel.

Clutching his well-worn manuscript in both hands as though it were a shield to ward off blows, the Reverend Boyle glanced around the room in a frantic effort to meet a sympathetic face. Not one of the men in the disbanding group would meet his desperate eyes, however. But the Reverend was not ready to concede defeat. He darted around the table to Professor Roget, who was just snapping his attaché case closed.

'Professor Roget,' the Reverend said in a sort of conspiratorial plea, unabashed by the embarrassed stares that he received from the men nearby, 'you were right, you know. I mean, in a way, you were. It's not what you think it is, not a fossil, but it is old – very old, Professor, as old as the world itself. Will you just look at this? Please? Read it? Then you'll see.'

In an obvious effort to be kind, Roget smiled and said, 'Your thesis on demonology, eh? Really, Reverend, I'm sure it would prove very interesting.' He took the battered manuscript from the Reverend's trembling hands. 'After all, if what we're dealing with isn't a demon, I don't know what is.'

27

After Anne Jackson told Sander that Dr Brokowski's blood sample showed him to be contaminated with Lawson's disease, she had gone into a hospital toilet and cried. She had known Dr Brokowski all her life. It had been he who delivered her son, Larry, he who had got her the job at the hospital when she was out of work and needed money. And now he himself needed help, and there was nothing she could do about it except cry.

She sat in the toilet cubicle and cried until she was exhausted, then got up and looked at herself in a mirror above a washbasin. She didn't like what she saw: the red swollen eyes and tangled hair. So she washed her face with cold water, put on lipstick, and combed her hair; then she went back to the lab, back to the microscope, the blood samples. It was her job. It was what she had to do, even if she had to stop now and then to dry her eyes of tears so she could see into the microscope.

For the most part, the job was fairly routine. The routine

always ended, however, when she found the strange and virulent amoeboid cells in a sample of blood, because the odds were that she would know the victim. This had happened twice within the last eight hours. Brokowski had been the last one; a few hours before that, however, she had discovered the amoeboid cells in a blood sample taken from Barbara Boxley, a young and pretty nurse who had also been a friend of hers. Now Barbara Boxley was in a straitjacket in one of the locked rooms in Wing C, raving like a lunatic, waiting only for the disposal unit to be completed at the Point Cabrillo lighthouse compound.

Anne had heard about the compound. She had heard the rumours about a disposal unit being built there because the hospital soon wouldn't be able to hold all the contaminated people, and what was to be done with them? They couldn't be treated. They couldn't be kept. Alive, they were only a source of contamination for others . . .

Another one. Sitting at the microscope, lost in ruminations and memories, she had been looking at the terrifying amoeboid cells on the slide for a long time before she realised – before her consciousness would allow her to realise – that what she was seeing was evidence that yet another member of the hospital staff had become contaminated.

The sudden flush of terror and dread set her heart hammering. Who would it be this time? Someone she knew? Another friend? She prayed not. She prayed silently and forced herself to be calm as she took the slide from the microscope and noted its identification number: J-54. Then, still with the tense composure of a spring wound to the breaking point, she turned to the forms on the table beside the microscope. In the left-hand margin of the form was a list of numbers, and to the right of each number was the name of a staff member.

She ran her trembling finger down the column of numbers, arrived at J-54, and saw the name: *Anne Jackson.*

She clapped her hand over her mouth to stifle a cry. She

closed her eyes and prayed fervidly, *Oh, please, God, please, not me*, but when she opened her eyes again, the name and number were the same. Anne Jackson was the one, and she was Anne Jackson, although she prayed, *Not me. Please, God, not me.* She thought of her son Larry, who was nine years old.

She frantically rechecked the number on the slide, rechecked the name, the number. Nothing changed. She thought for a moment that she might faint, but then she thought of her son again and knew she mustn't let herself faint. If she fainted, they would find out that she was contaminated and wouldn't let her out of the hospital again. They would give her a choice between taking the cyanide or being put in a straitjacket and taken to the compound. Either way, she would never see her son again, and she wanted to see him once more, just for a few minutes, that's all she asked, and then she would take the cyanide.

She knocked the stool over as she got up from the microscope. Some workers at nearby microscopes stared at her curiously as she hurried away from the overturned stool and grabbed her coat from a closet. She neither spoke to nor looked at anyone as she hurried out of the lab, her hand still over her mouth as if holding in a cry.

She met Sander coming down the corridor. She wanted to avoid him, but couldn't, so she stopped him and asked if it would be all right for her to go and see her son.

'Only for a few minutes?' she said. 'My son. He . . .'

It was then she blacked out for the first time. It was as if her brain had received a small electrical shock. For a brief moment, all her senses seemed to go dead, as if they had short-circuited. But then the blackout ended, and Dr Quence was saying, '. . . no harm. But you are coming back, aren't you?'

She assured him that she was, touched him good-bye, and then hurried out of the hospital. She walked across the parking lot and was getting into her car when the next blackout came. The motor was running and she didn't remember having turned on the ignition. She felt flushed and feverish, panicked, was praying, *Please, God, not me, not me,* and then, with the sensation of another electrical shock to her cortex, she blacked out again, just for a few seconds. When she came to, her feverish skin had begun to tingle, the tingling discomfort of having a limb go to sleep, except that now she felt it over her whole body.

There was a squeal of brakes, and someone shouted, 'Hey! Watch where you're going, for Christ's sake, lady!'

But she had to hurry. The cyanide pill was in her pocket. She felt it there, the little metal container. She just wanted to see her son once more before she took it. Just once. Just to say good-bye. 'Good-bye, Larry.' He was at the babysitter's. She would drive there and see him and say, 'Good-bye, Larry. Mother loves you, Larry. Remember that, Larry.'

She felt the crash, but hadn't seen it coming. She slammed against the steering wheel as the car slammed into something, careening in the street. The blackouts were coming faster and faster now. They were like a strobe light, black–white, black–white, black–white.

'Are you hurt, lady?' the man's voice said. 'You okay?'

'Yes. Of course. I am. I have to . . . see Larry. I have the cyanide here. I have . . . I'll take it . . . in time.'

She was running and her skin was tingling. The man shouted at her, but she was running. Perceptions came like the strobe light. Her brain was being jolted by electrical shocks, the currents surging through her body, tingling her skin, pulsing through her muscles in growing waves of strength. She ran. She knocked down an old lady. There were screams, shouts, running feet. She stopped, turned, saw flashes of her face in a mirror in a store window. Then it was she who was making the sounds with her mouth. She saw her face, her eyes burning back at her, her mouth opened to scream, but the sound that came out was a cry of horror and triumph.

FEBRUARY SEVENTEENTH

28 General Blanchard stood looking at the large map of Mendocino County. At eight o'clock the previous night, the night of 16 February, there had been twelve flags on the map. At ten o'clock there were twenty-five. Now, at twelve-fifteen in the morning of 17 February, there were forty-three flags. Was it going to continue doubling every two hours? At a geometric ratio? And spreading?

One of the map clerks cried, 'Sir!' and stuck a yellow flag into Ukiah.

It was Colonel Culbertson who gave voice to their dismay. 'Jesus Christ, Ukiah! Thirty-five miles away! It's spreading like – ' He didn't want to use the trite phrase 'wildfire', so he said, ' – like crazy,' and then realised that that was a poor word, too. 'Like the plague.'

'Worse,' Blanchard said. 'Even at its most virulent, the plague contagion wasn't absolute. There were always survivors. But this . . . ' He paused. 'There's no immunity. No way to stop it. If it gets into the large population areas . . .'

'Well, there's always *one* way to stop it,' Dblis said in a goading tone.

'That's right. There's always one way,' Blanchard agreed. 'God help us all.' He turned to one of his aides. 'Phone the communications centre. Tell them I'll be there shortly to talk to the White House.' He turned back to stare at the map. 'Corporal? Any details on that Ukiah contact?'

The map clerk touched his earphones and tilted his head, listening. 'It's kind of muddled, sir. The information I have is, a bunch of teenagers came on a mutant at a swimming hole a few miles west of Ukiah. Apparently quite a few of them got mauled.'

Blanchard was lost in thought. In an idle, speculative voice he said to no one in particular, 'If that's confirmed, it means we'll probably have to go to Contingency Plan B-3.'

Dblis nodded slowly, ponderously. 'That was almost foregone, right from the beginning. I'm sure the people in Moscow knew that, too.'

To Colonel Culbertson, Blanchard said, 'Call a general staff meeting.' He looked at his watch. 'My office, in forty-five minutes.'

The strain and lack of sleep were showing in the faces of the officers who had gathered in Blanchard's office. Their faces were white and puffy, but clenched with combative energy.

Blanchard, seated behind his desk, rubbed his eyes and said, 'Sorry to call you here at this hour. But I've just spoken to the President again. Told him the bad news: about forty-five minutes ago, we got a report that a mutant had appeared in Ukiah. That's over thirty miles from here, ten miles outside the quarantine area.' He frowned. 'So that's it. It got away from us.'

Everyone sat in a profound, despairing silence – all except General Dblis, whose eyes, behind those lashless lids, seemed to twinkle with a sort of I-told-you-so triumph.

Blanchard glanced at some papers in front of him and said, 'On what little evidence we have so far, contacts seem to be increasing at a geometric rate: doubling every two hours or so. If that's true . . .' He paused to organise his thoughts. 'Well, figure it out for yourselves: the number of reported contacts we have now is forty-six. If it continues to spread at a geometric rate, there'll be almost six thousand mutants by fourteen-hundred hours tomorrow. By eighteen-hundred hours, we might have as many as fifty thousand. And even that rate of increase is assuming that they remain in rural, sparsely populated areas. If they manage to get to the large population areas like Sacramento and San Francisco, the numbers will explode into many hundreds of thousands within twenty-four hours.'

Colonel Culbertson murmured, 'If the storm hadn't broken, we might've been able to – '

'The President isn't interested in reasons or excuses,' Blanchard said pointedly. 'He wants results, and he's depending on us to get this Goddamned thing under control before he's pressured to take retaliatory action.' He paused briefly before he added, 'So here's what we're going to do: first, extend the quarantine perimeter another fifteen miles – far enough to take in Ukiah. Second, I'm designating five of the largest towns in the quarantine area to be enclaves. We'll bring all the residents into the enclaves. Third, we declare the evacuated countryside to be a free-fire zone.'

'A free-fire zone?' Dblis asked. 'Like in Vietnam, eh?'

'That's right.'

'And kill everybody caught in the zone?'

Blanchard was blunt. 'Everyone found in the free-fire zone will be challenged, of course, and given an opportunity to come in voluntarily. If they don't, they're to be killed. Is that clear?'

Nobody responded.

And still with the unenthusiastic tone of a man who had nothing left to lose that was worth worrying about, Blanchard said, 'It's the best chance we have. Weather reports indicate that the storm'll pass early tomorrow morning. That means we not only can get the helicopters airborne, we can also call in napalm strikes from McClellen Field. We can begin blitzing the free-fire zone at dawn. We'll use the troops to protect and clean out the enclaves.'

Dblis nodded his approval. 'But if that doesn't work?'

Blanchard felt that Dblis was gently nudging him, and he didn't resist the direction. 'In that case, we'll have only one alternative, won't we?'

Still nudging him, Dblis said, 'Contingency B-3?'

'Yes,' Blanchard said as he again buried his face in his hands and rubbed his eyes; then he glanced up at the gloomy, silent men gathered in the office, and said, 'To tell you the truth, though, I don't think it's going to come to that. I think you men will be able to stop it before it gets that far. I sure as hell hope so, because if we do have to go to B-3 . . . well, it'll almost certainly mean war. Hardly any way to get around that, and the President told me to be sure and tell you men that he's not willing to see our country and every other country in the Northern Hemisphere go to ashes. We've *got* to stop this thing, do you hear me? Stop it here and now! If you want napalm strikes, you got 'em. All you want. We'll burn a fifty-mile swath around this whole Goddamned area if that's what it takes. But don't come back here tomorrow and tell me you couldn't do it because you didn't have the fire-power. Don't bring me excuses. Bring me results.'

Colonel Culbertson said, 'We'll do our best.'

'And your best had damned well better be good enough.' Blanchard said. 'From now on, it's *our* lives that are at stake.'

29

In the first faint grey light of dawn, the coastguard cutters could be seen: two grey hulks moving slowly in opposite directions about five or six hundred yards offshore. Small lights shone and flashed on their superstructures. In the sky above them were the last of the clouds that trailed like tattered banners behind the passing storm.

In that faint grey light the town of Mendocino resembled a miniature Dunkirk. Barbed-wire entanglements closed off the town on three sides, the ocean and the coastguard cutters closed it off on the fourth, and at the mouth of every road leading into the town a heavily guarded road-block had been set up.

The town was flooded with refugees. Most of the large public buildings – the library, the high school, the Arts

Centre – had been turned into living quarters for the refugees, where they were issued army cots, aluminium field kits, towels, soap, and a fungicide salve. Army field kitchens were set up at each refugee centre to feed the hundreds – and, by nine o'clock that morning, the thousands – of disgruntled and frightened people who had poured into the town in all stages of panic and unpreparedness.

The military bivouac area on the headlands had been busy all night, but with the coming of dawn the area exploded with activity. The helicopter gunboats began warming up at six o'clock, and thirty minutes later nearly all of them were in the air, whirling over the town as they dispersed, each to an assigned section of the quarantine area over which they would fly with their loudspeakers blaring, warning those who hadn't yet evacuated their homes that they had until nine o'clock to do so. After that, the area was to become a free-fire zone, and any civilians caught in it would be subject to being fired upon.

Sander had his telephone bell turned off, so he didn't hear about the evacuation until he got up that morning and turned on the television. He awakened Bobbi and told her about it. She tried repeatedly to phone her family, to make certain that they had been told to evacuate, but the phone circuits, overloaded, kept rejecting the calls. Between her attempts to phone, she went into the kitchen and hurriedly made some coffee and dropped some eggs into a frying pan.

Sander went into the bathroom to wash and shave, but once having caught the reflection of himself in the mirror, he stood for a long while and stared at himself. It struck him that he must look years older than he had two days ago. And he felt at least twenty years older. He felt dried-up and unreal, and everything seemed strangely frivolous. Bobbi seemed frivolous. Shaving seemed frivolous, too, as well as food and sleep and sex, or anything else he could think of. Including thinking itself. He tried to remember what it was like then, twenty years ago, when things still mattered, but even the effort to remember seemed frivolous.

'Here's some coffee,' Bobbi said, suddenly appearing in the doorway. She studied his reflection in the mirror. 'What's wrong?' But before he could respond, she said, 'What a dumb question.' She seemed very deflated. 'I guess I should say, "What's right"? '

He took the coffee, gulped a large portion of it, and then stared absently into the cup.

She said, 'I saw Jim Newman at the Seagull yesterday evening. He told me that he and those generals and some other men had actually talked to the President for over an hour about this.'

Sander nodded and began to lather his face.

Her eyes were hooded with dread. 'It's that bad, is it?'

He concentrated on his reflection. 'Bad enough,' he mumbled.

'I'm . . .' She faltered. 'All those soldiers and everything . . . like there was a war on, and now the President getting into it. I'm scared, Sandy.'

'Who isn't?'

'But I'm afraid we're . . .' She tried to smile. 'It may sound crazy, Sandy, but what I'm afraid of is, I'm afraid we're all going to die.'

He turned to her. She avoided his eyes because hers were suddenly filled with tears, which seemed to embarrass her. 'It's true, isn't it? None of us is going to get out of this alive?'

His first impulse was to comfort her, to hold her and assure her that they weren't going to die, but it just didn't seem to matter whether or not he did.

Suddenly she sniffed the air. 'The eggs!' she cried, and dashed for the kitchen.

After she had gone, he turned back to stare at his face in the mirror once more, and he realised that she was right. That was why he felt as if everything was so frivolous, why he felt aged and unreal and that nothing mattered. He was closing down. Instinctively, like some aged man, he had been closing down, phasing out his feelings, getting ready for death. Well, at least he had been given time to prepare himself. He was thankful for that, at least. That was more than Brokowski had had, more than Anne Jackson had had. He recalled how Anne had looked yesterday when he saw her in the corridor at the hospital, how agitated and panic-stricken she had been when she begged him to let her go home for a little while. She wanted to see her son, she said. He should have guessed what was wrong, but he didn't, so he let her go. She never came back.

As Sander was coming back through the living-room, he stopped to watch the television for a moment. The announcer was saying, '. . . other news, this important bulletin just in from Washington. There has been a nuclear explosion in northern China. One of our spy-in-the-sky satellites detected the explosion, which took place shortly after one o'clock last night, our time, in the vicinity of Nan Shan, a city only a few hundred miles from the Manchurian-Russian border. It is not known whether the explosion was that of a bomb or some other nuclear device, or whether the explosion was accidental or deliberate. However, since Nan Shan is a densely populated industrial city, military experts speculate that the explosion must have caused widespread devastation. Details are – '

Bobbi said, 'Sandy?' Tears were streaming down her face. 'I'm sorry, but the eggs are burned. I could – '

'Wait,' he said, signalling her to be silent. But by then the TV announcer had finished the bulletin and was reiterating the announcement of the local evacuation.

'Goddamn them,' Sander murmured.

'What?' Bobbi said. 'Who?'

'The stupid sonofabitches,' he muttered, still gazing at the TV screen.

'Who?'

'All of them!' he said. 'Our so-called leaders in this world. They're going to end up killing us all.' But his outrage, however bitter and strong, was slowly giving way to a terrible anxiety and curiosity. What could it mean, this nuclear explosion in northern China? Obviously, it hadn't been a Russian attack, or the Chinese would have retaliated immediately, and by now most of China and Russia would have been obliterated under a rain of nuclear missiles. What, then? Could it have been an accident? There was something – a hunch, intuition – that told him it wasn't, but his mind was too befuddled to guess what else it might have been.

As if desperately trying to find some way to comfort him, Bobbi said, 'I'm sorry. I could make you some more. It'd only take a minute. You should eat comething before you go.' But her real concern seemed to force its way out of her mouth in what was almost a comic *non sequitur*, 'Is it war? Is that what he was saying?'

Sander snapped out of his trance of befuddled fury, and in an answer that seemed to be even more of a comic *non sequitur* than hers, he said, 'No. No, thanks. I'll get something to eat at the hospital.'

Actually, he was glad not to have breakfast with her. It would have been too much like a mockery of everyday living, a forced and self-conscious attempt to recapture the almost slothful domestic contentment with which he and Bobbi used to loll around his apartment: have a leisurely breakfast, maybe read the newspaper, talk, make love, plan their uneventful lives. But that was a few days ago, in the old days, when they still thought they had some control over their lives. Now he knew better. Now he knew that their lives were completely at the disposal of powers that he couldn't even comprehend, let alone control.

Still, he had to keep trying. Even though he had no real hope of altering or even mitigating the catastrophe that the politicians and scientists and military meddlers had brought down upon all their heads, he felt there was no alternative but to keep trying. So he resisted the temptation to stay with Bobbi. He made his good-bye brief, and dashed down the stairs to his car, wondering if he would ever see her again.

He noticed that lights were burning in a great many houses, and as he drove through the commercial area of town, he saw that not only was every building lit up, the streets, too, were full of activity. The refugees were pouring in from the countryside, whole families with blankets and baskets and bundles of hastily gathered belongings, sleepy, crying children in tow, and expressions of confusion, fright and, panic.

He stopped at the road-block. On the other side of it was a long line of vehicles waiting to get in: trucks, cars, pick-ups, jeeps, and vans, all with their lights on and their motors running. Military policemen were going through the vehicles, searching them before allowing them into the town.

A white-helmeted MP lieutenant approached Sander's car. 'Sorry, sir,' he said, 'but you'll have to go back. No unauthorised personnel are allowed to leave.' Like the other soldiers, he wore gloves and his face was smeared with a fungicide salve.

Sander rolled down his window to speak to the lieutenant. 'I'm a doctor. I have to get to Fort Bragg Hospital.'

'Oh. Well, then,' the lieutenant said, 'you can go through. But you're aware, aren't you, that the countryside's being evacuated?'

'So I heard. How long's it been going on?'

'Since oh-one-hundred hours this morning. It's scheduled to end at oh-nine-hundred. After that, the rural area outside the enclaves becomes a free-fire zone.'

'How'll I get back from the hospital?'

'You'll need a red clearance pass. Once you have it, you'll be given an armed escort through the free-fire zone.' With that, he waved Sander through the road-block, but it was then that everyone began to hear the sound, and all activity along the line of refugee vehicles came to a stop as people stiffened with alarm.

At first it was like the sound of distant thunder. As it grew, however, it became high-pitched, a horrendous howling noise, and it was approaching at great speed. In those final moments, it sounded to Sander as if a train with its whistle screaming was bearing down directly upon them at full throttle.

They were jets. Six of them in formation, F-15 fighter-bombers. They came in low over the forest to the east of Mendocino, following the contours of the land. They were probably going five or six hundred miles an hour, and as they passed over the road-block at no more than three hundred feet altitude, everyone had to press their hands over their ears to keep from being deafened by the screaming roar. The planes swooped over the town and then pulled up sharply when they were over the ocean. They peeled off and fanned out as they turned, looping upwards into the grey morning sky. Trailing long plumes of smoke, they circled and headed back towards the shore, no longer flying in formation. The underside of each plane bristled with rockets and napalm bombs.

30

At each of the road-blocks surrounding the enclaves was a member of the Special Tactics Unit who had been trained to spot early-stage mutants. Accompanied by MPs, he checked every vehicle entering the enclave, and all passengers who showed any sign of irrational aggression and hostility were taken aside and questioned about any possible contact they might have had with a mutant. If they continued to be aggressive and hostile, or conceded that it was possible they'd had contact with a mutant, they – along with their families – would be handcuffed, if necessary, and loaded into the back of an army truck. They would be taken to the nearest hospital, where they would undergo blood tests and a two-hour quarantine. If contaminated, they would be put in straitjackets and taken to the compound.

The compound was an old coastguard station and lighthouse on the headlands about midway between Mendocino and Fort Bragg. It had been built as a training station for lighthouse attendants; shortly after World War II, however, when it became apparent that lighthouses of the future would be automated, the compound was closed down. But the buildings – three concrete barracks, a mess hall, numerous outbuildings, and the lighthouse itself – had been kept in good repair by the coastguard maintenance crew.

The Special Tactics Unit took over the compound and turned it into a disposal centre for persons in the early stages of mutation. Given the rapid rate of increase in mutants, it was obvious to the officers of *Operation Hatchet* that the hospitals in the quarantine area would very soon be unable to contain all the people who would have to be examined and quarantined, let alone the increasing numbers of mutants who were reaching the contagious stage. After that – after slime secretion had begun – the mutants had to be kept behind locked doors, and the hospitals would soon run out of lockable doors, as well. Besides, once secretion began, the mutants could not be medically treated, fed, or cared for. What else was to be done with them?

Colonel Thomas Parker, the commanding officer of the Special Tactics Unit, invoked Contingency Plan K-2. He kept an engineering company working on the buildings of the compound around the clock for two days. They hermetically sealed all three of the concrete barracks. They tore out all the windows and sealed them up with cemented bricks. They also bricked up the back door of each barrack, and the front doors were constructed so that they were not only soundproof, but airproof as well.

In addition, the engineers punched holes in the concrete buildings at ground level and ran pipes into the sealed interiors. The other ends of the pipes were connected to valves and gauges and tanks of chlorine Z3 gas.

These preparations had been completed by dawn on Sunday morning, 17 February, when Colonel Parker arrived at the compound to inspect the work and test the compound's efficiency. The test consisted of putting a dog into one of the buildings, sealing the front door, and then turning on the gas. As the gas spewed into the room, Colonel Parker and three junior officers watched the process on a closed-circuit television screen in the building that had once been the compound's mess hall. TV cameras and microphones had been installed in the reconstructed barracks so that the observers in the monitoring room could see and hear everything that went on.

Colonel Parker and his three junior officers watched the dog on the screen, and glanced at their watches to see how long it would take the dog to die.

While this was happening, soldiers in gas masks scurried around the building with gas-detection devices, checking the joints and corners for possible leaks.

The first group of mutants arrived by army trucks from Fort Bragg Hospital an hour later. There were twenty-two of them altogether; six were children. All of them were wearing straitjackets. Some were violently hostile and had to be dragged thrashing and cursing into the chambers. Others were weeping and begging. Still others walked, with the horrified passivity of zombies, through the doorway. Then the big, thick door closed behind them.

When Sander arrived at the hospital that morning, Carol Marvin at the reception desk told him that there was to be an emergency meeting of all high-level staff members in the cafeteria in twenty minutes.

'Any idea what it's about?' he asked her.

She shook her head, no, but said that the meeting had been called by Mr Hunter, the CIA man, and she had got the impression that it was important.

As Sander entered the cafeteria, he got himself a cup of

coffee and a Danish pastry before he went to join the others near the dais at the far end of the room. There were perhaps fifty or sixty people there – Hoffmann, Roget, Sheftman, and Yoshimura among them – and most of them, haggard and worn, were wolfing down doughnuts and coffee, smoking, talking, speculating, exchanging notes. One of the main topics of conversation was the news of the nuclear explosion that had taken place in China the night before, and it was Hoffmann who said that he was willing to bet he could guess the reason for the explosion.

Before he could share his speculations, however, S. Bradley Hunter entered the room, hurriedly made his way to the makeshift dais, and asked everyone to please give him their attention for a few minutes.

'General Blanchard asked me to call this meeting and inform you of a new and perhaps critical development in our fight against this disease.' In a small, dry voice, he added, 'Probably most of you have heard by now about what happened in China last night. For those of you who haven't, it's this: at exactly one-fifteen a.m., our time, a nuclear bomb was dropped on the city of Nan Shan, which is – *was*, I guess I should say – an industrial city with a population of about seven hundred thousand people. As of now, the city is a pile of rubble, and there's probably not a living soul within a hundred miles of it.

'At first, of course – that is, when we first learned of the explosion – we assumed that it had either been a nuclear accident, or that the Russians had attacked China. But it took the people in Washington only a few minutes on the hot lines to the Kremlin and Peking to ascertain that, in fact, it was neither an accident nor a Russian bomb. The Chinese bombed their own city.'

He paused for a moment, adjusted his rimless glasses, sighed with exhaustion. 'Now, some of you may already have guessed why the Chinese destroyed one of their own cities, and why that event is of critical importance to all of us here in this room. It's simply this: we are not alone. This disease that we're fighting here has also broken out in northern China.'

He paused again for a few seconds to give the astonished audience time to assimilate this information, then added, 'As near as we've been able to determine, the disease appeared in Nan Shan within about twelve hours after it first appeared here. Unfortunately, we know nothing more than that.' The tiredness of his small, dry voice deepened to a sort of ominous despair as he added, 'Now, of course, the most obvious conclusion is that the Russians released the disease simultaneously in Nan Shan and Mendocino. They vehemently deny having done it, of course, but if they did . . . *if*, I say . . . although,' he added parenthetically, 'there seems to be very little doubt about it now. Anyway, *if* they did it, and if, under threat of imminent nuclear annihilation from both the United States and China, they can be persuaded to admit it, then there remains a small ray of hope for us. Because, of course, if the disease is a Russian germ-warfare agent, then the Russians obviously already have an antidote for it. Otherwise, they would never have released it so near their own border. Right now the President is on the hot line to the Kremlin, trying to persuade them to back off from this suicidal confrontation by sharing the antidote with us. However . . .' He made a palms-up gesture of despair and futility.

'Anyway,' he said after a short pause, 'that's all I can tell you at this time. If there are no questions, you may all return to your stations.'

He waited for a moment to see if there were any questions, but the audience – with the exception of Professor Roget – sat in a dumbfounded and despairing silence. Only Roget seemed to have escaped the crushing depression caused by Hunter's information. He, in fact, seemed almost excited when he stood up and said, 'One question, please, Mr Hunter. Do you happen to know if the city of Nan Shan is in the ancient feudal kingdom of Hsiung-nu?'

'No, Professor, I don't. I'm not a China specialist. But I can see that you get the information, if you think it's important.'

'It may be,' Roget said. 'It may be *very* important. But don't bother. I can get it myself. Thank you,' he said, as he whirled and hurriedly left the room.

Some of the napalm strikes could be seen from Mendocino. The throngs of refugees and residents and soldiers on the streets watched one of the F-15s strike a target on the shoreline about three miles north of town. The F-15 made its approach from the sea and released one napalm bomb on the shoreline. The plane then pulled sharply upwards, while the oblong canister hurtled end-over-end towards its target, an old moss-encrusted farmhouse on the wooded ridge above Russian Gulch.

The bomb struck the ridge just below the house, and the liquid flames leaped upwards and forwards into a long arching fan, engulfing the house. The F-15 returned for a second pass and saw that the target had been destroyed.

Other napalm strikes were made near town as the morning wore on. Most of the targets were a few miles inland, in the area of the Pygmy Forest, and couldn't be seen from the streets or from the rooftops. But the spectators could see the F-15s dive towards their targets and pull up, and in a moment the black smoke from the flames billowed up into the grey sky above the horizon.

The helicopter gunboats were in the air, too, constantly coming into the headlands landing area to be refuelled and resupplied with rockets and bullets, then they were off again, swinging inland. They filled the late morning with the distant sounds of their clattering machine-guns and the occasional explosions of their rockets.

These scenes and sounds of a desperate open warfare increased the nervous tension that already existed in the town, and by late morning a spirit of lawlessness had begun in the people on the streets, especially among the refugees and the tourists who had been trapped in the area by the quarantine. Fights broke out among people who lined up to get into the town's two grocery stores. The store owners, by order of the military police, allowed only a small number of shoppers in the stores at any given time; otherwise, the stores would have been unable to handle the swarms of panic-prone customers. But at Mendosa's store trouble erupted when one refugee man, fearing that the supply of milk would be gone before he could buy any for his child, tried to crash the line and get into the store without waiting his turn. A fight broke out. People began yelling and shoving. In the turmoil, someone darted past the MP at the door, and when the MP turned to nab the crasher, someone else pushed him from behind; he fell and the crowd surged through the door, pushing and shoving and yelling, swarming through the store, trying to load their arms with as much of the already depleted stocks of food as they could hold. Women fought over the last loaves of bread, and men shoved women out of the way to get to the few remaining cartons of eggs.

The quick response of an MP patrol kept the crowd from becoming a rioting and looting mob, but the incident pointed up the need for special measures to keep the populace from getting out of hand. Those special measures included issuing riot guns, gas masks, and tear-gas guns to the MP patrols; declaring a general curfew to go into effect at nine o'clock that night, after which time no one would be allowed on the streets without special permission of the military authorities; and the closing and padlocking of all bars and restaurants. Also, two more jeeps carrying public-address systems were put into operation to patrol the streets, constantly urging the citizens to remain calm. They used the PA systems to tell the people that the army was bringing in shipments of food, so there was no need to worry, there would be plenty of food for everyone. They repeatedly assured everyone that the army had the situation under control.

No one believed them.

At the compound, monitoring was under way on the first group of early-stage mutants who had been herded and dragged into the first disposal chamber shortly after eleven o'clock that morning. An hour later, a psychologist – an army major – sat at a table in the mess hall, watching the closed-circuit TV pictures of the early-stage mutants inside the chamber. He could hear them, too. He took notes as he watched.

By noon the first mutant within the chamber entered the slime-secreting stage, and within twenty minutes, three more began to show visible signs of slime secretion. The chamber more and more became a hellhole of frenzied howling, thrashing about, curses, cries, screams. The ones among them who were in the earliest stages of mutation either had been terrified into catatonic trances, or had dragged and stumbled their way to the door, where they tumbled together and screamed their demands to be let out.

At twelve-thirty the compound's young commanding officer, a captain, stood in the monitoring room, watching the terrifying chaos in the chamber. Finally, he turned to the psychologist at the table.

'Hasn't this gone on long enough?' he asked.

The major glanced up from a note he was making. 'I'm sorry, Captain. I'm not exactly enjoying this, you know. We have to have all the information we can get.' He glanced up at the screen for a moment, then sighed and flung the pencil down on the table in a gesture of disgust. 'Oh, all right,' he said. 'You might as well get it over with.'

Without saying a word, the captain turned and left the monitoring room. The psychologist leaned back in his chair, nervously lit a cigarette, and watched to see when it would happen. The noise was too loud within the chamber to hear the gas when it was turned on, and of course it couldn't be seen or smelled by the mutants inside the chamber.

They never knew what happened. As the psychologist watched, the mutants suddenly began to wilt – the ones closest to the gas jets first, but within ten seconds everyone in the chamber had breathed it, and within another ten seconds they were all dead.

Twenty minutes later, when all signs of life had stopped, the chamber was cleared of the gas, the door was opened, and a squad of soldiers, wearing gas masks in case any of the gas lingered in the chamber, sterilised the interior with fungicide. Then they dragged the bodies out and burned them.

A large, crude crematorium had been hastily erected about a hundred yards from the chambers. It was made of four thick walls of firebrick. There was no roof. There was a rough, uneven grating made of crisscrossed reinforcing rods above the burners. A butane tank truck was parked nearby; a hose connected the truck to the burners.

The first long billow of black, greasy smoke rose above the crematorium early that afternoon. It could be seen for miles.

The second and third truckloads of early-stage mutants arrived at the compound while the billow of black smoke hung heavy in the grey sky. There were twenty-one mutants in the first load, twenty-nine in the second load. They were put into the second and third chambers while the first chamber was being readied for yet another load that would soon be on its way.

The pillar of smoke from the crematorium, though waxing and waning, continued to billow up all afternoon, a gigantic black funeral wreath in the overcast sky.

31

When Professor Roget left the conference in the hospital's cafeteria that Sunday morning, he went directly back to the mobile computer unit behind the hospital. It was a huge army van, filled with a complex array of electronic devices, among which were two computer terminals. One of the terminals was connected by telephone cable to Roget's computer at UC, Davis; the other was connected to the computer systems at the Chemical and Biological Warfare Research Centre at Fort Detrick, Maryland.

There were two programmers in the van when Roget entered. He gave them a chipper 'Good morning', and then said to one of them, 'Sergeant, do me a favour, will you, please? Find me a map of ancient China. Try the Fort Bragg library, the College of the Redwoods, the high school, wherever you have to look, but find me one, and hurry please.'

Then he sat down at an army field desk in one corner of the van and reached for the telephone. He gave the operator his phone number, which contained a code that allowed him to make top-priority calls. He told the operator to connect him with the Reverend Boyle in Mendocino.

Among the clutter of papers on the desk in front of Roget was the copy of the Reverend Boyle's thesis on pre-Christian demonology. Roget flipped through the manuscript as he waited for the operator to get the Reverend on the phone, which took almost five minutes, and then he said, 'Reverend? Listen. Can you come to Fort Bragg immediately? I want to talk to you about your thesis on demonology.'

A tremulous note of interest entered the Reverend's despondent voice when he said, 'You read it?'

'I looked at it, yes,' Roget said. 'And I have reason to believe it may be very important to us, but I need to ask you some questions, mainly about interpretations of ancient texts. Can you come?'

Slightly abashed now, the Reverend said, 'I'd be glad to, but they require something called a red clearance pass now to get through the road-blocks, and I'm afraid they wouldn't give *me* one.'

Roget said he thought he could arrange that. He instructed the Reverend to report to *Hatchet*'s headquarters in the Mendocino Hotel immediately, and after the phone connection was broken, Roget made a series of calls that finally cleared the way for the Reverend Boyle to come to Fort Bragg.

While waiting for the Reverend to arrive, Roget once again focused his attention on the battered manuscript. It was a very curious document. Predictably enough, the bulk of the text was concerned with references to demons that the Reverend had culled from various holy books and texts that predated the birth of Christ – Tibetan prayer wheels, for instance, and the *Upanishads*, the *Egyptian Book of the Dead*, as well as the *I Ching*, and, of course, the Old Testament.

None of these references held any interest for Roget. He had long ago assumed that demons were nothing more than the projections of pathetically primitive or deranged minds. But what had caused a perceptible increase in Roget's heartbeat was the picture of a bronze Chinese bowl. The Reverend Boyle's text explained that the bowl had been made in the feudal kingdom of Hsiung-nu in northern China during the year 1200 B.C. Imprinted into the sides of the bowl was a message in primitive ideograms from the early Chou dynasty, and among them was the ideogram for 'snail'. According to the Reverend Boyle's interpretation, the message read, 'Many men (people) snail water dragons (demons?).'

It was this particular message that Roget was contemplating when the sergeant returned from the Fort Bragg library with a map of ancient China contained in a history textbook. Roget hurriedly examined the map for the feudal kingdom of

Hsiung-nu, found it, and then suddenly slapped the map in a gesture of joyful triumph, because Hsiung-nu was, indeed, in northern China, and its principal city had been Nan Shan.

Roget went back to Boyle's thesis, to a section of the manuscript that dealt with the ways that prehistoric peoples recorded their visions of demons before the advent of modern written languages. In particular, what caught his eye was a pictograph: a series of crude drawings that had been carved into the walls of a cave by prehistoric cliff-dwelling Indians who had lived in what was now New Mexico. The author's interpretation of the pictograph appeared below it, and the words formed the message 'People become water demons'.

Water demons? In New Mexico? At first this interpretation seemed far-fetched to Roget, but then it occurred to him that the pictogram that the prehistoric Indians used for the word 'water' – three short, wavy lines – might have been the only way they had to convey the idea of 'wet'. Could it also have been the only way they had to convey the idea of 'slime'? If so, then the pictograph might have been interpreted to mean that the people became demons who were covered with slime.

The text went on to explain that, while this pictograph was only one of many found by archaeologists in the New Mexico cliff dwellings, it had been the last. After it had been carved into the wall of the cave, all the Indians had apparently abandoned their cliff dwellings in such a hurry that they left behind everything upon which their lives depended: their tools, their utensils, their crops – even their garments. Why?

The archaeologists who had excavated the site had been unable to explain the tribe's sudden and obviously panicked departure, but the Reverend Boyle, writing in the inflated prose of a pedantic graduate student, had offered his theory that the Indians had become possessed by demons, or had been chased away by demons.

Roget read on. He pored over pages of Egyptian hieroglyphics, pictographs from the Indus Valley in Pakistan, Sumerian cuneiform tablets, and Chinese ideographs, many of which, according to the Reverend Boyle's interpretations, were primitive reports of people who'd had encounters with demons, or had been possessed by them.

A timid knock sounded on the door of the van. When Roget's deep and excited voice boomed, 'Come in', the Reverend Boyle entered like a supplicant unsure of his welcome.

The two men seemed a study in contrasts. Roget's gnome-like body vibrated with the excitement of discovery, while the Reverend Boyle, angular and stoop-shouldered, had the doleful countenance of a condemned prisoner nearing his hour of execution.

'The reason I asked you here,' Roget said as he pulled another chair up to the desk, 'is this: I want us to go through this manuscript as quickly as we can, and have you point out to me every reference you can find – how shall I put this? – references to large numbers of people who were reported to have become demons at the same time. Especially where the demons were reported to be connected in some way with . . . well, with water. Wetness.'

'Slime?' Reverend Boyle said archly, and his sad, bloodshot eyes appeared to twinkle for a moment, if not with triumph, at least with vindication.

'Exactly,' Roget said. He placed the opened manuscript in front of the Reverend. 'Like this.' He tapped the picture of the Chinese bowl with its ideogram of a snail.

'Ah,' the Reverend said, 'Ah, yes. You see? I'm not so crazy, after all, am I?'

'I never thought you were,' Roget said, becoming slightly wary now, hoping that the Reverend wasn't going to waste any time with self-pity.

'The others do. They think I'm – '

'Well, then,' Roget interrupted in a chipper tone, 'let's get to work and see if we can prove them wrong, shall we?'

At first the Reverend Boyle was inclined to be distracted and desultory in his examination, but with Roget's constant encouragement and prodding, he finally became a little excited by the challenge of the task.

Counting the pictograph left by the cliff-dwelling Indians in New Mexico and the ideographic message imprinted on the bronze Chinese bowl, however, the Reverend was able to find only four instances of prehistoric demons that met Roget's criteria. The third was a report in cuneiform writing on a clay tablet from North Africa that dated back to about 6000 B.C. The fourth was a pictograph carved in a bone found in the Near East, which also dated back to about 6000 B.C.

'That's as far back as you can go,' the Reverend Boyle said. 'Before that, there was no such thing as written language of any kind.'

'Curious, isn't it?' Roget asked as he contemplated the notes he had taken during their examination of the manuscript. 'The approximate periods between outbreaks, I mean. If we count the disease that we have here on our hands today as an outbreak of, uh, "demonism", then the outbreaks seem to come at intervals of about three thousand years.' He tilted his head in a gesture of puzzlement and admiration. 'Curious . . .'

The Reverend Boyle eyed Roget with a sort of weary suspicion. 'What're you up to, Professor? You don't really believe that what we have here today is demonism, do you?'

'Believe?' Roget said. 'Reverend, I don't get paid to believe. I get paid to find out.' He abruptly pushed his chair back from the desk, a signal that the conference was over, and added, 'Thank you very much, Reverend, for your help. I'm grateful. Now, if you'll excuse me, I have to get busy and put this data into a computer, and then maybe I'll find out a little more about the nature of our affliction, whether it be demons or disease.'

The Reverend seemed to be lapsing back into a sort of self-pitying hopelessness when he said, 'Why bother? It will end soon.'

'End?' Roget asked. 'What will? The affliction?'

'The world.'

For a moment Roget stared at the Reverend in amazed silence, marvelling at the profound depths of the man's despair. Although not a religious man himself, Roget felt an impulse to give the minister a stinging rebuke for his lack of Christian faith and hope. However, he had no time for such nonsense. As he abruptly got to his feet, he said, 'I daresay you may be right, Reverend. Until then, however, I have work to do. If you'll excuse me now . . .?'

The Reverend, rising, once again accepted Roget's outstretched hand, and said, 'I'll be giving a special sermon this evening. You've read what my thesis has to say about this calamity, but you haven't heard the most important revelations. The Old Testament references are important, but it's the New Testament revelations that are crucial to this calamity. If you'd care to hear them . . .?'

'That so?' Roget said. 'Hmmmm. Well, maybe I will. First, though, if you don't mind, I think I'll find out what my computer has to say about it.'

32

The first glimmer of hope came at approximately four o'clock that Sunday afternoon, when Lacy Coors began to show signs of responding to a new antibiotic called actinomycin G. The new drug had been developed in the previous twenty-four hours by a team working under the direction of Captain Yoshimura, an immunologist with the Special Tactics Unit. Sander and Hoffmann and others had helped in the development of the antibiotic, but it had been Yoshimura who, hollow-eyed and feverish with exhaustion, had worked without rest for two days and nights and finally had done what most of his colleagues and co-workers had given up hope of doing. He had discovered a molecular variant of actinomycin that seemed to block the production of DNA in the quasi-fungoid organisms, thereby causing them to malfunction and die.

Lacy Coors was the mutant to whom the antibiotic was first administered. After she had been completely anaesthetised by a chloroform gas that was pumped into the sealed plastic capsule, a specially trained crew of medical corpsmen, gloved and masked, carefully lifted the canopy. A terrible stench of excrement and rot – a cesspool effluvium – suddenly filled the room. After she had been sterilised, Sander started an intravenous drip containing actinomycin G.

Fifteen minutes later they pricked the skin of her leg and took the first drop of blood for examination. Thereafter, a blood sample was taken every thirty minutes for two hours.

It was blood sample four, taken just after one-thirty that afternoon, in which the effect was first seen. Excitement began to build up in the lab as Yoshimura, Sander and Hoffmann examined the fifth and sixth blood samples under the microscope. Doctors and lab technicians had begun to gravitate towards the corner where the samples were being examined, and by the time Yoshimura received the seventh sample from the Coors mutant, a thin crowd had gathered around him, Sander and Hoffmann. The onlookers waited, almost breathless in a heavy silence of anxiety and hope.

Yoshimura stared into the microscope for perhaps half a minute, making adjustments now and then. When he looked up, there were tears in his eyes. He looked at Hoffmann and Sander. 'Take a look,' he said. Unable to contain himself, he nodded, tentatively at first, but with increasing vigour and affirmation as he saw the shadow of comprehension play across the haggard faces of the people gathered around.

'Congratulations, Captain,' Hoffmann said as he relinquished the microscope to Sander. He held out his hand to Yoshimura and said, 'I think you've just made yourself famous.'

It was a woman technician among the onlookers who first broke the spell of incredulous silence and immobility. She stepped forward and threw her arms around Yoshimura's neck, an act that set off a wave of excitement and renewed hope. The onlookers stirred, glancing at each other with wonder, and then began to shake hands and hug each other with sounds of laughter and sighs of profound relief.

The plastic canopy had been replaced over the gurney on which Lacy Coors lay, strapped and straitjacketed, and the anaesthesia had worn off enough so that her physical reactions could be examined and analysed.

The first change the examiners noticed in her was that the rate of slime secretion seemed to be diminishing. That was shortly after four o'clock. She was beginning to groan, still in that deep, subterranean tone of the mutant, and trying to thrash about in her bonds, so it was apparent that, even though slime secretion had diminished, her personality was still very much that of the mutant.

But at about four-thirty Sander thought he saw something: a change in her expression, a flicker of fear, perhaps, and fear was one emotion that had never before been seen in a mutant. He began to look more closely at her face. Hoffmann, Yoshimura, D. B. Sheftman, and Colonel Thomas Parker – among others – fell silent when they noticed the puzzled expression on Sander's face.

'Look,' he said. 'Her eyes . . .'

For a few seconds Lacy seemed to recognise him, and during those brief seconds it seemed as if she had reclaimed her eyes from the mutant, as if it were Lacy, and not the mutant, who looked at him and said something.

'Turn it on,' Sander told the technician who stood at the head of the gurney.

But by the time the switch was thrown, it was the mutant who was looking out of her eyes again, and the mutant who was cursing them with obscene fury.

Then again the slimy mask of her face suddenly and momentarily registered an agony of fear, rather than ferocity, and the mutant's hatred ceased to burn in her cloudy eyes as she struggled to focus on Sander.

'Lacy?' he called, his voice tremulous. 'Can you hear me?'

And in a voice that was without the mutant's rage, she stammered, 'San . . . Sandy?'

'Yes, Lacy,' he said, feeling a surge of excitement, an excitement that swept over everyone in the room. They all drew nearer the canopy and peered down at Lacy as though they were seeing her through a microscope.

Her voice had changed. Though still deep and growling, there was in it somewhere the sound of a young girl's terrified plea when she cried out, 'Sandy! What . . . what's happened to . . .?'

'Lacy, you've been . . .'

But suddenly Lacy disappeared again. The mutant regained control – had actually seemed to struggle with Lacy for supremacy over her body, her eyes, her mind – but though the mutant was back in control, it seemed weaker, more desperate.

It was perhaps two full minutes before Lacy came back into the eyes and the cursing and thrashing stopped. 'Sandy! Please! What're you doing? To me? I'm so, so, so. Thirsty. What's happening to me?'

Sander said, 'Lacy, you've been critically ill. Don't you know that? Do you remember – ?'

'What? What's wrong? Sandy, please! I'm so thirsty.'

'We'll let you have some water very soon, Lacy,' he promised, 'but if we're going to help you get well, you've got to help us. You understand, Lacy? Can you understand what I'm saying?'

'Yes. Yes. But, please! What're you doing . . . to me?'

'Listen to me now, Lacy. It's important: do you remember anything that happened to you? Anything at all?'

She seemed to be trying to figure something out, but then she groaned and looked at Sander with hurt, puzzled eyes, as if wondering why he was torturing her. 'What's wrong with me?'

Sander took a deep breath, as if summoning up his courage. 'Listen to me, Lacy. Do you remember what happened to you and Billy Boyle?'

She looked blank for a moment.

'You and Billy were parked on – '

She cried out. Her eyes had been feverishly dull and blank for a moment, but then comprehension broke through and she cried out, 'Billy! Oh, Billy! No, no, no, no!'

Her increasing hysteria caused Sander to become very stern. 'Lacy, stop it! You're safe now. You're safe. Stop it.'

The power of his voice apparently surprised her into silence for a moment, and when he saw that he had her attention again, he lowered his voice and said, 'You've had a terrible experience, Lacy, but there's hope that it's almost over now. You have to help us, though. Will you? Will you try?'

She snarled. The mutant was back.

The struggle continued on into the early evening, a struggle between Lacy and the mutant for control of her body and mind. The struggle racked her body and made her writhe with alternate fury and horror. She cried, she screamed, she begged, and cursed. And though the mutant managed to stay in control most of the time, the intervals when Lacy had control were growing steadily longer and more frequent. That the mutant was growing steadily weaker there was no doubt, but it put up a frenzied and powerful struggle.

It was shortly after five-thirty that Hoffmann was called from the room. He returned a few minutes later and asked Sander and Colonel Parker to step out into the hall with him.

'We have to go,' he told them. 'General Blanchard's called

an urgent meeting of some of the Executive Steering Committee members.'

'Leave?' Sander said. 'With this going on? Is it that important?'

Hoffmann nodded. 'I think so. I get the idea that it's something very big.'

33

The ten members of the committee who had been ordered to meet with Blanchard included Hoffmann, Sander, Colonels Culbertson and Parker, Newman, and General Dblis. They were ushered into Blanchard's office, and took chairs that had been placed in a half-circle facing Blanchard's desk.

'I asked you here,' Blanchard said as he, with his hands clasped behind his back, strode restlessly back and forth behind his desk, 'because an important decision's been made, and all of you have a need to know. Mind you,' he said, looking directly at Sander and Hoffmann, who were the only non-government-connected civilians there, 'everything discussed here will be considered top secret, and is not to go beyond that door.'

Sander and Hoffmann nodded that they understood.

'I'm going to be talking to the President again in a few minutes, and as things stand now . . .' His words trailed off as he nodded towards a portable blackboard that stood against one wall of the office. On the blackboard was a crudely drawn map of northern California. The new, enlarged quarantine area had been drawn on the board with red chalk, and there were two cities outside the red area whose names had been circled in red.

Blanchard strode to the board. He tapped a knuckle on the red-encircled city of Cloverdale. 'Were you all aware of this?' he asked, glancing at the civilians present.

Sander shook his head.

'It's gotten that far, has it?' Hoffmann asked.

'As of twenty minutes ago,' Blanchard acknowledged. 'That puts it about eighty miles from San Francisco.' Then he tapped the red-encircled town of Lakeport. 'Here, too. It's unconfirmed yet, but there's apparently been a mutant sighting here, about eighty-five miles from Sacramento.'

Again, he strode back and forth behind his desk. 'As we all know, this epidemic cannot – repeat: *cannot* – be allowed to reach those areas. So unless we come up with a miracle damned fast . . .' He glanced at Hoffmann. 'What about that antibiotic? How does it look at this point?'

Hoffmann scratched his unshaven chin with the stem of his empty pipe. 'Well, all I can say is that it still looks very good. It seems to be working.'

'Excuse me,' Colonel Culbertson said. 'I hadn't heard about that. You've come up with a serum that works?'

'An antibiotic,' Hoffmann corrected him.

'I hadn't heard about that,' Culbertson said in a vaguely complaining voice, as if he suspected someone of deliberately keeping him in the dark.

'We haven't made a general announcement, yet,' Hoffmann said. 'It's too early for that.'

'Or too late,' Blanchard said. 'How long would it take you to make enough of that antibiotic for, say, ten thousand people?'

Hoffmann hesitated.

'A rough estimate,' Blanchard said.

He glanced at Sander. 'Five days?'

Sander said, 'Captain Yoshimura would be the one to answer that, but I suspect it'd take at least that long.' Then he shrugged with resignation and hopelessness. 'In any case, it's obviously not going to make any difference in the spread of the disease. It's not going to be the miracle you need.'

'So we won't make any announcement at all,' Blanchard said. 'I want everything connected with that antibiotic to be kept secret.'

Hoffmann nodded understandingly. 'The only thing is, it might give everyone a little hope. It's done wonders for the morale of the hospital staff.'

'False hope. The fact is, gentlemen, that we have exactly' – he glanced at the clock on the wall, which was synchronised with the clocks in the NSC room at the White House – 'five hours and twenty-three minutes.' He paused and looked at them to see if they understood. 'We have until oh-one-thirty-five hours tomorrow morning, gentlemen, to stop it. If we haven't come up with a way to stop it by then . . .' He looked at the civilians in the room. 'Do you men know about *Operation Hatchet*'s Contingency B-3?' When it became obvious that they didn't, Blanchard said, 'It's the Chinese solution, the one they used on Nan Shan, the last resort: a nuclear strike.' He paused. 'And that's what'll happen at exactly oh-two-hundred hours in the morning, if we can't stop the spread of this disease before it gets into the big population centres.'

Sander felt that he was beyond feeling amazement, even surprise, but at least there was a hard edge of resentment in his voice when he said, 'A nuclear strike? You're going to call in a nuclear strike on us?'

'It's already been called in. If we fail to stop the spread of this disease, then at oh-one-thirty-five in the morning, three ICBMs will be launched from LeMay Missile Base in Nebraska. At oh-two hundred in the morning, the missiles will be detonated over the quarantine area.' He tapped the blackboard. 'Mendocino is ground zero for one of them. Out of the four MIRVed warheads, we'll take a fifty-megaton blast. It'll be at a very high altitude, so that the maximum destruction will be from the fireball. For a few seconds the temperature here will equal the temperature on the outer edges of the sun. The other two ICBMs will have Lakeport and Cloverdale, respectively, as ground zero, so that everything – every plant and animal and structure – within an area of about six hundred square miles will be burned to a cinder.

There won't be a tree or a building left standing, not an automobile or a telephone left unmelted.'

Hoffmann's voice caught in his throat when he said, 'What about . . . San Francisco and Sacramento?'

'The outlying suburbs of both cities will be scorched. Probably be some fires. But at least the cities themselves won't be destroyed – at least not by these missiles.'

'Radioactivity?' Hoffmann asked.

'Minimal,' Blanchard said. 'These'll be fairly clean nukes, and they'll detonate high enough so the possibility of radioactive dust clouds will be minimised. But that won't make any difference to us, of course. We'll all be dead.'

'How many people?' Sander asked.

'Within the total kill area, four or five hundred thousand. Probably that many more injured or burned so badly they probably won't live.'

'A million?' Sander said. 'A million people?' He slammed his hand down on the arm of his chair. 'A disease that hasn't proved fatal to even *one* person, and you're going to kill a million to stop it? What kind of insanity is this?'

Blanchard went white with fury, but his voice remained low and calm. 'We've got our choice, Doctor: either a million dead, here and now, or the disease takes over the whole country. And what's to stop it then? Why not the whole American continent? Are you willing to see that happen?'

Sander didn't respond.

'Are you?' Blanchard demanded; and when it became obvious that Sander wasn't going to answer, he took a deep breath before he said, 'The decision has been made. If it had been made earlier, there'd be fewer people who have to die. The Chinese stopped it at about seven hundred thousand deaths. How long do you want us to wait?'

Sander still didn't respond, but sat in a silence of baffled anguish and resentment, and it was Hoffmann who finally broke the awkward silence.

'It's been confirmed, then?' he asked. 'About Nan Shan,

I mean? It was Lawson's disease?'

Blanchard nodded. 'Confirmed.'

'And the nuclear blast stopped it?' Colonel Parker asked.

Another nod. 'As far as they know, yes, it appears to have stopped.'

It was General Dblis who spoke next. His tone was quite ordinary, and there was no trace of expression on his waxen face as he said, 'Have there been any new developments indicating that it's of Russian origin?'

'No.'

'What about the Chinese?' Dblis asked. 'I assume they have no hard evidence that it's Russian, or they would've retaliated by now.'

'That's right, they don't. They assume it's Russian, of course, but as long as there's room for doubt, they're holding back.'

'Do they have any reason to doubt it?' Dblis asked. 'Other than the negative one of there being no hard evidence, I mean?'

In an idle, speculative tone, Blanchard said, 'They're asking themselves the same thing we are: why Nan Shan? Why Mendocino? Why not Peking and New York?' He shook his head. 'As Mr Newman said last night, it doesn't make sense.' He paused for a moment, puzzled and distracted, and then abruptly walked around to the front of his desk. 'But that isn't our problem,' he said as he leaned back against the desk and folded his arms across his chest. 'Our problem is to stop this thing. That's why I've told you about the nuclear strike – so you'll be aware of the deadline and plan your operations accordingly. But I want to make it absolutely clear that it's top-secret information. It's not to go beyond that door. If news of it were to get out . . . well, I don't have to tell you what'd happen. Complete panic. People would stampede the road-blocks. And the worst thing of all – far worse than the strike itself – would be the failure of the strike. If people stampeded, we might not be able to stop them all.

Some would get through, carrying the disease with them. In that case, the strike would have been for nothing. We would have died for nothing.'

After a short pause, he added, 'I realise it'll be a terrible burden for you, knowing that you're going to die, and not being able to do anything about it. But if it's any consolation to you, nobody – *nobody* – will be allowed to leave the quarantine area. As of a few minutes ago, the air force and coastguard were given their orders: if anybody tries to get out by helicopter or plane, he'll be shot down. If people try to escape by boat, the coastguard will blow them out of the water. So let's not entertain any illusions about that, gentlemen; we're sealed in. Our fate is tied to the fate of this disease. If we stop it, we live. If we don't, we die.'

He turned and walked back around the desk. 'All right, then,' he said in a tone of dismissal. 'If any of you manages to think up some miracle, or happens to be vouchsafed one by God, I want to know immediately. Resume your stations.' He let the men get to their feet, and then he added, 'All except you, General Dblis. I'd like a further word with you, if you don't mind.'

After the others were gone, Dblis waited for Blanchard to speak, but Blanchard seemed suddenly interested in some papers on his desk.

Dblis cleared his throat.

Blanchard looked up. 'Oh, yes,' he said, as if he had completely forgotten about Dblis. 'Well, the fact is, it looks as if you've finally gone too far, doesn't it?'

Dblis sighed. 'All right, what is it? What am I being accused of now?'

'Would desertion be all right?'

Dblis didn't bother to disguise his disdain. 'Have you lost your mind?'

Blanchard got up and strode to the office door and flung it open. 'Captain Kane!'

The helicopter pilot had been waiting in the outer office.

He entered, closed the door behind him, faced Blanchard, and saluted. 'Captain Kane reporting, sir, as ordered.'

'At ease, Captain,' Blanchard said. 'Now, tell me again: you were asked to make an unauthorised and illegal flight tonight, were you not?'

'Yes, sir.'

'Who asked you to do it?'

The captain was sweating. He kept his eyes lowered and fumbled with his hat as he said, 'General Dblis did, sir.'

'Was General Dblis to accompany you on the flight?'

'Yes, sir.'

'Where were you supposed to take him?'

'San Francisco, sir.'

'Why San Francisco? Did he tell you?'

'Yes, sir. He said there was a plane waiting there for him, a jet that'd take him to Brazil.'

'And what inducement did he offer you to make the trip?'

'My life, sir. He said that . . . that there was going to be a nuclear strike against the quarantine area tonight, and that there'd probably be a nuclear war, and that the whole Northern Hemisphere would be destroyed. He said I could come with him to Brazil, where he had friends and money, and . . .' He shrugged, begging to be relieved from explaining further.

Blanchard looked at Dblis. 'Well?'

Dblis seemed indifferent. 'Lies, of course. All lies, and you know it as well as I do. Are there no depths to which you won't stoop to pursue this vendetta against me? I'm warning you, Thurston, if we survive this, it'll be *you* who'll be facing a few charges, starting with official misconduct and malicious prosecution.'

Blanchard nodded resignedly, as if he'd expected as much, then once more strode to the office door and flung it open. 'MPs,' he said, and when two MPs, a lieutenant and a sergeant, entered the office, Blanchard said, 'General Dblis is under house arrest. Take him to his quarters. If he tries to escape, you have my authorisation to shoot him.'

34

The three churches in Mendocino – the only public buildings that hadn't been taken over by the army – were filled to capacity that Sunday evening, and the Presbyterian Church was crowded to overflowing. News had got round that Reverend Boyle was going to give a very special sermon that evening at six. The church was filled by five-thirty. By the time the sermon began, people were standing all along the wall in the rear of the church.

A hush fell over the congregation when the Reverend stepped into the pulpit, a hush of hope and expectation. Much of the congregation was vaguely disappointed by the Reverend's appearance, however. He had never been an imposing man, and he was especially unimposing now, with his rumpled suit and haggard face. They had hoped for a man who could inspire them with his own strength and certitude. The Reverend failed in appearance to inspire anyone. Also, his first words made it quite clear that this was not going to be a hopeful, uplifting sermon, which they all wanted – needed – to hear. He opened the Bible, placed his palms down on the opened pages, and said in a voice that could hardly be heard in the back of the church, 'I have failed you all.'

There was some throat-clearing in the congregation, some foot-shuffling. A child whimpered.

'I have preached falsehoods. I have not told you the truth. For years I have come before you here, in the house of our Lord, and led you astray. I preached to you of a God who was forgiving, a God who was gentle, a God who was loving. I was wrong.'

When the child whined again, it was hushed. There was no more foot-shuffling. The listeners were straining to hear the surprising things the Reverend was saying. He seemed tense and feverish, as if he were suppressing some great fury.

'I led you to believe,' the Reverend went on, 'that the way of our God was a tree-shaded lane where sweet cherry blossoms wafted down upon you and me as Jesus led us by the hands like little children into a land of innocence and joy, where evil and sorrow shall be no more. If you sinned, you were assured of his compassion. If you stumbled and fell by the wayside, you could always be sure that he would help you up, wipe away your tears, and accept your repentance.

'No more!' he suddenly shouted, and slammed his hand down on the opened Bible. 'A calamity has fallen upon us, and, oh, my brothers and sisters, this calamity was willed by God. It was willed and foretold by he who sent the plagues against Egypt and caused the first-born of every family to be killed, innocent and sinner alike. He sent the Black Death against the great cities of medieval Europe and the dead and dying were hauled away, yes, hauled from the very churches where they had gathered to ask for God's protection. Hauled away by the thousands! The hundreds of thousands! All to be dumped naked and anonymous in collective graves. Innocent children screamed with their dying agony, and priests fell writhing in pain upon the very altars of their worship.'

He paused. Sweat was beginning to bead his forehead, and he was becoming visibly agitated by an uncertain mingling of fear and vindictiveness. Small, restless noises were heard among the congregation, who had had enough of calamity, who wanted comfort, not condemnation.

'And now,' he said in a lowered voice, 'there is another plague upon the world – a plague more powerful, more evil, more merciless and horrifying than the bubonic plague, whose victims were at least vouchsafed the blessed relief of death. But what of the plague that is upon us? Shall we die from it? No! Not yet! As foretold in Revelations, this is the time when – and I quote – "men shall seek death, and shall not find it; and shall desire to die, and death shall flee from them." That's the fate that our good, kind God has condemned us to.'

He faltered for a moment as if befuddled, as if he had forgotten where he was. He gripped the lectern with both hands, steadying himself, and a peculiar expression passed across his face. It came and went so quickly, however, and was so incongruous, that nobody was really sure he had seen it: an expression of impish delight, as if he had been on the verge of saying some naughty word but had suppressed the impulse.

'We read in Revelations six:thirteen, "And the stars of heaven fell unto the earth, even as a fig tree casteth her figs when she is shaken by a mighty wind." Yes, it happened here – here, in Mendocino. They fell, and were the avatars of a monstrous evil. "Meteorites" we called them.' He paused for a moment, and then in a voice of sarcastic mimicry, he added, 'Look! Aren't they pretty! Like heavenly fireworks.' Then in a booming voice of sudden disgust, he shouted, 'Bullshit!'

The word seemed to surprise him as much as it did the congregation, and to them it was almost like a slap. The listeners glanced at one another with wide questioning eyes, as if to confirm what they had heard.

The Reverend, recovering from his initial shock, murmured a sheepish apology for the vulgarity. Mopping his feverish face with a handkerchief, he explained that he hadn't been quite himself lately, and hoped they would forgive him.

Once he had regained his composure, he went on to tell them that the meteorites that had fallen upon Mendocino were more than just heavenly fireworks. On the contrary, he said, the meteorites had been the harbingers of their damnation.

' "And he doeth great wonders, so that he maketh fire come down from heaven on the earth in the sight of man." That's also in Revelations, where the end of the world is prophesied. A time of overwhelming calamities and plagues, and rivers that run red with the blood of the slaughtered! A time when "the nations are angry, and Thy wrath is come. And the time of the dead, that they should be judged". In chapter eleven, verse three, we're told that the Beast – the *Beast*! Satan himself! – shall ascend from the bottomless pit and make war against men. "The Beast", as we're told in chapter seventeen, verse eight, "The Beast that thou sawest was, and is not . . . behold the Beast that was, and is not, and yet is."

'Is this gibberish? No! It is prophecy, a foretelling of the time when the Beast shall return to make demons of men, as he has done at least seven times in the past. Oh, yes! This is not the first plague of demons, but merely the last. The Beast that *was* is the Beast that *is* once again. Oh, yes! The seventh seal is broken! Seven times he has risen from the bottomless pit to make war against man, and the seventh shall be the last. "And he causeth all, both small and great, rich and poor, free and bond, to receive a mark in the right hand, or on their foreheads – and it shall be called the mark of the Beast!"

'He is here! He has come among us again, that Beast, and for the last time. He walks among us tonight. Chapter fourteen, verse eleven: "And the smoke of their torment ascendeth up for ever and ever, and they have not rest day or night, who worship the Beast and his image, and whosoever receiveth the mark of his name." '

There was a brief dramatic pause. Reverend Boyle, sweating profusely now, glared accusingly at the congregation. Then he said in a vicious whisper, 'The Beast is the master! It was he who put the mark upon the mutants! He who sends them to stalk our forests and cities! To murder and contaminate! He who turns our loved ones into demons, and sets upon them the reeking slime of hell's own bottomless pit! The Beast! The chimera!'

Among the congregation, some were frightened and beginning to cry. Some muttered in bewilderment and anger. Others, a few who were sitting near the aisles, got up and left the church. But whatever their individual reactions, they all shared a growing astonishment at the sweating, hysterical clergyman who seemed to be cruelly flailing them with the constantly increasing terror of their nightmare world. What was the matter with him? Had his suffering driven him mad? It had certainly begun to seem so.

'And where has God been all this time?' he cried. 'Where is our merciful and loving and all-powerful Saviour? Has he willed this upon us, and then deserted us? Has he turned his back upon our cries? For help? While the Beast from the bottomless pit – even now! Even at this very minute – may be entering your homes to befoul you and your loved ones with his evil slime? Where is God? Where is that sonofabitch?'

A collective gasp went up from the audience. And with this blasphemy, they began to realise, slowly at first, muttering to themselves, that what was wrong with the Reverend might be even more serious than insanity. His voice was growing steadily deeper, and his eyes were beginning to burn with hostility.

And now people who weren't near the aisles were beginning to leave. A vague, befuddled panic began to flutter across the crowd.

'Where are you going?' the Reverend yelled at the backs of those who were departing. 'You can't face the truth, can you? Can you? You can't face the fact! That your God is in league with the Devil! That the angel of pestilence is God's angel!' He snatched the Bible from the lectern and shook it at the departing people. 'Face it! Your God is against you! Your God is a liar! A trickster! He doesn't give a shit about you!'

Then he laughed and ripped a handful of pages out of the Bible. He flung the pages to the floor. And with every passing second, the realisation grew among those who remained in the church, transfixed, that what they were seeing was a man turning into a mutant before their very eyes.

A woman screamed. At that, those who were leaving began to push at the people in front of them, trying to get out. Almost everyone was up, stumbling and pushing, and the tension in the church was nearing the flash point of panic.

Raging at them as they retreated, the Reverend shook his fist. 'Can't you face the truth? Can't you? Bastards! Fuck you! Fuck you and your God!' He ripped more pages out of the Bible and went through the motions of using them for toilet paper as he screamed maniacally, 'I wipe my ass on him!' He roared with mirthless laughter after completing each wiping gesture, and flung the pages at the departing congregation. When he was finished ripping the pages, he threw down the mutilated Bible and stomped on it. Then he ripped the lectern out of the pulpit and flung it aside. He flailed the air with his hands and shouted at the madly scurrying people, 'Run! Run and hide! But you can't escape . . . the Beast! The Beast is the master! He will . . . find you! He walks among . . . us! The Beast is the . . . master! Master! Master!'

As the last of the pushing and screaming congregation stumbled out of the church, two squads of helmeted soldiers who had been alerted by one of the fleeing congregation began to push their way in. With carbines and automatic rifles at the ready, the soldiers were quick to follow their lieutenant's orders to take up positions in the aisles and in the doorways. They aimed their weapons at the man on the dais.

'You there!' the lieutenant shouted. He held a .45 automatic at port arms. It was cocked. His face, like the faces of his men, was shiny with the protective fungicide salve. 'You there! Lie down on the floor. Face down. Don't resist and you won't be hurt.'

The Reverend shouted defiant obscenities. He reached down and, with the strength of many men, picked up the overturned lectern and flung it at the soldiers. It crashed into the seats near them.

'Fire!' the lieutenant shouted.

Each of the eight soldiers who carried carbines probably fired at least once, but when the two who carried the automatic rifles opened up, the spray of their bullets cut across the Reverend's body like scythes. Gushing blood from a score of wounds, his body, turning and falling, slammed against the large wooden cross at the rear of the dais. He clutched desperately at the crosspiece, trying to hold himself up. But now the bullets from the automatic rifles tore into his back and, exiting from his body, knocked large splinters off the cross.

'Cease firing!' the lieutenant shouted.

In the terrifying, cordite-smelling silence of the church after the echoes of the rifles had died away, the soldiers stood and watched the body of the mutant as it sank slowly to the floor, leaving a long smear of blood down the face of the bullet-shattered cross.

35

Bobbi was at the apartment. She had worked six hours that day as a volunteer at one of the refugee centres, and had returned to the apartment about an hour ago. She hadn't wanted to miss Sander in case he called from the hospital. She hadn't allowed herself to hope that he might actually come home, and so she was all the more delighted when he did. She ran to meet him at the door, embraced him, kissed him, and was moved almost to tears by the look of profound hopelessness on his face.

'I need a drink,' he said.

'Sit down. I'll make you one.'

But he followed her into the kitchen.

'Are you hungry?' she asked as she took ice cubes from the refrigerator. 'I could make you something.'

'No. I shouldn't stay long. Should get back to the hospital, I guess. But I wanted to tell you about Lacy.'

'So, that's it,' she said as she turned to face him, assuming from his expression that it was bad news. 'She's dead?'

'No, no, no. On the contrary, she's responding favourably to a new antibiotic we developed, the first one to be effective against the disease.'

'My God, you found a *cure*?'

'Maybe. Looks like we might have, anyway. Lacy's responding favourably, and so are a couple more test cases. With Lacy, slime secretion had stopped entirely by the time I'd left the hospital, and she was able to recognise people again, talk to them.'

Bobbi clapped her hands. 'Why, that's wonderful!' She rushed to him and threw her arms around his neck. 'Can I see her? I want to see her, Sandy. Can I talk to her?'

In a voice that matched the futility reflected in his eyes, he said, 'I suppose so. Why not?'

She was puzzled. 'But that's not it,' she said, scrutinising his face. 'There's something that you're not telling me, isn't there? Otherwise, you'd be happy that you finally found a cure.'

He sighed. 'It's too late. We didn't find it in time.'

'Too late?' She looked at him. 'What d'you mean?' And when he failed to respond, she said, 'What is it, Sandy? What's going to happen?'

'How about that drink?'

Apprehensive now, she went back to the sink, mixed him a Scotch-and-water, and said, 'At the high school centre today there was talk . . . rumours . . . that if the disease couldn't be stopped any other way, we were going to get . . . bombed. Like in China. They say that's what happened in China.'

He snorted. 'My, my, rumours sure get around, don't they? That comes from living in a small town.'

When she handed him his drink, she said, 'Is that it? Are they going to . . .'

After taking the first swallow of the drink, he said, 'Would you want to know? If it were true, I mean?' he tried to make it sound like a purely hypothetical question.

After a moment's reflection, she said, 'I guess it'd depend.' She turned back to the sink and did what she very seldom did: poured herself a drink, a strong one.

'On what?'

She shrugged. 'On lots of things.' She took a drink of the Scotch and shuddered, almost gagged, but held it down. 'But in this case, yes, I would, I'd want to know. Is that it, then? Have we got only a few hours left?'

He pressed the cold tumbler against his forehead. 'As of now, yes. Unless something happens . . .'

'But the antibiotic?'

'Won't stop it. A nuclear strike is apparently the only thing that'll do that.' He drained his drink.

Bobbi took another gulp of hers, shuddered again, and the shock to her throat caused her voice to break. 'How long?' She cleared her throat. 'How long have we got?'

'Till two o'clock in the morning.'

She glanced at the clock on the wall. 'Six hours? Only six hours?'

He nodded. 'I'm sorry. I shouldn't've said anything.'

'No, I'm grateful that you did. It's going to take a little while to get used to the idea, though.' Her hand was shaking when she tipped the glass up, drained it, and then put it down so she could embrace him. Her arms went around his waist and she pressed her face against his chest. She didn't want him to see the tears in her eyes.

'Anyway, it's supposed to be top-secret stuff. I wasn't supposed to tell anybody.'

'It's better that you did. Now's not the time to have secrets, is it, so I'll tell you one. I haven't told you before now because I was afraid you might not . . . Oh, hell, what difference could it possibly make now?' She was crying.

He stroked her hair. 'What is it, love? If it doesn't make any difference, then it won't hurt for me to know, will it?'

'It might,' she said. 'It might make things worse – harder for you – knowing that I'm pregnant, but that's it, I am. I didn't tell you before because I didn't know if you'd want it, and I wanted it. I wanted it so much, a child by you.'

'Don't cry,' he said, still stroking her hair. 'Let's not waste any time with tears. Let's not think about it.' But he was talking to himself as well as to her. He had emptied himself of hopes, prepared himself for death, and now he didn't want to think about how life might have been *if* . . . The irony was too grim to bear.

She made a strenuous effort to pull herself together, straightening up, bracing herself, wiping the tears off her face. 'Yeah, you're right. No time to waste on being sad. I just want us to be together till . . . it happens. I want to spend every minute we've got left, with you.'

'I should go back to the hospital,' he warned her.

'But why, if it's hopeless?'

'I don't know. Except just to keep fighting it as long as we can. When the time comes, I'd hate to think there was something more I could've done that I didn't do.'

'Then I'll go with you. I can see Lacy. I can help around the hospital. Anyway,' she said as she clung to him tightly, 'I'm not going to let you go unless I can come with you. I'm not going to be separated from you again.'

36

Chris Jordan came home for dinner that day and fell asleep at the table. He had been getting only three or four hours of sleep a night for the last three nights, and he could no longer hold his eyes open. He was practically asleep on his feet.

Marge managed to get him into his pyjamas and into bed. Determined that he was going to get some rest before he dropped, she turned off both the telephone and the radio unit. But before she turned off the television, she learned from a news bulletin that the Reverend Boyle had contracted Lawson's disease and had been killed in his church.

'It's suspected that there are at least four more mutants at large in the Mendocino enclave,' the newscaster said, 'and the army expects to apprehend them within hours. In the meantime, residents are warned to take every precaution: lock all windows and doors, and stay off the streets until the mutants are caught.'

Marge knew that if Chris learned the mutants were at large in the town, he would force himself to get up and join in the search for them, and for a few minutes she considered telling him. If the situation was getting that bad, maybe sleep wasn't so important, after all. Still, there were certainly enough soldiers in town to track down and kill four mutants, so what did they need with Chris? Let him rest for one night, at least; tomorrow he could begin again.

She made certain that all the windows and doors were locked, and she got Chris's pump shotgun from the office and took it with her when she called Adrianne to go upstairs to bed.

Adrianne asked if she could sleep with Chris and Marge that night because she was afraid to sleep by herself in her own room, and Marge said yes. She wanted Adrianne near. She didn't know what might happen, but she had a premonition that the growing menace and evil that seemed to lurk there beyond her windows in the murky darkness was coming closer to her and her loved ones.

'Wait,' Adrianne said, 'I have to get Pupo. He always sleeps with me.'

But the puppy was not in the house. He had been put outside earlier so that he wouldn't wet on the floor during the night, but he hadn't come back. Adrianne wanted to go and get him, but Marge wouldn't allow her to open a door to call the dog. Adrianne cried.

Marge said, 'Now listen to me! Stop that! He can stay outside for one night. It won't hurt him.'

'But, Mommy, he'll get cold, and he never – '

'No!' Marge said, raising her voice, feeling her fear edging towards hysteria. 'I said no! Now, Adrianne, be a good girl. We've got enough trouble without your making more. Now, come on, get into your jammies.'

So they went upstairs and went to bed. Adrianne got into bed beside her mother, who was in the middle. Chris was sprawled on the other side, snoring fitfully and loud.

Marge herself was soon asleep, turned towards Chris and cuddling up to him, but Adrianne was too upset to sleep. She kept thinking of the puppy outside in the cold, and soon she began to imagine she could hear him, a small whining sound coming from far away. She listened, and at times she thought it might be the wind, it was so thin and far away, but at other times she was sure that it was her puppy, probably downstairs at the door, crying to be let in. Adrianne wanted to wake Marge and ask her to go down and get the dog, but she knew her mother was very tired, almost as tired as her Daddy, in fact, because they were helping to fight some terrible thing that was happening. Adrianne didn't understand what it was, but she knew that it was some sort of terrifying sickness that turned people into monsters. It frightened her just to think about it, but it frightened her even more to think that her puppy might get the sickness if he had to stay outside all night. So she lay awake a long time, listening to the whines, and finally summoned up enough courage to go downstairs by herself and let the puppy in the house.

At last she slipped out of bed in the darkness and quietly, very quietly so she wouldn't wake Mommy or Daddy, tiptoed down the dark stairs to the kitchen. The whine was louder now, coming from somewhere in the backyard. She turned on the kitchen light and put her ear against the door leading to the yard. Yes, she could hear the whine clearly now.

She turned on the outside light before she unlocked the door and opened it a crack. It was then she saw the strange light in the sky. It was coming from a helicopter that was hanging low in the air about a block away from the house. A huge searchlight on the helicopter was shining down on the ground, flashing about as if searching for something.

She had hoped the puppy would be at the back door, waiting to come in, but it wasn't. 'Pupo?' she called softly, and heard the puppy's answering whine. She knew now that he was hurt. She had never heard him whine like that except when he was hurt.

She went outside to look for him. The ground was cold and wet on the bottoms of her feet, and she knew her Mommy would be very angry if she knew she had come out without her shoes, but the puppy was there, somewhere in the shadowy darkness beneath the ivy-covered arbour in the backyard, and she didn't want to go back into the house without him.

'Pupo?' she said. 'Here, boy. Come here.'

She found him where he lay near the dark edges of the arbour. He was sprawled grotesquely on the ground. He didn't wag his tail or run to meet her. He didn't move. He looked up at her, whining, and she knelt beside him.

'What's the matter, Pupo? Are you hurt?'

He was wet. There was a glistening substance on his fur, a shiny substance, and she got it on her hand when she reached out to pick him up. It was then she heard the noise, the phlegm-rattling sound of breathing, coming from the darker shadows in the back of the arbour. Peering searchingly into the shadows, she saw a huge man trying to hide in the darkness under the arbour. He was staring at her. He was naked and covered with a glistening sheen of slime.

She screamed.

Marge was the first to hear the screams. 'It's Adrianne!' she shouted. 'She's downstairs!'

Chris, jolted awake, jumped out of bed, knocking over the bedside table; then he had to hesitate for a moment to get his bearings. Marge was scrambling out of bed. She raced to turn on the light, crying, 'It's Adrianne, oh, my God, something's wrong with Adrianne!'

Chris dashed for the door.

'The shotgun!' Marge cried.

It was standing beside the door. Chris picked it up without breaking stride and threw a round into the chamber as he rushed down the stairs, two and three at a time. When he entered the kitchen, he held the shotgun at his hip, ready to fire.

Adrianne had dashed screaming for the house, but the mutant had caught her just as she came through the kitchen door. He had caught her, picked her up, and was hugging her to him, placing a hand over her mouth to keep her from screaming.

Chris couldn't fire when he first entered the room for fear of hitting Adrianne, but as soon as the mutant saw him, he dropped the child and lunged for Chris with a furious roar, a roar that was cut off abruptly by the greater roar of the shotgun. It was aimed at the mutant's face, and it was at point-blank range. The mutant, with his face a sudden mask of blood and splintered bone, was knocked backwards by the blast, and before he finally fell sprawling in the open doorway, he had been shot twice more, both times in the chest.

After standing over the mutant and putting another charge of buckshot into his head to make certain he was dead, Christ turned to Adrianne, who was crumpled on the floor, crying and trembling and trying to wipe the slime off herself. He laid the shotgun on the table and started to reach down for Adrianne.

Marge cried, 'Don't! Don't touch her!' She was standing in the doorway. 'Please, Chris, wait till I get it!' She whirled and raced to the downstairs bathroom, where the fungicide was kept in a plastic container. She was opening it when she ran back into the kitchen.

Chris snatched it out of her hands. He knelt above Adrianne. 'Close your eyes! Tight!' he told her, then poured the disinfectant over her in a stream. He touched her to turn her over, and Marge, near hysteria now, cried, 'Don't! Chris, don't touch her till – !'

But he did. He ripped her pyjamas off, flinging them aside, and poured the fungicide over her body and into her hair, which was matted with slime. Then he picked her up.

'I'm taking her to the bathroom,' he said to Marge. Adrianne, crying hysterically, threw her arms around his neck. 'Stay away from us,' he told Marge. 'Don't touch us.'

'I'll call an ambulance,' Marge said.

'No!' he ordered. 'You're not to call anybody!'

He took Adrianne into the bathroom and put her in the tub. He poured the rest of the fungicide over her head and down her shoulders, and washed the crevices of her body with it. She strangled and cried out when he poured it into her nose and around her mouth.

'Daddy, it stings!' she cried. 'Daddy, don't! You're choking . . . It stings, Daddy, it stings!'

'I know, sweetheart,' he said, holding her hands, 'but it's got to be done. Be brave, honey, it's got to be done.'

Finally, it was done, and he washed her off with hot, soapy water.

Marge stood in the doorway of the bathroom. Trembling and crying, she said, 'Please, Chris, we've got to get you both to the hospital. To a doctor.'

'No,' he said again in an uncompromising voice as he dried Adrianne with a towel. 'You know what'll happen if we take her to the hospital and she has it. You know where she'd have to go.' Then to Adrianne, he said, 'It's okay, honey, we won't let them take you. You're going to stay right here and I'll stay with you.'

Marge buried her face in her hands.

Chris wrapped Adrianne in another towel. She was sniffling and trembling now, in a state of shock. She didn't understand what they were saying about her. She hugged Chris as he picked her up and carried her out of the bathroom and up the stairs to her own room. He put her in her bed and covered her with an extra blanket. Marge started to help, but he motioned her away.

'Don't take chances,' he said. 'Stay away from us.' To Adrianne, he said, 'Sweetheart? Listen, I'll be right back.'

'Don't leave me.'

'I'll be right back. Mommy'll stay here with you.'

First he went downstairs to the kitchen and got the shotgun, then went back upstairs to his bedroom and took the small aluminium container from the pocket of his jacket. He carried it and the shotgun back to Adrianne's room. After leaning the shotgun against the door moulding, he crossed to Adrianne's bed and placed the aluminium container on the night table.

Marge, standing at the foot of the bed, was beginning a groan of horror that threatened to become a cry, until Chris said, 'Marge! Listen to me, now. We've got about two hours before we'll know. If she has it . . . Listen, now. If she has it, I'm not going to let them take her. They'd take her to the compound, and you know what's happening there. You've seen that smoke coming from there. I'm not going to let them do that to her.'

'But what if . . . ?' She was making a supreme effort to keep control of herself. 'The soldiers. What if they heard the shots? They'll come to investigate and – '

'That's why I want you to leave. Go next door, or at least downstairs. Tell 'em not to come up here after her. I'll kill anybody who comes up here to get her.'

'Leave?' she cried, incredulous and betrayed. 'Leave you? No, Chris! I won't do it. I'm going to stay here with you and Adrianne.'

When she moved towards him as if to embrace him, he recoiled and said, 'Goddamnit, Marge! There may be . . . if the soldiers come before we know for sure, there'll be shooting. You can save yourself. You can still do that. Don't be a fool, Marge.'

And now, finally in control, she said, 'No, I won't do it. I won't leave. You're the fool if you think I will.'

He sighed with a sort of infinite weariness, and when she saw that he wasn't going to argue anymore, she moved towards him with opened arms. They embraced.

37

Sander and Bobby arrived at the hospital shortly before dusk. He took her directly to the room where Lacy was being kept. Yoshimura was in the room, checking on Lacy's progress, which had been steady and increasingly more rapid as the weakening organisms lost their hold on her.

Slime secretion had stopped altogether, and Lacy was now beginning to look like herself again. Even her skin was apparently returning to a semblance of its normal cellular functions as the dying amoeboid cells relinquished their mutating powers.

But she was still strapped and straitjacketed. She had been bathed and her skin had been examined by an epidermologist from the Special Tactics Unit. Afterwards, the plastic canopy had been replaced on the gurney. 'Simply as a precaution,' Yoshimura had told Lacy, though everyone agreed that she was no longer capable of contaminating anyone.

'It stinks in here,' she told Bobbi when Bobbi asked how she was doing. 'This straitjacket is wet and slimy. Jesus, Bobbi! You can't imagine how glad I am to see you! Where're Mom and Dad? They all right?'

Bobbi stood at the head of the gurney with her hand lying on the canopy, a symbolic way of touching her haggard and horror-scarred sister. 'They're fine. They're staying in the high school centre. They – '

'What?' Lacy said. 'High school centre?'

'Oh, you don't know about that. Well, since you've been sick . . .'

While the sisters talked, Sander took Yoshimura aside and

asked him about the other mutants who had been administered the actinomycin.

'Responding favourably,' said Yoshimura, who looked very tired but optimistic. 'And we'll have enough of the antibiotic in a few hours to start treating a dozen more. In fact, it looks so good that Colonel Parker has ordered the compound to shut down.'

It was only with great effort that Sander could carry on conversations like this, knowing how futile they were, knowing that within a few hours, in spite of everything they could do, they would all be dead, not gassed at the compound or killed by the disease, but killed by the only method they had of stopping it. But there seemed no alternative to forcing himself to believe that something might yet make a difference, to go on talking, grasping at straws.

Professor Roget, very excited, hurried into the room. 'So there you are,' he said to Sander. 'They told me you were back. There's something I need to ask you.' His excitement was that of a little boy who has discovered a treasure and is dying to tell somebody about it. 'I've been trying to get Sheriff Jordan on the phone, but he doesn't answer, so I thought you might be able to tell me, since you were there at the Hopkins house. Did you happen to notice any *holes* about the place?'

Sander blinked. 'Holes in the ground?'

'Yes, yes, a hole in the ground. A well, maybe?' he said. 'Had anybody dug a well there?'

'I don't recall seeing one, but I wasn't looking for one, either. This is Bobbi Coors,' he said, nodding towards Bobbi. 'You might ask her. She used to live there.'

Bobbi had stopped talking to Lacy as soon as she heard the name Hopkins mentioned. She stared curiously at Roget, who turned upon her a face that was bright with hope.

'You lived there?'

She nodded. 'For a while last year.'

'Is there a well there?'

'Yes. Richard dug it last summer.'

'And how deep is it, do you know?'

She thought for a moment. 'Fourteen feet.'

'You're sure it's that deep?'

'Positive.'

Roget clapped his hands. 'That's it!' he said, and turned to Sander and Yoshimura, who were squinting with puzzlement. 'That's where the organism came from. The well.' There wasn't a trace of uncertainty in his voice. 'It came from the well.' He looked as if he could hardly contain his excitement, as if he might at any moment do a dance around the room.

Sander's voice betrayed his scepticism. 'You're sure of that?'

'I'm sure,' Roget said. 'I have solved the mystery of the organism's origins! I was only waiting to make sure about the hole on the Hopkins property. Now that I know, I'm going to phone General Blanchard. Why don't we make it a small staff conference while we're at it?' He glanced at his watch. 'I'll meet you in the small conference-lab in five minutes.'

Eight men showed up for the conference. Sander and Hoffmann were among them, as were James Newman, Yoshimura, Colonel Parker, and D. B. Sheftman. Roget, who sat at the head of the small table, got General Blanchard on the phone, then switched the call to monitor so that everybody could hear everything that was said.

'General Blanchard, I have some wonderful news for you,' Roget said. 'We're having a staff meeting here now, and you're on the monitor speaker, so feel free to interrupt at any time to ask questions of me or any of the others present.' He went on to name those present, and then launched into a dissertation by announcing that he had solved the riddle of the origin of the organism that was causing Lawson's disease.

'And let me say at the outset that it didn't come from outer space.' He glanced at Newman. 'Nor did it originate in a

Russian laboratory.' He looked at Hoffmann. 'The fact is, General, and it is a *fact*, my original hunch was right: the damned thing has existed right here on earth for at least thirty thousand years.'

He pointed to a map of the world that he had placed on a pedestal behind him. Different areas of the map had been shaded in with different colours, and many of the coloured areas overlapped on the edges. 'See that?' he said to those present, and then to Blanchard he said, 'Sorry you can't see it, General, but what the others are seeing is a map of the world that shows areas in which there have been previous outbreaks of Lawson's disease.' Then he quickly took a sheaf of papers from his attaché case. 'And here's the proof,' he said, holding the sheaf up as though it were the torch on the Statue of Liberty. 'Remember, General, that I said I was conducting a computerised study of the fossil spores that had a certain resemblance to this organism? My colleagues and I collected data from all over the world, put the data into a computer, and here's what we got.'

Blanchard took advantage of a slight pause to ask, 'Do I understand you correctly, Professor? This isn't the first outbreak of the disease?' His voice issuing from the monitor was thin and metallic.

'That is absolutely correct, General. There can be no doubt about it: the disease has been epidemic in different areas of the world at least seven times – seven *different* times – during the last thirty thousand years.'

Roget paused, accepting the stunned silence as an accolade. Like most short men and bantam roosters, Roget often seemed cocky. In his case, however, the cockiness didn't seem to be merely an overcompensation for his small physical stature. It seemed, instead, to be a self-congratulatory delight in his own intellectual prowess, about which he had no doubts at all.

'How did we do this?' he asked rhetorically, as though establishing a dialogue with himself. 'Well, first of all, by dating many hundreds of the quasi-fungoid fossils that have been found throughout the world – that is, by dating the sedimentary strata in which they were found. Also . . .' Here Roget paused again, as if trying to suppress a pixie-like smile, and then said, 'Well, General, do you recall Reverend Boyle's thesis on pre-Christian demonology? The one he tried to bring to the President's attention?'

'I'm not likely to forget it,' Blanchard said. 'Why?'

'Well, sir, believe it or not, it turned out to have some information that proved very valuable to us.'

'On demons?' Hoffmann asked.

'On Lawson's disease,' Roget said. 'You see, what he did – unknowingly, of course, but nonetheless did – was to document historically the last two outbreaks of Lawson's disease. In fact, it was due to his research that we were able to pinpoint the exact year and place of the last outbreak: it was exactly three thousand, one hundred and eighty years ago.'

'And you got that date from Reverend Boyle?' Blanchard asked in a voice that made it sound as if he were ready to dismiss the whole thing.

'We got this information from an inscription on a bronze bowl that came from the ancient feudal kingdom of Hsiung-nu in northern China, which is one of the locations where the last outbreak of Lawson's disease occurred. And for those of you who don't already know it,' Roget added archly, 'the principal city of Hsiung-nu was Nan Shan.'

Now there was no doubt that he had everyone's undivided and suspenseful attention.

'Luckily enough,' Roget continued, 'the Chinese at that time had developed both a calendar and a crude form of ideographic writing. That's how we know.'

Blanchard seemed to be mustering his last reserves of scepticism when he asked, 'And you've got scientific evidence to back that up? Something more than just an inscription on a bowl?'

'Indeed, we do,' Roget said. 'We have evidence to show

that there have been at least seven previous outbreaks, and they've appeared with what seems to be an astonishing regularity of about every three thousand years. Furthermore, the areas covered in each of the seven different outbreaks seem to be very small for a disease with such an irresistible force. As far as we can determine, the disease never at any time covered a whole continent, say, or even a territory as large as our own country. For instance, the yellow area on this map shows the approximate boundaries of the last outbreak that took place about three thousand years ago in this part of North America – which, of course, would probably make it simultaneous with the outbreak in China. Unfortunately, our methods of dating the spores by determining the age of the sedimentary strata in which they're found can't be done with any exactitude. In dating sedimentary strata, we usually have to allow for a margin of error of about two or three hundred years. Also unfortunately, the natives of this country at that time – unlike the Chinese – had developed neither a calendar nor a written language sophisticated enough to leave us any helpful historical accounts. However, there were some Indian pictographs found in a cave in New Mexico that seem to substantiate what we already know from our scientific data: that the disease did, in fact, appear in that area of the country at about that time.

'In point of fact,' he added in his most authoritative voice, 'as shown here on the map – the yellow areas – the disease covered an area from as far south as the Rio Grande to the northern coast of California. More specifically, Mendocino County itself. In fact, the Pygmy Forest.'

For a moment, having orchestrated this information to a climax, Roget paused, then added in a less dramatic voice, 'That's something I hadn't known till a few hours ago: that there'd been fossil spores resembling our quasi fungoid found right here in Mendocino County. They were found five years ago by a colleague of mine, Professor Robert Boler, who was in charge of a Geological Data Bank Programme for the Department of the Interior. The spores were found in a core sample taken from the Pygmy Forest at a depth of eight feet.'

He looked at Sander. 'That's why I wanted to know about the well, you see? Because that's where the spore came from that started this epidemic.'

Blanchard interrupted over the monitor. 'What's this about a well?'

'The well at the Hopkins house,' Roget said. 'It was dug deeper than eight feet, which marks a sedimentary stratum that was laid down three thousand years ago – at about the time of the last outbreak of this disease. Whoever dug the well, dug up a spore or spores that have lain dormant since the last outbreak. By a very lucky – lucky for it, not for us – confluence of circumstances and chances, the spore found the conditions right for germination.'

There was a momentary silence, then Blanchard said, 'And there was an outbreak of the disease in northern China at the same time?'

'Since the dates are so close,' Roget answered, 'I think it's logical to assume that the outbreaks were concurrent.'

'And do you have any idea how widespread the disease became in China?'

'No, sir. This is a computer-produced map based on the varying ages of the fossil spores that have been found in many different areas of the world. Unfortunately, we have no information about such spores being found in China. It's only been during the last twenty-five or thirty years that mycologists have begun to develop a real interest in this quasi-fungoid fossil, and during those years, as you know, sir, China hasn't been inclined to share any scientific information of any kind with us or anybody else. The only evidence we have that the disease appeared in China at that time is the inscription on the bronze bowl – that, and, of course, the obvious assumption that the disease recently recurred there, just as it did here, a little over three thousand years later.'

Unable to contain himself any longer, Hoffmann broke in by asking, 'But what's the meaning of this apparent three-thousand-year gap between outbreaks?'

With an elaborate shrug, Roget said, 'Who knows? The only thing we can infer, obviously, is that this highly evolved quasi-fungoid species – and that's what it is, gentlemen, make no mistake about it – it's a highly evolved but primordial life force, as old as man himself, no doubt. It's a species unto itself: not a mutation, not a chimera, but a very unique species that has coexisted with man for at least thirty thousand years, and probably from the time when man became chromosomally defined. In fact, without man, it obviously couldn't exist.'

He hesitated. 'But where was I? Oh, yes! Noah, you were asking about that three-thousand-year gap between outbreaks. Well, look at the map. Seven different outbreaks during the last thirty thousand years, each of them occurring at approximately three-thousand-year intervals. The last one occurred in China and North America in the year 1200 B.C. The one before that occurred in North Africa and the Middle East, approximately 4000 B.C. The one before that occurred in the Mediterranean area and stretched to what is now central Russia, and that was around 7000 B.C. That outbreak, by the way, also occurred in North America around Lake Superior, as you can see on the map. And so on – all at approximate three-thousand-year intervals.

'Well, then,' he added, 'it seems the only thing we can do is infer that it's cyclical. It apparently lies dormant for that period of time, then bursts out in a fury of virulence, and then just as mysteriously stops.'

Blanchard said, 'What stops it? I mean, haven't you got *any* idea?'

'None at all,' Roget admitted. 'And what makes it so mysterious is the relatively small areas that each outbreak covers. Obviously, the duration of each outbreak must be fairly short, or it would've covered – well, how long would it take to cover the whole continent at the rate it's going now? Of course, the population density among the primitives that lived here three thousand years ago was only an exceedingly small fraction of what the population density is today, so it wouldn't have spread as fast as it's spreading now. Still, I think it's safe to assume the outbreaks didn't last long, or the disease would've covered the whole continent.'

Blanchard said, 'So when you say the outbreaks were "fairly short", it's only a deduction on your part?'

'A logical deduction, yes, sir.'

Hoffmann said, 'What about dating the geological strata in which the spores are found? You said you couldn't be very accurate in that?'

'Except in special circumstances, when dating geological strata, the best we can hope to do is narrow it down to a margin of about two hundred years. But as I said,' he insisted, 'the outbreaks couldn't have lasted that long, or the disease would've spread throughout the whole continent. Especially in China. And we know that it didn't. Otherwise there would be numerous historical references to it in Chinese history and legends.'

Blanchard's tone had a get-down-to-basics tone when he said, 'Look here, Professor, there's something I want to ask you: how do you *know* the fossil spores you and your colleagues found are the same organism that we have here?'

Roget grinned. He obviously held a trump card. 'Very simple, General,' he said. 'We germinated them.' He paused for effect. 'You see, General, my staff and I, during the last few days, managed to locate over a hundred spores of this very unique species, and I asked my colleagues in the botany department of each university and college where the spores were being kept – I asked them to see if they could germinate them.

'Of course,' he said, 'they'd tried this before. It's routine, you see? When mycologists find any fossil spores, they attempt to germinate them. Routine experimentation. Well, sir, I discovered an amazing thing: no one had ever succeeded in germinating spores of this particular quasi fungoid – until now. Today, five of them germinated, and, General, they are *identical* to the organism that's causing Lawson's disease.'

Sander interrupted. 'But why didn't they germinate before? You said it was routine to try to germinate fossil spores when they're found?'

'Yes.'

'Well, then? If all the spores found in Mendocino proved to be viable today, why weren't they viable years ago when they were first found?'

'Exactly!' Roget said, and grinned again, this time in tribute to Sander's question. 'Why didn't they? That's the crux of the matter, you see? The spores left over from the last outbreak, the ones that were found here in northern California – they all became viable at the *same time*, after having lain dormant for a period of roughly three thousand years.'

Hoffmann said, 'Then the ability of the spores to germinate is a matter of periodicity, rather than opportunity?'

'Exactly,' Roget said again. 'To answer Sander's question, the spores didn't germinate before because it wasn't *time* for them to germinate. That's the obvious cycle, you see? Every three thousand years the spores become viable, and if they meet the proper conditions, they germinate. It's the same kind of cyclic principle that we see operating in the century plant, which blooms every one hundred years.'

'And if they don't meet the proper conditions for germination?' Hoffmann asked. 'Do they stay viable for another three thousand years?'

'No,' Roget answered. 'They die. They become true fossils.'

'Then only the spores from the previous epidemic are capable of germinating?'

'That's correct. That's what we learned when I asked my colleagues in the various universities to try to germinate all the fossil spores of this species that they had. The spores that were older than three thousand years didn't germinate. They had become true fossils. Therefore, you see, the propagation of this remarkable species is entirely dependent upon the spores produced by the preceding epidemic. That is at least one handicap that nature put upon it, to prevent it from completely overwhelming the human species.'

'You're sure of all this?' Blanchard said from the black monitor.

'Yes, General,' Roget said. 'I am positive.'

'I want to get on the wire to Washington immediately about this, but I don't want to waste the President's time with just another theory.'

Roget seemed a little piqued when he said, 'General, I tell you for a *fact*: the quasi-fungoid organism that's causing Lawson's disease has existed on earth for at least thirty thousand years, and there have been at least seven previous outbreaks of the disease that've occurred at intervals of approximately three thousand years. That much is indisputable.'

'Well, then,' Blanchard said after a slight pause, 'is there anyone there who *isn't* convinced by your findings? Professor Hoffmann, for instance – Professor?'

'Yes, General?'

'You thought the disease was caused by a germ-warfare agent. What do you think now?'

There was a short pause as Hoffmann, puffing on his empty pipe, deliberated the question, then said, 'His evidence is incontestable, and his conclusions sound. I was wrong. Professor Roget is right.'

'Thank you,' said Roget, obviously quite pleased with Hoffmann's endorsement.

Blanchard said, 'All right, then, how about you, Mr Newman? You there?'

'Yes, sir, I'm here,' Newman said.

'What about it? Still think it might be from outer space?'

'No, sir,' Newman said, without hesitation. 'I couldn't prove my theory. Professor Roget has proved his. I'm convinced.'

'So that's it,' Blanchard said in a tone of finality but of only slight relief. 'Thank you all, and especially you, Professor Roget. I have to hand it to you, you've done one hell of a job. Unfortunately,' he added in a more sombre tone, 'you can't tell me how long the outbreaks lasted, or what stopped them.'

Again Roget shrugged, and because he had no neck to speak of, his shoulders lifted almost to the level of his ears. 'No, that I cannot do. The best I can do factually is to set the outer limits of the last outbreak at about two hundred years' duration. As for what stopped it – who knows?'

'Two hundred years,' Blanchard said meditatively, then sighed and said, 'Hell, we don't have two days.' After another short pause, he added, 'We have only a few hours. So,' he said after taking a deep breath, 'your findings are not the miracle we've been looking for. However, I am grateful, and I congratulate you. At least we can consider the matter of its origin settled, and they'll be glad to hear that back in Washington. They'll be glad to hear that the Russians were telling the truth for once. Also, we'll see that your findings are relayed on to the Chinese, and, if they believe us, maybe we can head off a nuclear war. That's a tribute to you, Professor Roget. You have our deepest gratitude and admiration, I assure you.'

Roget beamed with pleasure. 'Well, I had a lot of help from a lot of people. And we'll keep working on it.'

'You do that, Prof – '

The general's voice suddenly stopped, cut off in the middle of a word. The line had gone dead.

When he realised what had happened, Roget picked up the telephone and flashed the operator. 'Hello? Hello?'

The switchboard operator spoke over the monitor. 'Yes, sir?'

'Operator, we were cut off. We were talking to General Blanchard in Mendocino. What happened that we were cut off?'

'Just a moment, sir,' the operator said, and left them sitting there in the silence of returning despair. For a while they had all been caught up in the excitement of Roget's discoveries, and with excitement had come a desperate flicker of renewed hope. But Blanchard had doused that flicker when he reminded them that Roget's discoveries hadn't really changed their predicament at all. Without the knowledge of how long the previous outbreaks had lasted, or what had stopped them, they were no better off than before.

'I'm sorry, sir,' the operator said suddenly, 'but all the lines to Mendocino are dead. They must be down somewhere. I'll check with the phone company repair crews and see if – '

'Hurry, please!' Roget said. 'It's important that I speak to General Blanchard again.'

'I'll do my best, sir,' the operator said.

'I'll wait at this number. Ring me back as soon as you get a line operating, do you hear?' When he returned the phone to its cradle, he sighed heavily and said to the others, 'There was something else I wanted to tell him.'

The others stared at him expectantly.

'Those caves in New Mexico,' he said. 'There've been excavations in them, and I understand they're a tourist attraction now. If that pictograph was right . . .'

When Roget's words trailed off into a morose silence, Sander finished the statement for him: 'There'll be viable spores in the caves.'

Roget nodded. 'Maybe we shouldn't wait for the phone to be reconnected. A messenger might be quicker. Those caves have to be sealed off. If the disease should break out there, too, we'd really be lost.'

38

The telephone lines that connected Mendocino with Fort Bragg were broken at twelve minutes after ten that night. The break was caused by a helicopter gunboat. A reconnaissance patrol of paratroopers had spotted one or more mutants in a cypress cove just north of road-block M-3. The patrol leader had brought his men back to the road-block and called for a gunboat strike on the cypress cove.

The helicopter was there within five minutes, and within five more minutes the cypress cove, lit by parachute flares, was saturated with machine-gun bullets and rocket explosions. One of the big sidewinder rockets slammed into a cypress tree, toppling it, sending it crashing against a telephone pole, and snapping all the telephone lines between Mendocino and Fort Bragg.

Even the hot line in General Blanchard's office was temporarily disconnected. The hot line – a direct telephone connection to the White House that didn't go through any switchboard or secretaries – had run through Fort Bragg, but after the cables were broken, the hot line was rerouted through Ukiah, an operation that took nearly twenty minutes to complete.

So it was 10.32 P.M. when Blanchard, using the reconnected hot line, reported Roget's findings to the President in the NSC room in the basement of the White House. Blanchard abridged Roget's report considerably, but he stressed that all the top-level scientists on the project were now certain that the organism that caused Lawson's disease was not a Russian germ-warfare agent.

'Well, I'm mighty glad to hear that,' said the President. He sounded exhausted, and it seemed that the more exhausted he became, the thicker his country drawl became. ' 'Deed, I am. And I'll have Hubert get on the hot line to

Peking immediately, if not sooner, 'cause it looks like they're just hours away from war with Russia. So you tell that Professor out there – what was his name? Roget?'

'That's right.'

'You tell him for me, Gen'al, we surely do 'preciate what he's done. What all of 'em's done. Fact is,' he said, and a note of dry humour crept into his voice, 'you can tell 'em that from now on I'm not going to go around calling professors pointy-headed intellectuals anymore. However,' he added, and now his voice was suddenly grim again, 'it doesn't do you people out there much good, knowing that it's not a Russian recombinant, does it?'

'No.'

'Doesn't put you any closer to stopping it, does it?'

'I guess not. We only know that it did stop. Unfortunately, we don't know how or why it stopped, and can't predict with any precision how long the outbreaks lasted.'

'Two hundred years, didn't you say?'

'That seems to be the extreme outer limit, yes, sir, although Professor Roget is convinced the outbreaks lasted considerably less time than that.'

'What was that, an educated guess?' the President asked with undisguised scepticism.

'Something like that.'

'And on the basis of that, can you honestly recommend that we postpone the strike even two hours, let alone two days, or weeks, or months?'

'No, sir.'

'I mean, do you think we can run the risk of *any* kind of postponement? Now, I realise that question puts you in a hell of a bind, seeing as how it's your life at stake, but just remember, now, I got the country to think about, Gen'al. The world.'

'I understand, sir, and, no, I'm not recommending postponement.'

'The fact is, Gen'al . . . ' There was an implicit warning in the way the President's voice faded and died. 'Well, about that strike, now. What it boils down to is this: everybody on the council here agrees that the situation out there is out of control. For instance, we got a report just a little while ago that a town called Boonville had so many mutants inside it that it was going to be abandoned. That right?'

'Yes, sir. The people there, the ones who aren't suspected of being contaminated, are being taken to the Cloverdale enclave in an armed convoy.'

'But sure as hell, there'll be a few contaminated people among them, isn't that right? So then there'll be mutants inside the Cloverdale enclave?'

'Very probably, yes, but that can't be helped. It's an impossible situation, Mr President, and that's the truth of it. There's just no way we're going to be able to control or stop this thing with – '

'My point exactly,' the President said, interrupting. 'So what it boils down to is this: subject to your approval, we've decided to move the strike ahead two hours.'

Blanchard automatically glanced at the clock on the wall. 'To twenty-four-hundred hours?'

'That's right – unless, of course, you have some compelling reason to wait. But the way things look from here, if we hold off till two o'clock, we run the very real risk of the disease reaching San Francisco. If that happens, we'll have to include that city in the strike, or let the whole country become contaminated.'

Blanchard nodded. 'You're right, of course. Well, then, as far as we're concerned out here, two hours could hardly make that much difference, I guess.'

'So be it, then,' said the President. 'I'm really sorry, Gen'al. Honest to God sorry. I'd about as soon die myself as have to do this, but . . . well, like I said, I got the country to think about.'

'I understand, sir. In your position, I'd do the same.'

'The Chinese had to do it.'

'Yes, sir.'

'Well, then . . .'

'I understand, sir,' Blanchard insisted. 'I concur.'

'You're a good man, Gen'al. God bless you.'

After Blanchard hung up the phone, he sat and stared at it for a long time, unblinking, hardly breathing, almost catatonic with fatigue and hopelessness.

39

The three ICBMs were scheduled to be launched from LeMay Missile Base near Black Hawk, Nebraska. Three missiles of the 3rd Strategic Missile Squadron had been chosen to make the strike on Mendocino because the Russian targets at which they had been previously aimed were at the bottom of the Strategic Air Command's target-priority list. So the three Minuteman missiles were retargeted for the northern California quarantine area. Their guidance system computers had been programmed with a high-altitude saturation pattern.

They had originally been scheduled to be launched at 0135 hours, Western Standard Time, on 18 February. However, launch time had since been moved back two hours, to 2335 hours on the seventeenth. Detonation time would be about two minutes before midnight on 17 February.

The ICBMs were in underground silos at Launch Complex Four. A maze of underground cables connected the silos to the blockhouse control room, which was a series of rooms carved out of granite fifty feet below the earth's surface. Inside the main control room was a vast array of electronic consoles, television monitoring screens, computers, clocks, telephones, radar screens, and banks of instrumentation indicators.

Six hours before launch time, the teams of technicians poured into the control rooms and into the missile silos to check out their communications channels and their electronic consoles. During the check-out, amber and green and red lights on the consoles flashed, bathing the interior of the blockhouse in a multicoloured glow. The lights and the flickering meters, the clipped voices of men speaking through headsets and loudspeakers, the closed-circuit television pictures of the three ICBMs in their silos two miles away – all combined to give the blockhouse the appearance of a spaceship.

The countdown officer, a major who was hatless like the rest of the team, stood on a raised concrete platform in the middle of the blockhouse, facing the battery of consoles and monitoring screens. He was standing behind a counter. Before him on the counter were telephones, microphones, and a panel of electronic buttons and switches. At precisely six hours before launch time – T minus 360 minutes – the countdown officer said, 'Arm and set safeties on Minuteman X-four, -five, and -eight.'

At eleven o'clock that night, Sander was getting ready to leave the hospital. There seemed to be no point in staying. Nothing more could possibly be accomplished in the short time they had left.

'Where will you go?' Hoffmann asked.

They were in Sander's office. They drank from paper cups filled with Scotch.

'They won't let you out of Fort Bragg, you know.'

Sander had taken off his smock and now wore his raincoat, on the lapel of which was pinned his red clearance pass. His brown hair was as rumpled as his coat.

'I don't know,' he said as he leaned across the cluttered desk and drained the last of the Scotch into Hoffmann's cup. 'Just get out of here – out of this stinking hole.' He glanced around the room. 'I hate this Goddamned place.'

'Do you really?'

'It stinks of failure,' he said. 'Of death.'

'Oh, come, come, Sander,' Hoffmann responded in a

slightly bantering but completely humourless tone. 'You're too much of a scientist to equate death with failure.'

He shook his head. 'Scientist? Not me. And I guess that's the reason I never will be. Scientists are the Fausts of our time. To you, knowledge is everything. To me, life is. And death is the failure of life. What else could it be?'

'The completion?' Hoffmann suggested.

Sander drained his cup, glanced at the clock. 'Two hours and forty-seven minutes to completion,' he said as he rose from his chair, his movements ponderous and laboured. 'I'd better be going. Bobbi's waiting for me in the lobby.'

'I'll walk down with you.'

Sander took one quick look around the office before he turned out the light.

As they were going down the stairs, Hoffmann said, 'Well, I envy you – having someone to be with, I mean. I think of Isa . . .'

They didn't speak again until they reached the lobby, where Bobbi was waiting at the reception counter. She was wearing a raincoat with a white scarf around her neck. Sander took her arm and the three of them moved away from the noisy and crowded reception area to a quieter spot near the guarded entrance. Sander turned to Hoffmann and held out his hand. Both men had the laboured movements of zombies, Sander especially. He had numbed himself, deliberately, and with the help of alcohol, because he was afraid and didn't want to panic as the clock ticked nearer the hour of their deaths.

Hoffmann said, 'Good-bye, Miss Coors – Bobbi. I'm sorry we didn't have a chance to know each other better.'

'Good-bye, Professor.' She shook his hand, and didn't trust herself to say more.

They had already turned to go when Yoshimura hailed Sander. 'There you are, both of you,' he said to Sander and Hoffmann as he approached. 'They told me you were leaving,' he said to Sander. 'I hoped I'd catch you. Excuse me,' he added politely to Bobbi, then turned back to Sander and continued the sentence, 'because there's something I think you ought to see before you go.'

Sander couldn't be sure, but there seemed to be a glint of suspended excitement in Yoshimura's voice, as though he believed that what he could do might still make a difference.

Seeing Sander's reluctance, he said, 'It may be important.' To Hoffmann, he said, 'Professor? I think both of you will find it most interesting.'

Sander said to Bobbi, 'Do you mind? I'm sure it won't take more than a few minutes.'

Bobbi nodded her assent, and they touched hands as he walked away, following Yoshimura and Hoffmann.

They hurried down the corridor of Wing C, past the room where Lacy was being kept, to a room where there was another mutant in one of the specially made capsules. This was the McGettigan mutant – a child, an eight-year-old boy named Morry McGettigan, who had gone up the Albion River on a mushroom hunt with his mother three days before. He had been one of the twenty-four mutants that had been kept in the hospital as a test case. He was in a room by himself.

As soon as the three men walked into the room, the boy began shouting at them, cursing, but the capsule's intercom was turned off and they couldn't hear him. The three men gathered around the plastic canopy and stared down at the boy. Then Sander switched his gaze to Yoshimura, who was on the opposite side of the capsule.

'Well?'

'Watch,' Yoshimura said. 'It'll happen in a minute.'

But Sander was impatient to leave. 'Couldn't you just tell us what it is?'

'It's better if you see it, and then we can decide if we agree on what it is. There,' he said. 'Watch now.'

A shadow seemed to flicker across the boy's slime-covered face. His curses faltered, and in his eyes for a moment, like a light pulsing on and off, the child's terror seemed to alternate with the mutant's hostility. It was the child's terror that lingered.

Yoshimura quickly switched on the intercom. 'Morry?' he said. 'Morry, do you remember Professor Hoffmann and Doctor Quence?'

The boy was whining. 'Why am I? Here? Where's my mother? I want . . . my mother.'

The realisation of what he was seeing hit Sander like a jolt of electricity. He and Hoffmann exchanged amazed glances, then he grabbed the clipboard that hung from the foot of the gurney. He thumbed hastily through the forms and graphs on the board, and said to Yoshimura, 'But he hasn't been on actinomycin.'

'That's right,' Yoshimura said. 'He hasn't. Now let's go across the hall.'

Across the hall was the room where two other mutants were kept, one an old man named Johnson, the other Richard Hopkins. They, too, were being held as test cases. But since they weren't under plastic canopies, they couldn't be approached closely, and therefore couldn't be given food, water, or medication. They had been without food or water for three days. Their wastes had spilled out on to the gurneys on which they were strapped, causing the sealed room to stink like a cesspool.

The three men stopped just inside the door.

'Please,' the old man said as soon as he saw Yoshimura. 'You said you . . . would . . . give me some water.'

'It's on its way, Mr Johnson,' Yoshimura said. 'An orderly will be here in a few minutes with food and water for you, and soon you'll be able to have a bath.'

Richard Hopkins said, 'Tell them to . . . hurry. Get us out of here.'

In a tone barely above a whisper, Sander said, 'My God! Them, too?' He and Hoffmann exchanged dumbfounded glances, and both made a conscious effort to suppress their growing excitement because they dared not believe that what the evidence indicated was true: 'Then it wasn't the actinomycin. It only *speeded up* the process.' To Yoshimura, he snapped, 'The cultures! Did you check them?'

'No. I went to get you and – '

Sander bolted out of the room, followed closely by Hoffmann and Yoshimura. In a pace just short of running, he dashed towards the lab. But first he stopped at the reception counter. 'Carol,' he said, 'you know where Professor Roget is? Get him! Have him paged. Tell him to report to the lab *immediately*. And see if you can get through to Mendocino, yet.'

Bobbi had left the visitors' sofa where she had been waiting and was now at his elbow. 'What is it, Sandy?'

'Haven't got time to explain,' he said as he whirled and hurried down the corridor.

Hoffmann and Yoshimura had got ahead of him, but he caught up with them just as they were entering the lab.

The lab wasn't as crowded as it was in the daytime, but there were perhaps fifteen technicians still there, and they all looked up from whatever they were doing when the three men burst into the room.

The cultures were kept in a far corner of the lab. Dr Ted Cassidy was there. He had been running some routine experiments with the cultures, but at the time that Sander and the others had come in, Dr Cassidy had just made a startling discovery. Sander could guess what it was, and Cassidy, when he looked up from the microscope and saw Sander and the others there, could guess what had brought them there in such a hurry.

'Then it's happening in the cultures, too?' Sander asked when he saw the look on Cassidy's face.

'Yes,' Cassidy said. 'The damnedest thing I've ever seen. They're all going dormant.'

'You've checked *all* the cultures?' Hoffmann said.

Cassidy nodded. 'All of 'em.'

'In both your youngest and oldest?' Yoshimura asked.

'*All* of 'em,' Cassidy said triumphantly. He looked at Sander. 'But you said "too" a minute ago. Does that mean it's happening in the patients?'

'Yes,' Sander said, and he could feel the exhilaration, the swelling hope, like floodwaters behind the crumbling dam of his scepticism. 'And all this time we thought the actinomycin was effecting the cure, when actually it was just speeding it up. What we've got,' he announced to everybody who had gathered around, but then decided to be more cautious, 'What we've *apparently* got is a spontaneous remission.'

'There's no doubt about it,' said Professor Roget, who had just entered the lab. Everyone turned to him. 'I've just been on the phone to a colleague of mine at the University of Colorado.' To Sander and Hoffmann specifically, he said, 'He happens to be the botanist who germinated the spores that were found in the Pygmy Forest five years ago. Well, he just got through to me on the phone, and told me that all the amoeboid cells in his cultures are turning into spores, and all the spores are going dormant.'

'It's finished?' asked one of the incredulous technicians who had gathered around. 'Is that what it means?'

'Yes,' Roget answered, smiling broadly. 'A spontaneous remission.'

'Why?' someone asked. '*How?*'

'The time factor,' Roget said. 'The periodicity factor. We knew that it became viable after every three thousand years or so, but what we didn't know was *why* it stopped, once it had broken out. Well, what stopped it was *time*. It – and I'm talking about it as though it were one gigantic creature, because that's essentially what it is, a *being* made up of all the millions of cells in the bodies of countless mutants – it sleeps for about three thousand years, then wakes up for a few days, a week, maybe, probably no more than two hundred hours, ravages the human species, and thereby produces enough new spores to ensure that it will survive for another three thousand years. Then a biological clock of some sort triggers all the cells in the vast creature to begin closing down at once, to go to sleep for another three thousand years.'

'It's *over*?' one of the technicians cried, and the cry set off a wave of elation that swept over the crowd. 'It's finished!' But then, as if it were too good to be true, he had to have reassurance. 'It really is, isn't it?' he asked Sander. 'It's really over?'

'It really is,' Sander said, though he himself was not quite able to take it in.

Jubilation ensued. It was like a victory scene after the end of a long and hard-fought war. There were shouts and handshakes and hugs. Some began to cry and others began to dance.

But Sander wasn't caught up in the jubilant mood. Turning to Hoffmann, he said in a voice edged with alarm, 'The missiles!'

40

At LeMay Missile Base, inside the blockhouse at Launch Complex Four, the countdown officer said, 'Stand by to initiate sequence,' and pushed a button on the panel that started and synchronised the countdown clocks. When he received verification from the silos that the countdown clocks had started, he said, 'Initiate sequence. Start telemetry evaluation.'

The next order he gave was to remove the silo covers. This operation could be seen on the closed-circuit television screens: pictures of the massive silo covers sliding smoothly back to reveal the missiles – each as tall as a five-storey building. Their lacquer-shiny surfaces gave them the ominous appearance of death-dealing machines from other worlds.

'T minus thirty minutes and counting,' the countdown officer said 'All personnel clear the silos.'

He received verification in ten minutes, and then said, 'T

minus twenty minutes and counting. Maintain silence, and no smoking in the blockhouse for the remainder of the countdown.'

He glanced at the bank of clocks on the left wall. The clock that kept Western Standard Time read 2315 hours – 11:15 P.M.

Sander and Hoffmann ran from the noisy lab and down the corridor to the reception counter in the lobby.

'Carol,' Sander said, interrupting her at something. 'Are the lines to Mendocino still out?'

'Yes, Doctor. The phone company says – '

'Can you reroute a call to Mendocino through Willets and Ukiah?'

Sensing the urgency of his request, she said, 'We could, but the lines are jammed and the calls are backed up for over an hour.'

'A top-priority call – how long would that take?'

Carol wasn't sure. 'Twenty minutes? I don't know. Maybe longer. The army's tied up every line.'

Sander glanced at his watch. It was 11:23 P.M. 'If the highway is open, we could drive there in about ten minutes,' he said to Hoffmann. But then he had another idea. 'Carol. Get me the Sheriff's Headquarters on the phone.' While she dialled, Sander turned to Hoffmann and said, 'The Sheriff's Headquarters can get through to Chris Jordan on their radio, and he can get the message to Blanchard.'

But all Carol got was a busy signal.

Hoffmann interrupted Sander's curses of impatience. 'Let's do it this way, Sander, just to make sure: you drive to Mendocino and I'll stay here and keep trying to get through on the phone or radio. That way – '

Sander shook his head. 'Blanchard might hesitate to call off the strike on my word alone. He'll probably think I've panicked, that I'm making it up. I'll need you for confirmation.' To Carol, he said, 'Keep trying.'

'Wait,' she said. 'It's ringing.' She handed the phone to Sander.

It rang for what seemed like minutes before the dispatcher finally answered. Sander identified himself and told the dispatcher to radio Chris Jordan in Mendocino immediately.

'We've been trying to do that very thing, Doctor,' the dispatcher said. 'But we've had no contact with him or Marge since early this evening. Either they're away from the radio, or they've turned it off.'

Sander had to think fast. 'Look. This is an extreme emergency. Keep trying to get him. If you do, tell him to get a message to General Blanchard immediately. He's to tell General Blanchard to cancel Contingency Plan B-3. Is that clear? *Stop Contingency Plan B-3.*'

'Yes, sir, I'll keep trying, but – '

'And have one of your deputies meet us at the Noyo River road-block in – ' he glanced at his watch, which read 11:27 – 'in three minutes.'

'I'll see what I can do, Doctor,' said the dispatcher in a tone of weary but grudging compliance. 'But the deputies are all out on other calls and – '

'Never mind the other calls!' Sander cried, nearly grinding his teeth. 'Just do what I tell you: have a deputy at the Noyo River road-block in three minutes.' He abruptly hung up the phone and turned to Carol. 'Did you hear what I told her?'

Carol nodded.

'Get on the phone, try to get a top-priority call through Ukiah to General Blanchard in Mendocino. Tell him what I told the sheriff's dispatcher: tell him to stop Contingency Plan B-3. Better get Roget up here to back you up on it. He's in the lab. Okay?' he asked, but before she could answer, he had already turned to Hoffmann. 'Let's get going.'

They started towards the door. Bobbi had been standing next to him since he came from the lab, and now she fell in beside him and Hoffmann as they started for the door. Sander stopped.

'Not you,' he said. 'You'd better stay here.'

'No,' she said. 'I don't know what's happening, but I'm going to stay with you. We agreed.'

He hadn't time to argue. 'All right,' he said. 'But hurry.'

As they raced towards the parking lot, Sander told Bobbi enough to satisfy her curiosity about what was going on, and the three of them, unified by urgency, climbed into the front seat of Sander's Mercedes. Sander raced the car through the streets of Fort Bragg, the streets deserted now except for occasional military vehicles, and reached the Noyo River road-block at 11:32, only to be told by the lieutenant in charge of the road-block that they wouldn't be allowed to go through.

Speaking to Sander through the opened window of the car, he said, 'I'm sorry, but I have my orders: no one is to be allowed through.'

Sander and Hoffmann got out of the car to argue with the lieutenant. They told him who they were, showed him their red clearance passes, and while they were arguing, Deputy Carl Gotlieb drove up and skidded to a stop in his patrol car.

'That's a no-man's-land out there,' the lieutenant was saying, still adamant but becoming a little intimidated by their insistence and urgency. 'And there're no more escort units to see that you get through in case the mutants – '

'But there won't *be* any mutants!' Sander said. 'It's *over*. I've told you the epidemic is over, damnit. The mutants are in a process of reversion, so they're – '

'I'm sorry,' the lieutenant said. 'I have my orders.'

'What's going on?' Carl said as he got out of his patrol car.

Hoffmann snapped, 'Lieutenant, do you have a field phone here? Get your superior on it, please; I want to talk to him.'

Sander said to Carl, 'Stand by. We want you to take us to Mendocino as soon as we get this mess straightened out.'

The lieutenant, growing more sullen and unsure of himself, took Hoffmann to the army van that stood beside the machine-gun emplacement on the shoulder of the pavement.

While Hoffmann was gone, Sander spent his time impatiently reassuring Carl and a few soldiers who had gathered around him that, yes, the epidemic was over, and there would be no more mutants. But they obviously couldn't reconcile his assurances with his desperation.

Hoffmann and the lieutenant emerged from the van at 11:37 P.M. 'We're cleared,' Hoffmann said. 'Let's get the hell out of here.'

The disgruntled lieutenant ordered the soldiers to open the road-block.

'Let's go with the deputy,' Sander suggested, and they hurried into the patrol car, Hoffmann in the front seat with Carl, Sander and Bobbi in the back seat.

'Get there as fast as you can without having a wreck,' Sander told Carl.

The tyres squealed as the car lunged through the opening in the road-block and started across the Noyo River Bridge.

The countdown proceeded without interruption until T minus thirty-one seconds, at which time the countdown officer gave the order to 'Push launch initiate', and the countdown was transferred from human control to computers in the ICBMs themselves. Thereafter, all directions came from programmes in the computers which sent out check signals. If the computer in any one of the missiles didn't receive proper answers, the countdown on all three ICBMs automatically stopped.

It happened at T minus eighteen seconds: a red light flashed on the console for ICBM X-eight.

A console operator said over the intercom, 'We have a red on warhead instrumentation, X-eight.'

The countdown automatically stopped.

The patrol car, with Carl Gotlieb at the wheel, was going sixty miles an hour by the time it crossed Noyo River Bridge, and by the time it got to the city limits, it was going eighty.

'Don't kill us,' Hoffmann said. 'It's necessary that we get there alive, if any of us are to live at all.'

Carl slowed down, at least on the curves, and he had his siren and red light going even though there wasn't another car on the highway.

'What's going on?' Carl wanted to know. 'If the epidemic is over, how come you're talking about us not living?'

'Wait,' Sander said from the back seat. He leaned forward to talk to Carl. 'Your radio – can you get the army headquarters on it?'

'No. Army radios are on a different band.'

'Try Chris, then,' Sander said.

'They've been trying to get him all night.'

'Try again.'

Carl left the siren off long enough to grab the microphone and say, 'Car ten to Station seven, you read me?' He steered the car with his left hand as they raced down the dark road. 'Station seven? Chris? Marge? Are you there? Over.'

Nothing but static.

'There's something wrong there,' Carl said in a voice filled with foreboding. 'It's not like Chris or Marge to turn the radio off. Never done it before.'

'After you drop us off in Mendocino, go by his house and see what's the matter,' Sander suggested. Leaning back in the seat, he clutched the side strap with his left hand, steadying himself on the tyre-squealing curves. His right hand was held by Bobbi, who clutched him as hard as he clutched the strap. Like a frightened child, she sat close to him, as if there were some security to be gained by body contact.

'Yeah, I will,' Carl said. 'But now what about it? I want to know why we have to get to Mendocino so fast.'

Hoffmann said, 'We're scheduled to take a nulcear strike at two o'clock this morning. We have to get to General Blanchard before the missiles are fired.'

The speedometer needle jumped from seventy to eighty. 'Hold on to your hats,' Carl said.

'No, don't get us killed or delayed by a wreck,' Hoffmann said. 'We have time.' He held his wristwatch to the lights from the instrument panel. 'The missiles are supposed to be launched at one-thirty-five, our time. It's eleven-forty-two now. That gives us time to get there without risking a wreck. If we should have an accident, word may not get through in time to stop them.'

Carl had already begun to slow down, but by then they were approaching the lights on road-block M-3 at the mouth of Lansing Street. Carl hit the siren again, loudly and insistently, as he neared the road-block, signalling the soldiers to hold their fire.

'Halt!' came the order from a loudspeaker when the car got within twenty feet of the road-block.

Soldiers came out of the floodlights to surround the car, their rifles and pistols at the ready. Badly frightened, they wouldn't have hesitated to fire at anyone who looked the slightest bit threatening.

A captain came to Carl's window and bent down to survey everyone in the car. 'What're you doing here?' he demanded. 'Nobody's supposed to be on this highway tonight.'

Hoffmann leaned towards the driver's side. 'We have to see General Blanchard, and we have no time to lose. It's a matter of the greatest urgency, Captain.'

The captain was doubtful. 'Wait here. I'll phone the CO and see what he says.'

Hoffmann was quick and emphatic. 'There's no time for that, Captain. You must let us through immediately. All our lives may depend on it.'

The captain had started to walk away, but turned to listen, then shouted into the lights, 'All right, open it up. Let 'em through.'

'T minus twenty seconds and counting,' said the countdown officer as his eyes constantly scanned the flashing consoles and monitoring screens.

Minuteman X-eight had been temporarily scrubbed. It had been disengaged from the remaining two missiles, and the countdown had resumed.

The only constant sound in the blockhouse was a low sibilant hum as the seconds ticked away to within twenty seconds of launch. The countdown was being conducted by the computers in the missiles themselves, and the countdown officer called out the seconds more and more often as they diminished.

'T minus eighteen seconds, and all systems are go.'

At exactly T minus twelve seconds, a fail-safe code from SAC headquarters was fed into the ICBMs' computers. Green lights flashed on the consoles, and the countdown officer announced, 'We have fail-safe clearance on both birds. T minus ten seconds and counting: nine . . . eight . . . seven . . . six . . . five . . . four . . . three . . . two . . . one . . . zero.'

Batteries of green and amber lights flashed on the consoles, and the countdown officer announced, 'We have ignition, both birds.'

On the closed-circuit television screens they could see pictures coming in from inside the silos – upward shots that showed the looped cables and hoses breaking away from the bodies of the ICBMs. Then the picture suddenly became blurred by white smoke, at which time there was a switch to other cameras on towers a hundred yards from the silos. Now, as a low rumbling roar began to be heard and the earth began to tremble, the picture showed the missiles thrusting slowly out of the earth like gigantic snakes slinking out of their holes.

'We have lift-off, both birds.'

A storm of dust and smoke obscured the images of the missiles for a moment, but even through the dust the blast from the nozzles could be seen. The images rapidly grew smaller as the missiles gained speed, and soon the fiery tails of the missiles were only balls of light on the screens.

'Switch to radar projection,' the countdown officer said.

The pictures were replaced with projections of grid-marked screens, across which a slow, sweeping line of light moved from left to right. The two missiles could be seen as blips rising slowly from the bottom-left corner of the screen. The two missiles still showed up individually on the screen when the countdown officer announced, 'Birds at sixty-five thousand, thirty-two-degrees arc, accelerating to five thousand.'

The two blips had begun to merge when, suddenly, they divided like amoebas.

'We have first-stage burnout, second-stage ignition. The birds are on their way. Detonation predictor shows fourteen minutes to target.'

Among the clocks on the blockhouse wall, the one that kept Western Standard Time showed 11:55 P.M.

At that moment the deputy sheriff's patrol car pulled up in front of Crown Hall Communications Centre. They had first gone to operational headquarters in the Mendocino Hotel, only to be told that General Blanchard was at the communications centre in conference with the President.

And the guards at the door wouldn't let them in. Rather than argue with them, Sander pulled out a small memo pad and scribbled a note that read, 'Epidemic is over, stop missiles,' and gave it to the corporal of the guard.

'Read it,' Sander said. 'Now take it to General Blanchard.'

But the corporal didn't take the note directly to Blanchard. He gave it to his superior, the captain of the guard, who took it to a mjaor on Blanchard's staff, who gave it to Blanchard. So almost another minute passed before Blanchard, with the note in his hand, flung the door open and faced them.

'What the hell is this?' he demanded. He held the door open and motioned them – Sander, Bobbi, and Hoffmann – into the anteroom that adjoined the main communications room.

At first Sander was merely puzzled by Blanchard's reaction. 'It's the miracle you wanted,' he said. 'The epidemic is over. The disease is finished.'

Blanchard looked at Hoffmann for confirmation. 'Is it true?'

'Yes, yes, yes, it's true,' Hoffmann said. 'It's kaput.'

'So suddenly? How's that possible?'

Hoffmann said, 'A spontaneous remission. It began a couple of hours ago, but we didn't realise until – '

Blanchard crumpled the note in his fist. 'God help us,' he groaned.

And now Sander felt more than mere puzzlement. In a voice constricted with dread and terror, he said, 'What's the matter? Are we too late?'

'Yes,' Blanchard said, glancing at his watch. 'The missiles were launched three minutes and fifteen seconds ago.'

41

Blanchard whirled and stormed back into the main communications room. They followed him, Sander saying, 'But you said . . . Goddamnit, you said the strike wouldn't take place until two.'

As soon as they burst into the room, they became the centre of attention for the people whose images were projected on the giant screen at the rear of the hall. Among the faces was the President's, with his familiar pugnacious frown and pomaded hair, a few strands of which had fallen in disarray across his forehead.

As usual the centre was brightly lit and busy with technicians, but at the conference table where Blanchard had been sitting were only three other men: Colonels Culbertson and Parker, and S. Bradley Hunter.

'What is it?' the President asked, staring into the camera at Blanchard. 'What's that all about, Gen'al?'

Blanchard rushed to the microphone on the table. 'Mr President, those missiles, they've got to be stopped!'

And now it was the President and all the top-level civilian and military officials with him who reacted as if they had been struck.

'What?' the President said. 'They've got to be *what?*'

'Stop the missiles!' Blanchard said, and it sounded like an order.

Hoffmann grabbed a microphone from off the conference table. 'There's obviously no time to explain, but you have to believe me, Mr President, the epidemic is over. It's through. You can stop the missiles, can't you? Can't they self-destruct?'

'Of all the Goddamned . . .' The President looked bewildered as he spoke to someone across the conference table from him, someone who couldn't be seen on the screen in Crown Hall. 'Well? What about it? Can they?'

'No,' said an emphatic voice from off-screen; then the camera turned to General Lyman Slater, the Pentagon's chief of air defence, a bald-headed little man with steel-rimmed glasses. 'No, definitely not. For security purposes, the Minuteman missiles can self-destruct *only* if they go off course. And the guidance system is unjammable. So once the Minuteman is launched, it's out of anyone's control. The only way to stop them is to shoot them down.'

The President looked hopelessly bewildered.

'Then do it!' Blanchard said. 'Goddamnit, get on it!'

But General Slater had already picked up the phone in front of him. He switched off his microphone as he began to issue a rapid-fire stream of orders into the phone. At the same time he was issuing orders to the military aides and civilian assistants who sat behind him at the conference table, sending them scurrying for exits and other telephones.

A multitude of voices was talking and whispering at the same time, but the President's came through most clearly when the camera turned back to him. 'All right, then, out there, did you get that? We're going to try to shoot 'em down. Looks like the only chance we have to stop 'em. We'll fire everything we have, and hope for the best. But, damnit,' he continued in the tone of a man who felt he had been betrayed in some way, 'what in God's name is going on out there, anyway? Why should that disease suddenly be over, just like that? What stopped it?'

'It stopped itself,' Hoffmann said. 'It's a spontaneous remission. It was *time* that stopped it, part of a three-thousand-year cycle.'

'It just stopped?' the President said, unable to comprehend what he was hearing. 'All on its own? Just *stopped*?'

It was Sander who said, 'It stopped because the biological clock built into its genetic code told it that it was time to stop.'

'And when did you first find that out?'

'At eleven-twenty-five, just a little while ago, that's when we became sure.'

'Well, then, damnit to hell, man, why couldn't you have gotten the news to us sooner? Just five or ten minutes sooner!'

There was an undisguised rage in Sander's voice. 'The phone lines between Fort Bragg and here are out, so we had to drive, but I'm sure we could've gotten here a few minutes sooner if' – and here his tone became accusatory ' – if we'd been told that the time of the missile strike had been advanced. If you hadn't moved – '

'All right, all right,' the President said guiltily. 'But, damnit, the situation out there had gotten completely out of hand, completely beyond control, and we had to do it or risk letting the disease get into San Francisco. I see now we should've notified you, but . . . well, we didn't think it'd do any good for you to know. I'm . . . I'm sorry.'

'You may be sorry,' Sander said, 'but it's we who're going to be dead if you can't shoot those missiles down.'

But the President had already turned his attention elsewhere – to somebody at his own conference table who was talking. It was General Slater again, who was saying, '. . . fourteen batteries of Nike and three batteries of Condor anti-ballistic missiles within range of the ICBMs. They'll commence firing in a few seconds, as soon as they get radar lock-in. Can we get a DEW Line projection on the screen?'

It was the Secretary of Defence who asked General Slater, 'How long have we got to get them?'

'Eight minutes,' Slater said. 'Ten minutes at best. We have to knock 'em out before they re-enter the atmosphere – at their eighty-five-mile apex, if possible. The deeper they penetrate, the more damage they'll do.' Then he raised his voice so the communications engineers and technicians would know it was they to whom he was speaking. 'Are we going to be able to get a DEW Line projection?'

From somewhere within the communications system an unseen electronics engineer said over a loudspeaker, 'We can give you a radar projection, but it'll have to be on both screens, here and in Mendocino.'

'Do it,' Slater said. 'Keep the audio channels open, but give us the picture.'

And almost immediately the picture of General Slater on the Crown Hall screen was replaced by a picture of a radar screen, the line of light sweeping across the grid lines. And the blip that lingered as the line swept across the screen was one that cast a pall over everybody in the communications centre – including the technicians, who hadn't known until then what the code phrase 'Contingency B-3' had meant. Now they realised what was happening, so they, too, watched the ominous blip on the screen, the radar picture of two Minuteman missiles that were hurtling towards Mendocino at a speed of fifteen thousand miles an hour.

Sander glanced at the WST clock on the wall. Slater had estimated that the missiles would have to be knocked out in ten minutes. If he were correct, then only eight minutes and fifteen seconds remained.

Suddenly eight more blips could be seen on the screen – smaller ones that were arching upwards towards the single, larger one.

The voice of General Slater announced over the loudspeaker, 'There they are, the first salvo of Nikes. They're from our base near Denver.'

But the seconds ticked away in a tense, palpable silence, and it soon became obvious that the Nikes weren't going to intersect with the ICBMs. Their angle of flight was such that they were flying in the same direction as the ICBMs – chasing them, but without the capacity to overtake them.

'The launch was too late,' General Slater said in a disappointed voice. 'The Nikes'll burn up as they fall back into the atmosphere and – But, look there! What we're seeing now are the Nike salvos from bases in Utah and Nevada. There'll be seven batteries firing from those areas.'

He was talking about a blizzard of blips that suddenly appeared on the lower-right side of the screen. Sander didn't try to count them, but he guessed there were thirty or forty of them, all slowly converging on an intercept angle with the onrushing ICBMs. Sander glanced at the clock again: six minutes and forty-eight seconds to go. He looked at Bobbi, who was standing at his elbow. She returned his gaze, and instinctively edged closer to him, but her eyes, as if drawn by a magnet, flashed back to the picture on the radar screen. She was holding the tips of her fingers over her mouth.

'Gen'al Blanchard?' It was the President's voice. 'Are you getting this radar projection out there all right?'

'Yes, Mr President. We're watching.'

Some of the smaller blips were merging as they moved steadily closer to the ICBMs, on collision course.

'The salvos coming in now, they ought to do the job,' the President said hopefully.

But even though the small blips seemed to merge with the larger one, and though they suddenly flared up when they exploded, the larger blip continued its way inexorably across the screen.

'They're missing,' the President said in a critical voice.

After a moment of silence came General Slater's sad admission, 'Yes, sir, they're missing. But it only takes one. If we get one of 'em, they'll both detonate, close as they are.'

The small blips were flaring up all around the ICBMs, flaring like matches, then quickly going out; but the larger blip emerged from the flare-ups undisturbed in its progress.

Colonel Culbertson was beginning to whisper over and over again in a sort of chant, 'Get 'em. Get 'em.'

The voice over the loudspeaker was Slater's: 'There's something! Looks like one of 'em has been knocked off course.'

The larger blip slowly split in two. The diverging portion began going off at about a twenty-degree angle.

'It'll self-destruct in about fifteen or twenty seconds,' Slater announced.

'Will both of them go?' some unidentifiable voice from the NSC room asked.

'No, not likely,' Slater said. 'It's timed so that it won't self-destruct till it gets a safe distance from the other. After all, we could hardly foresee the day when we'd *want* a self-destruct to knock out the others in a salvo.'

The large diverging blip suddenly flared up on the screen, flickered for a few seconds, and vanished.

'It's gone,' Slater said. 'At least eight western states got some light from that.'

But nobody in the communications centre had been looking out the windows to see the dull glow from the enormous fireball in the sky beyond the earth's atmosphere. They continued to stare at the radar screen, watching the remaining Minuteman still coming in, emerging unscathed and undeviated from the flurries of exploding Nike missiles.

'What the hell kind of defences have we got,' demanded the President, 'that we can't bring down one Goddamned ICBM?'

The Secretary of Defence said in a sort of apologetic voice, 'It's the PV shield – polar valence shield – a new device we installed in the Minuteman missiles last year. It's designed to fool the computer guidance systems in enemy antiballistic missiles and cause them to veer off and detonate as soon as they enter the range of the shield. We had high hopes for it, but it's apparently turning out to be more successful than we'd even hoped it'd be.'

Sander checked the time. Three minutes and five seconds left.

'But we'll get it,' Slater said with forced confidence. 'We'll get it. We haven't had the Condors yet. They carry a bigger payload than the Nikes, they'll be able to get close enough.'

Another minute passed before Slater announced that the new pattern of blips coming on to the far right of the screen were the Condor antiballistic missiles from a base near Sacramento.

But, once they converged with the Minuteman blip and flared up, it became apparent to everyone that they weren't having any more effect than the Nikes had had. The Minuteman came through them all, and soon something happened that brought a groan of despair from nearly everyone in the Crown Hall Centre: the Minuteman blip began an ominous nosing downwards.

'Get it! Get it! Get it!' Culbertson continued to chant, his whisper growing more fierce as the missile hurtled towards them.

The eight minutes were up. The Minuteman was re-entering the earth's atmosphere.

It was Blanchard who gave voice to all their worst fears, the inevitabllity of defeat, of death: 'It's coming in . . .'

Bobbi pressed her shoulder against Sander. He put his arm around her. She still had her fingers pressed against her lips, and now she was very quietly praying, 'Please, God . . . Please, God . . .'

There were perhaps forty more seconds of tension mounting steadily to the panic point, and then everyone was startled by a sudden shout from General Slater: 'A hit!' he cried. 'We got a hit!'

He had seen it before the others had. The Minuteman

blip suddenly expanded. It had been hit. The nuclear warhead exploded.

'We got it! We got it!'

Then came the light. Suddenly the darkness beyond the windows was gone, and an eerie light, nearly as bright as the sun, began to pour through the windows, growing, pulsing.

Bobbi buried her face against Sander's chest. He held her tightly and closed his eyes instinctively, turning away from the light; they automatically shielded their eyes, although the light was not bright enough to be blinding.

'Gen . . . Blanchard,' Slater was saying, but the communications system was crackling with a storm of static, causing Slater's words to come through in bits and broken pieces. 'Are . . . get . . . light out . . . now?'

'The light?' Blanchard asked, shouting to be heard above the roar of static. 'We're getting it now, nearly as bright as the sun.'

Slater was still trying to talk. '. . . be a right, th . . . I think. We . . . it high e . . . shouldn't cause you . . . trouble.'

The light was beginning to fade, still pulsing as it faded, and the static had begun to diminish, allowing everyone to hear Slater's voice a little better. 'You'll get the buffeting . . . a second. Don't . . . by any windows, just in case, but . . . think it's . . . bad enough to hurt anything.'

The light had gone when they began to hear the roar and feel the buffeting shock waves at the same time. As the low rumbling sound increased, windows and doors rattled, joints creaked and groaned, and there were metallic sounds of machinery and equipment clattering around them. The roar sounded like distant thunder.

'We got the buffeting now,' Blanchard said.

'How bad is it?'

'Not bad enough to break any windows yet, that I know of. It's easing up now.'

'That's the worst of it, then,' Slater said. 'And since we got it high enough, and it was a clean nuke, you shouldn't have any critical problems with radioactivity. So it's over,' he announced in a self-satisfied voice. 'You're home free.'

A din of voices from the White House began to come over the loudspeakers. Cheers could be heard, voices offering congratulations, exaggerated sighs, nervous laughter, and then a burst of laughter when the President drawled, 'Whoooeeee, boys, I think I'm gonna have to go change my pants.'

But no one in the Crown Hall Centre moved or spoke for a long time. The paralysing fear would not leave them so soon. It would be a while yet before their shock wore off and they could celebrate, before they could congratulate themselves on being alive.

Sander continued to hold Bobbi. She was crying.

FEBRUARY NINETEENTH

42 The burials of Chris and Marge Jordan and their daughter Adrianne took place in the early afternoon of 19 February. They were buried in the small Protestant cemetery on the headlands about halfway between Mendocino and Albion Flats. Bordered by Highway 1 on the east and the ocean on the west, the small patch of cemetery ground was studded with gravestones in the form of slabs and crosses and granite angels that stood on the rocky cliffs, gazing forever with unseeing eyes towards the vast expanse of sky and ocean beyond the ragged edges of the westward land.

It was a rare winter day of no clouds and no wind, a day of meadowlarks and pale, lemony sunlight. A herd of sheep grazed in the meadow below the graveyard, ewes that were fat with lambs soon to be born. Two brown does also grazed in the meadow. The does, mingling with the sheep, looked up now and then to appraise the throngs of people that had gathered in the cemetery, then, satisfied that the people were no threat to them, lowered their heads to munch again on the greening and rain-shimmered grass.

The graveyard was crowded with people who had come to bury their dead. The Reverend Boyle and his son Billy had been buried earlier that day, and other gaping holes surrounded by mounds of raw earth awaited the bodies of others, most of whom had died as mutants during the last hours of the epidemic.

Sander and Bobbi stood among the many mourners and watched as the three coffins that held Chris and Marge and Adrianne were lowered into their graves.

The Coors family – Bobbi included – had arrived at the graveyard earlier to attend the burial of the Boyles. Sander, who had been working at the hospital, hadn't been able to get away in time for the Boyles' burial, but he did arrive at the graveyard just as the mourners were dispersing slowly through the graveyard. As he approached the Coors family, Bobbi came to meet him. She took his hand.

'Come on,' she said. 'Dad'd like to say something to you.'

Hurley Coors met Sander with an outstretched hand. Shyly, and with an awkward smile, he said, 'I'm glad to hear about you and Bobbi. Congratulations.'

Bobbi's mother stepped forward to give Sander a quick kiss on the cheek. 'That's a welcome-into-the-family kiss, but it's also a kiss of thanks for saving Lacy,' she said.

'I'm afraid I can't take much credit for that,' Sander said.

'Yes, you can. You could've let them send her to the compound.'

Sander didn't respond to that. The compound was a subject that would probably cause him nightmares for years to come. Two hundred and thirty-four people had died there, and their ashes had been gathered up to be buried in a collective grave. Still, they had been a lot luckier than the Chinese. At last report, the nuclear blast over Nan Shan had cost over a million lives.

'How is Lacy?' Bobbi asked. 'Did you see her this morning?'

He nodded. 'Just a few minutes ago. She's fine. She'll be sent down to San Francisco tomorrow for the tests.'

It had been decided to send the survivors of Lawson's disease to San Francisco for a battery of tests, both psychological and physical, but what Sander didn't say was that there would probably be other medical complications, other after-effects of the disease, and that Lacy might be in the hospital in San Francisco for a long time. The disease had left encysted spores in the lymph nodes of all the reverted mutants, and there was no way of knowing how long it would take for the patients' epidermal cells to resume normal functions.

Still, the disease had run its course and no one had died directly from it, and satisfactory recoveries were expected in the many hundreds of cases that were now being transported to hospitals in the Bay area for tests and treatment. Lacy was among them, of course, as were Richard Hopkins and Anne Jackson. Anne had been found the morning before by one of the many army patrols sent out to comb the countryside for people who, sick and exhausted and in deep shock, were recovering from the condition of having been mutants.

'Christopher Jordan . . . Marjorie Jordan . . . Adrianne Jordan,' the minister intoned as he tossed a handful of dirt down on to the lid of each coffin. 'We leave your bodies here, but your souls are at rest with God.'

Sander stopped listening. It bothered him a little that the minister, so professionally pious, had never known Chris or Marge, had never even seen them. He had been sent up from Oakland to take Reverend Boyle's place, and now he was just doing his job. He was just one of the thousands of people – relatives, curiosity seekers, and news-media people – who had poured into the area since the barricades and roadblocks had been taken down late last night.

Sander looked up to watch the army trucks, a seemingly endless flow of them, as they roared past, heading south on Highway 1. The army was pulling out. The dangers of a global war were not over yet, but there were reports that tensions were easing everywhere. Even so, there were rumours that the soldiers who were now pulling out of Mendocino would be sent directly to the Middle East, where the dangers of conflict still seemed most acute – 'where', as General Blanchard had said that morning, 'there still seems to be a powder-keg situation'. Blanchard had been speaking at a meeting at Crown Hall, where all the men and women who had been engaged in the fight against Lawson's disease had been called together to be congratulated, praised, commended. Blanchard said that some of them – especially Roget,

Hoffmann, Sander, Yoshimura, and Sheftman – would receive Presidential Citations for their contributions to the fight. They were heroes, Blanchard had said. True heroes.

Sander snorted with disdain when he tried to think of himself as a hero. The others had obviously been pleased to hear that they would receive the decorations, but Sander didn't give a damn. All he wanted was to be left alone, to live and die in peace here in this out-of-the-way place. Let the others cherish the memory of having been heroes during one of the most challenging and exciting and important experiences in the history of the world; to Sander it had been only an ordeal that would haunt his dreams.

'Let us pray,' the minister said.

Like the other mourners gathered around the graves, Sander bowed his head, but he didn't listen to the minister's prayer. And though he stared down at the coffins in the graves, he wasn't really seeing them. What he was seeing were the three bodies as he had first seen them night before last, shortly after the nuclear explosion in the sky. He and Bobbi had been the first to leave the Crown Hall Centre that night, and as they were being driven home to Sander's apartment in an army staff car, Sander noticed when they passed the Jordans' house that two patrol cars were parked in the yard. One of the cars had its red and yellow dome lights flashing, and Carl Gotlieb was standing in the yard beside the car as if waiting for something.

Sander asked the army driver to stop at the house. 'Something's wrong there,' he said, and though it was only a premonition at the time, he knew it was true as soon as he saw Carl's face.

'They're . . .' Carl's voice caught in his throat. 'Doctor, I'm afraid they're all dead.'

Sander was out of the car and going up the walk as he said, 'Where are they?'

Carl followed him as far as the front door. 'Upstairs in the girl's bedroom. Listen, that flash of light a little while ago, was that the – '

Sander bounded up the stairs three at a time, followed closely by Bobbi. The door to Adrianne's room was open, but Sander stopped in the doorway as if he had run up against an invisible barrier. It was the bodies he saw. The three of them were stretched out on the bed, side by side, as if they had laid down to go to sleep.

Sander crossed to the bed. There on the bedside table, open and empty, was the little aluminium container that had held the cyanide capsules. Though he knew they were all dead, Sander reached down to take Chris's wrist, as if to search for a pulse. The flesh was cold, but the degree of rigor mortis indicated that they had been dead only a little while. Maybe an hour.

Sander didn't hear Bobbi come up behind him. He didn't know she was there until he heard her grief-stricken voice murmuring. 'Oh, my God. Oh, my God.' She leaned against the bedpost at the foot of the bed, and when she had looked upon the bodies long enough, she covered her face with her hands. But she didn't cry. One dry sob racked her body, but she had cried too much already. She had no tears left.

When the graveside service for the Jordans was over, the minister and many of the mourners, especially the deputies and their families, simply crossed the graveyard to another burial site, to another freshly dug grave that stood waiting for another coffin.

Sander and Bobbi drifted away from the burial scenes. They were strolling slowly towards the ocean when they heard James Newman call to them. He had been among the mourners at the burial of the Jordans.

'Aren't you two going back to town now?' Newman asked as he approached. His bushy red hair and beard were bright in the sunlight.

'We thought we'd go for a walk,' Sander said.

'It's such a beautiful day,' Bobbi added.

'Sure is,' Newman agreed, looking around as if to make certain that it was. 'Well, then, I won't be seeing you again, so I'll say good-bye now.' He held out his hand to Sander.

'You're leaving, too?' Bobbi asked.

He nodded. 'Flying back to Houston this afternoon.' He seemed very self-conscious, very young.

'Sorry to see you go,' Sander said. 'If you ever get back this way, drop in and see us.'

'I'll do that,' Newman said. He offered to shake Bobbi's hand, but she pushed his hand aside and gave him a hug and a quick kiss on the cheek.

'Write us a letter, will you?' she asked. 'So I'll know where to send the announcement when the baby comes.'

Her kiss had made him blush, so it took a moment for her remark to register on him; then he said, 'What? You mean you two are . . .' He was unable to decide exactly how to put it.

'Oh, it's all right,' Bobbi said. 'We're getting married. I asked him yesterday and he said yes. See?' She held up her left hand with the ring on it. 'It's Sandy's grandmother's engagement ring.'

'It's beautiful,' Newman said. 'Well. Gee, that's great, my congratulations. Well, then, I guess I'd better be going. Good-bye.'

'Good luck, Jim,' Sander said.

' 'Bye, Jim. Be sure and write.'

'I will,' he said over his shoulder as he turned and walked through the gravestones towards the parking lot.

Sander took off his coat as they strolled along the cliffs. He was dressed in a black suit and tie. He loosened the tie and slung the coat over his shoulder. The day was not overly warm, but the pale winter sunlight made it seem so, and there was no wind. Seagulls glided overhead. Now and then a meadowlark bobbled out of the grass, warbled its brief, sweet song, and then dropped back into the grass.

The ocean was calm. It seemed strangely at peace with the land and the unclouded sky. The tide was very low and the swells washed gently across the tidal pools, rolling over the rocks and spilling back into the foamy surf.

Bobbi took off her shoes and carried them in her hand. She was wearing a dark skirt with a black lace blouse and a grey knit shawl.

As they strolled along the paths, sometimes with their arms around each other, sometimes holding hands, they talked idly and luxuriated in their aimlessness.

'Seems like we haven't done this in years,' Bobbi said when they stopped for a moment and sat down on a rock. 'And what was it, only five days ago that it all started? Only *five days*? Seems more like five years.' She had picked up a handful of pebbles. She tossed the pebbles a few at a time over the edge of the cliff and into the surf below. 'God, what a long, strange trip it's been!'

'Well, it's over now.'

'Yeah. But I wonder if things'll ever be the same again? Think so? Think we can ever go back to being the way we were?'

Now and then above the sound of their voices and the gentle surf they could hear the faraway sound of a buoy.

As if he were only half-listening to her question, he said, 'Did I tell you that Hoffmann offered me a job?'

She searched his face to see what response he wanted. 'Oh? What doing?'

'Doing research at Stanford.'

'Researching what?'

Sander himself picked up a handful of pebbles and tossed them over the cliffs as he said, 'Research on Lawson's disease for the Department of Chemical and Biological Warfare.' He snorted. 'Can you believe it? They're going to see if maybe they can adapt it for germ-warfare application.'

She shook her head. 'No. No, I can't believe it. You are kidding, aren't you?'

'Not at all. They say China's sure to do it, so we'd better do it, too. And it pays well.'

With her face pinched and brows knitted, she said, 'And what did you tell him?'

He dusted his hands. 'Told him to go to hell.'

She nodded, smiling, and said, 'And I'm sure he will, the wicked man.' She rested her head against his shoulder, nuzzling against him, and said, 'I love you, Sandy.'

He held her close and stroked her hair. After another moment of silence, she pulled his face down and kissed him on the lips.

At first his response was without warmth or feeling. He kissed her merely to satisfy her desire, for he had none of his own. During the past few days he had shut down all his feelings, had emptied himself of desires. It had been the only way he had survived the ordeal, but now it was over, and, kissing her, he wondered if he would ever feel anything again.

Bobbi seemed to understand what was needed. She wouldn't let him pull away from the kiss. She pressed herself against him and opened her mouth for his tongue, insisting, urging. And as he kissed her, feeling once again the firm warmth of her flesh, he began to feel within his own flesh the stirring of old desires. It was like receiving a transfusion, the way heat and energy seemed to flow from her into him, as though it were her blood that coursed through his veins, and now he knew that everything was going to be all right again. Now he felt himself coming back to life.